Praise for *Cherry Pies & Deadly Lies*

"The first in an amusing new series features a fearless, reckless sleuth who unravels a complicated mystery while juggling her sex life and her future plans."

—*Kirkus Reviews*

W9-AXH-114

Cherry Pies
& DEADLY LIES

Cherry Pies & DEADLY LIES

A VERY CHERRY MYSTERY

DARCI HANNAH

MIDNIGHT INK
WOODBURY, MINNESOTA

MIDNIGHT INK

FIRST EDITION
First Printing, 2018

Book format by Bob Gaul
Cover design by Kevin R. Brown
Cover illustration by Greg Newbold/Bold Strokes Illustration

Midnight Ink, an imprint of Llewellyn Worldwide Ltd.

This is a work of fiction. Names, characters, places, and incidents are either the product of the author's imagination or are used fictitiously, and any resemblance to actual persons living or dead, business establishments, events, or locales is entirely coincidental.

Library of Congress Cataloging-in-Publication Data
Names: Hannah, Darci, author.
Title: Cherry pies & deadly lies / Darci Hannah.
Other titles: Cherry pies and deadly lies
Description: Woodbury, Minnesota: Midnight Ink, [2018] | Series: A very cherry mystery; #1
Identifiers: LCCN 2017061036 (print) | LCCN 2018001204 (ebook) | ISBN 9780738758480 (ebook) | ISBN 9780738757803 (softcover: acid-free paper)
Subjects: LCSH: Murder—Investigation—Fiction. | GSAFD: Mystery fiction.
Classification: LCC PS3608.A7156 (ebook) | LCC PS3608.A7156 C48 2018 (print) | DDC 813/.6—dc23
LC record available at https://lccn.loc.gov/2017061036

Midnight Ink
Llewellyn Worldwide Ltd.
2143 Wooddale Drive
Woodbury, MN 55125-2989
www.midnightinkbooks.com

Printed in the United States of America

To Dave and Jan Hilgers,
my extraordinary parents and the true "Blooms" of Cherry Cove.

One

Murder. What a detestable word. It's something a person doesn't normally think about, and rightly so. It's morbid, sad, senseless, violent, and utterly gruesome. Sure, it's good for the ratings on the evening news and sales of the morning papers, but not much else. People delight in reading about murder, but the only ones truly excited by it are news junkies and sickos. I wasn't a news junkie. And I was pretty darn certain I wasn't a sicko either. No, murder had nothing to do with me or my life and I dearly wanted to keep it that way. In fact, murder was the furthest thing from my mind until that untimely phone call from Mom. The moment the word tumbled from her lips it dropped like a cannon ball, turning my insides to jelly, demanding my attention; demanding I return home to the sleepy little lakeside village of Cherry Cove, Wisconsin.

It was a very untimely phone call indeed.

Earlier in the day, before Mom's earth-shattering call, I'd been in the kitchen of my tiny Northside Chicago apartment furiously baking. I ran an online bakery called *Bloom 'n' Cherries!*, online because I didn't have the capital for a storefront, and cherry-centric because I was born and raised on a cherry orchard. However, not wanting to pick cherries all my life, I'd turned to advertising instead. It was my life … well, up until a year ago February, when I'd been booted from my job as an ad exec in one of Chicago's largest ad agencies. Desperately trying to get my foot back in that tightly shut door, I was baking every dessert in my cherry arsenal. This was because I was in the grip of a plan.

It was the brainchild of my former assistant Giff, aka Gifford Mc-Grady. His brilliant idea was that I take my goods on the road and set up shop on Merchandize Mart Plaza outside my old office building. Mr. Black, my former boss, had a weakness for the smell of pert, tart red cherries oozing out of flaky crust, and Giff felt sure he would wander over to my stand. That's when I'd pounce. I'd give my final appeal for getting my old job back. Really, I had nothing to lose but the last remaining shred of my dignity.

For my little sojourn into streetside selling, I'd pulled out all the stops. My cherry arsenal was loaded and ready, bursting with cherry tarts, cherry squares, cherry scones, cherry cobblers, and my *pièce de résistance*, deconstructed cherry pie. This was my own creation. It was a layered confection starting with a crisp, lightly sugared phyllo pastry crust and topped with a layer of sweet almond cream, tart cherries, brandied cherry glaze, and toasted almonds. This layer was repeated, then topped with a dollop of fresh whipped cream and a perfect, plump cherry in a drizzle of glaze. It was pure mind-blowing, unadulterated taste-bud bliss! One bite and Mr. Black would forget I'd ever made *that ad*.

By lunchtime, my kiosk version of *Bloom 'n' Cherries!* was selling better than expected. My red-and-white-striped awning and cherry-bedazzled sign were hard to miss. But it was my array of yummy products, proudly displayed in clear plastic clamshells, with a fork on top held in place by a *Bloom 'n' Cherries!* logo sticker, that were the real hit. My stand was a novelty on the plaza. A line had formed. One hungry customer was just about to buy a slice of deconstructed pie when I happened to catch sight of Mr. Black. He was coming out the front doors of our towering office building, crossing the plaza to head for a cab. Giff, meticulously dressed, was striding in his wake.

Then the smell of cherries hit them both. Giff stopped walking. Two strides later, so did Mr. Black. The man turned in my direction. He saw me and frowned. Before he could run to his cab I waved, catching his attention. There was nothing for it now. He had made eye contact. He had to come on over to my stand.

"You know that man?" my customer asked, looking skeptical. His question was answered the moment my old boss stood before me, hands on hips, staring at my sign. Giff stood beside him mimicking his stance, grinning slightly yet flashing caution.

"Hello, darling," Giff said, the first to speak. "What a surprise seeing you here."

It wasn't a surprise at all. And Giff was a terrible actor.

Mr. Black stared at my sign. *"Bloom 'n' Cherries!,"* he said cautiously. "Cute. Very clever. I'm glad to see that after all this time you've finally moved on. Best of luck to you, Whitney Bloom." He turned to go.

"No!" I blurted, then caught myself. "Please. Sir. I want my old job back!"

I hadn't meant it to sound so desperate or so blunt, but there it was. There was no taking it back now. I watched as a frightful range of expressions flashed across my ex-boss's distinguished, middle-age face—shock, disbelief, horror, anger—until finally settling on laughter. Taking his cue, Giff laughed as well.

Knowing Giff's laughter was purely mercenary, I ignored him and settled my gaze back on Mr. Black. "Sir, this isn't a joke! I made a mistake, but should I be punished for it forever? This is America, land of second chances. All I'm asking for is another chance."

His laughter died away. "My dear Miss Bloom, this may be America, but I doubt that even our founding fathers would be inclined to give you a second chance after producing *that ad*. There's a picture of your face hanging in the lobby of the building, circled in red with a line through the middle. And even if you happen to slip past the guards, you won't be setting foot in the agency. The moment you were out the door we changed the locks. Why, you ask? Because you single-handedly destroyed a reputable brand by making it the laughing stock of the entire nation. The product has been pulled from every store, and the client has been ruined—bankrupt and left with a warehouse filled to the rafters with unsellable products. That, Ms. Bloom, is quite enough destruction for one lifetime. Cut your losses while you can. We're still trying to." He turned to leave again.

"Please, Mr. Black!" I launched myself across the table, grabbing his expensive suit coat by the sleeve. "I'm desperate."

Giff inhaled scandalously. "*Whitney*," he admonished, prying my hand from my ex-boss's coat.

Mr. Black was glowering. "Desperate? *You're* desperate?" he seethed. "We lost ten million dollars because of you. What in God's name were you thinking, making an ad like that and allowing the client to air it during the Super Bowl?"

"In my defense, sir, the client was very encouraging. And, all due respect, they loved my ad."

"Of course they did! They were a parcel of yoga-pant-wearing, granola-crunching, feminine product enthusiasts. But the Super Bowl is not about feminine hygiene, Ms. Bloom. It's about football, and all the things that go along with it—cold beer, greasy food, expensive cars, sexy women—everything that makes America great. It's neither the time nor the place to unveil a … a feminine hygiene ad! Didn't they teach you that at Northwestern?" His face was an alarming shade of red.

"It was never covered, sir. And it was a sexy ad," I pointed out.

"For the first seven seconds," he conceded. "The last eight were a horror show! As I told you fifteen months ago, you're finished! End of story!"

Impulsively he grabbed up a cherry square, plucked it from its clamshell, and took an angry bite. His face softened a measure as he chewed. He looked at the pastry in his hand. "Dear heavens above," he uttered. He looked at me again, clearly not knowing how to process the contradiction of physical anger and epicurean delight. "This … this is delicious," he said accusingly. "Really delicious!" he spat, as if it angered him. "Take my advice, Ms. Bloom; go back to the orchard from which you came. You have a gift for cherries and little else." He plucked two more clamshells off the table and stalked off.

Giff, stricken with silent apology, threw down a twenty, took one himself, and turned to follow.

"Holy gods of advertising!" exclaimed a male voice very close to me. It was my customer. I'd momentarily forgotten the line of people waiting to buy a cherry goodie. "Now that's a side of the legendary Richard Black you don't see. All things considered, that was particularly harsh, my dear. Here," he said, opening his wallet. He placed a crisp hundred-dollar bill on the table and picked up two clamshells of deconstructed pie, and a tart as well. "Keep the change. By the way, I thought your ad was hilarious."

Two

It was dark by the time I fought the traffic back to my small Northside apartment. Giff had called to apologize for his stunningly bad lapse in judgment. His apology was sincere enough, but I took offense when he started wheezing with laughter after regaling me with an uncensored version of Mr. Black's tirade after my brazen ambush.

"Whit, darling," Giff said, "look on the bright side. With the exception of one lowly little cherry square, you sold out today. *Bloom 'n' Cherries!* was a hit, and *that ad* helped. You may never produce another television ad again—and really, who needs the headache and all the sleepless nights—but I'll tell you something. You're a cherry visionary. Nobody can work magic on those pesky little stone fruits like you can. Also, and never forget this, angel, but you look absolutely fabulous selling cherries." The conversation degraded from there, and the call ended shortly thereafter when Giff reminded me of the one thing I didn't wish to be reminded of—the real reason I'd left Cherry Cove in the first place.

Men! They always knew how to push your buttons.

Once home in my over-priced shoebox apartment I flipped on the lights, kicked off my shoes, and crossed to the fridge. There I selected a fine two-dollar Chablis from my collection of budget wines and poured out a glass. While indulging in the feel of that first cathartic sip, I cast a predatory eye over the lone cherry square. *Dinner*, I thought, feeling my stomach rumble on cue. But dinner was just going to have to wait. I was angry, depressed, and feeling rejected, and the only cure for that was baking. Besides, I had an order to fill.

I pulled the remainder of my cherry stock from the cupboard and got to work on the pie dough first, sipping wine as I measured out the ingredients for five flaky crusts. I sifted the flour, cut in the chilled butter and Crisco with gusto (imagining it was Mr. Black's head), and, like a mad scientist, threw in the right amounts of sugar and salt. Next came the ice water, meticulously measured and blended last into the coarse mixture. I needed five pies, and I was doing my best to make every one of them invoke tears of pure epicurean joy at first bite.

After giving it a quick chill in the refrigerator, I attacked the dough, rolling out five large round disks. These I fitted into the awaiting pie tins with care, creating the first and most important layer of crust. Next I set to work on the piquant cherry pie filling.

Into my largest sauce pan went the sugar, corn starch, and cherry juice. Once the filling had thickened, I added the tart Montmorency cherries from our orchard and stirred in the fresh lemon juice and butter. This was then poured into the crusts, filling each tin equally. The last step was a woven checkered top crust with a dusting of sugar. After I'd placed a little foil around the edges to prevent the crusts from burning, it was time to send them into the oven.

The baking was going to take some time, and since I was still feeling glum I added more wine to my glass for good measure and seized the last cherry square. I took both over to the couch, where I plopped down like an overworked waitress at the end of a double shift. I was still feeling depressed. I wanted to drown my sorrows in cheap wine and gooey cherry pastry and wallow in the bittersweet glow of a good chick flick. Instead I made myself be a responsible adult, opening my laptop and checking my website to see if I had any new orders. I didn't. But what I did have was another message from my mysterious online friend, C-Bomb.

The sight of the absurd online name made me smile. C-Bomb had first contacted me through my website, stating his name was short for "cherry bomb" and that he was a self-proclaimed cherry connoisseur. Since having sworn off all heterosexual flesh-and-blood men some time ago, I felt there was little harm in instant messaging with a man I would never meet—one who had a way with words, seemed sophisticated, and had a real sense of humor about cherries. In short, C-Bomb was a charming enigma, one who entertained me with idle banter, subtle sexual innuendoes, and his thoughts on the red tart cherry. He knew a good deal about me, which came off at times as a little creepy, but in reality it wasn't hard to do given my website for *Bloom 'n' Cherries!*, my short but memorable career in advertising, and all the social media I engaged in. At times, it appeared my entire life was on display. His was not, and I found that totally sexy. He wouldn't even tell me his real name, or his age, or send me a picture. And googling the name C-Bomb elicited nothing but pages and pages of garbage. Strangely, I found that I liked that. Whoever he was, C-Bomb was mysterious. It gave my active imagination more fodder for fantasy, and with a name like C-Bomb the sky was the limit.

Hi, I typed.

So, how did it go? Did Mr. Black give you your old job back? he replied.

Unfortunately, no. They've not only kicked me to the curb, but changed the locks as well, or so I'm told. I hit enter and took another gulp of wine.

I detect a hint of despair. Perhaps you're forgetting the family business? Or the fact you have a passion for cherries? Did I ever mention that I've stayed at the Cherry Orchard Inn?

I sat up and stared at the screen. The Cherry Orchard Inn! It was the most charming, iconic inn located in Cherry Cove, and I should know. My parents owned that inn! It was the first time he'd mentioned it. I took another sip of wine and typed, *No. I had no idea. When was this?*

Tsk tsk. I'm not going to tell you when, nor will I tell you the name of the room. I will tell you that the view was spectacular and the food sublime, although I'm sure you're well aware of both. Oh, and did I mention that I met your parents, Jani and Baxter? Such nice people. So generous! And don't get them started talking about you, their charming daughter, unless you've got an hour to spare. Fortunately, I did, and I was all ears, especially when I learned about the man your mother thinks you should marry. Does the name Tatum Vander Hagen ring any bells? I was sorry to hear about him. However, the fact that you're not in Cherry Cove anymore does give a man hope. Am I wrong to hope?

I frowned at the screen. *I'm a little disturbed that you talked with my folks. And I'm not saying a thing about Tate unless you give me the date of your visit and the name of the room you stayed in.*

So you can look me up in the books and find my real name? Never!

How else am I to know who you really are?

Well that's the game, isn't it? I'm your enigma. Someday, Ms. Bloom, I shall sweep you off your feet and kiss you, and all will be revealed.

What? When? Where? You don't even know me ... do you? I found it utterly mysterious, erotic, and, if I was being totally honest, a little unsettling as well. The guy could be in his fifties, married with kids ... then again, he could be totally ripped, wealthy, single, romantic, and a wild beast in the sack. Swingin' dingles! It was thoughts like these that kept me typing with this stranger.

You know I can't answer any of those questions, he replied. *Let's just leave it up to Fate, that and the fact that there are no coincidences in life. By the way, thank you for sharing your deconstructed cherry pie recipe. It looks complicated. Maybe someday you'll make it for me.*

In order to do that I need to know who you are—unless you order it from the website. But I warn you, from this day forth I shall conduct a thorough background search on all who order that pie!

No. I mean in person. As I've told you, someday you will know who I am, but not today.

Oh, for cripes sake! Just tell me! I scream-typed, my mind swirling with all the possibilities. Frankly, none of them looked too good. Just then my phone began to ring. I glanced at the screen.

Mom.

Fudgesicles! I'd been meaning to call her all day.

It was late May and tourist season was just around the corner. This was the weekend our inn hosted its annual Cherry Blossom Festival, a fun-filled two days designed to showcase the orchard in all its full-blooming glory (nothing awakens the senses to the beauties of spring-time like a stroll through a blossoming cherry orchard). It was a weekend filled with gentle pursuits. Along with the usual activities our inn boasted, there was croquet on the lawn, tennis for those who were so inclined, and unrestricted strolling through the blossoming orchard followed by a visit to the cherry-blossom scented hot tubs. On Saturday at mid-morning there was a hayride through the orchard with a tour of the processing sheds, followed by lunch under a tent erected on the lawn. At mid-afternoon, this same tent hosted a wine and cheese tasting, showcasing cherry wines from around the country and the best local cheeses. Other cherry products were on display and sampled under the tent as well, every one of them sold at the inn gift shop. And it was under this same tent where the signature event of the weekend took place: the cherry pie bake-off. Anyone could enter, although it was usually the locals who competed. Competition could get pretty steep since the prize was a one-hundred-dollar gift card, bragging rights, and the honor of keeping the "Gilded Cherry" trophy for a whole year.

Mom had been excited about this year's festival and strongly suggested I come up for the weekend. I knew every room was booked and that they could use my help. But I also knew that if I showed up, Mom would insist I enter my deconstructed pie in the contest, and I just wasn't feeling it. Not this year. She'd called four times in the past two days, and somehow I'd forgotten to call her back.

I had ignored her calls.

I was a terrible daughter.

"Mom!" I said, answering the phone. "I was just thinking about you. I'm so glad you called."

If my voice was infused with enthusiasm, hers was anything but. "Whitney," she whimpered into the phone. "I'm so scared. I'm so scared."

At the tone of her voice the hair at the back of my neck stood on end and my insides turned to water. Mom was perpetually cheerful. She was never anything less than perky over the phone. "Dang it, Mom! Where are you? What's going on?"

"I'm at the inn," she whispered ominously, causing my entire body to prickle with foreboding. "Something terrible has happened. Oh, just terrible!"

"What? Mom, please, calm down and tell me what's happened."

"It was all going so well ... so well until they found him."

My hands were shaking. "Who? Mom, who did they find?"

"Jeb," she whispered over the phone. "Jeb Carlson, and he's very, very dead."

"Are you kidding me?" I cried. "Jeb?" Jeb Carlson, an older gentleman who'd lived in Cherry Cove nearly his whole life, managed our orchard. He was a sweet old guy, cheerful, friendly, and utterly indispensable to our family. He knew everything there was to know about cherries, and was also the head judge of the cherry pie bake-off. It was really too much to think about. "Oh my God! How did he die? Did he have a heart attack or something?"

"Murdered," she uttered into the phone.

My heart stopped for a beat or two at the impossibility of the word. It was unbelievable. Unfathomable. Nothing bad like that ever happened in the sleepy town of Cherry Cove. "Are you telling me that Jeb's been murdered? During the Cherry Blossom Festival weekend? Is this your idea of a joke, Mom? Because if it is, it's a pretty sick one."

"No," she said, and began crying. "No joke. I wish it was. And the worst part … the worst part is … "

Really, how could it be any worse?

"And the worst part is, it appears your dad is the murderer."

THUD! It was either my heart engaging or the other shoe dropping—either way, I felt shaken to the core. She was right. It was worse. Far worse.

Forgetting everything but the fact that I needed to get to Cherry Cove fast, I shut my laptop and began packing.

Three

$\mathcal{G}$iff was out clubbing with hot Jonny from Creative when I called him. The bass at the club was so booming loud it was a wonder he even heard his phone ring. Then I remembered he wore tight pants and always had his phone set to vibrate.

"Whassup, Whitney Bloom? Calling to hear me apologize again? Not gonna happen. The Giffster only apologizes once per f-up, never more. You know that."

"Yeah. No. We're good. I'm just calling because I need to bail on brunch tomorrow, and I need you to do me a favor."

"You what? Fail to launch tomorrow and like my flavor?"

"No. I said I have to bail on brunch," I yelled into the phone.

"Just a minute." I could hear him cover the mic on his phone. A moment later he spoke again; this time the bass was subdued, with only a few voices in the background, and there was the distinct flush of a toilet. "Okay, try it again."

"I'm calling to tell you that I can't meet for brunch tomorrow, and I need you to do me a huge favor."

"Why not? Oh! You're on a hot date!"

"No. It's nothing good. Family emergency. I'm heading to Cherry Cove."

"Oh my God," he uttered when my words finally sunk in. "Not Grandma Jenn? Not that cherry-loving free spirit? She's the coolest, Whit. Christ, I love the old girl to pieces." I could tell he was drunk, the maudlin tones cloaking his deep, expressive voice. It was an impressive show of emotion, even for him.

"No. No. Grandma Jenn's fine. It's my dad. There's a possibility he's murdered someone."

"Wa-wa-wa what!?" The voice on the other end shifted, filling with incredulity as it echoed off the bathroom walls. "Baxter Bloom? A murderer? Whitney, what the deuce is going on?"

"Hush!" I hissed. "For cripes sake, keep your voice down. I don't know what's going on, and the truth is, I don't have any details. And, of course, I don't think my dad's a murderer! That's why I've got go. The inn's booked for the weekend and Mom sounds like she's falling apart. I'm just calling to let you know I won't be there. Also, I need you to deliver some pies to the gastropub. I'll leave directions on the counter."

"No problem, sweetheart. Consider it done. Anything else?"

"Wish me luck?"

"Luck? Angel, you're not the lucky type, and even if you were, I've a feeling you're going to need a pinch more than luck for this one."

∞

Giff, although drunk, was undoubtedly correct. I wasn't the lucky sort. Things seldom ever fell my way, and if they did, it was usually because I'd yanked them first. And it was shabby of him to remind me of it! Hard work and a go get 'em attitude were my trademarks. Although at times I could get a little overzealous. But was that a crime? And, for the love of Pete, I was feeling extremely overzealous at the moment … or was it anxious? Definitely anxious! Murder, I'm told, will do that to a person. But the murder of an old friend and valued employee—during the Cherry Blossom Festival weekend—with Dad as the prime suspect? How messed up was that?

Another thing that was bothering me was the fact that I didn't have any details. Mom obviously had been in shock, and our conversation hadn't been long. I'd know all the details soon enough, I told myself, once I made it to the Cherry Orchard Inn.

After packing my bags, taking the pies out of the oven, and talking to Giff, I realized I needed sleep. It was a five-hour drive up to Cherry Cove from Chicago, and after the day I'd had I doubted I'd make it without driving into the lake. I needed a few hours under my belt, so I programmed the coffee maker and set my alarm for two thirty in the morning.

It was well before dawn when I hit the road, driving with a hot thermos of coffee on the seat beside me. The air was crisp, the sky strewn with stars, and the roads all but empty. Five hours straight north up the shoreline of Lake Michigan, and the entire way I was wracked with guilt. I hadn't been home in … dear God, had it really been eighteen months? I was a terrible daughter! And the thought that Dad might be thrown in prison for murder was more than I could bear. Tears blurred my vision as I sped out of the city in my cherry red Ford Escape. Every song streaming through my iPhone reminded me of home. Caffeine coursed through my blood as I pressed on the accelerator, crying, sipping coffee, nibbling dry cereal, and trying to wrap my head around the thought that somebody could murder a sweet old man like Jeb Carlson, and that anyone would think my dad was a suspect.

I watched the sun rise over Lake Michigan and shortly thereafter crossed the Bayview Bridge in Sturgeon Bay. I was on the Door

County Peninsula, that little nubbin of a thumb halfway up the great state of Wisconsin, poking into Lake Michigan. I continued north on Route 42, noting the beauty of the greening hills and thick woodland sprouting with new life. Half an hour later everything came into view, and I breathed a sigh of relief.

It never fails to take your breath away, that first sight of the cove opening before you through dense wood and cherry-scented air. The town of Cherry Cove started at the bottom of a substantial hill and sprawled along the north half of Cherry Cove Bay. The crescent shoreline, dotted with rock and sandy beaches, white gingerbread gazebos, and Victorian-style buildings bedecked with newly planted flower boxes and hanging planters, was as picturesque as a town could be, in my opinion. And I wasn't the only one who thought so. Cherry Cove had attracted the notice of plenty of high-end travel magazines as well, earning full-color centerfold spreads that beckoned tourists and residents alike. Flowerbeds lined the main road. Sailboats sat at anchor on the cool blue waters of the harbor. Beyond the bay sat a couple of islands, and beyond those the vast body of water known as the Green Bay. There was a red-painted barn, and a little Scandinavian-style log cottage covered with a thick sod roof, a nod to the Swedish and Norwegian settlers who came to the Cove in the late 1800s. Above the town, poking high over the tree-covered hills, was the white steeple of St. Paul's Lutheran Church.

I slowed down at the top of the hill, staring at the horseshoe bay and the awakening town beyond it, and took a deep breath. Cherry blossoms! On my left the sprawling Bloom Family Orchard came into view, every neatly pruned Montmorency cherry tree heavy with white blossoms. My heart beat a little faster at the sight. I was nearly home.

I turned onto Cherry Bluff Lane, a private road that wound its way along the rolling orchard until ending at the Cherry Orchard Inn out on the point. The inn was a large, rambling, modernized Victorian building with a wide wrap-around front porch and a cone-roofed, three-story turret on one side. It was surrounded by beautiful grounds and impeccable terraced landscaping. For all its size it was still a quaint inn, with only ten guest rooms that were named instead of numbered. Every room had a different theme. It was all part of the charm. The inn itself sat on a hill that overlooked the wide bay and the town of Cherry Cove dotting the far shore. I had forgotten what a magical place it was—the inn, the orchard, the processing sheds just visible in the distance, and the dense forest beyond—all occupying some of the best real estate in Wisconsin.

The magical feeling was shattered the moment I saw the police SUV parked under the portico, reminding me that the Cherry Orchard Inn was now the scene of a crime. It would forever be tainted as the place of Jeb Carlson's murder. The parking lot was full, and having no patience to even attempt to parallel park in the only space left (between a Mercedes and a Jag), I thought it safest to just snag the handicapped spot and be done with it. From there I ran under the portico, flew up the wide front steps, and bolted through the door.

The grand foyer, a spacious two-story entrance with a winding white staircase on the left spiraling to the balconied second floor, was empty. To the right was a cozy breakfast room. The French doors to it were open, and I could see that coffee had already been laid out on the antique sideboard in the back along with an assortment of sweet rolls, muffins, cherry pecan bread, and a bowl of fresh berries. The room itself, with six pretty little tables and several groupings around the stone fireplace, was empty. Beyond the grand foyer and the staircase sat the front desk. It was a modern piece, white with clean lines to match the window panes, the woodwork, and the stairs. Before me was the main dining room, and the patio beyond, but the French doors there were still closed. The dining room didn't open until nine.

The person working the front desk must have heard me come in. A moment later a familiar face emerged from the office door and stood behind the counter.

"Whitney!" Margaret exclaimed, surprised yet clearly troubled. She lowered her voice. "I heard you were expected, though I didn't think you'd come through the inn entrance."

"Good morning, Margaret. I saw the cop car out front. I thought they'd all be in here."

"No. Not here. Never here. And that fluffy-headed idiot was told to go straight to the family residence, and not to park out front for all to see. Though no one's up yet, thank heavens. We're trying to keep things as close to normal as possible here, under the circumstances. Your folks are in the family quarters. Go on back. I'll buzz you in."

Four

The family quarters were essentially two thousand square feet of private living space in the wing of the inn opposite the guest rooms. The bedrooms were upstairs, and the kitchen, dining room, sunroom, and Dad's office were on the first floor. I walked down the back hall toward its front door, wondering where everyone was, when all of a sudden Mom popped into the hallway in front of me. She had come flitting out of the kitchen bearing a tray of fluted stemware and a pitcher of mimosas. She apparently hadn't seen me coming from the hotel side, and turned in the direction of the sunroom, oblivious.

Either my mom had hit rock bottom and was planning on doing a little drinking, or she was hosting a brunch, which was odd, I thought, under the current circumstances. I hoped, for the sake of my poor father, it was the former and not the latter. "Mom!" I called out to her retreating back. At the sound of my voice she froze.

After a moment, the unflappable Jani Bloom swung her blonde braids in my direction. Her round blue eyes lit up with joy. "Whitney, darling! You're here! Oh, and I just love what you've done with your hair!"

It was the kind of greeting I'd expect if we'd just met for coffee, not one for the current occasion. I hadn't seen Mom in over six months. I hadn't been home in nearly eighteen. I had just driven five hours because I was told there'd been a murder at the orchard and that Dad was suspect number one. Apparently, none of that seemed to matter. Mom was ogling my hair as if it were spray-painted gold and dripping with jewels.

"That cut's so darling on you, so sassy and modern! It frames your beautiful face, highlights your big blue eyes, and is the perfect cut for those shiny blonde locks. I just love it!"

I'm not gonna lie. I was kind of in love with my sleek new face-framing bob as well. I thought it made me look older, more sophisticated—like an aspiring business woman should look. Not sassy.

Mom tilted her head to one side, smiled, and thrust out her tray. "Mimosa?"

Heavens, it was tempting. But what the devil was she thinking!? And who makes a pitcher of mimosas the morning after their husband has been accused of murder? I wasn't entirely certain what was going on, but whatever it was, did it really require a tray of mimosas? Either I'd been away too long this time or Mom was losing it. Likely it was a little of both.

"Ah, no thanks, Mom. Where's Dad?"

"Dad?"

"You know, my father? The man who, apparently, murdered Jeb Carlson last night? Do you remember our conversation, Mom? At all?"

Her blue eyes widened, then rolled sideways in the direction of the sunroom. Her cheeks flushed bright red. "Hush, darling," she said. "Not so loud. Of course there's been a murder, a terrible one, but we've all decided it's for the best if we keep it quiet—just for the weekend, you know."

"What?" I cried. "Mom, you can't just brush something like murder under the carpet! We're talking about Jeb Carlson here! He's not just anybody, Mom. He's family!" I was heaving with indignation as I spoke.

"Of course it's not okay!" she replied quickly. "And I know how this looks. I'm sick to death just thinking about it. But what's done is done. There's no use frightening the guests in the meantime."

I stared at her, and then my eyes fell to the tray of mimosas, the fluted crystal gently tinkling under her shaking hands.

"Dang it!" I breathed, and took the tray from her before she dropped it. "I'm sorry, Mom. I know how much this weekend means to you and Dad, just as I know how much Jeb means to this place."

"We don't want to do it," Mom said, looking ill. "We all want to mourn him, as he should be mourned, but we have our guests to think about. They paid a pretty penny to be here, and the festival must go on." She spoke bravely, but I could see through the façade. Her chin quivered and her eyes glistened with unshed tears. She then took a fluted glass off the tray I was holding and poured herself a mimosa. She gulped it down like water and continued reflectively. "It's just a shame that nice young couple staying in the Swan Suite, Ryan and Jillian McSweeny, had to stumble upon Jeb's body last night. You see," she said, staring at me, "the McSweenys snuck into the orchard for a little nookie-nookie under the blossoms and found poor Jeb instead, a big dent in his head and dead as a doornail." She hiccupped at the thought, stifling a flow of tears. "Imagine their shock at finding him like that."

She paused for a moment, pressing her knuckles to her lips to keep them from quivering. Her hand came away. "If they'd come straight to the front desk, we might have been able to contain the murder a little longer. But they didn't. They ran straight to the lounge, and you know how fast bad news spreads in a lounge. If they hadn't gone into the orchard last night," she continued, "Jeb's body might not have been found until later today." A slight shiver took her at the thought, but I really didn't see how that development could have made such a tragedy any better. "At least if we'd been the ones who found him, we could have done something about that mallet."

"Mallet? What mallet, Mom? You didn't say anything about a mallet last night."

She looked at me, frowned, and whispered, "Your father's croquet mallet, dear. The gold-plated one Dr. Engle gave him on his fiftieth birthday."

It was then that her words hit me with force. "Holy cobbler!" I exclaimed. "Tell me that Dad's mallet wasn't the murder weapon."

"I … I can't do that, dear. Oh, how I wish I could, but I can't. I can't because it was lying beside the body when they found him."

"And … and so they think it *is* the murder weapon?"

"It appears so," she replied, and bit her lip.

I could feel all the blood drain from my face. "But … but surely that doesn't mean Dad killed him, right? It just means somebody took his mallet. Who could have taken his croquet mallet?"

Mom looked stunned, like a deer in headlights. "Well, that's just the thing. Your father loves that mallet. He was using it before dinner, and he claimed he left it locked in his office after that. It didn't help matters any that he was seen arguing with Jeb a couple of hours before he was murdered. Oh dear, it doesn't look good. Not at all." Her lip began to quiver again. The reality of Jeb's death was finally breaking through her stoic Midwestern sensibilities.

"And whose idea was it to sweep this calamity under the table?" I asked.

"Well, I suppose Officer MacLaren is responsible for that. He wants all the guests to remain here while he looks into the matter—at least until tomorrow."

"Officer MacLaren?" The name sounded vaguely familiar, but I couldn't place it. "Who the heck is he?"

"Excuse me." At that very moment a soft, vaguely familiar voice came from the hallway somewhere behind Mom. "Perhaps I can clear that up for you, *Whit-less*?"

There was only one man on Earth who would have the nerve to call me Whit-less, even in such a teasing manner. Still holding the tray, I pushed past Mom, only to come face-to-face with a tall, trim, incredibly handsome ginger-haired police officer.

"Holy cobbler!" I breathed, staring unbelievingly into the face of my old friend and academic rival Jack MacLaren. Time, and the better part of a decade, had done wonders for him. He used to be a gangly, geeky, know-it-all boy and the top student in our school. I stood before him, marveling. "Either somebody's actually gone and made you a cop, or you like dressing up as one."

Jack took a glass off my tray, grinned knowingly, and poured himself a mimosa. He then allowed his honey-colored eyes to scan my body from head to toe. Amazement blazed, then gave way to a simmer of appreciation. I was pleased, purely from the shock of his reaction.

"Does it give you any satisfaction to learn that the uniform's real?" He raised an eyebrow, took a healthy swig of mimosa, and added, "Blame the folks down in Milwaukee if you like."

"Clearly, they have a sense of humor."

Lowering his voice, he replied, "Unlike the ad people in Chicago." He winked. Nothing could have humiliated me more.

"You ... saw my ad?" It was a stupid question. I regretted it the moment the words left my mouth.

"I did. Several times, in fact. I saw it watching the game. I saw it again the next morning, although not as an ad per say, and it popped up again during a video game I was playing. For the record, I thought it was very convincing."

Great. Was there any person on earth who hadn't seen *that ad*? Apparently not, and the fact that Mom's smile was beyond disingenuous was even more upsetting.

"However," Jack continued, grabbing my undivided attention once again, "you'll be happy to know that once the folks in Milwaukee realized their mistake, I moved up here. I'm Cherry Cove's only man in uniform. Actually," he said, pretending to think, "I'm the only cop stationed on the entire peninsula. But don't worry. I have backup. My boss resides in the police station down in Sturgeon Bay. Good thing I'm here, though. Right? Because there's been a murder."

Hearing the word again caused an electric bolt of dread to shoot down my spine. And the thought of Jack MacLaren as head cop on Dad's case sent the tray in my hands shaking like a paint mixer. Jack took it from me, a look of concern crossing his compelling adult features.

"Don't worry," he said, "I worked as a detective in Milwaukee. This isn't my first rodeo." The wink he tacked on to the end of this statement was as disconcerting as his grin.

Thankfully I didn't have long to contemplate it, because just then my father's booming voice rang out from the vicinity of the sunroom.

"Jani, for God's sake," he cried, "where'd ya get off to with those drinks? Young MacLaren's chomping at the bit to get on with it!"

"Dad?" I strained to see around the tall, alarmingly fit detective.

My dad, Baxter Bloom, a trim, successful, smartly dressed man in his late fifties, came bursting into the hallway. At the sight of me his feet faltered, his light gray eyes bulged, and his face turned the color of his sleek, silver-white hair. "Whitney?" he uttered, as if I'd just been resurrected from the dead. Apparently Mom, who'd never been known to keep a secret in her life, had failed to mention that I was coming home.

"Dad!" I ran forward to give him a long overdue hug. "Oh, Daddy! I was so scared when I heard they believed you'd murdered Jeb."

But here Dad stopped and cast Mom an accusatory look. "You told her, Jani? And after I told you not to?"

At least Mom had the courtesy to blush. "She has to know, Baggsie. You can't hide something like murder from your daughter."

"Oh, fer cripes sake! How many times do I have to tell you people? I didn't murder anyone!"

"I know, Daddy. I believe you. And I'm here because I'm going to find out who did."

Five

It was eight in the morning. Sunlight streamed through the wall of polished windows that looked out across the bay. It was going to be a beautiful, temperate day in Cherry Cove and I wasn't enjoying it in the least. I sat curled up like a fetus in a floral-cushioned wicker chair nursing a mimosa that I realized after the first sip was of the non-alcoholic variety. I cast Mom a look of extreme disappointment. I felt entirely cheated … or maybe it was the fact that the man in uniform sitting across from me in the sunroom was actually Jack MacLaren, my childhood friend. He had brains; I had to give him that. But finding him back home? I would have thought that after Milwaukee he'd have aimed a bit higher. After all, what respectable young man would choose to toss away the most productive years of his career in a sleepy little village like Cherry Cove? A lazy one, I mused, and realized that my father's fate rested in his hands. The thought, like the non-alcoholic mimosa I was sipping, was utterly depressing.

"Mr. Bloom," Jack said, leaning forward in his chair with a pen and notepad ready. The crumb-speckled plate on the table beside him indicated that he'd already polished off a piece of coffee cake—cherry, of course—and he was now on his second mimosa. I wondered if he realized there wasn't any alcohol in his own drink. Did he know the difference between ginger ale and champagne?

"I know this has been a troubling time for you, sir, but I need you to walk me through last night once again. Your initial statement was rushed, and since you've called your daughter up here from Chicago"—he cast a look at Mom—"and since she's stated she's going to be the one to actually find the person responsible for Jeb's death"—the look he gave me as he said this was dripping with sarcastic sweetness—"I'd like you to recall the events of last night with as much detail as you can remember."

Dad was clearly not looking forward to this, but really, he had no choice. Releasing a long breath, he said, "I feel … I feel just sick about Jeb's death. It's bad enough my croquet mallet was found by his body, but how are we going to get along here without him? Jeb was invaluable to us, MacLaren."

"I know, sir. As far as I know, there isn't a person in Cherry Cove who wasn't fond of him. I think you'll understand that for the sake of his life and his memory, we need to find out who's responsible for his death. Therefore, I'll ask you to bear with me as I ask you once again to state your movements between eight and ten thirty p.m. last night."

"Like I told you before," Dad said, "I was making sure everything was running smoothly at the inn. Dinner was a private affair. The dining room was reserved for the guests and any locals participating in the Cherry Blossom Festival. Dinner went until eight o'clock. After that I went into the lounge for a spell. A good many of the guests had retired there. I made my rounds, welcoming everyone, and sat for a while with the Hansons, a charming couple up from Green Bay. They come every year. We were catching up. Brisbane came by as well and sat with us. Shortly thereafter Gabby, our waitress, came over and handed me a piece of paper. It was a note from Jeb. He wanted to speak with me in private."

"That would be around eight thirty?"

Dad nodded.

"Is that a usual way for Jeb to communicate?"

"No. He usually comes to me himself, or sends me a text. I didn't have my phone on me at the time."

"You mentioned earlier that Mr. Carlson was in one of the processing sheds. Did you leave immediately or did you make any stops before meeting him there?"

"Went straight to the shed," Dad replied.

"Through the main doors of the inn?"

Here Dad hesitated. "No. Wait." A thoughtful look crossed his face as he replied, "I went to get my phone. The moment Gabby slipped me that note I realized, I didn't have it."

Jack's eyebrows rose in question. "So, you didn't go straight to the processing shed?"

"Once I found my phone, I did."

Jack then asked where he'd found it, to which Dad replied, his office.

"Your office in the family wing? Just down the hall from here?" Dad nodded. "Was it locked last night?" Dad shook his head. "Do you remember locking it when you left again?"

"Don't lock my office. Don't need to. It's in here," Dad said, indicating the family wing.

Jack scribbled something in his notebook, then asked, "After retrieving your phone, you went to meet Mr. Carlson. Where was he?"

"Outside the smaller shed, the one where we keep all our tractors, harvesters, and Gators. He was working late. Had to prepare the hay wagon for the orchard tour."

"Was he alone?"

"When I found him, he was. Erik had been helping him, but he'd sent the boy to the inn with the message Gabby gave me. Jeb thought Erik would head home after that, but he must have lingered a bit."

"You're referring to Erik Larson?"

Dad nodded.

Jack flipped through his notebook, landing on a scribbled page. "Erik Larson stated that he heard you two arguing last night. He came forward shortly after the body was removed from the orchard. What were you arguing about.

A sheepish look crossed Dad's face. He cast a sideways glance at Mom and finally said, "Wine. We were discussing wine."

"Wine?" Jack looked confused. "Why was wine significant, sir?"

"Because Jeb and I were dabbling in it."

"What?" It was the first time Mom had stirred since Jack began his questioning. "You were dabbling in wine?" Her high, round cheeks were glowing red with indignation. "And just what is that supposed to mean?" Obviously, this was news to her.

Dad cast Mom an apologetic look. "They make cherry wine down in the Door Peninsula Winery. Since we serve it here, we thought we could do better. Save some money as well. It's becoming quite a hot seller, and Jeb and I decided to make a few barrels from last years' harvest and see what all the fuss was about. We set up the whole operation in the old lighthouse. Jeb thought it would give our wine some mystique and enhance the flavor. We were going to call it *Cherry Point Lighthouse Winery*. I was going to hire Whitney here to design our label and help with marketing. We were going to unveil it at the wine and cheese tasting this afternoon. Anyhow, those were our plans. Jeb kept an eye on things for us. We didn't want to say anything until we had a viable product." He looked at Mom. "I wanted it to be a surprise, Jani. However, last night when I went to speak with him, Jeb looked pretty upset. He was downright troubled. When I asked him what was wrong, he told me that when he went to check on the wine, he found that someone had broken into the lighthouse and taken every last cask of it. Nobody knew it was in there!" he stated forcefully, looking squarely at Jack. "Nobody knew what we were about, and it was Jeb's job to keep watch! All that work and secrecy for nothing!"

Jack gave Dad a hard stare. "You never said anything about this last night. I suppose you don't have a permit to make wine or to distill spirits on the premises?"

"Well, not yet," Dad snapped. "Not until we know if we have a knack for it. What's the use spending more money?"

A wan smile crossed Jack's lips and he scribbled something in his notebook. "You say that you and Jeb were the only ones who knew about the wine in the old lighthouse. Obviously, somebody else knew about it too. Do you have any idea who could have taken the wine?"

Dad shook his head. "I tell my wife everything, MacLaren, and if Jani didn't know about our wine, why would you think I'd tell anyone else?"

"Not you, sir. Jeb. Could he have told anyone about the wine?"

Dad thought about that a moment. "I didn't think so, but I suppose he could have. Come to think of it, he did seem rather nervous when we talked—as if he wasn't telling me the whole story. Something was bothering him, but naturally I assumed it was the fact that all our wine had been taken."

Jack nodded and scribbled something in his notebook. "What did you do after speaking with Jeb?"

"We went to have a look at the orchard records in Jeb's office, to see if we missed anything. Then I went to the lighthouse to have a look myself. I stayed down there for the better part of an hour, searching the place. We had ten barrels in there, MacLaren. That's a substantial amount of wine. I can't imagine anyone taking that much. After having a good look around the old building, I walked along the shore, up and down aways, to see if I could figure out what happened and if whoever took it happened to leave one behind. But it was dark by then, and I didn't find much of anything."

"What time was this?"

"Oh, I don't know? Ten I suppose."

"I'm going to want to have a look at your operation," Jack told him. "Until I do, don't let anyone near the lighthouse. Also, and this may sound odd, but when you met Mr. Carlson, were you carrying your croquet mallet?"

"Of course not!" Dad looked affronted. "I did use it earlier, during the croquet tournament. After that I put it back in my office and went to attend to other matters of business."

"You said you went back to your office to retrieve your phone before you went to speak with Mr. Carlson. Do you recall seeing your croquet mallet in there?"

"Don't know. I wasn't looking for it. But I assure you I didn't touch it again after the croquet tournament. Why would I?" There was the slightest hint of challenge in Dad's voice. Jack wisely refrained from stating the obvious, which was that somebody had used it to murder Jeb. Instead, the detective came back to the topic of Dad's office and the fact that he had left it unlocked.

"Do you know of anyone who would have taken it from your office?"

Dad gave a glum shake his head. "I don't, but it wouldn't be hard to do. You know what it's like up here, MacLaren. Cherry Cove is still the type of place where folks don't feel the need to lock the doors, or much of anything else."

"That may be true, but now, after so brutal a murder and the theft of so much illegal wine, I believe things are about to change. Pity,"

Jack added, and the men exchanged a weighted look. It was then Jack asked what Dad had done once he came back from the lighthouse.

"I came back here to the family quarters and went upstairs to the bedroom. It had been a long day. With the doings of the festival, seeing to all the guests' needs, and the fact that I'd just discovered all our wine missing, I was exhausted. Jani came in shortly after I did. That would have been around ten thirty. Imagine our surprise when a short while later we got a call from the lounge. It was Gabby, her voice hysterical as she told me that the McSweenys had found a body in the orchard. That sent the hair on the back of my neck on end! We feared it was one of the other guests, and then doom struck when I heard the name Jeb Carlson." Dad looked more dejected than I'd ever seen him. He took a deep breath and hung his head.

Jack closed his notebook. "Mr. Bloom. Mr. Bloom, look at me, sir. What troubles me is that you have two hours—two crucial hours—that no one but you can account for. That in itself is not so unusual. However, when coupled with the fact that you were heard arguing with Mr. Carlson, and that your croquet mallet was found beside the body, you understand how this might look suspicious? But," he said, aiming a grim smile at Dad, "I'm not convinced we should close the books on this one just yet. You weren't the only person wandering about the grounds last night, and if you left Mr. Carlson back at the processing sheds around nine p.m., you obviously weren't the last person to speak with him. The Cherry Blossom Festival always attracts a crowd. I understand the inn's full, and that you have a substantial amount of staff working this weekend as well. Then there are the locals who participate in the festival and love to get involved." Jack closed his notebook, tucked it into his pocket, and stood.

"Last night it was too dark to see much of anything," he went on. "Today, hopefully, I'll be able to find a bit more evidence at the crime scene. With any luck I might even be able to convince a forensic unit to take a look. That will help." Jack locked eyes with my father. "Like I told you last night, I want the Cherry Blossom Festival to continue on as if nothing's happened, with the one caveat that nobody's to go near the crime scene. Nobody, and I mean nobody, is to go beyond the yellow tape." This he said looking directly at me. "To do so would be a crime. Is that clear?" He shifted his focus back to Dad. "Keep out of that part of the orchard. Until I can take a closer look at the body and go over the crime scene once again, I want everyone to remain here and continue on as if nothing's happened." Jack looked at his watch. "Right now, however, I have a meeting at Door County General with the county coroner. I'm bringing him our key piece of evidence, the croquet mallet found at the crime scene. Once I speak with him, and after he has a look at the mallet, I hope to have a better understanding of what went on here. Also, I'm going to need to take a look at your guest book as well as a list of all your employees."

"Of course," Dad said. "We keep all the employee records in Sorensen's office. I'll make you a copy." Dad got up, impatient to leave the room and the difficult line of questioning. He was nearly to the door when Mom broke in.

"Jack ... Officer MacLaren, why don't you go with Baxter and I'll see if I can't wrap up a little of that coffee cake for you? After all, it sounds like you're in for quite a busy day."

At the mention of coffee cake, a smile lit up Jack's face. "Thanks, Mrs. Bloom. I'd appreciate it."

"Well, it's the least I can do after all you've done for us." Mom took Jack by the arm and escorted him out of the sunroom. The moment Dad and Jack were out of earshot, Mom popped back in and wasted no time getting to her point.

"Whitney," she whispered, panic touching her face and constricting her voice. "Go with Jack. You know what he's like. He's a dear boy, but do you really feel he's qualified for this sort of thing? There are nineteen guests, not to mention the staff. Oh, sure, young MacLaren's good at handing out speeding tickets, finding the occasional stolen bicycle, and giving seminars on gun safety to hunters, but ... well, this time it's murder, and the murder weapon belongs to your father." Her eyes were tearing up at the thought. "Not to mention the fact that he lives all alone in that odd little station of his doing God only knows what all day."

"Jeez, Mom. Jack's a professional!" I didn't know why I'd picked that moment to defend him, but I had. Probably because the alternative was too ridiculous to even consider. "I know it's hard to believe," I added, "but he's obviously been trained for this."

"I know," she whispered, casting a nervous glance at the French doors to the hall. "But you're so smart and clever, Whitney." The look on her face, the utter confidence, was disturbing. "And don't forget," she pressed on, filling with pride and a suspicious amount of purpose—kind of like Mel Gibson portraying William Wallace as he rallied his ragtag lot of Scotsman to the slaughter—"you, Whitney Bloom, were number two!" Two fingers with cherry-red painted nails sprang to action in front of my face, as if I should be heartened by the thought that I had graduated second out of a class of only forty students. Mom clearly was not the competitive sort, nor was she living in the real world.

"Mom, that ... that doesn't mean anything," I protested, but she cut me off.

"Whitney, it's like this. It's apparent that Jack has reason to believe your dad might not have killed Jeb, but I don't want to take any chances. I can't run this place alone," she said, "and now there's the orchard to think about. And unless you want to move back home and help run this place, I think you should go with him to his meeting with the county coroner."

Fudgesicles! The woman had a point. I leapt from my chair, tossed back the rest of my virgin mimosa, and dashed out of the sunroom.

Six

hat in the name ... ?"

There was an incensed look on Jack's face the moment I ambushed the front seat of his police-issue Ford Expedition. Thanks to my hectic life in the city, and my penchant for disregarding time, I was forever chasing down cabs. I had gotten pretty good at catching them too.

"I thought ... " I said, and paused to buckle my seat belt. I then turned my brightest smile on him. "I thought I'd join you. No, no, don't step on the brake. I'm not getting out. Think about it, Jack. You have a daunting task ahead of you. I'm sure you're an able detective, and a fine policeman, but I think you're in a bit over your head here."

"Over my head?" he repeated, clearly insulted by the notion. It was then I recalled that Jack MacLaren didn't like to appear anything less than fully capable.

"I'm sorry to be so blunt, Jack, but let's face it. You're a small-town cop and murder is a big-time crime." I was trying to make a point. MacLaren was having none of it. Instead he lifted a ruddy brow, cocked his head, and looked utterly skeptical. For a detective, he was being pretty thick, I thought. "Listen," I cajoled, attempting to put him at ease. "I grew up on that orchard. I helped plant half those trees. I know those processing sheds like the back of my hand, as well as every nook and cranny of the inn. You need me. And for what it's worth, I know a thing or two about solving crimes." This last statement was a classic case of stretching the truth, something all savvy advertisers use to their advantage. I'd read a lot of mysteries and watched a fair amount of crime shows on TV, so I wasn't entirely ignorant about how to go about solving a crime. But I'd never been an active participant. Now, however, I was ready to roll up my sleeves and dig in, and in order to do that, I felt that I needed to see the body. I needed to know what had happened in the orchard. And I was determined to get my way.

Unfortunately, Jack wasn't taking me seriously. In fact, he was laughing so hard he had to pull off the road.

"Seriously, Whit," he said, as soon as he could breathe again. "I appreciate the offer, but what exactly is it you think you can do here?"

I crossed my arms, tilted my head, and said, "Look. In advertising we're taught to look at demographics in order to figure out a product's target audience. Anything can be solved by demographics, Jack, including the likeliest suspect for murder. Think of murder as a product to sell. The first thing you need to figure out is who needs that product … or, in our case, who needs that person dead? Who benefits most? Everything is a factor—age, sex, race, religion, political inclination, culture, education, income, family … what part of the country a person lives in. I didn't want to say anything back there, around my parents, but, um … I believe I can help you." I cast him a knowing look.

"Really?" For some reason, this too seemed to amuse him. "By putting your advertising skills to the test? Could you possibly be equating the murder of a man to a feminine hygiene ad?"

At the mention of *that ad* my face grew unnaturally hot. Dang it! Why did he have to bring that up again? Trying to ignore his ironic grin, I said, "Unlike you, I have a friendly face and a knack for getting people to talk. There are a lot of people staying at the inn, not to mention all the staff. Somebody must have seen something. I know you're going to need to talk with everyone there, everyone you can think of, to see if you can find someone with a motive. Why not let me help?"

The smile came off his face and his eyes hardened. "Are you telling me how to do my job? You the girl who ran off to Chicago to pursue a career in advertising, who created the most shocking Super Bowl ad of last year? By the way, how's that working out for you, Whit? Because I hear you changed jobs and are now selling cherry pies on the internet to pay your rent. This isn't a game. You may not care, but Jeb Carlson is dead—murdered on my watch!—in my town!—and I'm going to find the devil who did it. But I can't do that with you tagging along driven by your own guilty conscience."

There was some truth in that statement. That's why it hurt so much, and my face grew even hotter under his scrutinizing gaze. "Are ... are you calling me a loser, Jack?"

"No. Not a loser. Overreaching's the term I'd use. You always shoot for the stars and sail right over them, and when you finally land in reality, you can't accept it. You can't accept it and then you run away. And now you can't accept the fact that I don't need your help."

He'd cut too close to the bone this time, and he knew it. Curse Jack MacLaren for reminding me of all my faults and failures!

"Very well," I seethed. "Have it your way." I unbuckled my seat belt and reached for the door handle. "Go ahead and work this case yourself. After all, being by yourself is what you've always excelled at. And you're wrong about me. I'm devastated by Jeb's murder. He was a great man and a dear friend, and the thought that my dad is being blamed for it is more than I care to think about. I don't want to see him go to prison. A man like Dad couldn't survive it. It would destroy my family. But I doubt you even care about family. I doubt you care for anything at all but yourself." I pulled on the door handle.

Jack locked the door. "Whitney. Christ! I'm sorry. Please … don't … "

My plan had backfired, and so had his. And I didn't ever want to look at him again. All I wanted was to get the heck out of his SUV. I opened the lock and threw my shoulder into the door. Jack locked it again.

"Whitney, look at me. I haven't seen you in years and yet here we are bickering like kids again. It was kind of our thing—all the teasing, arguing, and challenging one another. I also recall that you were the only one to laugh at my jokes and had thick enough skin to be my friend. You of all people know I'm not an easy person to be around, and I'm afraid time hasn't helped that any. And it grows worse when I get frustrated and scared, like I am now."

With one hand wrapped around the door handle and the other wiping the tears of anger blurring my vision, I said, "You're … scared?" I didn't believe it.

He gave a solemn nod. "I am. Deadly so. There's a murderer on the loose in Cherry Cove," he added very softly, "and I have no idea who or where he is. I'm in charge of this investigation, yet I'm having a hell of a time getting backup. Jeb had the audacity to be murdered on a Friday night. Sturgeon Bay could only send one patrol officer to help me, the other four being busy with drunk and disorderly calls, and it took two hours to get an ambulance to the orchard because I'd already declared the body dead when I examined it, and a dead body is code for an ambulance driver to take his sweet effing time. And do you want to know the worst of it? I don't think your dad murdered Jeb. I believe he had little or nothing to do with the murder. However, thanks to a group of gossiping guests, plus the fact that your dad's prized croquet mallet was found beside the body, everybody has jumped to the obvious conclusion. Sergeant Stamper, from the Sturgeon Bay station, has been quick to call the whole mess a case of second-degree murder, and it might very well be. But I doubt it. I think something else went on in that cherry orchard."

I looked at him and sniffled. "Really? So … so you really don't believe my dad killed Jeb Carlson?"

Jack's lips pressed into a grim line and he shook his head.

"Then what do you think happened?"

"I don't know. What I do know is that I'm going to need to collect as much evidence as I can get. Last night, by the time I was called, it was too dark to see much of anything. I need to get out to the orchard and take another look, but first I have to head down to Sturgeon Bay. I called the county coroner last night and asked for an autopsy. I wanted it done right away, before Jeb's family comes up from Sheboygan to claim the body."

"Who's the county coroner?" I asked.

"Your grandma Jenn's neighbor, Doc Fisker. He's old but good, and he's susceptible to bribes." As Jack spoke, he jerked his thumb toward the back seat of his police SUV. I looked there and saw a familiar bakery box on the seat. "Cherry pie," Jack continued in answer to my unspoken question. "One of Grandma Jenn's. That pie is like gold around here. Shameless, isn't it? But that's how things work. If you want any real police work done, you bribe 'em with pastry. I should be on my hands and knees going over the orchard with a magnifying glass and a fine-tooth comb, but no, I'm buying cherry pie at the Cherry Orchard Inn instead. Things like this never happened back in Milwaukee."

"Were you happy in Milwaukee, Jack?"

He thought about it for a moment. "Yeah," he said. "For the most part I was."

"Then why are you here? I mean, if you were so happy in Milwaukee, why did you end up back in Cherry Cove?"

Jack lowered his head, pretending to look at his hands. "I came back," he said, turning to look at me, "because my dad got sick. Mom needed me here."

"Oh my God. I'm so sorry!" I covered his hand with my own. "Is he better? I always liked your dad, although I hardly understood a word he said."

"Oh, that was his accent. Scottish, you know. Raised in Glasgow, and although they claim to speak English there, they're really just fooling themselves." A soft smile touched his lips.

"No. I mean, there was that too, but your dad's really smart. He's probably the smartest man I've ever met."

"Yeah, Dad was pretty smart," Jack said. He looked out the window. "Was? Is he … ?"

"Last year. He was twenty years older than my mom—you know, well beyond the acceptable creeper range, right? But somehow they managed to make it work."

I had always liked Jack's parents. His mother, Inga, had been in her early twenties when she'd come to Cherry Cove from Sweden. Inga and my mom had both been waitresses at the Swedish Inn. Jack's father, a brilliant chemical engineer from Scotland, had come to Cherry Cove on vacation, dined at the Swedish Inn, and fell madly in love with Inga, or so my mother had told me. Inga was still one of my mom's closest friends.

"Naturally Mom was devastated, and I didn't have the heart to go back to Milwaukee," Jack continued. "That's when the good people of

Cherry Cove got together and demanded that the Door County Sheriff's Department put an officer on the peninsula. A short while later a position was created, and I was the lucky man to fill it."

"Jack, why didn't you tell me your father died?"

"Um," he said, pretending to think, "probably because you moved to Chicago and I don't have your phone number, or your address. Anyhow, I thought your mom would have told you."

It was my turn to look glum and utterly abashed. "She probably tried. I'm not very good at taking her phone calls these days."

He studied me with his soft, amber-colored eyes. I'd always thought Jack the heartless, selfish one between us, but apparently I was wrong. He'd given up his entire career as a detective in Milwaukee to be with his parents in Cherry Cove, while most of the time I was too self-absorbed to take even a phone call from mine. The thought hurt more than I liked to admit.

"Well," Jack said, breaking the silence with a touch of humor, "that sure sounds like an issue that's gonna require a lot of serious professional help. Unfortunately I don't have a psych degree, but I'll tell you what, Ms. Whit-less Bloom. If you think you can handle it, I'll even let you tag along with me to the morgue. But that's it. I heard you tell your dad you want to find Jeb's murderer, and I know you well enough to take that threat seriously, but for your own good I'm not going to let that happen. In spite of what you might think, police work is dangerous. And no civilian should stick their nose in a case involving murder. That being said, I admire your tenacity, Bloom. Do you still want to see a dead body?"

It was a challenge, one I accepted with a nod.

"Very well. Buckle up."

Seven

As Jack's Ford Expedition raced toward the comparative metropolis of Sturgeon Bay, I turned my mind to the real problem at hand: which was, quite simply, that I had no idea what I'd been thinking. A few minutes ago, thanks to Mom, I'd been convinced that I wanted nothing more than to insert myself into this troubling case of murder in the cherry orchard. Now that I had, however, I was having second thoughts. I mean, I was in an actual police car—correction, a police-issue SUV—with an actual qualified detective at the wheel—who was packing heat!—and who was bound and determined to examine a dead body. A DEAD BODY!

I didn't like dead bodies. I didn't even like seeing them on all the TV crime shows I watched, and those were fake dead bodies. Now the thought of staring at one—an old, baggy one with its head bashed in by a gold-plated croquet mallet—seemed beyond ghoulish. The thought sent a slight shiver of disgust down my spine, and I might have gaged as well.

Apparently Officer MacLaren didn't suffer any such qualms. In fact, if his face was any indication, I'd say he was actually excited by the prospect. He was explaining, in great detail, why it was imperative that he started with the body in the first place. As he talked I silently cursed myself for not conquering my bad habit of reacting before engaging in higher-level thinking. If I'd engaged my brain, I'd likely have been sitting before the fireplace in the breakfast room of the Cherry Orchard Inn enjoying a coffee and a cherry-filled croissant, not riding in a police car with a cop who was disturbingly pumped about viewing the body of a murder victim.

In retrospect, Jack had been right to question my qualifications for wanting to tag along. Advertising? What on earth had I been thinking? And if he'd just been an adult about the whole situation, he might have gotten his way. But he had to bait me with *that ad*. That and the fact that I could be a little overreaching at times. Giff liked to call it overzealous. Whatever personality affliction I suffered from, it had landed me here, right beside Jack, heading for Door County General and the morgue.

"So, how do you like living in Chicago?" Jack asked, once he realized I was no longer listening to his colorful narration on the more memorable dead bodies he'd come across during his career in Milwaukee.

"Oh, it's great. Chicago's great," I answered, offering what I hoped was a convincing smile.

"Yeah, but starting your own business is pretty cool. You've got to have a lot of drive to do something like that. For instance, I could never do it."

"You don't need to do it," I remarked. "You're a cop. You already have a pretty cool job."

With both hands on the wheel he flashed a quick grin. "Why thank you, Ms. Bloom, but what I meant was, when I'm not working I slip into bum mode pretty easily. You probably didn't know this just from looking at me, but I'm totally addicted to video games." This was punctuated with an ironic stare.

He was being kind, likely to make up for his earlier behavior. Besides, he was too fit to be addicted to video games. I played along and said, "Oh, I believe it. You and every man under thirty-five."

"Did I tell you that I've been to your website, *Bloom 'n' Cherries!*?" I was glad he was staring ahead through the windshield as he said it, because this I did find alarming. As if reading my thoughts, he added, "It's true. I don't know anything about advertising, but I have to say, the pictures on your site are pure food porn. You're good. You got me to order a few things, and I live right in the heart of cherry country."

"You ... ordered something from my site?" I wondered how I could have missed it.

"Yeah, but not under my own name, of course." He flashed an impish grin.

The moment he did, every nerve in my body came fully awake, every warning bell sounding off. Dear God, could Jack MacLaren be the infamous C-Bomb—the internet enigma I'd been chatting with ever since opening my online store? We'd flirted! Dear God, I'd said things to C-Bomb I'd never say to any man ... well, at least not to Jack MacLaren! Had Jack been trolling me? Had he been serious? Holy mother of embarrassment, I didn't even know how to process it. Then I realized he was staring at me.

"You okay, Whit? I didn't mean to alarm you."

"What ... what name do you use?"

His grin grew even wider. My heart sank like a stone and my cheeks burned with mortal embarrassment. Then, unable to contain his secret any longer, he said, "Inga MacLaren."

"Your *mother*?" That was a revelation. Inga ordered quite a bit and always had it sent to her house, not a police station. "You're ordering things from my site under your mother's name? Isn't that illegal or something?"

This made him chuckle. "Whoa there, PI Bloom. It's only illegal if I don't have her permission. And I'm sorry that shocked you. It started innocently enough. Inga is very cautious about buying goods on the internet," he added, using a comical Swedish accent that mimicked his mother's. "But she really wanted to support your business. I suggested she buy a prepaid Visa card, which she did. But she was still hesitant, so she came to the police station and wanted me to show her how to do it. Inga's not so great with technology, so I helped her order a few things from *Bloom 'n' Cherries!* and had it sent to her house. She loved your products so much that she has me ordering things for her all the time now. For the record, I thought they were great too. Have you ever considered opening a brick and mortar *Bloom 'n' Cherries!* at the inn? I know your grandma sells her pies at the gift shop, but you have to pre-order those. And you have a lot of products. You could totally make a killing during the tourist season and use your website for the off-season."

"I never really gave it much thought," I told him truthfully, still processing the fact that he'd ordered baked goods from *Bloom 'n' Cherries!* "I guess I've been kind of holding out hope for another shot at advertising. However, I don't see that happening anytime soon." Jack looked at me, his eyes full of question. *"That ad,"* I explained. "I really mucked things up good with *that ad.*"

"Maybe, but at least you got to produce a real TV ad, which is a lot more than most people can say. I'm sorry about that, Whit. And I'm sorry for what I said to you before. I didn't really mean it. It's more the fact that crime work can get very nasty sometimes. It takes a strong stomach, and sometimes when you're digging for answers, you uncover things you're not quite ready for—things that maybe you wish you hadn't uncovered in the first place." He saw the troubled look on

46

my face and was quick to add, "I'm not saying that's what's going to happen here. What I'm trying to say is that once you start digging, you have to hope for the best and be prepared for the worst."

Eight

$\mathcal{I}$ was still trying to process Jack's ominous words when we pulled into the parking lot of Door County General, a modest though relatively modern hospital of twenty-five beds. The sight of the hospital made my stomach moan out loud, protesting the morgue before my brain had the chance to … or maybe it was the heavenly scent of Grandma Jenn's cherry pie wafting from the back seat. I'd been smelling it for the last half hour. Suddenly I realized how hungry I was.

Jack, hearing the cry from my protesting stomach, had taken hold of the bakery box like a wide receiver, protecting it like the game ball. He gave me a large evidence bag containing Dad's croquet mallet to carry instead.

"I forgot to ask," he began as we stepped onto the elevator. He pressed a button. The doors closed and the elevator descended. "You've seen a dead body before, right?" He shifted the bakery box to his other arm—the one farthest from me—and held me in a questioning gaze.

"Yes. Of course," I lied, and felt compelled to add, "Chicago's full of 'em."

It was not the answer he'd been expecting. A curious smile touched his lips and he said, "Okay. Well then, I don't need to warn you about ... " The door opened and he stepped out, stopping in mid-sentence. I was waiting for him to finish his thought, to finish his warning, but he didn't, because just then Doc Fisker popped out of a doorway halfway down the basement hall. He spied us as we came out of the elevator, paused to shove the remains of what looked to be a Danish into his mouth, and wiped his hands on his lab coat.

"Oh, hey there, Officer MacLaren!" Doc Fisker waved as he ambled toward us, a wide smile lighting up his face. He was a heavy-set man in his late sixties, with a pouf of white hair on his head and eyes as round and inquisitive as an owl's. His thick glasses made them look even larger, which was always a bit disconcerting at first. "And is that Miss Bloom I see? Oh, fer heaven's sake! I haven't seen you around these parts in an age." He shook Jack's hand, then embraced me in an avuncular hug. Stepping away, he said to me, "I suppose you're tagging along because of that mess up there at you orchard, eh?"

In answer to his question, I held up the bag containing Dad's croquet mallet.

"So that's the culprit! Would've been nice to have had that right when the body came in." Doc Fisker turned to Jack and, lowering his voice, continued. "I know Baxter's a bit of a hot head on a golf course, but I've never heard of croquet inciting such rage. Were they playing for money, by chance?"

The question took Jack by surprise. "This isn't the result of croquet, Doc."

"Really? That's surprising. Because everyone around these parts knows that's Baxter's prized croquet mallet."

"Indeed. So why would Baxter leave it next to the body? That, dear doctor, is why we're here."

"Oh, a mystery! I do so love a mystery. I find there's always a rather mysterious element hanging around that old orchard. Why, I was up there earlier this spring and do you know what I saw? Jeb had those girls—Jenn, Jani, the Robinson girl, and a few of the younger waitresses—dressed in flowing white gowns with flowered wreaths in their hair, holding hands and dancing around the budding trees. Was suspiciously pagan. When I asked him about it, he said…" At that very moment, Doc Fisker caught a whiff of the pie in Jack's hands. The temptation was too strong. He didn't even have the willpower to fight through to the end of his own sentence. Instead he turned to Jack and rested his magnified blue orbs on the bakery box in nearly the same manner I had. And he'd just polished off a Danish!

"Oh, MacLaren, you wily devil. You've brought me one of Jenn's pies."

"Only the best for you, Doc. Fresh from the ovens of the Cherry Orchard Inn." Jack held the box up to his own nose and took a theatric whiff. "A legendary pie made from the cherries grown in Miss Bloom's own family orchard. It's what put Cherry Cove on the map."

"You're a shameless rascal, MacLaren. Forcing an old man to work on a Saturday … and on a fool's errand ta boot!" But even as the doctor spoke, he couldn't help grinning.

"There you go again, Doc, confusing shameless with appreciative." There was a twinkle in Jack's honey-colored eyes as he said this. "And if you must know, Miss Bloom and I don't believe that her father had anything to do with the murder of Jeb Carlson."

A troubled look crossed Doc Fisker's normally pleasant face. "Then ya better brace yourselves, my dears, because it looks a pretty convincing case to me. But don't take my word for it. I'm only the county coroner around these parts. Very well, MacLaren, Miss Bloom, if you insist. Let us pull on some gloves, unwrap the body, and do a little pokin' around, shall we?"

Nine

With my hands securely encased in latex, and my sweatshirt and jeans discretely covered by a freshly laundered white lab coat, I was as ready as I was ever going to be to face my darkest fears. I was about to view the very dead body of Jeb Carlson.

This thought had not stopped bothering me since I'd ambushed the front seat of Jack's car. But if I was going to insist on playing detective, the least I could do was follow through on my promise. I was going to need to look at a dead body without my hands covering my eyes, and I was going to need to listen thoughtfully as Jack and Doc Fisker made professional observations and discussed theories. It would also be helpful if I could add valuable input, or at least offer an intelligent remark or two. I thought of some of the intelligent remarks I'd heard on television crime shows when one of the actors discovered a dead body. Marks on the neck meant strangulation; a blue face indicated asphyxiation; a body under water was a drowning... a smashed-in skull meant a croquet mallet to the head. Dang it! Cause of death was always so obvious!

Thankfully Jack and Doc Fisker were oblivious to the sweat beading up on my brow or the slight trembling of my hands. In fact, they were engaged in a steady stream of small talk, leaving me to mentally prepare for what I was about to confront in the morgue.

"Really?" I heard Doc Fisker say just before he turned his curious, over-large gaze on me. "You lost your job in advertising after making *that ad*?"

"Ah," I began, pulling my macabre thoughts back to the conversation. "Yes."

"Actually, Miss Bloom has a thriving online business now," Jack added, snapping the fingers of his own latex gloves for a better fit. He cast me a grin and grabbed hold of a gurney. "She's put all her advertising skills to good use, isn't that right, Whitney?"

I suspected he was teasing me, but I was too nervous to do anything but nod in agreement as I followed them out of the medical examiner's office. We then headed down the hall, past a lab, and stopped before what was obviously our destination.

"An online business," Doc Fisker mused, picking up the conversation again. He paused to slide his ID card into the lock. The door opened and an attendant waved us through. "I don't buy much of anything online. Don't trust it with all that identity theft stuff. But now that I think on it, my wife purchased something online once. It was that book. Have you read that book, Miss Bloom?"

With only half a mind engaged in their conversation, I replied, "I don't know, doctor. What book are you referring to?"

"*Fifty Shades of Grey*," he said with an alarmingly straight face. Jack, caught off guard, missed a step. He also couldn't help himself from throwing a questioning look my way. I ignored him.

"No, sir. I haven't yet had the pleasure."

"Well, the wife did, and let me tell you, she really enjoyed it." A cottony tuft, resembling a slightly electrified albino caterpillar, wiggled behind the thick glasses.

The attendant opened another door for us and I was hit with a blast of cool air. We were now in the morgue proper. Dr. Fisker stopped before one of the many stainless steel doors of the body cooler. "Well, it's your lucky day then, isn't it?" This pronouncement was punctuated with a grin that definitely had no place inside a morgue. "Because I just happen to have a copy in my office."

As the doctor talked he opened the little door, revealing two fish-belly pale bare feet. On one big toe was a tag. After a quick perusal of the tag, he cried, "Got 'em!" and gave a hearty yank on the drawer.

My own body, meanwhile, was taken with a violent shudder. I wasn't entirely certain if it was due to the sight of the body draped beneath the white sheet or the mental image of the elderly Mrs. Fisker lounging poolside while reading S and M erotica. It was very likely a result of both.

"Just don't read it out loud on the trip back to Cherry Cove," Doc Fisker continued as he made ready to lift the sheet, "unless, of course, you want to." The bushy eyebrows wiggled suggestively.

Jack, poor thing, blushed to the roots of his red hair.

My stomach churned, making a distressing noise.

Doc Fisker chuckled and threw back the sheet.

The sight was revolting. It was Alien-Autopsy-meets-Walking-Dead disturbing! The fact that the dark, lifeless eyes were staring directly up at me only made it worse. Beyond the angry black bruising and dented skull was the indistinguishable face that for the last seventy years had been animated by the soul of Jeb Carlson—curator of our cherry orchard and a true gentleman. There was no doubt in my mind that the poor thing had indeed blocked the business end of a croquet mallet with his head. He had a bruise the size of a dinner plate to prove it.

"Poor old bastard," Doc Fisker said. "Quite the character. You probably didn't know, but that book I'm giving you, well, this old trailblazer had it last."

"Whaa … whaa …?" Unable to form words, I looked at the doctor. "Oh dear," I said, then collapsed on the hard tile floor of the morgue.

Ten

I awoke in a strange bed. My head was throbbing. And it took a moment or two before I realized where I was. But once I saw the retractable curtains, and the carts full of medical supplies and machinery, I suspected that I'd landed myself in the emergency room of the hospital. Then I remembered why, and groaned. Had I really passed out in the morgue? How embarrassing! Mortifying, really. Then my mind traveled back to the last thing I'd seen, which was Jeb's face ... or what was left of it after it blocked Dad's croquet mallet.

The mental image was gruesome, and I had to close my eyes for a moment to block the sting of fresh tears. It was a terrible way for a man to die. So violent and unnecessary. And the thought that Dad might have possibly done that to the poor old guy was too much to contemplate.

But I had to. That's why I was here. I was here to prove that Dad couldn't have done such an unspeakably gruesome act against his friend. I wanted it to be true, but what did I really know of my dad? There was that old saying that a person can never really know what another person is thinking. Was there some deep, dark side to Dad that he kept hidden? I mean, I was aware the man lived with a good amount of stress. There was always some emergency at the inn or the orchard that needed handling. He wasn't exactly a hothead, but every now and then he allowed anger to consume him. Mom would always say that Dad needed to blow his stack so he could let off some steam, then he'd settle down and focus on the problem at hand. This apparently wasn't a secret—even Doc Fisker had commented on it. Dad was an avid golfer. He loved the sport, and yet he was known far and wide as a habitual club-tosser. Could he have tossed his croquet mallet in anger?

Then there were those unsettling two hours of time, during which Jeb was murdered, when nobody but Dad could account for his whereabouts. That thought depressed me more than all the others. The ache in my body intensified and I suddenly felt heavy as lead.

A moment later, the sound of a television caught my attention. The person in the bed next to me was watching the news. And the story of the hour was the murder at the Cherry Orchard Inn.

I sat up with a start. The effort intensified the throbbing in my head. I brought a hand up to investigate and found that I had a lump the size of a golf ball front and center. It hurt like a freakin' sonofagun. The only blessing was that I was still in my own clothes, thank God. Ignoring the pain, I swung my legs over the side of the bed and threw back the curtain.

"Oh, my!" My abrupt entrance had startled the elderly woman in the bed next to mine. I felt a little guilty when I saw that a blob of Jell-O had wiggled off her spoon, landing in her coffee. "Hello there, dear," she said, seemingly unfazed. "You're awake. Nurse Sheila said you took a nasty tumble and cracked your head. I fell too, only I won't be springing out of bed so quickly this time."

"I'm very sorry to hear that," I said, and truly meant it. She seemed like a nice old lady. Under any other circumstances, I'd undoubtedly be a bit more attentive. But the news had grabbed my full attention.

"Isn't it just terrible," she said, her bright old eyes wide with morbid intrigue. "There's been a murder at the Cherry Orchard Inn. Can you believe it? Baywatch News had been up there all morning. They've got that woman reporter, Greta Stone, there now."

"What?" I cried. Unfortunately, she wasn't lying. It was surreal watching the live feed from the TV cameras as a Barbie-esque blonde stood in the familiar parking lot with the inn perfectly framed behind her. She was speaking to the cameras.

"The details are still unclear, but this is what we know so far. Last night, orchard manager Jeb Carlson was found dead in the cherry orchard by Ryan and Julia McSweeny, a young couple staying at the inn for the annual Cherry Blossom Festival. There are no suspects yet in custody, but the name Baxter Bloom, owner of both orchard and inn, has been put forth by an anonymous source as a person of interest. The cause of death is still unknown, and the local authorities are keeping a tight lid on this ongoing investigation. But don't worry, I'm going to personally stay here until we can get to the bottom of this Blunder Under the Blossoms. Reporting from the Cherry Orchard Inn, for Baywatch News, this is Greta Stone."

"Oh, that Greta Stone is a sly one!" the old lady exclaimed, then took a sip of her Jell-O coffee. "She's hot on the trail, that one. It's only a matter of time before she draws out the details. And I bet they're juicy."

In one painful clench, my heart emptied of all blood and my throat felt dry as sand. It was terrible! It was a nightmare! Poor Dad! Without another thought, I headed for the door.

"Wait! You can't just run out of here like that, dear! Not with that lump on your head. What am I to tell Nurse Sheila?"

"Umm ... thanks?" I said noncommittally, and dashed out the door.

Eleven

$\mathcal{I}$ needed to find Jack, and we needed to get back to the orchard. It was barely mid-morning, but all hell was breaking loose. I escaped the ER without incident, found a stairwell, and descended into the basement two steps at a time. I was running down the back hallway when I saw Jack emerging from the Medical Examiner's Office.

"Hey," Jack said upon seeing me. "You okay? Nasty lump. That's gotta hurt. I was just about to come up and see how you were doing."

Truthfully, I'd already forgotten about the pain in my head. "I'm fine," I assured him, bending over to catch my breath. "Listen, we've got to get back to the inn. It's been on the news. The press is already there. Can you believe it? They're calling it 'Blunder Under the Blossoms'! I was in advertising, Jack. That's the kind of thing that sticks to a business. That's the kind of thing that ruins lives! This is a PR nightmare."

He stood a moment, studying me through narrowed eyes. "That incident in the morgue … clearly, you're not cut out for this."

"Are you listening to what I'm telling you, Jack? The press is there."

"Of course they are. It's murder," he stated, holding me in a scrutinizing gaze.

"You knew they were there?"

"They were tipped off when the body came in last night. It's bound to happen. They have police scanners and informants in every hospital. Unfortunately, and you might not want to hear this, but it's journalists' job to report the news. However, I specifically told your parents that under no circumstance were they to talk with the press, and they won't. Don't worry."

"What? Don't worry? *Are you insane?* How am I not supposed to worry? You saw the body! You know what happened. Even a toddler could see that my dad killed that man! How can you look so calm?"

"Because," Jack said plainly, "I'm not a toddler." It seemed he was about to elaborate on this when Doc Fisker walked out of his office. The man was eating a huge piece of cherry pie on a very tiny paper plate.

"MacLaren, it's been a pleasure, m'boy," he said. "I'll sign the paperwork and wait for your call before I send it over, just like you asked. And Miss Bloom." He turned to me, paused, and shoveled another gooey bite of pie into his mouth. "Whoa Nelly!" he exclaimed, his large blue eyes growing even larger. He wiggled the little plastic fork at my forehead. "You've got a nice egg on your head. Came down hard and cracked it on the table before we knew what happened. You'll want to put some ice on that." He took another bite. "Don't be a stranger. Oh," he exclaimed, parking his tiny fork deep in the flaky pie crust. "I meant to give you this." He withdrew a disturbingly well-read copy of *Fifty Shades of Grey* from the pocket of his lab coat. His finger left a smudge of cherry pie filling on the cover. I didn't want to touch it, let alone take it. Jack suffered no such qualms and took it for me. "When you're done with that," the doctor instructed, "pass it along to your mother. She'd get a kick out of it."

"Thanks, Doc," Jack replied, doing a remarkable job of looking professional. "I'll see to it that Miss Bloom follows your orders to a tee. But for now, I think it's best that I get her out of here. Look at her head. I've heard of people passing out in a morgue before but didn't think it was true. Now we know." The idiot grinned. The doctor did too. Jack then cleared his throat, took my hand, and pulled me along to the elevator.

The moment the doors closed he dissolved into a fit of laughter. "I'm sorry," he said, gaining control of himself once again. "Doc Fisker. Gotta love the guy, but he's one disturbed old dude. Pie in one hand, chick-porn in the other. That's what happens when you cut open dead bodies all day for a living." He shook the book at me in a mocking way. The elevator door opened and we stepped out. "Do you want this?" he asked.

I shook my head. "It's all yours."

"Oh, no-no. Only sci-fi and comic books for me." He grinned, winked, and disappeared into the ER waiting room. A moment later he popped out again, bookless.

"Come along, Whit. Let's get you something to eat," he said, grabbing hold of my hand again. "As I was saying—or at least as I was beginning to say until I got distracted—you cannot enter a morgue on an empty stomach, especially when viewing the body of a friend or loved one. Doesn't work."

"But Jack, we don't have time to eat. We need to get back to the inn."

"And risk you passing out again? I think not. Dear God, your stomach's been growling like a rabid dog ever since you landed in the front seat of my car, and now you have a very unsightly lump on your forehead. First rule of crime investigation: eat a good breakfast."

"How can I eat knowing that the press is going to rake my parents over the coals?" My forehead throbbed at the thought.

"They're gonna try. And damaging details will begin to emerge. It's how it works, Whit. But don't worry."

"Don't worry?" I cried helplessly. "My dad's going to be lynched, and my mom will be left to run both orchard and inn, and let me tell you, I don't think she's up for it."

"Whit, don't fret just yet. It's not a bad thing the press is there. It'll get the guests talking. Everyone who has something to say about the murder will undoubtedly come forward and talk to the camera. People can't resist the thought of being on TV, especially when they think they have some little but important tidbit to share. I hope the reporter talks to every guest staying at the inn. Makes my job easier."

"Jack!" I admonished, standing beside his SUV. "Are you listening to yourself? My father ... " It was hard to wrap my head around the thought, but I'd come halfway to it and now I had to finish it. "My father probably murdered a man last night in his own cherry orchard! And now you're going to sit back and let the press interview the guests so they can destroy what's left of his dignity?"

Jack bent his head and looked me in the eye. "You believe your father murdered Jeb Carlson?" It appeared he found this interesting. That he did was like a blow to the stomach.

"Oh my God!" I breathed. "I saw the body before passing out! I'm not an idiot!"

He considered this a moment, then wisely added, "I never thought you were, but you did pass out. You didn't get the full story. I now know something that only Doc Fisker and the murderer know, and thanks to that man's weakness for your grandma's cherry pie, it will remain a secret for a while longer yet."

"What do you know?" I asked, flabbergasted.

Jack opened the car door for me. Only when I was seated and buckled in did he say, "What I know, Whitney Bloom, is exactly what I suspected in the first place. Your father didn't kill Jeb Carlson."

Twelve

To say that the words Jack uttered were a relief would be an understatement. I may have passed out in the morgue prematurely—and what I'd seen in there would certainly forever be seared in my memory—but the entire episode had left me with a new appreciation for the importance of good detective work. It caused me to ponder the fact that Officer MacLaren might not be quite as inexperienced as Mom thought him to be. He had followed a hunch and had used cherry pie as a bribe. That spoke of cleverness. The fact that he was withholding the secret he'd uncovered from me until I'd eaten was downright maddening. The man was not above extortion.

Therefore, moments after leaving the hospital, I found myself sitting in a quiet booth in the back of a local Sturgeon Bay establishment called Ed's Diner. The waitress, a sturdy middle-aged woman named Marge, knew Jack by name.

"Morning, Marge," he said to her with a bright, innocent smile. "My friend Miss Bloom here will have the Big Breakfast: eggs overeasy, extra bacon, pancakes instead of toast, a glass of water, coffee, a bag of ice, and two Tylenol if you've got 'em." The elderly waitress looked at me in a pitying way, nodded, and scribbled on her notepad.

"Wait," I protested, attempting to break in and change the obscene order to something a little less full-blown gluttony (I had a rule never to eat so much in public!). Our waitress, however, didn't appear to hear me. She was entirely focused on Jack. "Just a black coffee for me, Marge." Jack gave his lean, uniformed stomach a meaningful pat. "Criminals hate a fit cop. Hate it even more when you run their asses to the ground." He cast the waitress a playful wink.

"Oh, is that so?" A look of extreme skepticism appeared over a pair of bedazzled drugstore readers. "And here I thought that's what your pricey SUV was for, *Officer MacLaren*."

"There's that too, Marge. But criminals are a little harder on a truck than your average kamikaze deer. And unlike the unfortunate deer, criminals have lawyers."

Marge cracked a smile for the first time. "So what happened to you then, hon?" she asked, pointing a shocking-pink painted nail at the throbbing lump on my forehead. "Did the fit detective run you to ground as well? Or was it his handy SUV?"

I smiled up at her. "Neither, I'm afraid. I got this little beauty in the morgue." That sent her off in a hurry. A moment later I was scarfing down every morsel of the giant breakfast while Officer MacLaren nibbled on a piece of bacon and nursed a coffee.

"Can't have you passing out again," he remarked, watching me eat.

"Not likely to happen," I assured him with a mouthful of pancakes. "I've just conquered my fear of morgues and dead bodies."

He thought this was amusing. "No one conquers that fear, but I would've appreciated it if you hadn't lied to me. If you'd just told me that you'd never been to a morgue before, or that you'd never actually seen a dead body, I would have at least stood beside you. Had I been beside you and not across from you, I might have prevented that lump. There's no shame in admitting the truth, Whit. But there can be real danger in trying to be something you're not."

I stared at him, my head throbbing, my eyes bulging, my mind racing. "We both know that you would never have taken me with you if I'd told you the truth."

"True," he said, and took a sip of coffee. "And now you know. But Whitney, this is where it ends."

"Not quite," I reminded him, and pushed away my empty plate. "You said that my dad didn't kill Jeb Carlson. So who clubbed the poor man to death?"

Jack shrugged. "It wasn't the croquet mallet that killed him."

"I don't believe that for a minute. I saw the man's head—right before I passed out. The bruising was monstrous. Are you absolutely certain?"

"Pretty darn," he replied. "Would you care to venture a guess as to what actually killed him?"

I took a sip of coffee, thinking. Unfortunately, I had nothing. He undoubtedly knew I had nothing but was insisting on testing me. "Well," I began, "if it wasn't a blow to the head that killed Jeb Carlson, I'd say … " I thought a moment, then decided to throw caution to the wind and offered, "He was strangled."

"Really? Strangled? That's what you're going with?"

"I thought I saw some bruising around his neck, just there." As I spoke I indicated my own neck. But Jack wasn't buying it. In fact, he looked amused.

"You didn't have time to look at Jeb's neck before you passed out, did you?"

"Not really, no." The mere mention of my little accident was still humiliating.

"I thought you might be interested to know that all the bruising you saw, encompassing the entire left side of Jeb's face and not his neck, occurred postmortem. It happened after Jeb was already dead."

A shiver of disgust rippled through me. "Are you sure? Who would do such a thing to a harmless old man?"

"A murderer," Jack added levelly. "Not your dad, at any rate. What Doc Fisker and I discovered was that Jeb was poisoned first. He was dead before the mallet struck. Which means that whoever poisoned him went to some trouble to make it appear that your dad was to blame."

"Are you saying that someone's trying to frame my father for murder?"

"That's exactly what I'm saying. Do you know if your dad has any enemies, Whitney? Is there some reason a person would want to damage his image, or try to get him out of the way?"

"No. At least, I don't think that there is. My dad's a great guy. Everybody loves him."

What Jack thought of this I couldn't be sure. His face was as smooth and reflective as pond water. He thought for a moment before adding, "Then there's the possibility that this might not be about Baxter at all. Maybe it really is about Jeb, and your dad was just an easy target to pin his murder on. Did Jeb know something that he shouldn't have?" It looked as if he was asking me this. I shrugged my shoulders in response. "Did he have a secret worth dying for?" Jack continued. "Did he make an enemy who might want him dead?"

"Let's say he did. It makes the most sense to me."

"That's wishful thinking, Whit. The truth is, we don't have enough evidence to support either theory. However, one thing we do know is that whoever the murderer is, they're not a stranger. We're dealing with someone who knows their way around the orchard, someone who knows the relationship between Jeb and your father; someone who knows that your dad has a prized croquet mallet that he keeps in his office."

"Oh my God" was all I could say, suddenly feeling ill. I shouldn't have eaten so much. "I never considered that."

"This is what I tried to warn you about, Whitney. This is what makes investigating so dangerous. Murder, in most instances, is a very personal crime. You might not wish to acknowledge it, but the chances are good that you know the person who did this."

"You … you don't think it could be one of the guests?"

"We can't rule them out just yet, but in my experience, it's unlikely. Then, too, you've been away from here for quite a while. Maybe you won't know who this person is."

"If that was supposed to make me feel better, it doesn't."

"Could be a new friend of Jeb's," he offered by way of apology. "A girlfriend, perhaps? You heard what Doc Fisker said. Jeb was the last person to have *that book*." I didn't like where Jack was going with this. To be fair, neither did he. He took a sip of coffee, as if the bitter taste would erase the words from his tongue. I did the same. It didn't help. "However," he finally said, after thinking a moment, "I'm inclined to think it has something to do with the wine they were making in secret."

"The wine!" I exclaimed, suddenly remembering about that.

"Exactly. If nobody knew about it but the two of them, why was it missing?"

"Maybe Jeb took it himself and hid it, before telling Dad it was gone."

"If he hadn't been poisoned, it might be a consideration. If Jeb in fact stole the wine and then your dad found out, it might be plausible that he would have used his croquet mallet in anger. But Baxter's a smart man. If he was going to murder his orchard manager, say in a fit of unbridled passion—and say that he just happened to have his croquet mallet in hand—he wouldn't leave it in the orchard"

"Of course not! Dad's smarter than that." For some reason this thought enlivened me.

"Everyone knows it's his croquet mallet," Jack went on. "Even the couple who found the body recognized it. Doc Fisker and I did a cursory check of the grip and shaft for fingerprints, and there's plenty. He's sending it off to the lab, but I'm not holding my breath. Our killer has proven himself to be very clever, and a clever criminal would know to wear gloves."

"You said Jeb was poisoned first. Do you know what kind of poison was used, or how it was given?"

Jack gave a curt nod. "Doc Fisker identified it as cyanide poisoning. Apparently Jeb had ingested it. Very lethal stuff."

"How lethal?" I asked this because I knew next to nothing about poison, let alone the one Jack had mentioned.

"Obviously it was lethal enough to kill a man."

"Yeah, I see that. But where does it come from? How does one get it? And how did the murderer make Jeb ingest it?"

Jack shook his head slowly and shrugged.

"Okay. Jeb was poisoned," I said. "Let's think about this. According to Dad, most of the guests had retired to the lounge. However, the McSweenys sneak into the orchard for a little nookie-nookie, as Mom put it, and happen to stumble upon Jeb's body. What do we know of the McSweenys?"

"I spoke with them last night," Jack said. "They're from Milwaukee, in their early thirties, been married two years, and appeared to be in shock at having discovered the body. It could all be an act, of course, but I don't think so. They looked too nervous when they spoke about the croquet mallet. They'd been playing in the tournament that evening and recognized it as belonging to your father. Of course, what they reported isn't sitting well with any of the guests. Nobody wants to stay at an inn owned by a murder suspect. However, I made it perfectly clear last night that no one's to leave until we have a bit more information to go on."

"And so the Cherry Blossom Festival continues," I said darkly. "Are the McSweenys still suspects?"

"Everyone's a suspect, Whitney, even your parents, until I can prove they had nothing to do with the murder. To do this I need to substantiate all alibis. I need to find out who had a motive. Most importantly, I need to find the real killer."

"I wish I could have seen how the crime scene looked," I said.

Jack raised a curious brow and took out his phone. "I don't know what good it'll do, but here," he said, handing the phone to me. "I took these last night. They're a bit unsettling, but now that you've been fed and are sitting down, I think you can handle it."

It had been dark when the body was found, which only exacerbated the sinister quality of the pictures. Illuminated by the bright flash of a cell phone camera, they were positively gruesome. It turned my stomach to see them. Again, I regretted wolfing down that big breakfast. To witness Jeb's body like that … lying on a blanket of the tender white petals he'd cared so much for in life! His face looked similar to what I'd seen in the morgue, only more livid. I zoomed in, looking closely at the body and the petals beneath it. It suddenly struck me that something didn't seem quite right. It took me a moment more to realize what it was.

"Jack, there's something odd here. See by his right hand? I'll bet my life those are cherry pits."

Jack took a look. "Okay. What if they are? It's a cherry orchard."

"There aren't any pits in a cherry orchard, at least none that are that clean. You've seen the machine we use to harvest the cherries. There are two components to it—the hydraulic shaker, which clamps onto the trunk of the tree and travels down the left side of the row, and the collector-conveyer, which travels down the right side at the same time. The two machines work together, coming from either side of the tree until they overlap near the base of the trunk. When the machines are in place, the shaker goes into action, removing every ripe piece of fruit. The fruit, with some leaves and branches, falls into the collector-conveyer, where it moves up the belt and is deposited in a water-filled collection tub. Nothing falls on the ground. That being said, consider the fact that it's spring right now. The cherry harvest takes place in mid-July. And these pits look like they're lying on top of the blossoms, not under them. That would only happen if someone put them there."

"So you're suggesting that the killer was eating cherries?"

"No. These are sour cherries, and people generally don't like to eat them raw. Even if they did, all our cherries go through the pitter first. And, for the sake of argument, even if these pits were from the Bing variety, whoever was eating them while murdering Jeb would've likely spit them on the ground in a random fashion. These are all clustered together—as if they've dropped from his hand."

Jack took another look. "My God, Bloom," he said appreciatively and leaned back in the booth. "I can't believe I missed that. I'm going to need to take another look at the crime scene. First, however, I've asked your father to take me to the old lighthouse storeroom to have a look around. And while I'm doing that, I'll let him in on what we discovered this morning at the morgue. He'll be relieved, to say the least. But Whitney, I don't want the poisoning to become public knowledge just yet. Got it? Someone went to a lot of trouble to make it look like your dad killed Jeb in a fit of rage, and this person is still out there. I want the murderer to believe we're none the wiser. It'll make him bolder and hopefully he'll slip up. Like I said, I have a feeling whoever stole all that wine is somehow involved in the murder."

Suddenly I too had a pressing need to get into that old lighthouse and have a look around. This, however, I would never admit to Jack.

He glanced at his watch. "All right, Whit, you good?" I nodded. Jack stood and picked up the check. "My treat. And Whitney, now that you know the truth, I need you to be extra careful. But for the fact that we're old friends, I never would have taken you to the morgue this morning. I shouldn't have indulged your curiosity, but I did. Don't make me regret it. If you want to help, the best thing you can do is go back to the inn, pitch in wherever your Mom needs you, and stay vigilant." He then took my phone and added his number to the contact list. "No snooping around, got it? However, if you should happen to see anything suspicious, or hear anything that might be of use on this case, call me. This isn't a game. That lump on your head, you got that witnessing what this person is capable of."

Thirteen

My head was reeling with all the new information I'd learned at Ed's Diner. Jeb hadn't been clubbed to death, he'd been poisoned with cyanide, something I knew little about. I had to believe that being poisoned was a terrible, agonizing way to die, and yet as scary as that thought was, the fact that the murderer had tried to frame Dad was somehow possibly worse. It meant familiarity. It could easily be one of the guests. Dad said most came back every year. Yet Jack was inclined to believe that the murderer was local, and very familiar with both Jeb and Dad.

And then there was the oddity of the cherry pits. If they had fallen from Jeb's hand, why was he carrying cherry pits to begin with? I didn't know. I might never know, but I did know, with near certainty, where he had gotten them. It was the one small detail I had purposely refrained from telling Jack. A girl, including one endowed with probing curiosity, needed to keep some secrets to herself. Especially if that girl had no intention of listening to her high school friend, even if he was a cop.

As Jack drove back to the Cherry Orchard Inn in contemplative silence, I sat beside him in the passenger seat thinking of the crime scene. According to his description it was in the back of the orchard, not far from the processing sheds, and now clearly marked with yellow caution tape. I would have no trouble finding it, but that was hardly a thing I would tell him. I was also curious about the poison used. Jack obviously knew a great deal about this poison. His reticence on the subject was proof enough. He didn't want to talk about it, for the obvious reason that he didn't want me to know. Because he knew that if I knew, I'd keep digging, and rightly so. He knew this because this was exactly what the old Jack MacLaren would have done. And self-proclaimed obsessive video game junky or not, he would never drop a stimulating subject before examining it to death.

I was just about to covertly read up on cyanide poisoning on my iPhone when my phone rang. It was Giff. He was using FaceTime, his favorite form of communication, especially since he knew I could see that he was lounging on my bed with a stack of *Cosmos* beside him. It was all for show.

"Hi there," I answered, smiling at the screen.

"You driving? Jesus!" he exclaimed and leaned away from the phone. "Your forehead! Looks like an alien's about ready to pop outta that little egg."

Jack, overhearing, laughed.

Giff's eyes widened. "The lady is not alone? I hear a voice ... a decidedly male voice. Well, don't keep me in suspense, princess. Introduce me."

For his own entertainment, I was sure Giff was hoping it would be Tate. Giff knew all about Tate, and I suspected he had a bit of a man-crush on him as well. Dashing his hopeful look, I said, "I'm riding

shotgun in a police SUV. Say hello to Detective Jack MacLaren, Giff."
I turned the phone for a quick face-to-face introduction.

Jack took his eyes off the road for a second and waved. "Nice to
meet ya, Giff." With eyes back on the road, he added, "And don't
worry. I'm not arresting her, not yet anyway. We went to school together. And, for the record, I had nothing to do with that lump."

"Well, isn't that a shame … on both accounts." This reply elicited
another grin from the driver. "I used to work for her. Apparently she
thinks I still do." Giff raised his voice slightly and added, "I've delivered your pies, angel. You now owe me all the juicy details."

Jack cast me a look of warning as I turned the phone back to me.
The moment I did, Giff raised his brows and waved his hands theatri-
cally under his face while mouthing *HOT COP ALERT*. For some reason this made me blush. It wasn't like that, not at all. This was Jack
MacLaren.

"Okay, you want details?" I asked, ignoring the inappropriate teasing. "They're gruesome." I then proceeded to tell Giff a little about
the murder—just enough to repay my debt. He knew the victim's
name, he knew that Dad was the prime suspect, and I had regaled him
with my disastrous visit to the morgue, which enchanted him. What
he didn't know, however, was that Jeb had been poisoned first.

"It's disturbing, isn't it?" I remarked.

In true Giffster style, he replied, "Truthfully, angel, what I find
even more disturbing than murder is the fact you have a cherry pie
bake-off at the inn tomorrow afternoon and no judge. I'll be there in
five hours."

The screen went blank. He'd ended the call. It took me a moment before I realized that Gifford McGrady had just taken care of

one of the many nagging problems plaguing the inn, and my aching head.

Now to find the murderer. I googled "cyanide poisoning" and began educating myself.

Fourteen

The internet is a remarkable thing. What's even more remarkable is being able to sit beside a cop in his own car and access information he has no idea you're accessing. When Jack asked what I was doing, I replied, "Facebook. You have your obsessions, I have mine," which wasn't a total lie. I did like social media. I had to engage to promote *Bloom 'n' Cherries!*, but I was in no way obsessed with the thing. The moment he turned away, I started reading about cyanide.

Basically, death by cyanide is asphyxiation on the cellular level. The cyanide molecule CN prohibits cells in the body from absorbing oxygen. Without oxygen, cells can't produce energy, and without energy, muscles like the heart quickly use up their energy stores and die. The thought made me shiver. Cyanide can be inhaled as a gas, absorbed through the skin in liquid form, or ingested in crystal form. There's real danger of cyanide poisoning in a house fire due to the burning of plastics. That wasn't likely to have happened in Jeb's death, I thought, since there'd been no sign of a fire at the crime scene and no indication of soot in the mouth and nasal passages. Besides, Jack had told me that Jeb had ingested the poison. I then looked to see how the poison was made. I was disturbed to find that cyanide is relatively easy to acquire and quite simple to make. It's commonly found in pesticides and some industrial cleaning products. And, a bit closer to home, it's also found in the pits of common foods like almonds, apricot kernels, and apple seeds. If a person eats too many apple seeds they can have mild exposure symptoms, like a rapid heartbeat, shortness of breath, and dizziness. Greater exposure causes death, and it doesn't take long to die. In World War II, high-ranking members of the Nazi party used to carry cyanide capsules to commit suicide if they were caught. I remembered reading about that when I was a kid. But it was the mention of fruit pits that got me thinking. There wasn't much on the page I was reading, so I did another quick search and found the answer I was looking for.

"Wow," Jack breathed, pulling me from the webpage. I quickly turned off my phone. "You weren't kidding about the press infiltrating the inn," he said. "That's Greta Stone up there. She's the heavy hitter from Baywatch News. Mostly because she has a way of getting men to talk. She's a shameless flirt."

"I gathered," I replied, glancing at the attractive woman who'd promoted Blunder Under the Blossoms. Precariously balanced on red four-inch heels, she was leaning close to a pudgy, middle-aged man. The long, slender legs the heels were attached to seemed to sprout from under a very tight, very short, leave-nothing-to-the-imagination skirt. "That poor man," I remarked. "He thinks he has a chance, doesn't he?"

"That's the thing about men. We all do. But remember what we talked about at the hospital?" Jack asked. "Greta and her team are just doing what they do best, which is drum up scandal and interview anyone willing to get before the camera. You know what they say: nobody can pump a man like Greta Stone." Registering the look on my face, he clarified. "For information, that is."

"Oh, really? And how would you know this?"

Jack parked the car, turned off the ignition, and turned to me. "It's common knowledge … and a little bit based on the fact that I know her." The look on his face suggested something more than a working relationship.

"You *know* her? Greta Stone?" I didn't know why, but for some reason I felt a flash of jealousy. Most likely because Ms. Stone was drop-dead gorgeous! "How well?" The fact that Jack didn't answer this question was probably for the best.

I glanced out the windshield again, slightly miffed and more than a little skeptical.

"Don't dwell on it," he advised, reaching for the door handle. "Besides, you have Giff. He's what a lot of woman would call 'a real looker.'"

"What? I'm not dating Giff! Giff's gay!"

"Oh, so you do know. I wasn't sure you'd picked up on that." Jack flashed a grin and opened the door. "Okay," he said in a near whisper, "whatever you do, don't look directly at her. Just head for the family entrance and keep your head down. Got it?"

I nodded and exited the car. A moment later I felt Jack's hand on my back—a warm, strong hand. "Come on," he whispered, proceeding to guide me through the crowded parking lot and away from the view of the front porch. "Hopefully your dad's still waiting for me. I'm anxious to have a look at that lighthouse."

We were weaving our way through parked cars, keeping low and aiming for the left side of the inn, when a throaty voice called out from above. "Officer MacLaren! Jack, I know it's you!" The voice was unmistakable; the sound of it caused the hand on my back to stiffen. Jack kept walking, pushing me toward the three-story turret where a shaded pathway awaited leading to a private gate. "Don't turn around," he whispered. "Greta's onto us."

"Officer MacLaren! You're the law here in Cherry Cove. You were the responding officer on this case. I'd like a word with you, Jack! More importantly, I'd like to know why you're avoiding me and who you're trying to protect!" The sharp ping of high-heels skittering down stone echoed around us.

"Here she comes," I whispered.

Jack picked up the pace.

"Will Baxter Bloom, the wealthy owner of the Cherry Orchard Inn and Bloom Family Orchard, be charged with the murder of Jeb Carlson?"

Now that question pissed me off! I stopped and was about to turn around when another voice caught me by surprise.

"Whitney!"

My name, uttered by a voice I hadn't heard in a very long time, rocked me to the core. I spun around, stunned, and saw the one face I never wanted to see again. The face of Tatum Vander Hagen, my ex-boyfriend. The man who had broken my heart.

It was incredible! I had to do a double take to make sure I wasn't hallucinating. Nope, I wasn't. It was Tate, and he was driving one of the inn's three Gators. What the devil was he doing here? I'd only been home a few hours, and the fact that he looked so at home on the bright green-and-yellow utility four-wheeler wasn't sitting too well with me either. He'd just rounded the building from the other side and was racing across the parking lot toward us. He skidded to a stop three feet from where we stood and cried, "Quick, jump in."

I was horrified to find that I wanted to. Curse his arresting Norse god good looks! He was smiling, flashing dimples—the kind you just wanted to stick your fingers into and wiggle a bit. I'd worked hard to resist those captivating cheek dimples but, for the love of cobbler, they were a powerful weapon. He knew it, too, and yet seeing that I was still hesitant, his smile faltered.

"Jesus, Whit, I'm not going to bite."

I glared at him and hissed, "What the devil are you doing here, Tate?"

"What the devil happened to your forehead?" he countered.

"An accident," I snapped, tired of getting horrified looks about it.

"Sorry to hear it. Your mom's waiting for you. Look, it's either me or her," he said, pointing to Greta Stone. The woman was now clipping at speed through the parking lot. It was kind of impressive, considering she was wearing such obnoxiously high heels. The way I saw it, there wasn't a whole lot to choose between. I was still deliberating when Jack made the decision for me.

"Get in," he commanded, shoving me toward the Gator.

"Good man, MacLaren." Tate gave a nod coupled with a sly grin. He appeared keenly aware of the situation. "Sorry bro. Only room for one in this Gator. Besides, looks like your girlfriend's hot to chat with you."

"Take Whitney," Jack said. "Get her out of here. I'll handle this." He turned, glanced at Greta, and looked back at Tate. "Former girlfriend, bro."

"Yeah, bro. Whatever. Brace yourself now." Tate winked. Jack groaned and slapped the hood of the utility vehicle.

With a two-finger salute, Tate stepped on the gas, abandoning Jack to the mercy of his former hot girlfriend and man-eating reporter, Greta Stone.

Fifteen

"What are you doing here?" I was so befuddled I just had to ask the question again, all while glaring at the hunky blond-headed man next to me. He was the type of man it was hard not to stare at, and that was part of the problem. Tatum Vander Hagen, or "Vander Licious" as he was known in the cove, was the reason I'd avoided coming home. We'd started dating in high school, then dated on and off again throughout college, and then had a bout of serious dating after graduation until a year and a half ago. I'd come home for the weekend to surprise him and found him in bed with another woman. We had a long history, Tate and I. My parents still adored him, but I was not about to get sucked into his lethally alluring, deep-set Scandinavian blue gaze again.

His focus was conveniently straight ahead—as if he didn't already know every nuance of the grounds by heart. "Look, I know this is a shock to you. It's a shock to us all. The short answer is that I'm here today because Jeb isn't. I've volunteered to conduct the orchard hayride. Baxter wanted to do it, but he's been a sack of nerves all morning.

Besides, he's a murder suspect and the owner of the inn. Not sure the guests want to spend that much time in his company just yet."

As much as I hated to admit it, it did make sense. "Okay, but why you?"

Tate looked affronted. "It's what friends do, Whit. And because your mom asked me. I'm not going to tell her no."

Mom! I should have known. She'd always harbored hopes that one day Tate would be her son-in-law, and I had squashed that dream. I'd never told her the real reason why. She assumed it was because of my need to pursue a career in advertising, and I'd let her believe it. Now that I was home again, she was meddling. Well, it wasn't going to work.

"Listen," Tate said, "I know things are a little strained between us right now, but the truth is your folks are like family to me. And with you down in Chicago and your brother off to God only knows where chasing ghosts, they need someone here they can rely on in a pinch, and that someone is me. We're a close-knit community here in Cherry Cove."

He wasn't exactly lying, and that's why it hurt to be reminded. And Tate was right; Cherry Cove was a very tight-knit community. Although it was a tourist town with a population that swelled into the thousands during the summer months, the actual number of permanent residents was less than three hundred. Most were families who'd lived here for generations, and a few brave newcomers. Tate was a local boy. Our parents had been friends ever since I could remember. And when the Vander Hagens decided to retire to Florida, Tate stepped up and took control of the Cherry Cove Marina, the Vander Hagen family business. He also lived in the home he'd grown up in, a modest ranch house beside the marina. Tate was a good son. My younger brother and I had been more selfish. I'd left the orchard in search of fulfillment in advertising, and Bret had left to study film and television production at Columbia University in Chicago. My brother was now host of his own international ghost-hunting show, which aired on a cable channel. Since he traveled so much for the show, Bret returned home even less than I did. Tate, meanwhile, was now the sole owner of his family's marina, and I knew that he loved it. This was also part of the problem between us. He'd been content to stay in the Cove. I'd needed to spread my wings and experience life beyond our sleepy little village.

I looked at him again, and, in a softer voice, asked, "Do friends abandon each other to the mercy of a crazed reporter?"

"You're referring to MacLaren?" Tate allowed the creases at the corners of his generous mouth to deepen. "Had to make an executive decision. MacLaren understands. The dude's a cop. Takes his life in his hands every day, or so he tells me. It's what he signed up for. And I think you'll agree, he handled the situation like a pro." Again, the smile.

"Like a pro? He looked terrified. I've never seen him so nervous."

"Neither have I. Begs the question, what did she do to him? Whatever it is, I think it's good for him. Everyone has to face their demons sometime. It builds character."

I looked closely at Tate, noted the way he talked about Jack, and hit upon an unlikely conclusion. "Don't tell me the two of you actually hang out together?" For some reason, I'd never pictured Tate and Jack as friends. Of course, they'd always known each other—we'd all gone to the same high school—but Tate was older. He was also louder, a bit brash, outgoing, and had his own group of rowdy friends. But the ease with which he and Jack had just spoken led me to believe that things had changed between them since I'd last lived in Cherry Cove. Jack's pursuits and friends were always the kind that escaped notice unless you knew what to look for, and Tate never did.

"You find that surprising?" he asked, stopping to avoid hitting a group of guests walking across the back lawn. They were heading for the large white tent that had been erected for the festival. A group of young men and women from the restaurant were busy setting up tables and chairs and putting the finishing touches on what looked to be an elegant outing. The tables were topped with white linen and cherry blossom centerpieces. At one end, a bar was currently being stocked. Beside it was a large circular table where later in the day platters of local cheeses, artesian breads, and crackers would be served.

I looked back at Tate. He was resting his hands on the steering wheel, staring at the tent and the seemingly endless expanse of dark blue lake beyond. "We both live here, Whit," he continued. "MacLaren's a solid guy. He really knows his micro-brewed beers. Besides, he keeps his police boat in one of my slips. But enough about MacLaren. MacLaren's boring." He turned and held me in his magnetic gaze. "Let's talk about you, me … and the fact that you're back here in Cherry Cove."

"Ah … " I'd be lying if I said my heart wasn't tripping away double time, because it was. It was my primal reaction to the man. My head, however, knew better. Tate had said it was good to face one's demons, and, dear Lord, I was trying. However, instead of building character, I was more afraid of losing my self-respect. I shook the thought away and told him, "There is no *you and me*. Remember? From what I recall it was you, me, and whatever trampy summer floozy happened to find her way aboard your boat."

"I've changed since then," he stated softly. "So have you." Then the corners of his mouth lifted slightly. "And I probably should have changed the name of that boat. It would have saved me a lot of trouble. It drew them in like flies, and I was flattered by the attention. But Whitney, you must know that you were the only one I ever wanted aboard the *Lusty Dutchman*. You were the best first mate I ever had."

Why did he have to remind me of that now? Of course I was the best first mate he ever had! I was young, impressionable, and totally in love with him. Those were the moments one never forgot; and they still had the power to infiltrate my dreams. My cheeks grew unnaturally hot at the thought of Tate and his aptly named sailboat.

"I took you for granted back then," he added, "and that was wrong of me."

I waited for a teasing grin, but it never came. I was suddenly struck by the unlikely idea that maybe, quite possibly, Tatum Vander Hagen had finally grown up. He was nearly thirty, and I'd read enough women's magazines to know that men at nearly thirty tended to think of marriage and raising a family just a little bit more than they did of engaging in meaningless sex, orgies, and one night stands, although I was pretty certain they still did that too. But I supposed it was bound to happen sometime for Tate. However, his timing, as usual, was horrible. The sad truth of it was, I wasn't getting any younger either. I should have been thinking of marriage and having babies too; and perhaps if I'd made something of myself by now, I would be. Tate was offering me an olive branch. It was tempting to reach out and grab hold of it, letting myself get caught up in the dream. But I couldn't allow that to happen, especially not with Tate. Then, too, there was the fact that I lived in a shoebox apartment in Chicago. I baked cherry pies to make ends meet. I had failed at advertising, and I longed, just once, to find real success. I mean, how was I to be trusted with a baby when I couldn't even be trusted with a feminine hygiene account? The thought depressed me.

"Listen," I said, still looking squarely at his handsome face. "We're not going down this road right now. Jeb Carlson was murdered in the orchard last night and you're suddenly remorseful about us—about the way we ended? What's wrong with you?"

"Jesus, Whit, you think I'm not torn up about it? Jeb was my mentor. I've known the guy all my life, same as you. And then there's your dad. Baxter's in a heap of trouble. I'm sick just thinking about it ... and thinking of you, with your mom here, trying to run this place all by herself and your dad in prison. And you," he added with a deprecatory look, "what's wrong with you? It took an old man dying to bring you back to the orchard. Maybe if you'd made it a point to be here more often, this wouldn't have happened."

I was agog. "What?" I uttered, my anger subdued by a bolt of white-hot guilt. Could it be true? I could feel the sting of tears, and my chin gave a slight tremble.

"Damn it," he cursed. "I didn't mean that. Look, we're all a little on edge right now. And seeing you, why, I don't mind telling you it's like a ray of sunshine peering through a thunder cloud. I'm going to say it again and I don't care if it makes you angry, but I've missed you, Whitney."

"You do know that I'm only home for a short while ... just until we can lay the matter of Jeb's death to rest and set the inn to rights again."

"I'm aware, but about that ... what was the deal with you and Mc-Copper back there, anyhow?" Although Tate's voice was conversational, the look in his eyes was anything but. Confusion? Displeasure? Perhaps a flare of jealously? Yes, most definitely jealousy. Alpha dog jealousy. It was so foreign a look on him that it made me smile. This made Tate flinch. He turned from me and concentrated once more on driving aimlessly across the lawn while trying his hardest to not hit any of the guests. "Baxter said you went to the morgue with MacLaren today."

"I did," I replied. "I wanted to see the body for myself."

"Talk about messed up." Tate gave a disparaging shake of his head. "Why'd you want to see the body?"

"I thought there might have been some mistake. After hearing what happened last night—about that couple finding the body, and the fact that Dad's croquet mallet was lying beside it—I just felt that something about Jeb's death didn't add up." I didn't mention that Jack had thought so too, or the fact that he'd been correct in his suspicions. And because Jack had been correct, everyone at the inn was now to be treated as a suspect, including my ex-boyfriend.

"Wish you'd talked to me about it first," Tate said, his voice losing all trace of flirtation as he spoke. "Could have spared you the trouble. I saw the old man's face last night. Very nasty. And it does add up, Whit. Baxter was playing with that mallet all day, and he most likely had it when he was heard arguing with Jeb over that secret wine they were making that got lifted."

My heart stilled a moment at the mention of the wine. "How do you know about any of that?" I demanded. "That wine was a secret endeavor between Jeb and my father. No one was supposed to know they were making wine."

"You'd be surprised at what people know around here," Tate said cryptically. "I also happen to know your father explodes into fits of anger over troubling things. He could have hauled off and chucked his mallet in anger, not knowing Jeb was in the orchard. I've seen him throw his golf clubs tons of times. Do you know what I think? I think poor old Jeb was in the wrong place at the wrong time and caught the business end of Baxter's mallet square in the face. And if that isn't terrible enough, Sorensen confided to me last night that Baggsie might very well lose the inn over it."

I was alarmed not only by Tate's candor but by how much he knew about Dad, Jeb, and their secrets. He knew far more than I did, including the fact that a murder at the inn might be more devastating than anyone thought. My parents couldn't really lose the inn over it, could they? It was more than I cared to consider, and just the mention of it set off a wave of sweat-inducing panic. Then I looked at Tate.

"Sorensen?" I asked. "Who's this Sorensen you're talking about?" It was the first I'd heard the name.

"Brock Sorensen. The new business manager. He works for your dad."

I remembered hearing something about Dad hiring a Sorensen a while ago, but I'd been too busy with my own affairs to give it much thought. Then I thought of something else. "Last night, after the body was discovered by the McSweenys, who went out to the orchard to check out their story?"

"We all did," he replied.

"The entire inn went to look at the body?" It was a morbid thought.

"No. What I meant was, after the McSweenys came back to the inn believing they'd found a dead body, we all kind of freaked, especially when we realized that Jeb was nowhere to be found. I went with Briz to investigate, and when we found Jeb ... " Tate's eyes began welling up with tears. "When we found the old guy looking like that, we couldn't leave him. It was ... " He looked at me. I was moved by the genuine look of distress seizing his handsome features. I'd never seen Tate so overcome with emotion before. "It was totally barbaric," he finished.

I reminded myself that Tate didn't know Jeb had been poisoned first. Or if he did, he was doing a very good job of keeping it a secret. It was something to consider. Another thing to consider was the latest name I didn't recognize. "Who's Briz?" I asked.

"A friend of mine, Carleton Brisbane. He's an independently wealthy businessman who has a sweet yacht that he keeps at my marina. Met him last year. Stayed nearly the whole summer, he loved Cherry Cove so much, and when he heard about the Cherry Blossom Festival, he just had to come. Made his reservation the very day he heard of it. Didn't realize there were going to be so many couples, though. Thought there'd be more single women here. I mean, there are a few. There's the three in the Cherry Suite up from Sheboygan for a girls' getaway, and also a couple of older gals. The kind who wear sweaters with little cherries all over them."

"Nothing wrong with that," I added.

"And then there's the ladies in the Woodland Suite from Whitefish Bay, but those two aren't into men, if you know what I mean. And of the three in the Cherry Suite, two are divorcees in their forties and currently in their male-hating phase, and the other is a … well, she's not exactly Briz's type."

I raised a brow at this. "Sorry to hear it. Well, no one can really predict who's going to make reservations for such an event. But I think I remember Dad mentioning that name.

"Yeah. Briz is a friend of your dad's as well. We all hung out quite a lot last summer. Briz is a golfer, and, like I said, he has a sweet yacht."

I recalled how easily impressed Tate was. Then again, a wealthy man with a yacht might not be such a bad catch for a girl who baked pies for a living. I flashed Tate my sweetest smile. "And he's single, you say? You must introduce us."

Apparently Tate had never considered this before, and, from the look on his face, the thought wasn't sitting too well with him. Deciding to let the matter drop, I asked, "Who else came out to the orchard when they heard about the body?"

"Your dad, of course, and Dr. Engle, Brock Sorensen, Briz, and me. It was just the five of us. No one else."

I thought about that. I'd known Dr. Engle and Tate for a very long time. The other two I'd never met, and that made me instantly suspicious of them. "Tell me, was anyone eating cherries when they went to the orchard?"

Tate raised an eyebrow at this. "Not that I know of. Christ, we were all so full from that amazing dinner Boner whipped up that I don't think anyone could've stomached eating cherries."

Boner—or more correctly, Bob Bonaire—was head chef at the inn's renowned restaurant. Bob was a kooky guy but an excellent chef, and had acquired the nickname Boner very early in his career. Obviously, it had stuck.

"Tate," I began, placing a hand on his arm. I wanted to get his attention but instantly realized my mistake. Dang it, if I didn't feel the living warmth of his skin, or how my heart quickened at the thought of what secrets lay hidden behind his sensuous smile. For my own self-preservation, I removed my hand instantly, but it was too late. We had both felt it. "Hahem." I cleared my throat and scooted over as far as I could without falling out of the Gator. "I appreciate you telling me all this, just as I appreciate you saving me from that reporter. I don't think I could have stomached talking with her just now."

I was trying hard to ignore the heat in Tate's eyes. He'd let his gaze settle on my hand a moment before looking me in the eyes again. His foot, I realized, had come off the gas. The reason, I saw, was that we'd finally arrived at the private back entrance to the family quarters. Tall grass and wildflowers flanked the pathway, and the faint yet distinct smell of cherry blossoms tickled my nose.

"Do you really need to go in?" he asked through his soft, insinuating smile. "You could just come with me. I'm heading over to hitch up the hay wagon to the tractor right now. Come with me, Whit. Help me conduct the tour. No one knows more about this orchard than you do. Then, afterward, we can have lunch on the lawn with the guests. Or we can wait until three o'clock and join the wine and cheese tasting. What do you say?"

It sounded heavenly: a ride through the orchard followed by lunch. I wouldn't have minded a little wine and cheese tasting either. In spite of my visit to the morgue, the lump on my head, and the fact that there was a murderer on the loose, it was a glorious day. And wine and cheese were my kryptonite. I could feel myself growing weak under Tate's alluring gaze, and I hated myself a little for it. This is how it always happened, I reminded myself, until my inner voice was lulled to silence by those pleading eyes and adorable cheek dimples. Tate was charming. In my current state I was putty in his hands, and he knew it. I needed a support group to battle the likes of him. I needed the voice of reason to slap me in the face, but no one was about. It was just Tate and me ... alone in a Gator. "I ... I suppose I could ... "

Tate's foot was hovering over the gas pedal, ready to engage, when I heard my name. We both turned toward the house at the same time. And when I saw my two best childhood friends running across the patio calling to me, I was taken with a wave of relief and another of joy.

My prayers had been answered. My support group had arrived.

Sixteen

Shoo! Shoo!" cried Hannah Winthrop, running toward Tate and waving him away like a flock of meddlesome geese. Moments before, at the sight of my friends, I'd alighted from the Gator, shocking Tate and leaving him in a predicament like a fish in a barrel. Although it appeared all in good fun, there was a thread of seriousness in Hannah's swift, mother-hen actions. My besties knew what Tate had done to me, and like true friends, they always had my back.

Tay followed Hannah's example, running after Tate as well and chiming in with "Move along, lusty dutchman. There's an orchard tour that needs a guide, and you volunteered. Besides, we don't want you scaring Whitney off so soon. She's just come home."

Tate, recovering quickly, flashed them a rueful smile. He then tossed me a private wink and hit the gas. For the first time since coming home, I breathed a sigh of relief.

Although my friends and I talked weekly, it had been a while since I'd seen those two grinning faces. The second I did, the hands of time stilled for a moment, bringing me back to Mrs. Olafson's third grade class where the three of us had met. Tay and Hannah were still my dearest friends, but life had taken us all in different directions. I was the bird that flew the coop, heading for the big city and a career in advertising.

Tay, aka Taylor Robinson, stood all of five-foot-two inches, was incredibly hip and chic, and had a flair for design. Her clothes were unique and artfully put together; her hair was kept short and dyed a color red not normally found in nature; and she had a sharp wit and brand of sass we all admired. After high school, she had left Cherry Cove to study art and cultural anthropology at the University of Wisconsin; she'd come away from the experience with a deep and thorough knowledge of antiques, relics, and highly-sought-after gadgets of the past. Now, at the ripe old age of twenty-eight, Tay was the owner of Cherry Cove's trendiest antique boutique, Cheery Pickers.

Hannah, on the other hand, was in many ways Tay's polar opposite. She was a six-foot-tall willowy blonde with an open, cheerful nature. Hannah had gone to a four-year university like the rest of us, in her case to study business, but only found that she hated both college and studying. She was too much of a free spirit to be corralled in classes all day, and time was something to bend, not adhere to. After two years of giving it her all, Hannah dropped out of school and fell in love with yoga instead. She moved back to Cherry Cove and opened a small studio called Yoga in the Cove. She not only had freaky flexibility but quite a following on the peninsula.

For all the stretching, meditation, and mindfulness that Hannah practiced, you'd have thought she'd be the definition of centered and calm. But she wasn't. She was like a pinball whizzing through a neon-lighted game board full of paddles and spinners, bouncing here and there on a whim. Yoga kept her centered, but all the coffee she drank, and the chaos that surrounded her, made her a blast to hang out with.

"Look at you two!" I said now, embracing them both. "Aren't you a sight for sore eyes! But what are you guys doing here?"

"Are you kidding me?" Tay replied, her chic red hair ruffling in the breeze. "This is an emergency!"

"Yeah. Poor Jeb. And he'd just signed up for my Yoga for the Inflexible class." Hannah gave a sad shake of her head. She popped right out of sorrow and flew into panic. "And it's the Cherry Blossom Festival! The inn's in a tailspin! We've come to help out, Whit. And when your mom told us you were coming home this morning, we had a feeling Tate would try to ambush you." Both of them stared at me, oozing concern. I wouldn't dare say it lacked reason.

"I love you guys," I told them, grinning nonchalantly. "But seriously, did you really think I'd fall under his spell so easily? Ladies, the city's changed me."

Tay laughed. "Yeah, we know. It's changed Tate too. Don't worry, my friend, we've got your back."

Mom and Grandma Jenn had just finished an emergency meeting with the staff when we walked inside, and although my grandma knew I'd come home, it took her by surprise. The moment she saw me she leapt from her chair and ran over, crying joyfully, "Whitney! Whitney! Whitney!" A heartbeat later I was wrapped in her comforting, deceptively strong arms. I didn't know how much I'd missed her until that moment. I'd always thought Grandma Jenn resembled Helen Mirren, with her lovely white hair and pretty face, but she had a spirit all her own. She was one of those ageless women, youthful, vibrant, and full of good old-fashioned wisdom. "Oh, how I've missed you," she said. "And we're so glad you've come. Dear Heavens!" she exclaimed, getting a good look at me. "What happened to your head?"

I brushed a finger against my forehead, nearly flinching at the flash of pain. "This silly thing?" I said breezily. "I had a little accident this morning. I kind of passed out in the morgue and cracked my head."

Mom, Grandma Jenn, and Hannah looked horrified. Tay, however, burst into gales of laughter. It was infectious. "That's not a great start, Whit," she admonished after regaining her composure. "But the good news is that MacLaren actually took you there in the first place. That means he trusts you. You should feel special."

"Oh, he didn't want to take me," I told them. "I sort of shamed him into it. The whole thing was Mom's idea."

"Jani!" Gran admonished.

"I told you, Mom." Mom turned to address her mother. "If we want to get to the bottom of this murder, Whitney's our only chance. She got into the morgue!" This she exclaimed as if it proved my investigating qualifications. Truthfully, I was a little flattered by their amazement.

"I did," I said. "And this little battle wound is not without its reward. Mom was right to send me with Jack, because I did learn something in that morgue besides the fact that I don't have the stomach for looking at dead bodies. I've been sworn to secrecy by Jack, but I feel you four can be trusted. What we learned at Door County General is that Dad's croquet mallet didn't kill Jeb Carlson. He was poisoned first."

Mom was the only one relieved by this news. The rest understood the darker meaning of this revelation, which was that a murderer adept in the use of poison was still on the loose. This sparked a new conversation. I brought them up to speed on what I'd learned, including the secret wine Dad and Jeb had been making in the lighthouse and Jack's picture of the crime scene. Mostly, however, we discussed our concerns for the weekend, mainly how to keep the guests safe. Then Mom hit on the one subject I'd been dreading—the cherry pie bake-off on Sunday.

"Now that you're here, dear, I really think you should make your deconstructed pie and enter that in the contest. Some of the contestants have pulled out already. We want to show them there's nothing to worry about. And your pie will make a statement. I'll bet no one has tasted anything quite like it either. It'll turn heads, and you'll have every member of the Cherry Cove women's league clamoring for the recipe."

"Mom, I don't know if that's such a good idea."

"Why not?" she asked, frowning.

"Because Giff volunteered to fill Jeb's shoes and be the judge. I told him about the murder. Giff is horrified, but he wants to help us out."

"Gifford?" Mom asked. "But that's wonderful, Whitney. He's such a darling young man. I'm sure Gifford will do a wonderful job."

"So, Giff's really coming?" Tay asked. Her face lit up at the thought. Giff was no stranger to Cherry Cove, and he and Tay had a bit of a thing going on. They made the perfect couple, really, both having a love of fashion, art, and antiques. Giff was the only one who really appreciated all the nuances and artful touches Tay used in her boutique, and the two could sit around for hours discussing things I'd never heard of. They were definitely two peas in a pod. Unfortunately, they both liked men.

"He's on his way now," I told them, "and if I enter the cherry pie bake-off, Giff will hardly be an impartial judge. He'll want me to win, if for no other reason than to get his hands around the great Gilded Cherry trophy."

Hannah giggled. "Actually, you still can enter the contest, Whitney. It appears we have two judges this year. It was the second thing I thought about when I heard of Jeb's death—the first being how terrible it was. But that pie contest is the finale of the whole weekend! Jeb, if he was here, would have wanted the tradition to continue."

"That's true," Mom added, nodding her head. "This is cherry country, Whitney. Everyone looks forward to the bake-off. All the other orchards clamor for the title. It's quite competitive, you know."

The moment the words left Mom's mouth, it got me thinking. The judge of our cherry pie bake-off was murdered in his own orchard—poisoned, actually—and the whole thing made to look like Dad's fault. Could there be a connection? Jack hadn't mentioned anything. Probably because he hadn't considered it. But I had, and a burning desire to get into the orchard and view the crime scene consumed me. It was a moment before I realized that Hannah was speaking to me.

"I asked him to be the judge, and he said yes. Isn't that wonderful? We now have two judges—two impartial judges—which means that you absolutely should enter the contest, Whitney."

"She's right," Grandma Jenn added. "And since your folks are up to their eyeballs in problems just now, and since the hotel kitchen will be working double time, why don't you come to my house and bake your pie? After all, I have a lot of cherries on hand." She smiled.

"Okay," I said, feeling irrationally nervous about the whole affair. "But who's this other person who agreed to judge the contest?"

"Weren't you listening?" Hannah chided. "Briz. Tate's friend?" Her eyes widened in sudden recollection. "That's right. You haven't met him yet. I'll have to introduce you two. He's rich, worldly, ruggedly handsome, and beyond dreamy. He ticks all my boxes," she added, counting his virtues on her fingers. "He's perfect for me. Now all I have to do is convince him of it." This she punctuated with a wry grin.

How could I say no to that grin? "Okay," I told them. "I'm in. However, right now I need to take a little stroll through the orchard before Jack returns. Tay, Hannah, would you two ladies care to join me?"

"Of course," Hannah declared, jumping to her feet. "It'll be just like old times."

Seventeen

$\mathscr{I}$'m so excited you agreed to enter your pie," Hannah said the moment we stepped out the door. "It's about time we got some new blood in there. It's always the same old ladies and housewives with their time-honored recipes. Nothing's wrong with that, of course, but it's time for a change. It's time for a millennial shake-up, don't you think?"

"Have you even tasted my pie?" I asked, heading for the gravel road that skirted the lawn and led into the orchard.

"Not yet, but I hear it's amazing."

"It's sinful," Tay chimed in, "and so cutting edge it'll have all the gray heads spinning."

"It's tough to break with tradition," I mused. "Everybody has their idea of the perfect cherry pie. Should it be sweet? Should it be tart? Should it have a double crust or lattice crust, or any crust at all ...?"

"Should it contain cherries soaked in brandy?" Tay added with an ironic grin. "Most definitely! It's not every day you can eat a pie and cop a buzz at the same time."

"Really?" Hannah was enthralled. "You can get drunk off Whit's pie?"

"No," I said. Cutting a sideways glance at Tay, I added, "At least normal people don't. But what I mean is, my pie doesn't exactly look like a normal pie. We should probably blindfold the judges."

"Yeah, and feed them by hand with little forks," Hannah added. "I volunteer to feed Briz." A dreamy look appeared in her light blue eyes.

I stopped walking and looked at her. And then I giggled.

"Okay, Whit, stop laughing," Hannah said, her fair skin blushing bright pink. Hannah blushed easily. And with her long white-blonde hair, she couldn't hide it either. She resembled a strawberry cupcake topped with white icing. "For goodness sake," she hissed, turning even darker, "he's right over there."

She pointed to the tent on the lawn where the orchard hayride was getting underway. The low sides of the large flatbed trailer had been festively decorated with scallops of pink and white crepe paper. The trailer itself was covered with bales of hay, and on the hay sat boisterous passengers, each one holding a glass of wine or a bottle of microbrewed beer. It looked like the party was getting started. I could see Tate's bright blond head on the far side of the trailer. He was helping a female guest board. I knew that in a moment he'd climb onto the tractor at the head of the wagon and begin the tour. He'd loop around to the front of the inn, cross the main drive, and drive down the gravel road that led to the front of the massive orchard. And since my friends and I were heading to the one spot in the orchard forbidden to all but the authorities, it was imperative that we weren't seen, especially by Tate. Tate would be angry, and he'd tell Jack for sure.

"Quick! In here!" I said, and scrambled to get behind the thick hedgerow of yew bushes. Tay followed. Hannah, however, stayed where she was, seemingly mesmerized by an unseen force.

"Hannah!" Tay hissed. "For the love of Hogwarts, stop waving at that sexy man and get your double-jointed butt in here."

"Sexy man?" I flashed Tay a sideways glance and a grin. Tay had a type, and as far as I could tell, the hayride was void of any that fit her tastes. With the exception of Giff, Tay liked her men tattooed, long-haired, and with an aversion to wearing a shirt.

The questioning look in my eyes wasn't lost on her. "Carleton Brisbane," she whispered. "Even I have to admit he's uber yummy."

"Isn't he just, though?" came our friend's airy voice from the other side of the bush. "So far he's resisted my charms. Oh dang," she said with a decided lack of concern. "I've been spotted. Tate's waving me over. Now he's holding out a bottle of beer. Ladies, looks like I'm going to have to take this one for the team. *Save yourselves*," she added mockingly as she left us.

Curiosity got the best of me. Who was this incubus that could induce our friend to abandon us in the middle of a plan? It was unheard of. I dropped to my stomach and peered beneath the bushes.

At first all I could see was a trailer full of slightly drunken guests. Most, I could tell, were couples, snuggling close together as they shared a hay bale. There were a few small groupings of women plunked down between them—the women Tate had described to me. I saw a group that looked to be the friends on a girls' getaway sharing a bottle of wine; two heavy-set older women who were either spinsters, widows, or librarians; and two others, much younger, who were either best friends or lovers. It was hard to tell, but my advertiser's eye was always quick to categorize people into age groups and stereotypes. Then my gaze fell on a man who looked nothing like the rest.

So this was Carleton Brisbane. No wonder our friend had been quick to abandon us. He was no man-child but the real thing—a true, clean-shaven, smartly dressed, ruggedly handsome dude. His black hair was rich, glossy, and expertly cut to frame his strong face and highlight his bright aquamarine eyes. Although he looked at home casually perched on a bale of hay, he was more the type one found sauntering out of the pages of a country club lifestyle magazine, selling polo saddles and cologne that smelled like money. He wasn't a young man, not like Tate or Jack. No, this man was older, polished; worldly. I had to applaud Hannah. Her taste in men was improving.

"That's Briz," Tay whispered, nudging me in the ribs as if I hadn't guessed it already. She was peering beneath the bushes as well. "She had a thing for him all last summer, but he never took the bait. Tall bendy women can be very intimidating to a man."

A muffled laugh escaped my lips. "True," I said, "but that man over there doesn't look like he's intimidated by much. See? He's welcoming her aboard with open arms. My guess is he's a player."

"Aren't all men?"

Tay and I watched Hannah climb aboard the hay wagon. She looked winded but happy sitting next to Briz on his fun-size hay bale. Her happiness struck a chord in me, and automatically my gaze shifted to Tate. As if sensing my eyes on him, he turned and stared straight at the bushes we were hiding behind. The bright eyes, so open and so artlessly direct, made me flinch.

"Time to go," I said, and sprang up like a flushed hare. Then, with the utmost care, Tay and I made our way to the scene of the murder.

It was hard to fathom violent death when walking through a sea of white, fragrant cherry blossoms. The serenity of the orchard was misleading, especially when a gentle breeze came, coaxing the petals from the branches in a blizzard of satiny snowflakes. The scent, and the feel of the petals against my cheeks, sparked the echo of an old memory. Suddenly I was a child again, riding on my father's shoulders through the cherry blossoms.

"I'm certain that at the heart of every fairy tale is a cherry orchard," he had told me. "For there's nothing on earth more magical than walking through a cherry orchard in bloom. But the flowers are only the beginning, Whitney. When the flowers fade away, that's when the real magic begins." He'd been talking about cherries, of course—how they're born at the heart of every blossom and grow throughout the summer months until finally turning into a plump, beautiful red burst of summer flavor. I, however, had thought he was talking about something entirely different. So I was thinking of princesses and knights in shining armor—one dashing knight in particular—when Tay, being far more grounded in reality than I ever was, stopped walking. It was then that I noticed the yellow crime scene tape.

It stuck out like a kindergarten painting at an art show.

The effect was sobering, especially when considering that the man who'd tended the very orchard we were walking through had left us here, on this very spot.

"Damn," Tay uttered, her deep brown eyes full of fearful wonder. "It's so beautiful and yet so ghastly."

"I know," was all I could say. Then I reminded her not to touch anything as I lifted the yellow tape.

It was like entering another world, the darkness at the center of the fragrant white fairy tale. I stared at the ground. It was covered with white cherry blossoms, crushed and blood-spattered where Jeb had fallen. Then I recalled the body I'd seen in the morgue, and the pictures on Jack's phone. "My father didn't do this," I said aloud, because there was no way he would have. No Bloom would ever dare violate the sanctuary at the heart of our business, at the core of who we were. The cherry orchard was sacrosanct. I suddenly understood all the fear and sorrow in my mother's voice during that horrible phone call that had brought me here.

"I know, Whit," Tay said, coming to stand beside me. "No one who knows your dad could possibly believe it. Besides, you said that Jeb was poisoned first."

"I did," I agreed, and knelt beside the bruised petals, searching for the tiny reason I'd come here in the first place against Jack's warning. It didn't take long. I knew what I was looking for. Remembering the picture he'd shown me, I searched the area where Jeb's lifeless hand would have been. And there they were—a scattering of clean, dry cherry pits.

"Oh my God!" exclaimed Tay.

"I know. They don't look like much, but I have a hunch about these," I told her, picking up a cherry pit.

"No. I'm not talking about cherry pits. I'm talking about that!"

I looked to where she was pointing, at the ground a few feet away from where the body had been. It took me a moment, staring at the pile of twigs, until I saw what she'd seen. The twigs were not random. They'd been meticulously placed to form an eerie, pagan-looking stick face—a face whose soggy, sour-cherry eyes were staring up at me. The hair on the back of my neck stood on end.

"That ... wasn't in the picture Jack showed me," I uttered, backing away.

"I wonder why not?" Tay pondered, staring at the face on the ground as if it were an interesting piece of artwork and not the ominous pile of sticks that it was. "It seems a pretty significant clue to me. This looks suspiciously pagan."

"I agree. That's what I don't understand. Why is it here?"

"Maybe Jeb did this?" As she spoke she knelt beside the twig-face. "What if he was trying to tell us something before he died?"

"Like in *The Da Vinci Code*?" I asked through narrowed eyes, recalling the gruesome opening scene of the movie. "Really? You think a man who was poisoned had time to run out here, gather twigs, and make a spooky-looking face complete with cherry eyes right before he was clubbed in the head with my dad's croquet mallet? It doesn't make sense. And on the off chance that he did, what was he trying to tell us anyway?"

"What his attacker really looked like," she said with an unhealthy amount of confidence.

I raised an eyebrow. "Jeb's killer was a bark-faced tree man? Even you have to admit, Tay, that twigs are hardly the medium to capture a face. Wouldn't it have been easier for him to take out his phone and snap a picture?"

"Maybe he did," she said, standing up. We were both thinking the same thing.

"Where's his phone?" I asked. "Did he have it on him when they found him?"

"Now that's a question you're going to have to ask Jackie McCopper. You might also want to ask him about this twig-face here and why he didn't mention it to you earlier. I'm going to leave both up to you."

"Thanks," I said disingenuously, and took a picture of the eerie face, careful not to disturb it. "I might be able to pick his brain without being obvious. Right now, though, we need to go to the processing sheds. See this cherry pit?" I held up the one I'd taken from the ground. "In the photo, these were lying near his hand. I think Jeb was holding cherry pits when he died."

"Why would you think that?" she asked. "We're in a cherry orchard."

I explained the significance of the cherry pits to her, just as I had to Jack. "So, you see," I continued, "these shouldn't be here. This is why I needed to see the crime scene in the first place. Because I do think Jeb was trying to tell us something—only it wasn't what his murderer looked like. It was how he was killed."

"He choked on cherry pits?" Tay looked a little confused. "First they said he was hit in the head by a croquet mallet, then you said he was poisoned, and now you're telling me he choked on a handful of cherry pits?"

"I didn't say anything about choking. I've done a little research. Cherry pits, dear Tay, in the right hands can be turned into deadly cyanide. And in the processing shed, the one containing the cherry pitter, I'll bet there are a whole lot of cherry pits—enough to make a lethal dose of the stuff. My guess is that Jeb was somehow poisoned, and when he realized that my dad was going to be blamed for his murder, he grabbed a handful of these and ran into the orchard, hoping to reach the inn before the poison took hold."

"Oh my God," Tay breathed. "Poor Jeb. Who would do something like that?"

"I honestly don't know, but that's what I'm going to find out."

Eighteen

Somewhere in the distance, the tractor rumbled and the sound of muffled laughter hit our ears. I knew that Tate had started the cherry blossom tour out by the main road, driving to the very front of the orchard. There he would let the passengers off to wander under the oldest fruit-bearing trees on the property. Once the guests were back on board he would continue, driving up and down a few of the long, dense rows of blossoming trees. Eventually he would veer off into our wooded acreage and travel down a scenic trail. There he'd hit upon the clifftop road, giving the guests a spectacular view of the seemingly endless lake and a few of the islands that sat at the head of Cherry Cove Bay. From there they'd continue down a winding gravel road that would bring them out to Lighthouse Point and the Cherry Cove Lighthouse. Since this was part of the crime scene, the guests would not be allowed inside. After a quick blurb about the old lighthouse, Tate would continue another half-mile down Lighthouse Road to the processing sheds, the last part of the tour before bringing the guests back to the inn. Today, however, the sheds were also off limits. Hopefully Tate had supplied enough alcohol so that nobody was too disappointed. From the sound of the tractor, I could tell the tour had just entered the woods. I sent Hannah a quick text, asking her to alert me when they were at the lighthouse.

As Tay and I made our way toward the processing sheds, we were aware that we were the only two souls in this part of the orchard. And yet, ever since finding the crime scene and stumbling upon that eerie twig-face, the area had taken on a menacing air. I thought it was just me—just my highly suggestive imagination—but Tay had sensed it too. We both had the feeling that someone or something was watching us. Twigs snapped. Tree limbs rustled. Rogue burst of petals blew into our path. And every time we looked, no one was there.

We'd nearly come to the end of the long row where Jeb's body was found. The sheds sat just across the way, separated by a swath of grass and a hundred feet of crushed gravel. We were walking steadily toward the buildings, looking for any noticeable sign of footprints, when the sound of a tree limb snapping nearby spooked us into a mad dash. It was crazy. Our imaginations had gotten the best of us. Because, once again, no one was there.

"Holy Hogwarts! What the deuce is wrong with us?" Tay asked, breathing heavily while blocking the shed door with the weight of her body. It was a logical precaution, in case our imaginary pursuer thought to follow us inside. "You have an excuse," she continued, pointing an unsteady finger at me. "Your brother hosts that sketchy ghost show on cable, so crazy obviously runs in the family. But I'm sane. No one was actually there, right?"

"No one that I could see," I said, ignoring her sarcastic remark as I flipped on the light and headed for the cherry pitter. "It's probably just the fact that we stumbled upon a pretty creepy pile of sticks next to the place Jeb died. And," I said, turning back to her, "if it was the restless spirit of Jeb Carlson trying to reach out to us from beyond the grave, clearly whatever he was trying to tell us fell on deaf ears. We're a couple of fraidy-cats. Tay, forget the door. Come look at this."

I'd entered the processing room, a climate-controlled area where every glorious cherry grown in our orchard was washed, pitted, and deposited into ten-gallon containers. Once they were in the containers, the proper ratio of sugar was added. From there the cherries were sent to the refrigerators to sweeten before either being bottled for use in cherry pies, or dried and packaged for use in other baked goods or snack products. It was a big operation, and nearly all of it automated. But it was the industrial cherry pitter I was interested in.

It was a vast, ingenious machine. The cherries, coming in straight from the orchard, were washed and then dumped into a large holding bin. Once they were in the bin, a special conveyer, divided into trays four feet long by one foot wide and covered with holes the size of cherries, would pass through the bin, loading each cherry into a separate hole. The loaded conveyer would then pass beneath a block of thin steel rods, each one lining up with the tray of cherries. The pitter would come down and de-stone the entire tray at once before dumping the cherries onto another conveyer belt, which then carried them to the awaiting ten-gallon containers.

From all appearances, the entire operation had been meticulously cleaned after last summer's harvest, yet I was hoping my hunch would be correct. I went around to the other side of the machine, opened the hatch to the pit collector, and pulled out the bin. It was spotless. Of course it would be, I thought, chiding myself. Jeb would never let a bin full of sticky cherry pits sit all winter.

"Wow," Tay remarked, standing beside me. "That's clean. Not a pit left in sight. So where did they go?"

"Probably some landfill," I remarked, thinking.

"You guys don't use them to plant new trees?"

"No, not anymore," I said. "All new stock is grafted from existing trees. Fruit trees have been so genetically modified over the years that you never know what traits are carried on in the pits. Grafting new stock directly from existing trees is akin to cloning. It keeps the flavor of the cherries consistent and unique to the orchard."

"Look at you. I love it when you talk cherry to me. But I still don't get it. Where did the cherry pits at the crime scene come from then?"

I looked at her and shrugged. "Got me. I thought Jeb dropped them, but maybe the cyanide poison that killed him wasn't made from cherry pits at all. Unfortunately, cyanide isn't too hard to come by." I paused to pull the cherry pit I'd taken from the scene out of my pocket. "See how this pit looks remarkably clean—like it's been washed and dried? Maybe Jeb was actually thinking of germinating these."

"Then again, maybe not." Tay inspected the pit through narrowed eyes. "I want to think your initial hunch about these pits was correct. Something about that crime scene doesn't add up. Let's keep poking around."

We left the room and continued searching the building. I glanced into the walk-in refrigerators, which were empty, and walked into the store room where some of the lighter equipment was kept, including rows and rows of reusable ten-gallon containers and boxes of plastic liners. Next we poked our heads into the stockroom, which now only contained our private stock—all the cherries we used at the inn and what was sold in the shop. Nothing looked suspicious. We continued searching and then decided to split up. I would search Jeb's office while Tay volunteered to poke around the employee break room and kitchen. Before she left, she asked, "So how's it done?"

"Making cyanide from cherry pits? I was just reading about it on the way back from the morgue. Cherry pits don't actually contain cyanide—they contain a substance called amygdalin. When a cherry pit is chewed or crushed, the amygdalin is released. This also isn't a big deal on its own until the enzyme beta-d-glucose is released. It's contained in the cherry pit too, and also in the digestive tract of humans. The beta-d-glucose enzyme breaks the amygdalin down into a couple of compounds, hydrogen cyanide being one of them. But the amount in one cherry pit is relatively small. One cherry pit won't kill a person. That's why maybe my theory is wrong. If somebody was going to make enough cyanide poison from cherry pits to kill a person, they'd need to use at least fifty, crush them, and suspend the mashed pits in spirits or some type of liquid."

"Sounds like a lot of work. Then again, what better place to find a lot of cherry pits than at a cherry orchard." Tay cast me a knowing look and started down the hallway. She paused long enough to add, "Did you know that historically, poison is considered to be a woman's weapon?"

I stood before Jeb's office, noting that the door was already open, and reached in to turn on the light. "Is it?" I answered. "I imagine that historically, poison was used by anyone who wanted to inflict an anonymous death. Think of the Borgias," I called after her, and then stared at the scene before me. It felt surreal—a moment frozen in time, one of the last fleeting acts of Jeb Carlson's life. The crime scene might have been in the orchard, but I had the feeling that it had all begun here.

On the desk was a typical working clutter of papers and bills, equipment catalogues, an open can of Coke, a golf magazine, and the black screen of a desktop monitor shut down for the day. And then there was the still-life violence of the scene: Jeb's comfy leather high-back chair abandoned with haste against the wall, and on the cement floor a highball glass that had burst into jagged shards. Beneath it was a dark splatter mark that had all but dried, indicating that there must have been a little liquid still left in the glass when it was dropped. There was little doubt in my mind that whatever had been in that glass had likely killed him.

As I stared at the mess on the floor, Tay, from the vicinity of the break room, was still going on about the history of women and poison. I was only half-listening as I walked further into the office, careful not to touch anything. I recalled that Jack hadn't been in this room yet. Last night he'd been too busy with the actual body, the hysterical guests, my frantic parents, and the bloody croquet mallet. Murder in Cherry Cove wasn't a common affair, thank goodness, and poor Jack said he'd had a heck of a time getting the support he needed from Sturgeon Bay to properly investigate. I knew that eventually he would work his way around to the processing sheds, and I also knew that me coming here wasn't going to sit well with him. It was a risk I was prepared to take, though, since this room confirmed the autopsy findings. Jeb Carlson had been poisoned here before he ran into the orchard. But by whom? How was it done?

I took out my iPhone and snapped a few pictures. That's when I spotted the container on the other side of the desk. The lid was askew, showing the lip of a plastic liner. I left the broken glass to peer inside the box. I inhaled sharply. The box was full of clean, dried cherry pits—just like the ones found at the crime scene.

"Hey, Whit," Tay called from the kitchen as I was snapping a few more pictures of the cherry pits. "You're gonna want to take a look at this!"

I ran from the office, my heart racing with a painful, excited fear, and found Tay in the break room. She was staring into a garbage can. "What's up?" I asked.

"You said one cherry pit isn't enough to kill a man. How about a few hundred?"

"What?" I ran over to the garbage can. Scattered among the remains of food wrappers, water bottles, and a brown banana peel were a whole lot of what looked to be pulverized cherry pits. They looked damp, as if they'd been soaking for a while in some kind of liquid. Without thinking I reached in and scooped out a handful. Tay looked disgusted. It was disgusting. But I'd learned, in the few short hours since donning the hat of an amateur sleuth, that sometimes detective work required one to do disgusting things, like visiting a morgue or sift through break room garbage. I narrowed my eyes at her and sniffed the cherry pits. I was hit with the distinctive smell of rum.

"They've been soaked in rum," I said, dropping the pulverized pits back into the garbage.

"Nice work, Sherlock, but I can smell that from here—rum and rotting banana peel. You didn't actually need to dive in there to figure it out, but I'm kinda impressed you did."

"I forgot that you're a rum aficionado."

"I've told you thousands of times, every good weekend is fueled by rum."

"Well … not every good weekend. Not for Jeb. That's got to be the source of the poison."

Tay twisted her lips in a troubled expression. "I had a hunch something was up when I found a blender in the dishwasher."

"A blender?" I was impressed that the sight of a blender had caused her to open the lid on the garbage can.

Then Tay added, "Well, not just a blender. Among all the plates and coffee mugs, I found a strainer and funnel. I thought it a bit odd. And it's just our luck that whoever did this ran the dishwasher. Everything's spotless. Not a fingerprint left behind."

Abandoning the garbage can, I went to the dishwasher to investigate. I pulled out the lower rack and took a picture of the blender among the plates. I did the same with the top rack where the funnel and strainer were. I then looked in the bottom of the dishwasher by the drain, pulled out the collection screen, and found what I was looking for: a few granular pieces of pulverized cherry pit. "As if we needed it, here's further evidence. Who'd be brazen enough to grind the cherry pits right here in the processing shed?"

"What I want to know," Tay said, "is where they got all those pits in the first place? I've checked all these shelves. There's a few bags of dried cherries, cherry granola, herbal cherry blossom tea, and a ton of coffee. The fridge is stocked with water, soda, and a few abandoned lunches."

"From a box in Jeb's office," I told her. "I found one full of clean, dried cherry pits just like the ones in the orchard." My phone buzzed then. Hannah had sent me a text. The orchard tour had left the lighthouse. I looked back at Tay. "I have no idea why he'd have a box of pits, but I'm sure whoever did this got the pits from that box, ground them up, soaked them in rum, and somehow got Jeb to drink it." I then remembered the open can of Coke sitting on Jeb's desk.

We both ran back to the office. Tay swore when she saw the broken glass on the floor. I sniffed at the can of Coke on the desk. It was half full and, as far as I could tell, only contained Coke. That's when Tay opened a desk drawer.

"Bingo!" she cried. "A bottle of rum, and I'll lay odds it's been tampered with."

"Don't touch it," I warned, and snapped another picture. "Jack told me that murder is usually a personal crime. He might be right. Whoever did this knew Jeb's habits. They knew he was keeping dried cherry pits in his office, and they knew he liked to have a drink after work. Who knew Jeb was a rum and Coke kind of guy?"

"What are you doing?" Tay asked.

"Sending Jack a text. Although he's forbidden me to snoop around, he did ask me to let him know if I came across anything suspicious. We just found the actual murder weapon. I have to let him know."

"Wait!" Tay warned. "Don't send it yet." She was biting her lip, looking extremely troubled. "You're not going to like this. I wasn't going to tell you either—not until you said that whoever did this knew Jeb's habits. I found the base of that blender in one of the cupboards, Whit. Whoever owned it had a label maker, and they put their name on it. According to the label, that blender belongs to Jenny Lind."

"Grandma Jenn? That's ridiculous. Why would she leave it here? And why would she know anything about Jeb's habits?"

"You don't know?" Tay cried. Seeing that I didn't, she added, "I hate to be the one to tell you this, but if anyone knew Jeb's habits, it would be your grandma. They've been engaged in a torrid affair for the last two years. I even stumbled upon them one night. They were skinny dipping in the lake near Jenn's beach. And let me tell you—"

"Nope," I said, cutting her off right there. I didn't need to hear any more. "Why didn't you tell me?"

"Probably because it's none of my business. They've been friends for years, but they were keeping the affair secret. Maybe Jeb was two-timing her and she found out."

It was then I remembered the look on Gran's face before we'd left for the orchard. Had it been remorse? Guilt? Whatever it was, I felt even more sure that she knew something she wasn't letting on. Tay was right—I needed to get to Grandma Jenn before Jack did. I deleted the text message.

"Do you hear that?" Tay asked. It was the sound of drunken voices raised in bawdy song. Tate was leading them. "The orchard tour. We need to move fast."

Nineteen

Having just discovered the source of the poison that killed Jeb, and the fact that Grandma Jenn's blender was involved, Tay and I felt a pressing need to leave the processing shed and get back to the inn as quickly possible. We made for the front door, hoping to beat Tate, who'd be coming from the other direction. From the sound of the tractor I could tell that he was still on Lighthouse Road, although he was swiftly closing the distance. Tay poked her head out the door, making sure the coast was clear. I was about to slip by her when she blocked me with her arm and quietly shut it again. "Dammit," she breathed.

"What? Tate's here? Already?" I couldn't believe it.

"Not Tate. It's far worse. Jack's here, and he's got the crime scene unit from Sturgeon Bay with him. We can't go out there—especially not with that!" She pointed to the base of Grandma Jenn's blender tucked under my arm.

I had to admit, it didn't look good. It looked like I was trying to tamper with crime scene evidence, which I most definitely was. It was becoming a disturbing habit. After all, I'd taken a cherry pit from the crime scene in the orchard, and now I was lifting the base of the blender that had been used to make the poison. What the heck was happening to me? All this sleuthing was getting under my skin. I was growing shifty. I was suspicious of nearly everyone and everything. Heck, even the orchard seemed menacing to me now. Truthfully, I'd never considered taking anything from the processing shed … until Tay had dropped her secret little bombshell on me. Jeb Carlson and Grandma Jenn having a torrid affair! But really, all the signs were there. Had I been paying more attention to my family, I might have figured it out myself instead of being blindsided by the salacious details. But I'd now heard them. There was no unhearing that kind of thing.

And I had seen the look on Grandma Jenn's face when she'd heard we were going to the orchard. Then, too, there was Tay's offhanded remark about poison being a woman's weapon. Would Grandma Jenn even know how to make poison? Of course she would! She was smart, charmingly devious, knew everything there was to know about cherries, and was alarmingly well-versed in weird Scandinavian superstition. She also had the internet. But would she knowingly harm anyone? I couldn't believe that she would. So why was her blender in the break room kitchen? Why had it been used to pulverize cherry pits and steep them in Jeb's rum? Why had it been so thoroughly washed in the dishwasher? Those questions had prompted me to grab the blender. Mother-loving fudgeballs, I had to! It had my gran's name on it! What else was a granddaughter to do?

Probably think more clearly before covering crime scene evidence with her fingerprints, I mentally berated myself—after the blender was already in my hands.

There was nothing else for it now. I had to get to Grandma Jenn before Jack came pounding on her door, which he eventually would. There was a gold mine of evidence in Jeb's office. And Jack was a good detective. I may have pointed out the cherry pits at the crime scene to him, but I was pretty darn sure he was well-versed in cyanide poisoning, including all the ways to make it.

Beyond the door came the crunching of boots on gravel. Jack and his team were swiftly approaching. If he found me in the processing shed with the blender in my arms—after warning me not to snoop around—he'd likely have me arrested. Heck, I'd have me arrested.

"Quick!" I whispered to Tay, and we darted back the way we'd come. We were in the break room when we heard Jack's voice. It sent a wave of pure terror shooting through me. He was in the building, briefing the people who'd accompanied him.

"Is there another way out of here?" Tay croaked in a panicked whisper.

"There's the side entrance the employees use. Come on." I headed for the back hallway.

Tay grabbed my arm and stopped me. "Put that damn thing back," she hissed.

"I'd love to. But my fingerprints are all over it." Which was the God's honest truth. And there was no way I wanted Jack to find out I'd been here.

However, I imagined he would be happy to learn I was being punished for my momentary lapse in judgement, because while Jack and the investigative unit from Sturgeon Bay were slowly sweeping through the building, working their way toward us, Tate and the orchard tour had finally arrived. They were staying well clear of the police as Tate gave a little spiel about the processing sheds, which was wise. Unfortunately, he'd parked the hayride six feet from the side door. Sneaking back into the orchard with the clunky crime scene blender tucked under my sweatshirt was no longer an option.

We were squatting beside the door when I whispered a new plan. "We could wait until Tate leaves, but it's risky. Jack might find us first.

Therefore, I propose we shoot for the woods, make our way down to the shoreline, and work our way back to the inn from there. Okay?"

"Sure. No problem," Tay whispered back sarcastically. "So, we just saunter out there like no big deal, waving to Tate and the twenty other people with him while you try to hide that blender under your shirt? Are you nuts?"

I held up my iPhone. "You forget. We have a team member on board. I'm sure I can induce Hannah to tear herself away from Briz long enough to create a diversion."

Tay's eyes flew wide with caution. But it was too late. I'd already pressed send, cringing slightly as I did so. After all, the message—*Imperative! Create Diversion NOW!!*—could be interpreted in many ways.

For Hannah, it apparently meant a random, blood-curdling scream in the middle of Tate's narration. It was a hell of a diversion. Unfortunately, everyone inside the building heard it too. I distinctly heard Jack swear. And neither one of us could ignore the sound of boots running in our direction.

"Okay. That'll work," Tay said prosaically. Keeping low, we both slipped out the door.

The moment we were out, Hannah saw us. A new urgency hit her when she realized that we needed to make it into the woods. I caught the ghost of a grin as she jumped to her feet and began high-stepping while flailing her arms like propellers. "Bees! Bees! Bees!" she cried, much to the jaw-dropping horror of everyone. "Oh God, the pain!" Bless her, it created quite the panic.

We ran, then, fast as our legs would carry us. No sooner had we landed in the shelter of the woods than the door we'd just exited flew back on its hinges.

"Stay down," Tay hissed. "It's Detective McSpeedy. He looks angry ... yet remarkably fit. He's not even breathing heavily. Impressive."

I peered through the screen of dense foliage and saw Jack leap onto to the hay wagon with a heroic disregard for the imaginary bees. Everyone on board was freaking out. Tate was already there, trying to console Hannah. And then I noticed the one man sitting idly on his hay bale while the chaos swirled around him. It was Briz, and the full force of his magnetic gaze was on me. The moment he realized I was looking at him from my hiding place behind a screen of spring foliage, he smiled. He had a very charming smile.

∞

Our trek through the woods was swift, made even quicker by that lingering, unsettling feeling that something or someone was watching us. Our cherry orchard bordered a state forest. There was a good deal of dense, beautiful, state-protected woodland between our property and the next town over. And there was no telling what creatures were foraging in it. Bears were not uncommon, although I had never heard of anyone being attacked by one ... yet.

When Tay and I reached the family quarters of the inn, we learned that the orchard tour had already unloaded. While Tay went to clean herself up, I stood in the shadow of the high hedgerow, looking to see if Grandma Jenn was somewhere under the tent. A crowd had gathered, Tate's bright blond head sticking out like a beacon among them. Hannah was there as well, enjoying herself. Good for her, I thought, and smiled at the fact that no one seemed particularly concerned that she hadn't been disfigured or seized with anaphylactic shock from the bee incident.

Lunch was about to be served, and for this reason my eyes were drawn to the group of cute high school waitresses milling by the bar. I supposed they were awaiting drink orders. And while they waited the busboys were there to keep them company. It made me smile, the innocent flirtation of the young people. It brought to mind my own high school days and the many years I'd worn the same apron. The Cherry Orchard Inn had always made it a priority to hire local kids for the dining room, where they worked under the more experienced managers. I realized it had been a long time since I'd paid attention to the wait staff. The faces were all unfamiliar, but it looked like they were a close-knit group of friends.

Then, however, like a herd of deer turning in unison toward an unsettling sound, all the young heads swiveled to a spot on the patio. I turned as well and saw another young man approaching, although he wasn't as young. He was a bartender, near my own age and running a little late for his shift. And with that black hair, movie-star look, careless smile, and beautifully made body, they would forgive him a few minutes, I mused. Heck, they'd likely forgive him anything short of murder with that face. I had to commend head chef Bob Bonaire for hiring this man. When the tourists descended on the Cove, this bartender would have quite the following. I allowed myself one more look and then stepped back from the bushes. Grandma Jenn wasn't under the tent. A short while later, I learned from Mom that she'd gone to her own house for lunch.

Before me was a very distasteful task, one that I needed to confront alone. Leaving Mom in the dark, and Tay beside her for moral support, I took my crime scene blender base and got in my car. It was time I paid my gran a long-overdue visit.

Twenty

Grandma Jenn lived in a charming little Cape Cod less than a mile from the orchard. It sat at the end of a long gravel driveway, nestled in the woods and right on the shore of Cherry Cove Bay. She had moved there years ago, after selling the old Victorian mansion to my parents. I liked her house. It was quaint, cozy, and smelled like everything good from my childhood. It was the perfect home at the perfect distance—not too far from the orchard and only a short walk to the center of town. Although she'd grown up in the grand old Victorian, I really couldn't imagine her living anywhere else but here. I got out of my car with the blender base and knocked on her door.

"My dear girl," she said a heartbeat later, immaculately dressed and framed in the doorway, "it's about time you came for a visit. I've made sandwiches. Turkey, avocado, and sprouts, your favorite. I see you've found my blender."

The fact that she'd been waiting for me was a little unnerving. Taken off guard, I was speechless and willingly handed over the blender as I followed her inside.

She whisked me across the tiled entryway and down the hall, straight toward the large windows of the great room. Her house was just as I remembered it, full of sunlight and warm inviting smells. Beyond the windows sat her patio, and her rose garden about to bloom. The lake, flanked by greenery, red, pink, and white blossoms, and the stolid branches of oak and cedar sparkled in the distance like a sea of precious gems. On the patio a little wrought-iron table had already been set, topped with a flowered tablecloth, cloth napkins, delicate china, and silverware. Sandwiches awaited, along with a pitcher of iced tea with fresh mint leaves floating on top. It was strangely reminiscent of the tea parties we used to have when I was young. I didn't know how much I'd missed this place, or her, until that very moment. It all came crashing down on me like a rogue wave on an unsuspecting beach, leaving me helpless and humbled. And I hated myself for the questions I was about to ask. I suddenly remembered Jack's prophetic words: *Sometimes when you're digging for answers, you uncover things you're not quite ready for—things that maybe you wish you hadn't uncovered in the first place.* This, I thought grimly, was definitely one of those times.

"What a terrible thing it is," she began, breaking the silence while motioning for me to take a seat at the table, "the death of an old friend. It tears at your heart. I want to scream. I want to cry. I want to mourn him as he should be mourned, but there'll be time for that later." She poured me a glass of tea and sat down as well. "So, you've found out that we were having an affair."

The bluntness of her statement caused me to lose control of my jaw. It dangled. And I hastily took a sip of iced tea, hoping she wouldn't notice. My gran was never one to beat around the bush, but dang it! This was hardly the topic I wished to discuss over tea and sandwiches. Then again, from her point of view, it was a wise opening gambit. Get it out in the open. Thrust the eight-hundred-pound gorilla in the room under the spotlight.

I drank half the glass of tea before replying, "Yea, I might have heard something about that." She folded her hands and raised her eyebrows, prompting me to expound, "Okay, I just heard about it—from Tay of all people. Gran, why didn't you tell me?"

"For the simple reason, my dear, that it's none of your business. And mostly because your life is so full already with adventures of your own. Why bother you with my affairs? I'm very little bothered with them myself."

"I appreciate that, Gran, but since you and Jeb Carlson were more than just friends, unfortunately now it is my business. You knew that if I went to the processing sheds I'd find the cherry pits."

She set down her glass and gave a slow nod. "When you mentioned they were at the crime scene, I knew that if you went to the main processing shed and looked in Jeb's office, you'd find them. I had no idea you'd find my blender as well. I'd forgotten my name was on the darn thing. But you've only brought part of it, dear."

My stomach was churning, and whatever appetite I might have had was now lost. It was unbelievable, the thought that this sweet old lady could have poisoned her geriatric lover. "Gran," I breathed, "my God, why did you do it?"

She gave a little sigh. "Because he wanted to start drinking more smoothies," she admitted. "I've been experimenting with a tart cherry one. I made Jeb sample it one evening, after a bout of vigorous hanky-panky. Not only did he love the taste of it, why, it perked him right up. In fact, he called it his fountain of youth. Made him feel as frisky as a twenty-year-old again." She giggled. "Tart cherries do wonders for arthritis, you know, and with a little ginkgo biloba in the mix it keeps the memory sharp. Then too there's all the antioxidants from the berries I add and that burst of carbohydrates from the vanilla ice cream."

I shook my head like a dog in a bath, attempting to unhear the part about the vigorous lovemaking. That little detail I wouldn't have minded her omitting. And, truthfully, I was a little shocked that she was using ice cream in a smoothie—it was more like a cherry milkshake. Undeniably delicious, however, and with added health benefits. I shook my head again and focused. Although she was having an affair with her former employee and pumping him with a youthful elixir clearly designed for the more physical aspect of their relationship (I shivered at the thought), on the bright side, there was no clear admission of guilt that I could tell. "Okay," I said, "so you lent him your blender so he could make smoothies—"

"Not only my blender," she cut in. "I measured out all the ingredients and put them in freezer bags. All he needed to add was the ice cream."

"That's really thoughtful of you," I said, and meant it. "Okay, but I'm confused. Where do the cherry pits fit in? Did you add them to the smoothie as well?"

"Of course not!" she chided. "No person in their right mind should be eating cherry pits. You might not be aware of this, but cherry pits are poisonous."

I stared at her a second too long. "I know they're poisonous!" I said, as if I had known it forever and not just a few hours. "That's why I went to the crime scene. That's why I went to the processing shed. Remember when I told you and Mom that Jeb's death was made to look like it was caused by Dad's croquet mallet, but really he'd been poisoned first?"

"Yes, but I thought that was for Jani's sake. We all know what a hothead your father can be when he gets a club in his hand, golf, croquet, or otherwise."

"I wasn't lying for the sake of Mom, Gran! Jeb *was* poisoned. And when I found the cherry pits at the crime scene I grew suspicious. You just admitted that the cherry pits were yours. I found a box of them in Jeb's office."

"Just one box?" She tilted her head. "There should be more than one box."

"I don't know. There probably was. I didn't look. I was a little astonished by the fact that Jeb actually had a box of clean, dried cherry pits in his office. I'm nearly certain those pits are what killed him."

Her hand flew over her mouth and she uttered, "Oh my God," as if the correlation between Jeb being poisoned and the box of poisonous cherry pits had just been made. Maybe that ginkgo biloba wasn't all it was cracked up to be.

"Gran, let me be blunt," I said, and forced her to look at me. "I'm not going to judge you. I know that men can take your heart, rip it out of your body, and dance on it without a thought to your feelings. But I need to know, did you or did you not grind up a bunch of cherry pits, soak them in rum, and put the poison-infused rum back into the bottle in Jeb's desk, knowing he'd drink it?"

I interpreted the look she gave me to be more along the lines of incredulity rather than an admission of guilt.

"Of course not!" she cried. "Why would I poison Jeb when I loved him? He was my soulmate … although we could never live under the same roof."

"I thought Grandpa George was your soulmate?" I said accusingly, feeling very protective of Mom's dad. He'd died when I was young, but he was a good, kind man.

"Well, of course he was, dear." She patted my hand to console me. "Georgie was a wonderful man, but he's been gone a long time. A woman gets lonely, and Jeb has been a good friend nearly all my life. It was when his wife died that we found each other, in the biblical sense. But we both valued our independence, and we preferred to keep it strictly professional on the surface. For many years I was his boss, you know. That kind of thing is quite scandalous. Besides, it made all the furtive lovemaking—"

I held up a hand. "Got it. No need to elaborate. Remember, I'm not here to judge you. And for what it's worth, I think it's great you and Jeb found one another. But Gran, if you didn't use those cherry pits to poison Jeb, why were they in his office?"

The pencil-darkened brows disappeared under the white hair. "I'll show you. Wait here just a minute." Grandma Jenn disappeared into the house and returned a moment later carrying a long, rectangular strip of what looked to be sewn fleece. She deposited it in my hands. I'd assumed it was a scarf, but it was sewn on the edges and had some weight to it.

"What's this?" I asked, examining the brightly colored material. I saw that the ends were rounded, with little pockets sewn in for the hands.

"That's my contribution to the church bazaar. I've been keeping it a secret so that nosy Edna doesn't steal my idea and take all the credit for it. This, dear, is a therapeutic neck wrap. I felt that cherry pits had to have some use, so I came up with these. I fill them with a mix of clean cherry pits and cherry blossom potpourri and then sew them up. Pop it in the microwave for two minutes and you've got a warming wrap that feels and smells divine. Jeb was helping me. He cleaned and dried all the cherry pits from last summer's harvest." She paused, then, her robin's egg blue eyes filling with tears. "I had no idea anyone would think to use them to poison him. I never would have asked him such a thing had I known."

I went to her chair and held her. "Oh Gran. I'm so sorry. I'm so sorry, and yet I'm so relieved to learn about these," I said, wrapping the therapeutic neck warmer around my neck. It made her smile. "But I need you to think, now. Who else knew about the cherry pits? Who knew about Dad's croquet mallet, and his temper? Most importantly, who would want Jeb dead?"

She looked at me, her eyes vibrant with stifled tears. "No one," she uttered. "Jeb had no enemies. Everyone loved him." And then it hit her, that wisp of a thought, seemingly irrelevant until it wasn't. "Oh … my … goodness," she uttered.

"Gran, what is it?"

"I didn't think of it until now, but Jeb might have been acting a bit strangely. Two days ago, right when we were all knee-deep in preparations for the Cherry Blossom Festival, Jeb came into the kitchen and pulled me aside. That wasn't a usual thing for him. He seldom disturbed me at work. But I could tell something was bothering him. He told me that he needed to talk with me in private. He said it was very, very important. He used the word 'very' twice!"

"Did he? And what did he need to talk to you about that was so very important?"

"Well, that's just the thing. I don't know." Her chin began to quiver and then her eyes welled with tears. "I don't know, and I was too busy to talk with him—too busy to give him the time of day, and now he's gone. I'll never know!"

"Gran. Think. This could be important."

"I know, and I just brushed him off and told him that I didn't want to see him until after the weekend. You see, I'd assumed, as always, that he was just lonely and wanted to come over for a meal and a little … overnight affection. It had been a while since we hooked up."

I closed my eyes and forced the image from my head. "Okay. Interesting but not overly helpful. Gran, what if Jeb had stumbled onto something he wasn't supposed to ... something he saw or overheard while preparing the orchard, or wandering the woods?" Then another thought hit me. "Gran, did you know about the wine they were making in the lighthouse?"

A sheepish look crossed her face, and she nodded. "Jeb told me," she admitted. "We didn't keep secrets from one another, only from the world about our relationship. I knew Jeb and Baxter were making wine. It was bringing Jeb such joy."

"Tate knew about the wine as well," I told her.

A perfectly penciled brow arched. "Oh?" she said. "Well, I suppose that he would. Jeb and Tate were very close. In fact, Jeb relied on Tate for a good many things, including his recommendations when it came to hiring summer help at the orchard. You might not know this, but Tate coaches the high school basketball team. He's great with the kids, and those boys were nearly undefeated this year ... until their record was tainted by scandal. Tate was devastated, but you can get more information about that from your old friend Jack. Do you think whoever murdered Jeb knew about the wine?"

"It's definitely a possibility," I replied, thinking.

"Oh, Whitney," Grandma Jenn suddenly gasped, resting her silver-white head on her hands. "How absolutely dreadful. Jeb must have heard something and was trying to tell me about it! I feel just terrible about brushing him off. The least I could have done was to listen to him."

"It's better you didn't," I said, placing a hand on her trembling shoulder. She'd been under a lot of stress lately and hadn't even been given the time to properly mourn the loss of her soulmate. "Maybe if you'd listened to what Jeb had to say, whoever killed him would be after you too. Jeb wouldn't have wanted that, and neither would I. There's nothing you could have done to prevent what happened, Gran."

"Maybe not," she said, looking unconvinced. "But there's something very, very evil going on here, and I don't like it one bit."

Twenty-One

Why had Jeb Carlson been murdered? Poisoned with cyanide, struck in the face with a gold-plated croquet mallet, and left in a cherry orchard with a sprinkling of cherry pits and an eerie twig-face. What was the purpose of all that?

Everyone had immediately thought Dad was to blame. For those who didn't know him, it was an obvious leap of the imagination. After all, nobody could account for his whereabouts during the time of the murder. He'd been heard arguing with Jeb an hour before the body was found, and, to add insult to injury, his croquet mallet appeared to be the murder weapon. It hadn't helped any that he also had a history of sudden, violent outbursts when losing at sports involving croquet mallets, golf clubs, or tennis rackets. Using a croquet mallet as a murder weapon was a violent act, a man's swift act of vengeance. Given all these clues, it could be that the murderer was framing Dad, as Jack pointed out, and perhaps only using Jeb as a means to an end.

Then, however, there was the discovery that Jeb had actually died of cyanide poisoning and not a club to the head. Poison was a subtler way to murder a person—a woman's way, according to Tay. The fact that the murderer used cherry pits to create enough cyanide spoke of knowledge—not just about cherries, but about cyanide poisoning as well. Was it an accident that Grandma Jenn's blender had been used? Or had the murderer intentionally wished to pin the blame on her, making her appear the diabolical plotter?

I had to admit, finding all those clues in the processing shed had sent me into a panic sweat. Thank goodness Gran had nothing to do with it, and I truly believed that. There was an unmistakable sadness haunting the fine lines of her eyes. As we talked, she was trying to be her usual joyful self, but the deep, personal loss was hard to mask. And as much as I hated to acknowledge it (purely for my own silly reasons), I believed she really had lost her soulmate. Which raised another question: Did the murderer know that Jeb and Grandma Jenn were having an affair? Could it have been female jealousy? An old woman scorned, perhaps? Did it have something to do with the cherry pie bake-off that Jeb organized and judged every year? Or was Jeb's murder due to another matter entirely?

Grandma Jenn said that two days before his murder, Jeb was acting strangely. He'd been nervous, agitated by something, and wanted to speak with her in private. That wasn't like Jeb at all. So, what had he seen or heard that had made him so nervous?

Instantly a face jumped to mind, but not any human face. The face I was thinking of was made of twigs—an eerie pagan relic staring from the crime scene like a ghoul. Had Jack seen it too? I would have remembered if it had been visible in the photos, because that's not the kind of thing a person forgets. However, just because the twig-face wasn't in the pictures didn't mean it hadn't been there the night of the murder. Jack could have kept it to himself, which would be just like him. Then again, if it had been there, why hadn't anyone else mentioned it? Tate had gone to the crime scene. Dad too, and yet no one mentioned seeing the face. Had Jeb seen it before he was murdered? Or what if that face hadn't been there at all until today? Clearly this was a matter that begged to be explored.

I thought about Jeb and that odd twig-face as I walked along the lakeshore. After what had turned out to be, once the business of murder was cast aside, a nice lunch with Grandma Jenn, I decided to leave my car at her house and head into town. I needed to do a little thinking without the distraction of the Cherry Blossom Festival ... or of Tate, Jack, and that really hot bartender guy who was popping into my thoughts far too often for my comfort. Dang it! What the heck was wrong with me? This sleuthing business was really beginning to take its toll on my nerves. And I'd only been at it one morning! I wondered if Jack was having better luck making sense of it all. Then I reminded myself not to think about Jack. Instead I took out my iPhone and sent a text to Hannah and Tay asking them to meet me.

I continued along, passing the gingerbread charm of Candy Cove, the local candy store. A little way down from this was A Yarn Good Time, a home-spun little shop containing everything imaginable for the fiber arts. I passed three charming B&Bs, two beaches, a sporting goods store, the post office, the library and town hall (both in one building), the Cove Café, notorious for serving a cinnamon roll the size of a dinner plate, and Swenson's ice cream parlor, an old familiar haunt and the site of my first date with Tate.

A wave of nostalgia swept through me at the sight of the white wood-frame building with its cheerful red-and-white-striped awning. Swenson's served the best ice cream, burgers, and fries on the peninsula. I made the mistake of glancing at the patio. The red umbrellas had already gone up, reminding me that summer was just around the corner. At the back sat our old table, the one Tate had always requested because it was quiet, out-of-the-way, and had a spectacular view of the cove. Did I really miss him, I wondered? Or was it just my longing for a meaningful relationship? Either way, it was best not to dwell on it. I didn't have time to dwell on it. I was in the middle of a murder investigation.

Prying my eyes from Swenson's, I focused instead on the old turf-roofed Scandinavian gift shop next door. I noticed that it had been altered a bit. Then, as I rounded the gentle curve of the street, I gasped. Not only had it been altered, but it was now the police station! Oh, for cripes sakes! Had the whole village gone mad? Who puts a police station in an old-world Scandinavian log cabin? Apparently Cherry Cove does, and the thought wasn't nearly as shocking as spying Jack's SUV in the parking lot. Immediately my hand came up, shielding my face as I ran along the sidewalk. I was on a mission and had no time for a run-in with Detective McNosy. And then I heard the screaming.

My legs stopped working. I turned in the direction of the hideous noise and saw, to my horror, two little billy goats. They were perched on the thick grass roof of the police station, and they were staring right at me. Then they began screaming again, not bleating like normal goats. Apparently Jack had inherited not only the old Scandinavian gift shop but its crazy, hell-spawned animals as well. Wanting to giggle and enjoy the spectacle, I began running again instead, because the police station door had started to open. I ducked into Uncle Joe's grocery store, bought the few supplies I needed, and continued on my way. A few minutes later I bounded up the front steps of Cherry Cove's most iconic retail destination, Cheery Pickers.

I was always a little taken aback when first entering Tay's store. It was a candy store for the senses, smelling of scented candles and filled with the most eclectic collection of boutique clothing, home décor, eye-catching art, unusual antiques, handmade pottery, and costume jewelry. I'd taken only a few steps when I spied Tay's mom behind the counter. At the sight of her I smiled and waved, remembering, as the name formed on my tongue, not to call her Mrs. Robinson any longer. Two years ago we'd been specifically instructed to use her first name, Char. This was because the name Mrs. Robinson, as Tay had drunkenly informed us one evening, was nearly synonymous with an older woman seducing a younger man, thanks to an old movie called *The Graduate*. None of us had seen it, but we giggled all the same, because Mrs. Robinson—err, Char—had started dating a man four years older than her daughter. Char and Todd were now engaged, which seemed to amuse Tay more than it annoyed her, probably because whenever they were together she lovingly referred to him as Daddy.

Char ran around the counter and gave me an enthusiastic hug. The woman was fifty-two. Thanks to favorable genetics she looked forty-two, and because she was a shameless cougar, she dressed like a club-hopping thirty-year-old. "Whitney! Look at you!" She stood back and cringed a little at my disheveled Northwestern sweatshirt and blue jeans. It was a small blessing I was having a good hair day. It gave her artistic eye something to latch onto. "Cute hair," she remarked without any enthusiasm. That topic exhausted, she lowered her voice. "So good of you to come home and help your parents at a time like this. Terrible news about Jeb. How are your folks holding up?"

"They're shaken, but managing fair enough."

"No doubt they are. And," she continued in hushed tones, flashing a mischievous grin, "word on the street is you're matching wits against MacLaren. Good girl. My money's on you, kiddo. Tay and Hannah are in the office waiting for you."

"Ladies," I said a moment later, sauntering into Tay's surprisingly neat office. I held up my bag of goodies from Uncle Joe's. "I've brought us some thinkin' juice." I pulled out three bottles of wine, then upended the bag, depositing a box of Oreos on the desk. "And our favorite chocolate, cream-filled disks of inspiration. This," I said, holding up the dry-erase board, "is for me."

"Oh! Oh! We're going to make a suspect board like they do on TV." Hannah, face beaming, grabbed the box of Oreos.

"Exactly. Only in advertising we call it an idea board. However, suspect board is a more appropriate name for what we're about to do, I suppose. It's the same principle, though. We're going to do a little brainstorming. We're going to throw out any and all names, theories, and ideas associated with Jeb's murder, write them on the board, and see if anything jumps out at us. It's a way of seeing the forest through the trees, and, my friends, we have a lot of trees."

"I like it," Tay agreed, setting three wine glasses on her enormous lion-footed desk. Hannah uncorked one of the bottles and began pouring, while I opened the pack of markers and began writing everything we knew so far on the board.

"To Jeb," Hannah said somberly, raising her glass. "So vibrant in life, so mysterious in death."

Tay raised her glass as well. "Amen. And if you're watching from above, dear Jeb, how about a little help finding the bastard who took you from us?"

I picked up the other glass. "My sentiments exactly," I added, and clanked glasses all around. Then we set to work.

"What compels a person to take another person's life?" This I asked while mulling over all the puzzling facts.

"Anger," Hannah offered, then shoved an Oreo into her mouth. She washed it down with a swig of Chablis and blurted, "Hatred."

139

"Okay, but we haven't found anyone who clearly hated Jeb."

"No. But your dad was angry with him. They were heard arguing."

"They were making illegal wine in the old lighthouse," I reminded her, writing it down. "Whoever our murderer is, I'm convinced they know about that. They also know about my dad's anger issues and where he kept his croquet mallet."

"Love, sex, and jealousy," Tay rattled off. "Those can all be powerful reasons as well."

"Indeed." I wrote my grandma's name on the board. "At the crime scene in the processing shed there was plenty of evidence that appeared to link my gran to the murder." I drew a line from Grandma Jenn to the blender and the cherry pits. "These belong to Grandma Jenn. She even knows you can make cyanide from cherry pits, but after talking with her, I know she didn't do it. She and Jeb were having an affair." This I said looking straight at Hannah, hoping to shock her. The sheepish look on her face only confirmed that she'd known all about it too. "Am I the last person to learn about it?"

"Yep," Hannah quipped. "Even Jani knows. Rumor is she saw them one night having dinner at the bowling alley. Jeb and Jenn were holding hands under the table."

"Great. Okay, but look. My gran isn't the murderer. She loved Jeb and, by all accounts, it was a happy relationship. There's no motive. Could Jeb have had other women on the side? Or maybe an old flame who was jealous of Grandma Jenn—jealous enough to kill Jeb and frame her for murder? She did mention a name of someone who bothers her ... does the name Edna ring any bells?"

"Edna Baker? Yeah, she's the town busybody. Moved here a couple of years ago and wants to fit in like a local." Tay reached across the desk and refilled my wine glass. "I do believe the old girl had the hots for Jeb. She was always baking him pies and muffins, trying to soften him up. She desperately wanted to win the cherry pie bake-off and throw it in Jenn's face, but your grandma has that title in the bag."

I nearly choked on a sip of wine. "Because she and Jeb were lovers?"

"Well, yes," Hannah replied, grinning. "But that's not why she won every year. Whit, her pie's legendary. It *is* the best, but not only because of her crust and filling—it's because of the cherries she uses. She told Edna once that she gets them from one special tree in the orchard that only she knows about. I think it's just stuff, but I do re-member Jeb saying something about Edna sneaking into the orchard last August. She was poaching cherries. Had a whole pail filled before Jeb found her."

"Wow," I said, and wrote Edna's name on the board. Something large and oddly soft hit my leg. I looked down and saw Tay's enor-mous cat, Izzy. He'd been aiming for the empty wine bottle on the floor behind me and missed. Taking no notice of me, or my leg, Izzy shook his head and made another attempt. This time he was success-ful. The wine bottle hit the floor and rolled. Izzy pounced on it, trap-ping it between his big, fuzzy paws. Then, to my astonishment, he tried to stick his head inside the bottle, finally settling on the fact that only his tongue would fit.

"I don't have a cat, but is that normal?" I asked.

Tay peeked around the desk. "Not really," she informed me. "Char's spoiled him. She's made a habit of letting him lap up a sip or two of her wine. Now he thinks he's a sommelier. The little fur ball is compelled to sample every bottle."

"Well, he won't get much out of that one," Hannah added, and grinned.

Tay, working her computer like a high-tech goddess, printed a pic-ture of Edna Baker. "From the Cherry Cove Women's League," she informed us, handing it over. "She's a real peach, that's for sure. Slightly reminiscent of a bulldog, in both looks and tenacity."

"Oh!" I exclaimed, getting a good look at the picture. "Those eyes are so intense."

"Yep. That's our Edna. Once she sets those eyes on the prize, there's no deterring her." Tay grinned.

"Edna Baker is definitely someone I need to have a little chat with."

"That's all well and good," Tay interjected, staring at the board. "But Edna Baker is seventy years old. And while using poison from cherry pits might be her favorite pastime, I seriously doubt that she's capable of taking a club to a man's face. Besides, she would have had to be at the inn last night to take the croquet mallet from your dad's office, and she wasn't there. When Edna enters a room, believe me, you can't help but know it."

"Point taken. But I still don't think it would hurt having a little chat with her." I turned to Hannah and asked, "What about the two who found the body, the McSweenys?"

"I had a fine talk with them on the orchard tour. Nice couple. They both claim to like yoga, but clearly one of them is lying." Hannah rolled her eyes. "Oh, you mean regarding murder? I don't think either one of them is a likely suspect. Again, there's no motive. This is Ryan and Jillian's first visit to the Cherry Orchard Inn, and I'm sorry to say it'll probably be their last. And who could blame them? Stumbling upon Jeb's body like that? It'll haunt their nightmares long after the taste of cherry pie fades from their lips. Besides, I doubt they would have gone through the trouble of stealing your dad's croquet mallet and framing him for murder. Although they might want to now, after being made to stay through the weekend by MacLaren."

I stood with arms folded, staring at the board. It was like a bad day in advertising. We were racking our brains, trying to come up with suspects and motives, and every one of them was falling flat. Nothing was sticking. Then Tay handed me another picture. At first glance I thought it was a sun-gilded GQ model. Then I realized the man in the picture was Tate. I had to admit he was a very photogenic man.

"Jesus, don't stand there ogling it. Tape it to the board!" Tay ripped off a piece of tape and handed it across the desk. "Like it or not, Vander Licious is a suspect. Think about it, Whit. He was there last night. It's undeniable that he still has a thing for you. And since the two of you broke up, he's become chummy-chummy with your folks. If that's not a little odd, think about the fact that his friendship with Jeb gave him access to all the buildings, including the old lighthouse and Baxter's office."

"He did know about the illegal wine they were making," I remarked, adding him to our suspect board. "And he was at the inn last night. Okay, let's say he's a suspect. What's his motive?"

"I don't know," Tay said, looking pensive. "But if he had one he could have snuck off for a few minutes to do the deed. He could have easily made the poison, put it in the rum bottle, waited for Jeb to drink it, and then dragged the body into the orchard and clubbed him over the head. He has the strength to do it. The question is, why would he do it? He and Jeb were good friends. Tate helped out at the orchard whenever Jeb needed him."

"I know. Grandma Jenn told me all about it, including how he used to recommend some of the high school kids he coached to work on the orchard. I didn't even know he coached basketball." I found the thought of Tate as a murder suspect far more depressing than I should have.

"You know what this means," Hannah asked softly. "You're going to have to talk with him. Jack likely won't even consider him as a suspect due to their budding bromance. They're friends, and for a geek like Jack to have a friend like Tate, it has to be a little blinding."

"I think you're underestimating Jack." I don't know why I suddenly had the urge to defend him, but I did.

"Hannah's right, Whit. This could be your moment to finally best him."

I considered this. But Tate wasn't the only person worth looking in to. As unlikely as they were, there was Dr. Engel, Dad's closest friend; Brock Sorensen, his new business manager I had yet to meet; and Hannah's current heartthrob, Carleton Brisbane. Brisbane was a long shot, but he might know something, being Tate's friend. All these men had been at the inn the night of the murder, but none of them had a motive to kill Jeb as far as we knew. Yet the names were there, and all of them deserved a closer look.

We were discussing our suspect board when Char walked into the office. Like a well-trained truffle pig, she'd smelled wine, and she'd brought her own glass to the party.

"I just thought I'd pop in and see how you girls were doing," she said while helping herself to a glass. She took a long sip and stared at the board. "I don't want to say anything here, but there is another reason for murder other than sex, love, jealousy, hate, and anger. You're forgetting money, fear, and embarrassment."

I was stunned we hadn't thought of these and quickly added them to the board. "Okay, some new motives. Did anybody fear Jeb? Had he embarrassed anyone?"

Here Char quirked a perfectly plucked brow. "Well, it's likely nothing, but there is one woman who isn't a fan. Are you familiar with Lori

Larson?" I shook my head, having never heard the name. "She's lived on the peninsula for years," Char went on. "Has a small farmhouse off of Old Stage Road. Lori fancies herself a cook, but she isn't. She's the queen of the frozen pizza, or so Joe tells me." She tipped her stylish brown curls at the grocery bag on the floor, indicating the Joe she was referring to. "She works as a real estate agent. A couple of years ago her husband got fed up with the fact that she was never home and left her with the farm and the kids. She barely has time for those kids of hers, let alone the farm. And now, due to a hefty load of guilt, she's convinced she's the next Martha Stewart. The moment her husband left her she began entering all the local food contests to prove her domestic skills. Last year, bless her, she actually won second place for her strawberry jam at the county fair." Char tipped back the last of her wine, picked up a bottle, and poured another.

"She's come a long way," she continued. "At least her jam has, but her baking is so ungodly terrible her own goats aren't even tempted by it. Unfortunately, the first baking contest she ever entered was the cherry pie bake-off Jeb holds every year at the Cherry Blossom Festival. Because she had a cherry tree in her yard, she convinced herself she could make a pie good enough to win, having never baked a cherry pie before in her life! It looked a hot mess, and when Jeb took that first bite, he nearly broke a tooth on a cherry pit. He had to spit it out after realizing Lori hadn't bothered to pit any of the cherries. He was highly annoyed, especially after Lori admitted that she didn't know you were supposed to remove the pits first. Apparently, she doesn't eat cherries. Her ignorance, as you can imagine, sent everyone into fits of laughter. Jeb, after that initial shock, made a little joke, saying that he never thought cherries would be the death of him ... until he took a bite of Lori's pie. He said no more on the subject, but the incident embarrassed Lori to the core. She never forgave him that."

Twenty-Two

$\mathcal{E}$rik Larson. I had never met the kid, yet thanks to his mother and her pit-riddled cherry pie, and the fact that he worked on our orchard, he'd now landed at the top of our suspect board. If his mother had an ax to grind with Jeb Carlson, chances were good Erik knew about it. Heck, if he loved his mother enough, he might even have taken matters into his own hands on her behalf. The thought was unsettling.

From the picture Tay printed off, Erik looked to be a handsome, blond-headed youth, slightly reminiscent of a young Tate. But the eyes and mouth were all wrong. Tate most definitely knew him, since according to Hannah, Erik had been on the high school basketball team Tate coached, which was how he'd landed the job at the orchard. It was all so convenient, I thought. I suddenly recalled the huddle of high school kids under the white tent, knowing for certain that the tall blond-headed boy chatting-up the perky tawny-haired girl had been Erik Larson.

I'm not gonna lie. By the time our mission to talk with the boy had crystalized in our brains, none of us were in any condition to operate a car. Hannah, having started pre-gaming on the orchard tour, had drunk nearly a bottle of wine by herself and was taking a nap on the floor, curled beside the giant fur ball, Izzy. Tay, faring better than the rest of us but with a case of the giggles, took out her phone and snapped a picture. "This is totally going on Snapchat."

"No," I said, grabbing her arm. "No social media right now." I lowered my voice and whispered, "We're in the middle of an investigation." I marveled at how cool that sounded coming from my lips.

"Right," she said, giggling as she shoved the phone back in her pocket.

In order to talk with Erik, I needed to get back to the inn. My car was at Grandma Jenn's, of course, which was just fine under the circumstances. I wasn't in any shape to drive. I'd planned on picking it up later when I went to her house to bake my cherry pie for the bake-off. And right now the inn, perched on the bluffs across the bay, seemed unnaturally far away. It was also up hill. I turned to Tay. "Do you have some breath mints and, like, a bike I could borrow?"

"Bike?" She laughed. "Kids have bikes. I have something better." She pulled a tin of breath mints from her drawer, took a handful herself, shoved them into her mouth, and handed the container to me. "Mom." She turned to Char. "I need you to keep an eye on the store for a while longer. And Hannah too. Wake her up in an hour. She has a hot date with Briz tonight at the inn." We both started giggling.

"No kidding," Char remarked, looking impressed. "Didn't think she was his type."

"I don't think she is," Tay said. "But don't ruin the fantasy, Char. Okay?"

A moment later, with fresh breath and our heads clearing, Tay and I rode through the town, sandwiched together on an ancient Vespa scooter. It might have had the whiff of a Thelma and Louise moment—two besties with wind-tousled hair racing through the town on a mission. But we were only topping ten mph, and the laughter from the passing cars killed it entirely. Also, we were wearing bulky helmets. Char insisted.

"Lance found this little beauty for me," Tay called back over the ear-splitting PUT-PUT-PUT of the engine. Lance Van Guilder was her current boyfriend. "I've been training him to be a savvy picker. Found it in some guy's barn and traded him an old suit of armor for it."

This may have sounded like the farmer got the better end of the deal—a suit of medieval armor for a rusty, smoke-spewing bucket with wheels. But by all accounts it was an even trade, considering that Lance—with his long light brown hair, arms the size of tree trunks, and nearly-always-shirtless look—was a professional jouster on the renaissance fair circuit. The armor he wore was his own creation. And, according to Tay, his wasn't the most accurate lance in the tilt yard.

"Nice," I called back, holding on for dear life.

We had just crested the bluff, after puttering up a substantial hill, when Jack's police cruiser pulled in front of us, lights flashing. An explosive "Dammit!" erupted from Tay and she pulled off the road.

"What are you two doing?" Jack asked, emerging from his SUV. He was wearing street clothes. I don't know why it came as a shock to me. Maybe because they suited him so well.

"We're driving to the Cherry Orchard Inn," Tay offered in her sweetest voice. "Is there a problem with that, officer?"

"No. But you were going twenty miles per hour under the speed limit, and it's only twenty-five. That's difficult to do. And that scooter isn't exactly built for two. I thought maybe I could lighten the load a bit by offering Whitney a ride."

I needed no more invitation than that. I felt a modicum of guilt abandoning Tay, but it was all for a good reason. I was desperate to pick Jack's brain. I needed to know if he had seen the eerie twig-face in the orchard.

Out of a concern for safety, and maybe even a flash of chivalry as well, Jack insisted Tay ride ahead of us. When we were back on the road he casually remarked, "I saw you walk into town."

I feigned a look of surprise. "Really? Well, I needed to get a few things." Having no wish to elaborate on what I'd been doing, I was quick to change the subject. "So, how's the investigation going? Any new suspects? Oh! I have a question for you. During your investigation, did you come across anything like this in the orchard?" With the twig-face filling the screen of my iPhone, I turned it to him, paying close attention to his eyes.

Puzzlement, and something a little darker, seized his features. He pulled off the road, threw the SUV in park, and took the phone from my hand. "Where'd you see this?"

"Ahhh, in the orchard," I replied, breezily.

"Where in the orchard, Whitney?" He sounded curious, and not in a good way.

"Nowhere near the crime scene," I lied, secretly crossing my fingers. Grandma Jenn had told me a long time ago that if you told a lie and crossed your fingers it negated all the bad juju. I believed her. "Tay and I were trying to join the orchard tour, and, uh … you know, we kind of ran into it. I heard you were working with the Crime Scene Unit today and wondered if you guys happened to come across anything like it. Do you recognize it?"

"No," Jack said, and the way he said it, I believed him. "But I am curious." He then reduced the image on the phone. Dang it! I hadn't seen that coming. The full picture came into view, including a strip of yellow caution tape visible in the top right corner. "You *were* at the crime scene," he said accusingly, glaring at me through narrowed eyes. "I told you, Whitney. Stay out of this."

"Look, Jack. It's my family orchard. I can hardly stay out of this. Besides, I wanted a closer look at those cherry pits."

"So you went to the crime scene after I told you not to? You didn't touch anything, did you?" I was quick to shake my head. "And you saw this ... there?"

"We did. Didn't you?" Apparently, he hadn't. The thought sent the hair on the back of my neck on end.

"What time did you see this?" he demanded. "Do you remember?"

"About the same time the orchard tour set off. Eleven, I believe."

"Well ... that's impossible. I was there around noon. And I can clearly tell you that this wasn't there."

"What? But wasn't it there last night?"

"No," he said, and gave his copper-colored hair a convincing shake. "I've never seen anything like this before, not in that orchard anyway. And I wouldn't believe it was ever at the crime scene if it wasn't for this." He pointed to the tell-tale yellow tape in the shot.

"Maybe you missed it last night?" I suggested hopefully. "After all, it was dark, and finding Jeb like that must have been a shock to you."

"That's all true. But I didn't miss it, Whit. I have a powerful flashlight, and I taped off the crime scene myself. If that had been there, I would have known it."

"Are you saying that someone put this eerie face there between the time Jeb's body was removed last night and this morning, when Tay and I found it, and then took it down again before you and your team came to investigate? Why would anyone go to the trouble?"

Jack fell silent. Then, "Whitney, listen to me. This is very important. Right now, I don't care that you were at the crime scene. What I care about is who else was in the orchard with you besides Tay."

"Well," I said, slightly frightened by the intensity in his eyes, "there wasn't anyone with us. We were the only ones in that part of the orchard. Everyone else was with Tate on the tour."

"Are you sure?"

"I'm not exactly familiar with all the guests, but yeah, I'm pretty darn certain ... " I was about to insist that we'd been entirely alone when I suddenly remembered the eerie feeling that had come over us the moment we discovered the twig-face. Tay and I had been certain we were being watched. The word "ghost" came to mind, or "unsettled spirit," but it was hardly a thing I'd suggest to the likes of Jack. "All right," I said, because he was going go ask, "we didn't see anybody, but once we found the twig-face, we both felt ... well, odd. We had the feeling that someone or something was watching us. We also heard sounds—the snapping of a twig, the rustling of leaves as if something was brushing past them. It sounded like a person or animal was following us. But Jack, nothing was there. Believe me, we checked."

"What did you do then, once you saw this?" He pointed to the eerie image on my phone.

"I'm not proud of it, but we ran."

"Where to?" When I didn't answer, he guessed it. "You went to the processing sheds, didn't you? Christ, Whit. You were there before me. Tell me you didn't touch anything."

"Yeah. No. Of course we didn't," I lied again, crossing my fingers. "We were scared. We thought the processing shed would be enough to deter whatever was following us."

He thought about this a moment, coming at last to the obvious conclusion. "I know you two did a little poking around in there. Just couldn't resist it, could you? Remember, Whit, I know you. Don't lie to me. What did you find?"

"I imagine we saw pretty much the same things you did. Shattered glass on the floor of Jeb's office, an open can of Coke on the desk, a bottle of rum in the drawer that had been tampered with, and a box full of dried cherry pits, just like the ones I pointed out to you at Ed's Diner. I had to go to the sheds—when I realized cyanide could be made from cherry pits, I needed to see if my theory was correct. It was. All the evidence is there in that shed. I know you probably saw that all those dried cherry pits in Jeb's office belonged to Grandma Jenn. She told me the box had her name on it. But don't worry. She had nothing to do with his murder. I've already talked with her. She was having Jeb clean and dry them for her. She was using the cherry pits to make therapeutic neck warmers for the church bazaar."

Jack's puzzling smile seemed a bit out of place until he said, "Excellent. Well, that clears that up. But I should tell you, Whit, your grandma was never a murder suspect."

"What?" That got my goat. "Well, why ever not?"

"Ah ... " He pretended to think, then thrust three fingers before my face. "Three reasons, actually. One: we now believe Jeb died in his office, and she's an old lady who lacks the strength to carry the body from the scene of the crime to the orchard. Two: no motive. Beside the fact that Jeb was invaluable to the orchard, he and Jenn were in a romantic relationship. They were crazy about each other."

"You knew about that?"

"Of course. Everybody knew. I'm surprised you didn't. And three: Jenn's alibi checks out. She was in the inn kitchen with your mom and Bob Bonaire during the time the murder occurred. They were prepping the Saturday menu. She and your mom were baking cherry pecan bread. But you're right, Whit. Cherry pits are significant here. It's like the murderer is toying with us, using them as an ironic statement or something. And this," he said, indicating to the eerie twig-face. "I have no idea what the meaning of this is, but the fact that only you and Tay have seen it alarms me. Someone was in that orchard with you, Whitney, and I don't like it. Remember, Jeb's killer is still out there. And whoever it is, they're familiar enough with this place to know their way around the orchard and processing sheds."

"Erik Larson," I blurted, thinking of the boy Tay and I wanted to talk to.

Curiosity animated Jack's features. "What about him?"

"He works on the orchard," I said, and briefly explained to Jack what Char had told us about Lori Larson and her embarrassment two years ago during the pie bake-off at the Cherry Blossom Festival.

"Interesting. So you think an eighteen-year-old kid murdered his employer due to a slight his mom suffered two years ago? Whit, if that poor kid went around murdering everyone who's ever made fun of his mother's baking, there wouldn't be a soul left in the entire village, himself included. He's merciless on the woman."

"You obviously know him," I said. I might also have sneered a little at his overwhelming confidence.

"Of course I know him. I make it a point to get to know all the kids around here." From the way Jack said this, one would think him the embodiment of Officer Friendly. He grew serious again, adding, "Then too, Erik Larson's no angel. A couple of years ago, when his parents were going through a rough patch, I caught him and his buddy Cody Rivers stealing bikes from vacationers and selling them on Craigslist. They were using the money they made to buy beer and pot. Earlier this year, young Mr. Larson was involved in a scandal at the high school involving the use and distribution of steroids. Wasn't the only one using them either. When Tate found out, he was beside himself. He had to report it, even knowing the whole team would be suspended. Was a real pity, too, because we were leading our division.

Believe me, Whit. I've already talked with Erik. For all his faults, he's a sweet kid. I don't for a minute suspect him of murder. But he was with Jeb last night, helping him prepare the hay wagon for the orchard tour. Then, after delivering the note to your father, he stuck around waiting for his girlfriend to finish her shift."

"A pretty girl with tawny-blonde hair?"

"Yeah," he said, mildly impressed. "Kenna McKinnon's her name. Everyone on the staff was pretty freaked out last night, especially the high school kids. I thought Erik might have seen something out of the ordinary. But he was too distraught by the incident to be much help. I believe he was in a state of shock when we spoke, which isn't unusual. Jeb was something of a mentor to him."

"And you think it's safe to allow the high school kids to work today?"

Jack nodded. "We're not dealing with a serial killer, Whit. Jeb Carlson was the target. Only I still don't know why."

I suddenly recalled my conversation with Grandma Jenn. She'd said that Jeb was acting strangely before the Cherry Blossom Festival began. She thought he might have stumbled upon some troubling information. Or, as Jack had suggested earlier, maybe he knew somebody's wicked secret. Knowing Jeb, he might have even poked his nose a little too far into the matter, never realizing he'd be made to pay the price. But what had he stumbled upon? I looked at the picture of the twig-face on my iPhone and felt even more confused.

"Whitney. Whit?" I hadn't realized Jack was speaking to me. "You look a bit out of it. Are you okay?"

"Yeah," I said. "Just tired. I think the hours are finally catching up with me."

"Really?" he remarked, putting the car in gear. "I thought it was the wine."

Twenty-Three

I saw MacLaren pull off the road. What were you guys doing back there … or shouldn't I ask?" Tay smiled teasingly and alighted from a front porch rocking chair.

I cast her a look that expressed a sarcastic *really?* and pulled her with me through the front doors of the inn. "I asked him about this." I flashed her the twig-face picture on my phone and kept walking. "He's never seen it before, which means that you and I are the only ones. Come on." I beckoned, slipping behind the front desk and through the door leading to the family quarters. "I need to change. I've got a new plan."

My bedroom was on the second floor. As I opened the door, Tay stopped on the threshold and giggled. "A Victorian love nest, that's what this is. Jani's really outdone herself on this one."

I gave my old room the once-over, feeling a bit like a guest as I stared at the lovely, white antique furniture, the vases of brightly colored flowers, the china tea set delicately perched on a table by the window, the lace curtains, and the tester bed swagged in wreaths of flowers and pink chiffon. It was flowery, feminine, and overtly romantic. "I don't know,"

I mused, grabbing up my suitcase from the floor and plopping it on the bed. "I kind of miss the shocking pink walls and the boy-band posters. Mom couldn't wait to rip them down the moment I graduated college."

"Can't say that I blame her." Tay flopped on the bed and lounged on the decadent array of pillows like an Egyptian queen. "What do you think she's trying to say with a statement like this?"

"I haven't a clue. Nor do I care to guess. She told me these were all leftovers from the inn—as if that's a legit excuse to rip all the hot, broody men off my wall."

"Whit, she has an eye for decorating. And from the looks of this I'd say she's hoping to inspire some romantic feelings in her romantically stifled daughter."

"Yeah, well," I began, rummaging through my bag, "I'm not romantically stifled. I've just quit men for a while. It's no different than dropping carbs from your diet. Sure, you crave them, but it's far healthier to go without."

Skepticism was written all over Tay's face, helped along by a dramatic eye roll. I held up a flouncy, knee-length sundress and proclaimed, "My new plan. Erik Larson is working today, bussing both the wine and cheese tasting and dinner. We're gonna find this kid and ask him some pressing questions."

"Ah! We're going to do a little mingling." Tay ginned.

"Sober mingling," I reminded her. "It was fortuitous Char mentioned him. I told you that you and I are the only ones to have seen that eerie twig-face, but what if Jeb had seen it someplace as well—or maybe overheard something in the orchard he wasn't supposed to? Erik worked closely with Jeb and was with him in the processing shed the night he was poisoned. Erik was the one who delivered Jeb's note to my dad. Then, shortly thereafter, Erik overheard Dad and Jeb arguing, and he told Jack about that as well. We know that Dad was upset about the missing wine, but what if the wine was only one of the issues they fought about? Grandma Jenn told me that Jeb was acting strange and had asked to speak with her in private two days earlier. She never got the chance to find out what he was worried about, and maybe Dad didn't either. I think Jeb saw or heard something in the orchard that troubled him, and he wanted to bring it to my dad's attention. But being a notorious hothead, Dad might have been too torqued up about the missing wine to hear whatever else Jeb wanted to tell him. Jeb's no longer here to tell us what was going on, but Erik is. He might know what Jeb knew ... or he might be the one causing all the mischief."

Tay sat up with a start. "Well, don't just stand there. Put that thing on!"

The wine and cheese event was always a big hit. It was open to the public, and, being that it was a lovely Saturday afternoon in late May, the event appeared to be a very popular destination. The overflow parking was full. Cars were lining the winding drive all the way down to the main road. I would have liked to think everyone had come for the wine, cheese, and other cherry products showcased under the tent, but I had the suspicious feeling that the overly large crowd was due in part to morbid curiosity. Murder, I mused. It was as titillating in these parts as a Friday night fish fry.

While Tay threw on one of my old dresses, I popped in to the kitchen to have a word with Dad. The large crowd had sent the kitchen into a tizzy, and he and Mom were helping out, putting the finishing touches on yet more giant platters of cheese, assorted breads and crackers, and fresh berries to be brought to the lawn. A tall, lanky dark-haired fellow, whom I recognized as one of the bartenders, was talking with Dad. Apparently extra cases of cherry wine were needed under the tent. As I walked over to the long counter Mom and Dad were working at, the bartender gave a slight nod in my direction and left. My parents turned. Smiles of joy, and perhaps relief, broke out on their faces.

"No need to stop on my account," I said, sidling up to the counter. I picked up a box of gourmet sesame crackers and began adding them artfully to the tray beside Dad's slices of neatly shingled cherry Gouda. Mom was arranging plump strawberries, raspberries, and huge blackberries on a platter surrounding a bowl of the inn's signature candy: creamy squares of dark chocolate infused with tart cherries. Everything looked delicious. "You always said that there's no time to stop in a busy kitchen. I just came down to see how things were going, and to ask how you two are holding up."

"We're so glad you're here," Mom said, and I could see that she meant it.

"And now that I've spoken to MacLaren," Dad chimed in, "we're both doing a little better. It was a relief to know that my croquet mallet wasn't the murder weapon. But still, poison ... " He gave a disparaging shake of his head. "What a terrible way to die."

"I agree. And that's partially why I'm here." It was then that I asked Dad if the stolen wine was the only thing that Jeb had wanted to discuss. He was quick to acknowledge that it was. Then, however, he looked up from the cheese tray.

"Maybe there was something else? Jeb told me there were 'strange happenings' about. Damn right there was, I had told him. The lighthouse had been broken into and all our wine was gone! That's what I imagined he meant. Could he have meant something else?"

"I think maybe there was something else." I took out my phone and showed Dad the picture of the eerie twig-face at the crime scene. "Have you ever come across this before?"

"Dear God!" he exclaimed. "What a horrible little image. It has a pagan air about it, and are those cherries for the eyes?" A look of mild disgust crossed his face.

Mom, not wanting to be left out, craned her neck to investigate. It was instantly apparent that neither one of my parents had ever come across such a thing before. And they were unsettled to learn that somebody had placed it in the orchard at the crime scene after the fact.

"Whitney. Stay out of the orchard," Dad commanded. "In fact, no one's to go in there until Jeb's murderer has been apprehended. Is that clear? I know it's the Cherry Blossom Festival, but this is beyond the pale. I'm going to make an announcement. Then I'm going to see to having the whole orchard cordoned off. What are you up to, or shouldn't we ask?"

"Oh, you can ask," I said with a grin. "Tay and I are about to join the party on the lawn. There's a young man I'd like to have a word with."

When one is a woman standing five foot seven in heels, and her friend is even shorter, finding a person in a crowd is a bit like finding a needle in a haystack. Space under the tent was at a premium. Tay, however, was undeterred and declared that we needed to start at the bar and work our way to the back from there; she said that the wine would help us blend in. It was a good plan until we caught sight of Hot Bartender Guy. He looked cool as a cucumber standing behind the outdoor bar, popping cork after cork and filling up glasses like a champ. The moment he noticed us staring at him, he stopped pouring and grinned.

"Ladies," he said, appearing before us as if we were the only souls waiting to be served. "And what is it you'll be having now? Will it be the white, or the red?" His smile was as mesmerizing as his Irish

160

accent. I hadn't expected that. The scene from earlier in the day came flooding to my mind—all the young waitress had been hovering around this guy, giddy with excitement, and no wonder. His soft, lilting accent and full-on charm were impossible to resist.

"Wha … what do you suggest?" I asked, and went to lean an elbow on the bar in a coolly alluring posture. Unfortunately, the bar was wet. My elbow slipped right off, and I hit shoulder-first instead. It was not elegant or remotely cool. Hot Bartender Guy, adhering to the time-honored traditions of his profession, pretended not to notice.

Instead, he leaned in and softly replied, "Well now, love, that would depend on you. If you'll be wantin' a hint o'cherries, I suggest the white. If, however, you're feeling more *adventurous*"—the word was thick with innuendo—"the red is the choice for you."

"Oh, the red. Defiantly the red," Tay and I offered in near unison. He poured out two glasses and handed them across.

"How much?" I asked. I could see he thought this a ridiculous question.

"Complimentary, o'course, on account of you being the boss's daughter." He gave us a wink and turned to go.

It was then that I thought to ask if he could point us in the direction of Erik Larson. "And what is it you'll be wanting with the young lad?" he asked.

"Oh, we only want to talk. We need to ask him a few questions."

The light green eyes, like mossy pools glinting from the depths of a deep dark forest, narrowed slightly. "Well then, if that's all, he'll be that-a-way, I suspect." Hot Bartender Guy pointed into the crowd. Not very helpful.

"Thanks," Tay said, and stuffed a fiver in his tip jar.

With wineglasses in hand we circulated among the guests, engaging in small talk and getting a bit sidetracked with all the delectable cherry-inspired products—the local cheeses, the crackers begging to be doused with cherry spreads, cherry salsas, and cherry jams. We found Jack beside the fruit and chocolate table, shortly after he'd announced that the orchard was closed until further notice. Not wanting to look suspicious, we hovered there, making small talk and overindulging in dark chocolate pregnant with dried tart cherries. It was then, while in the middle of a conversation about the upcoming cherry pie bake-off, that I saw a patch of light blond poke above the crowd and disappear. Certain it belonged to the young man we were looking for, I excused myself and headed for the exact spot in the crowd I'd last seen the bright head. Once there, however, there was no sign of him.

Tay came beside me. "Where'd he go?"

"I have no idea, but one thing's for sure. That kid can move."

We then talked with each harried waitress we passed, which was a mistake. Every one of them had seen the kid in a different location, a location he was no longer in.

"Over there," I told Tay, spying three busboys chatting by a bussing station at the far side of the tent. Two of them were quite young, probably fifteen or sixteen. The dark-haired boy with them was definitely older. Eighteen or nineteen was my guess. Likely the same age as Erik. When they spied us walking toward them, the dark-haired kid picked up a bin and disappeared into the press of people. The younger two—a stocky boy named Pete Gunderson, we learned, and a slender redhead named Trevor Macintosh—were eager to talk. The Gunderson boy was certain Erik was in the boathouse making out with his girlfriend, Kenna McKinnon. Young Mr. Gunderson also informed us that it was best we wait until they returned. He'd made the mistake of surprising them once and had gotten a bloody nose for the effort. The boys chuckled at the memory. Then, as if spooked by something, they both picked up their bins and went back to work.

"Interesting," Tay mused. "So, do we go to the boathouse or wait it out?"

"Oh, we definitely go. The kid's supposed to be working!" Incensed, I put my wineglass in one of the bins and headed for the back of the tent. Tay followed. We'd taken no more than fifteen steps through the crowd when I felt her hand on my shoulder. I looked up and saw Erik Larson standing behind a tent pole. Beside him was the other busboy, the black-haired kid who had slipped off the moment he spotted us. The two were discussing what looked to be a troubling matter. It was highly suspicious. I was about to sneak up on them when Tay made the mistake of calling out his name.

Erik turned, saw us, and bolted through the crowd. His darkhaired friend disappeared as well.

"This way!" I cried, chasing after the bright blond head bobbing through the press of people. He was young, athletic, and used the guests and overflowing tables to his advantage. He crashed into Pete Gunderson, knocking the boy to the ground in an explosion of glassware. Mrs. Schneider, the guest staying in the Cabbage Rose Suite, shrieked as a full glass of wine exploded from her hand. It appeared that the kid was circling through the crowd, heading back to the rear of the tent. The miscreant meant to give us the slip and disappear into the woods, a sure sign of guilt as I saw it. Well, not on my watch, mister!

I decided to cut him off, and began working my way to the side of the tent where I could spring out of the crowd and give chase. I moved as fast as I could, cutting left to avoid a group of people chatting. A dang tent pole was right before me. I clapped a hand onto it and flung myself around. But I made it only halfway before slamming headlong into a man. The next thing I knew, I was on my backside staring up into the shocked yet dashing face of Mr. Carleton Brisbane.

Twenty-Four

iss Bloom! Are you all right? And here I was begging Officer MacLaren for an introduction. I never meant to knock you off your feet." He paused, grinned slightly, and added, "Well, not literally anyway. Carleton Brisbane." He leaned down and smoothly offered his hand. "It's a pleasure to finally meet you."

I would have replied, but I was still paralyzed with awe. I'd seen the man from a distance and thought him attractive; close-up, he was movie-star dazzling. I now understood Hannah's obsession and felt a little guilty that my thoughts were not as pure as my smile. Nor could I deny the swarm of butterflies that invaded my belly under his dazzling, intimately focused gaze. I should ignore the butterflies, and this man as well. What kind of friend was I that I even entertained the thought of dangling a toe in my bestie's clearly marked territory? But he was flirting! I didn't have to flirt back, however, I sternly reminded myself. I should listen to my gut instinct and run away as soon as I could.

Instead, smiling like a love-struck simpleton, I took his hand and replied, "Whitney Bloom. And I assure you, Carleton, the pleasure's all mine."

A forced cough at that very moment alerted me to the man standing beside Carleton Brisbane. It was Jack. Although his hand was covering his mouth, his face was a study of patronizing admonishment.

I felt embarrassed, and ashamed, and yet found myself unable to let go of Carleton's strong, supportive hand. Holy cobbler! I was like the vampy friend in every bad reality TV show. I was barely upright, adrift in a flood of confusing thoughts, when a force like a tiny hurricane hit me from behind. There was only one direction for me to go—straight into Carleton Brisbane's arms. They became the only two things holding me upright. Remarkably, the man was still standing; remarkably, I found that I didn't want him to let me go. It was all so confusing… until Tay's admonishing voice broke the spell.

"Whitney, for cripes sake! Now's not the time to… Oh, hey Carleton. Jack. What's up?" At the sound of Tay's voice, Carleton released me.

"I was about to ask you the same question," Jack said, taking a step forward. Somewhere inside our old high school buddy a switch had flipped, making him look remarkably like a hard-nosed detective. "It's quite the gala," he continued. "Should you two really be dodging through the crowd, upsetting the guests and swinging around tent poles? You're apt to give folks the wrong impression. For instance, they might think you're chasing after the busboys again." This he said with a pointed look at me.

"Well, they might, but they'd be wrong." With a quick look at Tay for support, I launched into a harmless falsehood. "If you really must know, Jack, we're working. Dad's short-handed and we volunteered to case the event, you know, to see where help is needed. It seems that one of the busboys has abandoned his post."

"I can only imagine. Let me guess. Erik Larson? Kind of hard to miss the kid, especially with you two in hot pursuit and him running like the devil." He shot me a look of stern disapproval before adding,

"I doubt he's coming back, which means that a busboy opportunity has opened up for you, Whitney."

Rising to the challenge, I told him, "I'll get right on it, but first may I have a word with you, Jack?" Without waiting, I took him by the arm and led him outside the tent. Groups of people dotted the vast lawn, and yet there was no trace of Erik Larson.

"So what's this all about?" he asked.

"I needed to talk with Erik Larson."

"And I told you earlier that I already have. Last night for twenty minutes. I have his statement at the station. The kid's pretty shaken up, Whitney, but he's not the murderer. Don't take this personally, but did you ever consider that he might not want to speak with you?"

"Oh, I know he doesn't. He's made that quite clear. The moment he caught wind that Tay and I were looking for him, he hightailed it out of here. If that isn't suspicious behavior I don't know what is."

"Whitney, Erik Larson is under no obligation to speak with you, and believe me, he knows you're the boss's daughter, just as he knows you and your friends are poking your noses into things you shouldn't be."

"That's your opinion, Jack. But I think something else is going on here. When you spoke to him last night, you didn't ask him about that twig-face. You didn't ask him because you didn't know about it. But I think Erik knows about it. I think he might be the one who put it in the orchard in the first place, trying to scare me off. Now why would that boy, whom I've never met, want to scare me?"

"Scare you? Whitney, now you're just sounding paranoid. He's a kid. Jeb was not only his employer but a mentor to him as well. All the kids here are a little on edge right now. Think about it. A man was murdered in the orchard last night, and they're here working today. I'm here to keep an eye on things. Imagine my surprise when I saw you and Tay racing through the crowd after Erik. I thought something was happening. Now I see it was just you meddling again. The boy ran. He doesn't want to talk to you. Do us both a favor and stay out of this. Okay?" Without awaiting my reply, Jack turned and stalked back to the tent.

I stayed there a moment longer, scanning the grounds. Where would Erik go? Would he hide in the woods, or make for the forbidden orchard? I turned in the other direction and stopped. The Cherry Orchard Inn's boathouse was a mere hundred yards away, sitting at the edge of the shore and extending into the bay. Pete Gunderson had said that Erik was there earlier, making out with his girlfriend. It was worth a look.

I walked down to the shore and entered the darkened building, thinking that I probably should have brought Tay with me. It was always cooler in the boathouse, and oddly peaceful due to the lulling sound of lapping water. Dad's hulking cabin cruiser was moored to the dock. High in the rafters, suspended on pulleys, was the family sailboat. The sails were stored in a locker on the other side of the building, along with two canoes and ten kayaks used by the inn's guests. Because the lighting was dim at best, I went to the nearest light switch and flipped it on.

A pale, aqua-blue glow filled the room, casting wavelike shadows along the walls and ceiling. I'd turned on the underwater lights. It wasn't my first choice, but it was enough, a calm, indirect brightness that gave the illusion that things were moving. I walked around, peered in Dad's boat, and called Erik's name. Then the muffled sound of running made me look up. A shadow shot across the wall, heading for the door. With my heart pounding in my chest, I grabbed a canoe paddle and followed. The door never opened. I spun around and saw something move in the bin that held the life jackets. Gripping the paddle tightly in one hand, I took hold of a life jacket in the other. Then I flung it aside. Two masked eyes peered up at me, and then jumped. I dropped the paddle with a high-pitched yelp as the creature scampered past me and climbed into the rafters. It was only a raccoon, but I was spooked. With my heart pounding uncomfortably in my chest, I ran out of the boathouse, confident that Erik Larson wasn't there.

Back under the relative safety of the tent, I heard my name. It was Hannah. She'd finally arrived for the wine and cheese tasting, looking happy and refreshed from her little nap on the floor of Tay's office.

"Whitney! Where've you been?" Her tone was admonishing, but her face exuded pure joy. Then she noticed my pallor, and quite possibly the sweat beading on my brow. "Good heavens! You look as if you've seen a ghost … which is ridiculous. It's broad daylight." She gave my cheeks a hard pinch, explaining that it was to bring the color back to my face. "There now. Much better. Okay, follow me. There's someone I want you to meet."

There was no great mystery who this person was, yet my heart sank nonetheless when I saw him—the suavely handsome Carleton Brisbane. He was standing beside Tay, chatting amicably, yet the moment he saw us approaching I realized it was not my pretty friend that he was staring at, but me. Tay cast me a cautioning look right before Hannah pushed me forward, declaring, "Carleton, this is Whitney Bloom, our best friend and the daughter of the couple who own this place." She then turned to me. "Carleton said you two met earlier but then you ran off after some busboy." Hannah wrapped her arm around Carleton's and gave a dramatic eye-roll. "Whitney's always running off like that. After graduation she ran off to Chicago, but now she's back. And we couldn't be happier! Have a glass of wine with us, Whit. Carleton was just telling us that he's a huge fan of *Bloom 'n' Cherries!* Were you aware of that?"

"No," I said, genuinely surprised.

Carleton gently removed Hannah's arm from his and said, "It's true. I have a thing for cherries. I blame it on my mother, God rest her soul. Every year she used to make me a cherry pie for my birthday. I hated cake, you see, partially because nothing I'd ever tasted compared with her cherry pie. It's been years since she passed, and every opportunity I get, I try to find a pie equal to hers. Hers was the best … until I tasted yours. Your grandma's isn't half bad either." He winked, obviously knowing that my pies and Grandma Jenn's were remarkably similar. "In fact," he continued, "that's part of the reason I'm here this weekend. I discovered the Cherry Orchard Inn last summer and found it utterly charming. A true cherry of a place," he decreed and gave a little laugh. It was a bad pun, and yet I found myself thoroughly delighted with him for uttering it. "And when I heard about the Cherry Blossom Festival, well, I just had to be part of that too. I must tell you how sorry I am about the unfortunate turn of events that's overshadowed the weekend. However, I consider the fact that you're here—the woman behind that remarkable website, *Bloom 'n' Cherries!*—to be the silver lining to the tragedy. And here I must add that you are far lovelier in person than that picture of you on your site. I know all about that because I'm one of your loyal customers."

"Wow," was all I could say, because the wheels of my mind were spinning. Could Carleton Brisbane be my mysterious online friend C-Bomb? Holy cobbler, he just might be! His initials were CB—possibly the reason he called himself C-Bomb. Also, there was an air of mystique about him. Even though he was older, it wasn't in a creepy way, and he was rich, dashing, and had a yacht. My hope meter soared.

Carleton, noting my delight, rewarded me with his most disarming grin. Hannah, staring at us with extreme displeasure, frowned.

"And do you know what else?" Carleton pressed on, leaning so close I could smell his fruity-wine breath. "I've been asked to be the judge of tomorrow's cherry pie bake-off. Imagine my surprise when Hannah asked me. Of course, I agreed. How could I not when I heard that you were entering one of your fabulous pies?"

It was unbelievable. Carleton Brisbane was most definitely flirting, and Hannah, standing possessively beside him, was furious with me. Her fair cheeks flushed bright as sautéed cherries. Her lips pursed to one side of her mouth, and her light blue eyes darkened in warning. Hannah was tall and flexible. It was a warning not to be ignored.

"I ... I am," I said, and gave a nervous laugh. "But there are a lot of great cherry pies in the competition. And you won't be the only judge. There's another man joining you who also considers himself to be quite an expert on cherries. I imagine the two of you will have the time of your lives tasting all the entries." That said, I made a point of glancing at my wrist. "Oh, would you look at the time! Carleton, Hannah, Tay, it's been a pleasure, but I really must go."

"Yes. Yes, you must," said Hannah, giving me the eye.

Remarkably, they all politely ignored the fact that I wasn't wearing a watch.

Twenty-Five

I had chased Erik Larson away, was scolded by Jack for doing it, and had possibly just flirted with my best friend's man. It was shaping up to be quite the day in Cherry Cove, I mused, feeling slightly guilty on all accounts. But I was not about to be deterred from my purpose. Although all the people who'd gathered under the tent for the wine and cheese tasting appeared to be enjoying themselves, the wait staff's demeanor told another story. All the young waitresses and busboys were working hard, but they appeared nearly robotic as they went about their duties. True, the recent murder had something to do with it, but I got the feeling there was a bit more going on. There was no youthful joy or pleasant camaraderie, only a palpable tension in the nervous faces and furtive looks that passed between them. Determined to get to the bottom of it, I decided to embrace my cover story for real. I grabbed an apron from the wait-station and tied it on. Of course, I had no intention of actually waiting tables. I just wanted to get close to the boys who were avoiding me, and there was no better way to do that than to join their ranks. Smiling, and with my best foot forward, I picked up a tray and made for Erik Larson's raven-haired friend.

He was across the room, clearing glasses and plates from a crowded table. I gave a quick look around to see where Jack was. Thankfully he was at the back of the tent, scanning the crowd while drinking water from a plastic cup. The moment I looked his way our eyes met. Jack, no doubt, was keeping an eye on me as well, and that eye could only be described as suspicious. I wasn't in a mood to be bullied in my own backyard. I cast him a sardonic grin and held up my tray. I don't know if he bought it, but I wasn't about to stick around and wait for him to come over and berate me. I needed to speak with the boy I assumed to be Cody Rivers.

"Cody, isn't it?" I said, sneaking up on the young man from behind.

At the sound of my voice, the kid froze. His bin of tableware, I could see, was half full. He picked it up and slowly turned around. "Yea," he said. Then the dark eyes lowered and he tried to slip around me.

I stepped in his path. "Wait. Listen. I don't know what you think I'm going to do here, but I'm definitely not going to hurt you. If anything, I'm here to help you, Cody. My name's Whitney, and I just want to ask you a few questions about last night."

There was fear and perhaps loathing as well in the young man's eyes as he looked at me. He then looked away, scanning the crowd as if searching for someone. "No," he finally answered in a harsh whisper. "You're working for him, aren't you?" By "him" I could tell he meant Jack. Why was he afraid of Jack? Then I remember Jack telling me that he'd caught this kid along with Erik last summer stealing bikes from tourists and then selling them on Craigslist. While this young heartbreaker was clearly no angel, I hardly believed he could be afraid of Jack. Still, the fear behind his eyes looked real. I needed to set his mind at ease, which I had a God-given knack for doing.

I gave a soft chuckle. "You think I work for him? Ha. Hardly." I rolled my eyes for dramatic effect. "Officer MacLaren is an old friend, but I definitely don't work for him. And I'm not a detective. I want to talk with you for my own reasons. Do you know who I am?"

"Yeah," he said, shifting nervously. "You're the daughter. You're the one who made *that ad*." The way he said it, the pointed look and oozing challenge, were no mistake. He meant to take a swing at the low hanging fruit of my previous career.

Truthfully, I was a little shocked he'd gone there, but he had. The gloves were off. Pushing my rising anger aside, I took a deep breath and calmly replied, "Yes. I made that ad. Interesting you remember it. You're hardly my target audience ... unless, of course, you have a disturbing interest in feminine hygiene products." I gave him the probing eye. He shrank a little, his black brows furrowing with open disgust. "Don't worry," I told him breezily. "I don't judge. In fact, I'm kind of flattered that you mentioned it. But enough about my ad. I'm here because you're a smart kid, Cody, and because Erik Larson is your friend. Did you work for Mr. Carlson as well?" He gave a quiet nod. "No one can work for a man like Jeb and not care for him even a little bit. Look. I don't know what's going on here, but clearly something's going on. I've never seen a group of young people acting so skittish. I'm even okay with the fact that you're not willing to tell me what it is just yet. But I am going to insist that you take a look at a picture and tell me if you recognize it. Okay?"

As I reached for my iPhone, I noticed his shifty black eyes scanning the tent area. A moment later they stopped, focusing on one of the waitresses, the pretty tawny-haired girl I recognized as Erik's girlfriend. I wanted to have a word with her next, but first, the picture. I opened my phone and went to retrieve the shot of the twig-face. "Here," I said, turning the screen to the young man, only to find he was no longer there. I swore inwardly. Not again! Like his friend, Cody had slipped away. Another moment of frantic searching and I found him halfway across the lawn, heading for the kitchen. I looked back at Kenna and realized that she was gone too. Tucking the tray under my arm, I resolved to follow Cody. I'd only taken two steps before I found myself surrounded by a thirsty group of patrons, every one of them telling me at once which wine they'd like to sample next. I had no choice but to attempt to take their orders.

Walking through a thirsty crowd with an empty drink tray was not exactly the best disguise for blending in. Everyone seemed to be hounding me now, and I had no choice but to head to the bar. I had over twenty drink orders, and I honestly couldn't remember what they were, but I had to attempt to look like I was working. Then I spied a familiar head bent over a case of wine and dropped my tray on the bar.

"Hey, Lucky Charms," I said, dropping a little playful banter as well. "How about grabbing me a bottle while you're at it."

Although I was tired, perplexed, and utterly confused by the drink orders, this time my elbow was firmly planted on the bar. The man behind it, however, wasn't the man I'd been expecting. Irish hottie was gone, and in his place stood the tall, lanky bartender I'd first seen in the kitchen.

"No problemo, babe," he said, displaying a crooked grin. "Here you go. Want some company drinking that?" He winked. I blinked and hastily shook my head.

"Oh, no. Sorry. I mean … I didn't mean 'no.' What I meant was, I was expecting someone else."

He twisted his lips in what I thought might be a sneer and said, "Don't you all. Unfortunately, Lucky the Charmer is on a break. I'm here now."

"Right," I said amicably, and then asked him to fill twenty glasses with whatever he felt like filling them with, because I honestly couldn't remember what was ordered.

I was about to attempt to lift the overburdened tray when Tate appeared beside me.

"Hey, lovely. Whoa. Tell me you're not going to try to carry that thing? In your condition, it's not going to end well."

I ignored the compliment in favor of the insult. "*Condition?*" I was about to ask him just what he meant by that when I noticed the man standing next to him.

"Easy, darling," Tate was quick to add, employing his dimples to their fullest effect. "I meant nothing by it, only that it's been a long time since you waited tables, and that tray is an accident waiting to happen. Besides, I came here to introduce you to Brock Sorensen. I don't believe you two have met. Brock is Baxter's new business manager, and I think you should listen to what he has to say."

"Yes," I said, pleased to finally be putting a face to the name, especially since his was a name that had made our suspect board, falling under the category of Person of Interest. Truthfully, I knew little about Sorensen other than the scant details Dad had told me. He was supposedly a top-notch accountant and a capable business manager. Bill Lundquist, the man he had replaced, had been a kindly family friend in his mid-seventies. Sorensen was younger by far, somewhere in his mid-thirties was my guess. He was a trim, lean, trendy, beta-male type with man-scaped facial hair and black-rimmed glasses. In advertising, his demographic would be comfortable in an urban setting, fond of craft-brewed beers and a prime target for a Whole Foods campaign. Brock's hair was a nondescript color, hovering between dark blond and light brown; it was hard to tell which in the shade of the tent. But his eyes were definitely green, a color set off to good effect by the slim-fitting electric green polo he was wearing, tucked firmly into his form-fitting black slacks. Sorensen smiled and thrust out his hand.

"It's a pleasure to finally meet you, Brock," I said, shaking hands. "Your name keeps popping up in conversation. I heard you were one of the unfortunate souls who went to the orchard last night with my dad."

Brock gave a grim nod. "Yes," he replied. "The single most disturbing night of my life. Poor old man."

"I can only imagine." I glanced at Tate. He had picked up two glasses of wine, one of which he handed to me. I took a small sip, thinking. There was really no nice way of asking tough questions, so I decided to be kind, but direct. "If you don't mind me asking, Brock, what were you doing last night before you learned of Jeb's murder?"

"Damn, Whit. You sound suspiciously like MacLaren." Tate, casually resting against the bar, cast me a pouty look. "Sorensen isn't a suspect."

"It's all right," Brock was quick to say. "I'm a stranger to Miss Bloom. It's perfectly natural that she has questions." He then picked up a glass from the bar as well, a crisp white, and took a meditative sip. "I stayed for dinner," he bluntly admitted. "In fact, I eat dinner at the inn any chance I get. It's one of the best perks of this job."

"I can only imagine. Not a bad perk for a single man."

"Oh, Sorensen's married," Tate put in, and gave the accountant a playful punch on the shoulder.

"I am," Brock admitted, rubbing his shoulder. "But my wife's a strict vegan and my kids have a lot of food allergies. As you can imagine, our diet at home is pretty restrictive. I applaud my wife's veganism. Sometimes I even enjoy it myself. Mostly, however, I find that I'm too tempted by all the delicious smells wafting into my office from the inn's acclaimed restaurant. They grill a mean New York strip, you know. I'm not strong enough to resist it." He flashed a mischievous grin. "After dinner last night I went back to the office at the inn to finish up some paper work. I don't know if you're aware of this, Miss Bloom, but when I took over after Bill Lundquist left, I found that the books were in bad shape. The poor old guy probably thought he was helping your folks, but in reality, what he was really doing was fudging the numbers, making it appear that the inn and orchard were turning a profit. Once I'd reconciled the books as best I could, I learned that this lovely enterprise is bleeding money twice as fast as it's being made, and thanks to a slew of pesky mishaps that have been occurring lately, things are getting worse."

My heart, so intimately linked to this extraordinary place, reacted to the news before I did and began pounding painfully in my chest. The cherry orchard and inn were in trouble? I'd never entertained that thought. "Pesky mishaps?" I croaked, feeling nearly as ill as I had when hearing the news about Jeb.

"Silly, annoying things, Miss Bloom—"

"Please, call me Whitney."

"Whitney," he said, and launched into a litany of things that had gone wrong since the first of the year, when he'd taken over. New reservation software had been installed in January. In March it had gotten hacked, resulting in lost reservations and compromised credit card numbers. The mishap had shaken the confidence of potential guests, and there were a handful of lawsuits pending. In April, when the health inspector came to inspect the restaurant kitchen, he opened the door to the walk-in pantry only to find a spontaneous infestation of rats. The rats got spooked and scurried into the kitchen proper. It took five hours to kill them all and another two weeks before the inspector would come back. The rats had obviously been planted there, but no one could figure out by whom or why.

Then there were smaller incidents. Cases of cherries had gone missing and small amounts of money had disappeared as well—fifty dollars here, a hundred there. Unique room accents and the odd antique had also been reported missing by the maid staff. Jack had been alerted to these minor incidents, and all the employees had been questioned, but no one was ever charged. Brock told us that Jack believed guests might be to blame for the missing decorations, which wasn't so unusual, but that he found the missing money and the cases of missing cherries more troubling. Those were still under investigation. But lately the incidents seemed to have stopped, Brock reported. Everything had appeared to be running smoothly again until last night, when Jeb Carlson was murdered.

Brock appeared clearly stumped by what he referred to as "this string of bad luck." Ironically, when I asked the question, he admitted that all the problems—with the exception of the flagrantly padded account books—began after he took over. He seemed acutely aware of this but not overly troubled. What was troubling, however, was the fact that my parents hadn't bothered to mention any of this to me.

Tate, with a grim set to his lips, leaned in. "Whit. I know you love this place. I also know that you'd do anything to help your parents. That's why I thought you should know what's really been going on here."

Although my head was spinning with this new information, I was moved by the fact that Tate had made the effort to introduce me to Brock Sorensen. "Thank you," I said, and squeezed his hand.

I won't lie. It felt good to touch him, and to lean on his familiar, quiet strength. But this was my problem, and I eventually had to let go. Tate was trying to win me back, and he had just taken the first adult step in doing so. I appreciated that. Regarding Brock Sorensen, however, there was something about the guy I didn't entirely trust.

"Thank you," I said again, as my mind chewed over this new, troubling information. "I appreciate you telling me this. However, as much as I'd love to stay and chat, I have a tray of wine to deliver."

With half the glasses removed, I lifted the tray and walked into the crowd, heading for the table of thirsty guests. I was nearly there when the young busboy Gunderson suddenly appeared before me, blocking my path.

An awkward grin lit his blunt, childlike features as he said, "He told me to give you this. He thinks you're hot." I was confused until the thick, dimpled hand shoved a crumpled note in the pocket of my apron. Before I could ask "who?", he was gone.

I set the entire tray of wine on the crowded table and walked out of the tent. There, in the privacy of the open lawn, I opened the note and read the hasty scrawl.

Tonight. Processing shed. 9 p.m.
Come alone.

I stared at the note, wondering who it was from. Pete Gunderson had said that the sender thought me hot, but staring at the cryptic lines, I doubted that was the case. I half hoped it was from the Irish bartender, but why a note? Clearly he was confident enough to ask me in person. No, I thought, high schoolers delivered such notes under such pretenses. This I knew because back in the day I'd written quite a few myself. I then thought of Cody Rivers and Erik Larson. It was likely that one of them had asked Pete Gunderson to deliver the note. Which one was ready to talk, I wondered, staring at the words a little longer.

Then, however, I was struck with the unsettling feeling of being watched. I looked up and across the empty lawn. One of the bushes in the thick screen of greenery near the woods rustled. It was either the wind or someone was definitely watching me. I placed the note back in my pocket and went to find Tay.

Twenty-Six

"You're not going alone."

It had been the argument of the past few hours, ever since I'd showed Tay the note. Tay had insisted we show it to Hannah as well, believing it would be akin to extending the proverbial olive branch, and she'd been correct. Hannah was still miffed at me for hitting on Briz, and upset at Briz for flirting with me. The poor thing was driving herself bonkers with jealousy over a man she wasn't even dating. Showing her the note, however, had snapped her out of it. Our old friend was back and ready for adventure. It was a slight relief … slight because the whole notion of meeting a stranger in an empty building on the whim of a note was unnerving. Who had written it? Why did they want to talk with me? What if it was a trap? These were all questions we had no answer for, but we weren't about to let that stop us.

The wine and cheese tasting event had come to a successful end, yet Erik Larson was still missing. Cody had reappeared but kept his distance. I didn't try to speak with him again, partly because the note might have been his, and partly because he was seriously busy. Erik's absence had continued throughout the Cherry Blossom Barbecue Dinner, held on the torch-lit patio. Many of the guests were still lingering there, stuffed with cherry-glazed baby back ribs, loaded baked potatoes, gilled corn on the cob, and the inn's signature Cherry Cove Salad (lettuce, pink lady apples, dried tart cherries, toasted pecans, and grated mozzarella cheese tossed with homemade poppy seed dressing) while contemplating large fresh-baked slices of Grandma Jenn's famous cherry pie. We had skipped the pie. It was 8:45, and I was in my room with the girls, changing into a pair of dark jeans and a black hoodie.

Picking up the conversation, I argued, "Whoever it is won't talk if you two show up with me. I mean, you can come with me, just not inside the processing shed. I don't want to scare the kid away."

"Okay. But I still think you should be packing heat in case it's not a kid." Tay, having gone home to change, reached into her handbag. "Here," she said, and pulled out a hefty pistol.

"Holy cobbler! I'm not taking a gun."

"Jeez, Whit, it's not real." She cast me an admonishing look. "It's an airsoft gun. Todd hides it in Char's naughty drawer."

"How on earth would you know that?" Hannah asked, her tone striking a note between mild disgust and delicious scandal.

"Because, obviously, I saw him put it in there. I thought he was playing in my mom's unmentionables and called him a perv. He pulled out the gun and shot me. It stings like a sonofafudge, but it's not lethal. See? It's got an orange tip. Not lethal."

"He shot you?" Hannah was aghast.

Tay shrugged.

I eyed the gun, took it, and said, "Yeah. Sure." I shoved it in the back of my waistband like a real detective. It felt pretty cool.

We were about ready to leave my room when Hannah piped up, "I still think we should tell Jack."

"Heck no!" Tay blurted, spinning to face her. "He's been bewitched by a slice of Jenn's pie. I saw him sitting at a table on the patio staring at it like he used to stare at that skanky reporter Greta Stone. Let him enjoy the moment. Besides, this is our lead to follow. Not Jack's."

Taking that as our cue, we left my room and headed for the processing shed.

A single light, yellow with age and choked with moths, illuminated the front entrance of the building. The sun had set before we left the inn, and now the entire blooming orchard and the processing sheds were cast in the last purple glimmer of twilight. Somehow, standing beneath the old porch light, it seemed darker. The utter quiet that permeated our senses reminded us that we were indeed alone. It was 8:59.

Hannah, seemingly fascinated with the knot of moths fluttering around the light, suddenly looked at me. "I don't have a good feeling about this."

Tay, monitoring the time on her phone, looked up as well. "Ditto. What if it's a trap?"

"Ladies. We've been over this. You'll be able to hear everything I do over the phone. Also," I said, giving my backside a pat, "I'm packing nonlethal heat. At the first sign of trouble I'll hightail it out this door. I promise. Until then, stay here and listen in." With my phone on mute, I clipped it onto a short lanyard and placed it around my neck with the microphone poking slightly above the neck of my hoodie.

"Nine o'clock," Tay whispered.

I gave the girls a nod, opened the front door of the shed, and slipped into the building.

It was black as night inside.

I stood a moment, waiting for my eyes to adjust. Once they did, I saw that the only source of light in the cavernous processing room was an exit sign above the doorway leading to the break room and

Jeb's old office. I didn't know who I was meeting, or where, but I figured, due to the utter silence, that they most likely weren't by the heavy machinery.

"Hey," I called out softly, walking through the dark room. "Anybody here?"

Nothing.

My progress wasn't swift. The deserted building was downright eerie, and the farther away from Tay and Hannah I traveled, the more the hairs on the back of my neck began to prickle. If someone was waiting for me here, they were being awfully quiet about it.

I thought of Jack then. Why hadn't we told him about the note? He was the law around here. He was the man investigating this case. And yet here I was, walking through a creepy building where a man had been murdered the night before, all because of my competitive nature and a stupid note. I stood under the exit sign and glanced into the back hallway.

Then I froze. It was a sound, soft and insubstantial as a baby's breath. Someone was in the building with me.

I drew the airsoft gun from my pants and held it before me. "Hello?" I uttered tentatively, peering into the darkness. I was just about to take a step into the hallway when sound erupted, violent and vicious as a dog attack. It came from the break room. "Somebody's in here," I cried to my phone, and ran for the break room door.

I thrust it open with my shoulder. The moment I did, the door on the far side of the room closed. But someone was still in the room, someone or something that was flopping against the hard tiles like a gaffed fish thrown onto the rocks to die. With heart pounding, I pressed a hand to the wall, searching for the light switch. I found it, flipped it on, and gasped in horror.

There on the floor, foaming at the mouth and seizing with a violence I'd never before seen, was Cody Rivers. The poor boy had been beaten to a pulp. Beside him, and somehow even more unsettling, was another creepy twig face.

I ran to him, took out my phone, and turned it off mute. "Hannah! Tay, are you there?"

"Whit, My God! What's happening?"

"It's Cody Rivers. I think he's been poisoned. Call an ambulance, and call Jack. I'm going to try to make him vomit. Then we need to get him out of here!"

"Copy that."

I left Cody for a moment to search the kitchen drawers for something I could use to trigger his gag reflex. He was convulsing too violently for me to use a finger. I grabbed a thick-handled wooden spoon, held him tightly against my chest, and pried his mouth open. Once the nasty business of purging was over, I left him on the floor while I went to find the wheelbarrow. Cody was a tall, well-muscled young man and there was no way I could carry him out of the building alone.

With Todd's gun in hand, I left the break room and headed for the processing room. The way this time was backlit by the lights I'd turned on, yet this caused the heavily equipped room to appear cavernous and dark. I'd barely stepped across the threshold when I heard footsteps. They were moving fast along the far wall, behind the extra storage bins and the forklift. There was still somebody in the building. Ten-to-one it was the murderer. Shaking, I aimed the gun at the sound. Then I saw it briefly, a hulking, shaggy shadow flitting across the wall toward the break room. I closed my eyes and pulled the trigger.

A flash like a bomb exploded in the darkness. The impact launched me off my feet, flinging me across the cement floor on my backside. "Holy cobbler!" I cried, momentarily blinded and stunned. I sat up, shook my head, and looked at the pistol gripped tightly in my hand. Nonlethal? Really? That's when I realized that fire was raging through entire front of the building. The thing belonging to the racing footsteps was nowhere to be found.

"Oh my God!" It was Hannah. She was screaming over the phone that was still dangling around my neck. "Whitney! Are you all right? There's fire!"

"Sort of," I cried, scrambling to my feet. I dropped the gun and ran for the wheelbarrow. "I guess that means you guys aren't coming in here to help me."

"We tried," Tay replied, sounding frantic. "The door was locked. What happened?"

I grabbed the wheelbarrow and was about to dash for the kitchen when I slowed down. "I'm not sure. Guys, this is important. Did you happen to see anyone leave the building?"

"No. I told you, the front doors are locked. We can't get in. We've been here the whole time, trying." Tay fell silent, then said, "Oh my God, Whitney! Is somebody in there with you?"

"Maybe," I said, and for the first time in my life, I understood what real fear felt like.

Smoke was filling the room, billowing on the ceiling while the fire spread like a voracious hunger. This was not the time to panic, I told myself. Killer or not, I needed to get Cody in the wheelbarrow and out the back exit.

Pushing the wheelbarrow toward the break room, two things crystalized in my mind. Someone had started the fire, and that same person had beaten and poisoned the boy, using, no doubt, the cyanide that had killed Jeb. What the hell was going on here? No wonder the kids were acting so strangely. They were afraid to talk. They were afraid to be seen with Jack or me. Now I understood why. Even though Cody had taken precautions by passing that note, someone had found out, and that someone had gone to extreme measures to silence him. Once back in the break room, the sight of the handsome kid alone on the floor, bloody and unconscious, made me sick with guilt. Thankfully there was no sign of the other.

"Hannah," I said, having muscled the boy into the wheelbarrow. "I'm bringing Cody out the back exit. Can you meet me there? Tay, stay and wait for Jack. Also, we're going to need the fire department."

"Got it."

I wheeled Cody out of the break room with caution. I then peeked into the hallway. Once I was certain no one was there, we ran for the back exit. I spun the wheelbarrow around, intending to pull it out of the building behind me, and depressed the door handle. However, when I threw my shoulder against the hard metal slab, it didn't budge. I did it again. I did the same thing two more times, all with the same result. The door wasn't locked, but it didn't budge. Something was blocking it.

"Hannah!" I cried. "Hannah, are you there?"

She screamed my name, alerting me that she was. "Oh my God! The door's blocked! One of the Gators has been backed into it and I can't find the key."

Then she echoed the words that were already ringing in my ears. "Whitney. My God! You're trapped in there!"

Now I knew what the killer had done. I was confident that whoever it was, they were no longer in the building with me. They were no longer here because it was a trap, and Cody, the poor boy, was the bait. The twig face glaring up from beside him had been my warning. I was trapped in a burning building with a dying young man. There was no way Hannah could pull a vehicle as heavy as a Gator away from the door by herself, and I doubted we had time to wait for help. I might survive it, but Cody would die for sure. There had to be another way.

Then I remembered the forklift.

It was risky, but it was our only chance. With a new plan running through my panic-stricken brain, and my friends crying at me over the phone, I wheeled Cody back to the kitchen. There I soaked all the towels I could find and threw them into the wheelbarrow with him. Once Cody was covered, I pushed him into the burning, smoke-filled room and made for the forklift.

With a burst of adrenaline strength, I hoisted him onto the narrow floor of the forklift, rearranged the wet towels, and climbed onto the seat. I then wrapped a towel around my own head as well. It had been a while since I'd last operated the forklift, but it all came flooding back. Driving a forklift isn't at all like driving a car. In fact, because of its compact weight distribution and the fact that it steers from the back wheels, it works almost the opposite. I remembered that much at least, and turned it on. I threw it into reverse and backed up into the room as far as I could while aligning myself with the burning front door. Then I stopped, put it in drive, and took a deep breath.

"Tay," I cried above the roaring fire into the phone. "Stand clear of the door. We're coming through!"

Twenty-Seven

Smoke filled the building, stinging my eyes and burning my lungs. I propped Cody up, making sure he was safely inside the forklift. Holding him firmly with one arm, I gripped the steering wheel with the other. There was only one chance to get this right. If I missed, or if the fire hadn't weakened the door enough, we'd crash and burn. It was a terrifying thought, but there was nothing else for it. I raised the fork to the level of a ramming rod and said a quick prayer. Then I stepped on the gas.

The forklift rocketed toward the blazing door. Anticipating the jarring impact, I stomped hard on the pedal and screamed.

We hit with a force like a compact car running headlong into a parked semi. A loud crash, a rush of swirling fire, a moment of weightlessness anchored by a white-knuckled grip, and more screaming. Then I felt the cool night air on my skin and opened my eyes.

I was still screaming. So were Tay and Hannah. Then I saw Jack standing beside them, and stopped. Relief swept through me at the sight of them all. My madcap plan had worked. Jack was beside the forklift the moment it came to a halt.

"Christ, Whit," he cried, his face red and contorted with anguish. "You should have told me about the note!" That was all he said on the matter because his entire focus then turned to the unconscious boy slumped at my feet.

"What the hell happened?" he demanded, lifting Cody down.

"Poisoned, I think. And beaten. He was convulsing and foaming at the mouth when I found him. I made him vomit, but he's in a bad way."

"I can see that. Christ, he's not breathing. I'm going to start CPR. Tay, help me. Hannah, get the hospital on the phone. Whitney, are you okay to run?" I nodded, feeling I could run for miles with all the adrenaline pumping through my blood. "Good," he said. "You're the fastest we have." He then tossed me his keys and sent me for his cruiser. The ambulance was coming all the way from Sturgeon Bay. Jack's plan was to meet it on the road. It was the best plan we had.

I took the keys and ran, bolting down the gravel road and plunging into darkness. It struck me then that Cody's attacker was still out here. Fear scoured my nerves once again, but I pushed it aside. There was no time to be afraid. A kid's life hung in the balance. With tears streaming down my cheeks, I made for the lights of the inn.

I was halfway down the road when I saw the shortcut. It was a lit pathway connecting the orchard to the parking lot. Without another thought I turned off the road in favor of the narrow, winding trail instead.

It might have been a mistake. The trail wound through a wooded stretch, and although it was lit, dimly, with decorative lampposts, the thick pines that lined the path appeared black and spooky. It made me run even faster. Only when the trees thinned and I caught sight of Jack's police-issue SUV in the parking lot did I breathe a sigh of relief. Unfortunately, that was when I caught a whiff of cigar smoke.

"What's the hurry, Ms. Bloom?" a languid, vaguely familiar voice said from the darkness. The voice startled me. And when I saw the shadow emerging from the pines, I grew scared. It was the shadow of a man, and it was blocking my path. I was running too fast to stop and was too afraid to try. I left it up to the spooky shadow to move, and it didn't. I ran full-tilt into the solid, cigar-smoking form of Brock Sorensen. The impact sent us both reeling to the ground.

"Oh, for Pete's sake!" I cried, scrambling to my feet. "What the devil are you thinking, jumping in front of me like that?"

"I ... crap!" he breathed, grabbing his cigar from the walkway. He gave it a little flick, then put it back in his mouth. "I thought you'd stop," he said, straightening. He took a puff and brushed the pine needles off his pants.

"Well ... I didn't. I couldn't! And I'm sorry, but I can't stand here and chit-chat. There's been an accident at the processing shed. I have to get Officer MacLaren's cruiser."

"Jack? Is he okay?"

"Jack's fine. It's a young man," I told him, and took off for the parking lot, aiming the key fob at the SUV as I ran. The doors unlocked. The lights came on. I jumped into the front seat, buckled up, and stuck the key into the ignition. I was just about to throw the car into reverse when Brock jumped into the passenger seat beside me.

Pulling the cigar from his mouth, he tossed it on the pavement and shut the door. "I'm coming with you."

My heart was still racing, and I didn't have time to argue. Every second I delayed was a second Cody couldn't afford. Sorensen was the business manager, after all. He'd probably hired the kid to begin with and had every right to tag along. So why was I so unsettled by his presence? Because moments ago a boy had been beaten and poisoned, and the processing shed set on fire, and this man had been standing off the pathway in the shadow of the pines smoking a cigar. He'd looked unfazed.

What did I know of Brock Sorensen? What did any of us know of him? He was new to Cherry Cove and therefore a mystery. What if he was the man behind everything? What if he was coming with me to finish off the poor boy, silencing him once and for all? Everything was a possibility, and yet everything seemed so absurd. Besides, I didn't have time to think on it further. Cody was dying. I threw the car into gear and stepped on the gas.

∞

The moment I pulled up to the burning processing shed, Jack gathered the young man into his arms and ran to meet us.

"Oh my God!" Sorensen cried. "It's Cody Rivers!" He jumped out of the cruiser and ran to assist Jack.

The fire truck was just arriving when we left. Hannah and Tay volunteered to stay behind and bring everyone at the inn up to speed on what had happened. With Jack and Brock in the back of the SUV again performing CPR on Cody, I turned on the sirens and raced toward Door County General. The moment I spotted the ambulance on the highway speeding toward us I flicked my high-beams and pulled over. They knew we were coming. I prayed they were prepared.

"I'll ride with the boy," Sorensen volunteered, climbing into the back of the ambulance with the EMT. The pallor of his skin was ashen, and he looked scared ... or perhaps, I mused darkly, it was guilt we were witnessing. I hated myself for doubting a man Dad had put his faith in, but I couldn't help it. Somebody had pummeled Cody's body and forced him to ingest poison. I had narrowly missed the killer. And then I found Sorensen lurking in the shadows off the pathway—almost as if he'd been waiting for me.

"We'll lead the way," Jack told the driver. "I'll call dispatch and have them contact the boy's parents."

Jack climbed into the SUV, made the call, and took the wheel. He pulled in front of the ambulance and turned on his emergency lights.

"Is … is that prudent, do you think?" I asked.

He looked at me as if I was from Mars. "We're going eighty and the speed-limit is fifty-five. Yes, the lights are prudent."

"No. I'm sorry. I mean, do you think it's prudent allowing Brock Sorensen to ride in the back of the ambulance?"

"Why would that be a problem?"

"Because somebody found out about that note."

"Yes. And unfortunately that somebody wasn't me."

"I'm sorry about that, Jack. It was wrong of me, but my point is that whoever knew Cody was going to talk to me went to extraordinary lengths to make sure he couldn't. They were still in the building when I found him. I saw the would-be killer's silhouette as he ran through the processing room just before it exploded in fire. He must have slipped out the back door, because when I tried to do the same it was blocked. Tay said one of the inn's Gators was parked against it, trapping both Cody and me inside. I was making such a racket up front with the fire that she never heard the Gator. Now, to my point. The killer couldn't have gone far on foot. Then, when I ran to get your cruiser, I stumbled upon Brock Sorensen lurking in the shadows by the tall pine trees—the ones flanking the parking lot. He was just standing there, smoking a cigar."

"The man likes his cigars," Jack said. Then, thinking, he added, "Wait. You think Sorensen was the person in the processing shed with you?" His ruddy brows furrowed at the thought.

"I don't know. It was too dark to tell who was there. But what if he was? What if he was the one who beat and poisoned Cody? Wouldn't he want to make certain the boy never talked again? Don't you think it's convenient that he offered to ride in the back of the ambulance with him?"

"Not if you consider that he's also the business manager of both the inn and the orchard. He has a vested interested in this place and the staff."

"But why was he in the orchard—that late at night?"

Jack thought a moment. "I don't know." His eyes shot sideways at me while he drove. "Do you think Sorensen poisoned and bludgeoned Jeb as well?"

"I have no proof, only suspicion. But think about it? He was at the inn last night. He has access to Dad's office and the processing sheds. He could have put the poison in Jeb's rum, knowing he'd drink it. Then he could have taken Dad's croquet mallet and followed Jeb back to the processing shed. After Jeb drank the poison he could have clubbed him in the head and dragged him into the orchard. He'd have the strength to do it."

"He would," Jack agreed. "He could have done all those things, but what's his motive?"

"That I don't know, but he did tell me all about what's been happening at the inn. He told me about the new software getting hacked, the rats in the kitchen, and the string of petty thefts. All of it seems to have started since he took over. Don't you find that a little suspicious?"

Jack cast another quick glance my way, then fell silent. The knuckles of his hands were white as they gripped the wheel.

"Jack? Jack, are you okay?"

"No," he replied very softly. "No, Whitney, I'm not."

Twenty-Eight

*J*ack was distraught. This was his case, the biggest he'd ever had since becoming the Cherry Cove police officer, and he was feeling overwhelmed. I didn't blame him. The death of Jeb Carlson had been bad enough. Although he knew that the killer was still on the loose, he'd never expected one of the young employees to be the next target. But we both knew why. All the fear, all the caution the young employees displayed suddenly made sense. They knew who the killer was, and the killer had been watching them. Had the killer been watching Jeb Carlson too?

"Cody's a good kid," Jack added, staring at the dark road ahead. "He took quite a risk sending you that note. Dear God, Whitney, I hope you're wrong about Sorensen."

"I hope so too," I said. "But if he is the murderer, I doubt he'd do anything stupid around the EMTs. Right?"

Jack gave a solemn nod. "If the boy survives, I'm posting a guard outside his door."

Once at the hospital, Cody was rushed to the ICU and treated for cyanide poisoning. He also had a concussion from the beating he'd received and multiple cuts and bruises. Jack, Brock, and I were relieved to learn he was breathing on his own again. However, he was in a coma. The ER doctor on duty was hopeful that Cody would have a full recovery, stating that my quick actions purging the boy of the poison had tipped the odds in his favor. Had I waited a moment longer, Cody Rivers, like Jeb Carlson before him, would be dead—another victim to lay at the feet of the Cherry Orchard Inn. I was relieved to learn that he would live, but the thought of how close to death he'd come shook me to the core. Another thought haunting my every waking moment was that this soulless killer was still out there, lurking in the shadows of the orchard and inn—or perhaps even worse, hiding in plain sight.

While Jack talked with Cody's parents, I decided to turn my attention to the puzzling Brock Sorensen. "I'll get some coffee and sandwiches," I told Jack. "Brock's coming with me." This was news to Sorensen, but he got the hint and gave a nod. I looked back at Jack. "You take your coffee black, don't you?"

"I do," he replied, flashing a look of caution. "Although a double shot of Mr. Daniels just now wouldn't go amiss."

"I know what you mean. I'll see what I can do."

"Do you need a ride back to Cherry Cove?" Sorensen had been talking on the phone as we walked to the hospital cafeteria. His conversation had just ended. "It's been a terrible night," he remarked. I had to admit, the guy looked haggard. "Don't know how long MacLaren'll be with Cody's parents. Don't envy him either. My wife's coming to get me. Just wanted to know if you'd like a ride back with us."

For curiosity's sake, it was tempting. However, Hannah had texted that she was coming to pick me up. "Thanks for the offer, but I already have a ride. I'd like to meet your wife, though."

Sorensen missed a step before casting me an emotionally charged look woven with overtones of amusement. "Curious, are you? I already told you that my wife's a vegan. What I failed to mention was that she's also a germaphobe and a bit OCD with a vacuum. We have the cleanest floors in the Cove."

And her husband poisons harmless old men and boys, I thought to myself. Outwardly, however, I smiled. "You paint such a charming picture of your wife. Can you blame me if I'm curious? So, Brock, how do you take your coffee?"

"Decaffeinated, with soy milk and three packs of Stevia."

I stared at him a heartbeat too long, realized he wasn't joking, and turned to the woman behind the counter as Brock strolled toward the cashier. "Two black coffees, another with cream and three packs of sugar, and three of your freshest sandwiches."

A minute later, as the cashier rang us up, I handed Brock the cup of creamy white coffee. "As I've been so pointedly reminded today, life is short. Live a little."

He stared into the cup and frowned. "This looks caffeinated and fatty."

"Exactly. That's why it's so delicious. Are you sensitive to caffeine or lactose intolerant?"

"Not particularly, but Gwyneth is."

"But not you? And yet you suffer. That's a heck of a cross to bear, Brock. Well, tonight your secret's safe with me. Don't stare at it. It's not like it's poison or anything. It's coffee."

This last statement was enough to pull his pensive gaze from his cup while eliciting a grimace. I could tell that he didn't appreciate the way I was staring at him either.

"No, it's not poison, Whitney. Forgive me if I seem a little tired of the word." He took his coffee and walked over to a table. I followed him.

"Damn. I can almost understand why there's a Starbucks on every corner. I feel like a kid who's finally found where his mom's been hiding the real cookies, and not the tasteless, gluten-free, sugar-free ones in the cookie jar, if you know what I mean." Apparently enjoying the taste of real coffee for the first time, Brock dropped his gaze back to the creamy liquid.

"Glad you like it. I'm a bit of a coffee evangelist. I drink far too much of the stuff and consider myself an expert. In my opinion, there are only four ways to serve coffee: black; with cream; with sugar; or with both—unless you want to add a shot of alcohol or liqueur. That's different. Nothing, however, is more wholesome than good old fashion cane sugar. And soy? That's a bean, not a mammal. We have no business milking it. Same with the almond. It's a nut, and yet we milk that too. O the hubris of man!" I mocked, staring levelly into Sorensen's green eyes. "I have no idea how one goes about milking such a thing, but it can't be humane—although all my vegan friends will argue that one till the cows come home." I winked, then tossed in a disarming grin.

Brock was smiling too. He was truly enjoying his sugar-laden, fatty, caffeinated beverage. His endorphins were fizzing over; his defenses were down. It was time to attack. "So," I began, "I have to ask you a question. What were you doing on that path tonight?"

Behind the black-rimmed glasses, his eyes grew wide. "Why? You don't think I had something to do with Cody?" When I didn't answer, he added, "Whitney, I know we've only just met, but I'm a little offended."

"I'm sorry, but you have to admit that the timing was suspicious."

"Not to me. I had no idea anything was amiss at the processing sheds. It's dark out. The orchard was deemed off limits to guests and no one was supposed to be in there. By the way, what were you doing at the sheds?"

"That Pete Gunderson kid passed me a note. I was to meet someone in the processing shed at nine p.m."

"Who?" he asked. "Cody? Did Cody write that note?"

"Well, at the time I didn't know. It didn't say. But the point—"

Brock leaned in, cutting me off with a cry of "What? You were passed a note to meet an unnamed person in the same place Jeb was poisoned last night and you went—without telling MacLaren? That, Whitney, is the height of recklessness." His look was so admonishing that I blushed. "You're lucky you weren't killed as well," he added.

Oh, but I almost was, I thought bleakly, casting him a hard look. My curiosity had nearly been fatal. Was he playing me? Or was he genuinely concerned? I took a long sip of coffee and replied, "I'm well aware of the foolishness of my actions, and I regret not handling the situation better. But I need to ask you again. What were you doing hiding in those pine trees near the parking lot?"

An ironic smile crossed his lips. "I was trying to smoke a cigar— a Cuban—until I saw you running down the pathway. I had no idea what you were doing out there or what you were running from. I didn't mean to startle you, Whitney." He drained the last of his coffee, set the empty Styrofoam cup on the table, and continued. "You admitted a moment ago to having a passion for coffee. Well, cigars are my guilty pleasure, only I have to sneak them. Imagine what the wife would say if she caught me with one of those between my whitened teeth?"

I had to admit, given what he'd said about his wife, it did make sense. I gave a nod. "But why there?"

"At the end of my workday I like a little peace and quiet before I go home to crazy town. Don't get me wrong. I love my family, but I have a two-year-old and a four-year-old at home and a lovely yet utterly neurotic wife. Those pines have become a bit of a sanctuary for me—off the beaten path yet close enough to the parking lot. Smoke too close to my car and Gwyneth would undoubtedly smell it. Lord knows I don't need another lecture."

"It must be hard to have to live like that. I don't understand it, but then again, I'm far from being married. Let me ask you this instead. While you were lurking in the pine trees with your Cuban did you happen to see anyone coming down the pathway other than me?"

"None running as fast as you, but there were people—diners, guests, employees—all heading for their cars. However, if the killer was in the processing shed when you arrived, why would he make for the parking lot when there are so many other places to go? Think about it, Whitney. Heading for the parking lot from that direction would look highly suspicious."

"Heading there alone, maybe. But not if he slipped in with a group of diners or guests." I thought for a moment. "Brock, did Cody have any enemies? Has there been anyone at the orchard or inn acting a little strange lately?"

"That I wouldn't know," he replied, and began messaging his forehead. "In my opinion, everyone's been acting a little strange lately." He smiled wanly. "You might want to talk with Bob Bonaire, though. Poor overworked Boner. If you want to know anything about the younger employees, talk to Boner."

Jack looked haggard when I met up with him in the ER lobby. He took one look at the sandwich and coffee in my hands and sighed happily. "You're an angel," he said, taking his food. "So, did you learn anything from Sorensen?"

I shook my head. "The man confuses me. I can't read him. There's a sneaky, shifty quality to him that appears to be the result of his overbearing wife. He told me he was out by those pine trees smoking a cigar, because he has a thing for cigars and doesn't want his wife to know about it. He could be telling the truth, or it could be a convenient cover."

"If it's any help, I've met his wife. She's a beauty. That's the attraction. But if I were in the man's shoes I'd have strangled the witch by now. I've never met a more controlling, passive-aggressive soul in my life. I think Sorensen's hanging on to an unhappy marriage. If Gwyneth turned up dead, it'd be a no-brainer. But murdering an old man and attempting to murder a boy ... what's his motive? Sure, he has access to all the offices and grounds, but Sorensen's job is to make sure the inn and orchard make a profit. Very few people I know seek to destroy the hand that feeds them."

"Generally, that's true," I agreed. "Unless the person is insane."

Jack grinned at my cynicism and took a sip of coffee. "Damn. I really thought there'd be some whisky in here."

"They're a little short on whiskey down in the cafeteria, but I did have my eye on some heavy sedatives in the pharmacy. Then I remembered you were driving."

"Good call," he said. "First, however, I'm meeting with Sergeant Stamper and Officer Jensen from the Sturgeon Bay department. They're helping with the investigation." He sat down in a nearby chair to eat his sandwich.

"Cody knew something," Jack continued, turning to me. "I saw it in his eyes last night after I was called to the scene. I didn't think much of it then, but I had the feeling that he knew something about the murderer but was too afraid to share it. Also, he never told his parents about Jeb Carlson. Imagine your boss turning up dead in the very orchard he managed? I don't know about you, but when I was Cody's age I would have taken the news straight to my parents, hoping they'd help me make some sense of it all. Cody, however, never mentioned a word of it. His folks learned of Jeb's death this morning on the news. And now, after our little chat, they know Jeb Carlson's death was due to poison and not a mallet to the head as the news is still reporting. That little tidbit didn't sit too well with them under the circumstances. Those poor people are fit to be tied, and I can't say that I blame them. Had they known Jeb was murdered, and that his murderer was still on the loose, they would never have let Cody come to work today. God, Whitney, what have I done?"

"You can't possibly blame yourself for this, Jack." I looked at him, at his strong profile, and felt a surge of pity. "You're trying to find the murderer and therefore everyone who was at the inn last night must stay until they've been cleared. Right? Besides, the Cherry Blossom Festival is in full swing. Holy cobbler!" I breathed, thinking of something I hadn't told him. "There was another twig-face. It was in the processing shed, right beside Cody. I nearly forgot about it until now."

"What? Are you sure? Because if so, it means that either Cody's been making them, or our killer has. And right now, my bet is on the killer." Jack looked intently at me. "Whitney, why would the killer be targeting you with these faces? It makes no sense. You don't even live here any longer."

"You think I'm the target?" The thought was highly unsettling. "I don't think so," I was quick to assure him. "Isn't it more likely that the

Twenty-Nine

*D*id ... did he make it?" Hannah was gripping the steering wheel so tightly I thought it might pop off in her hands. I realized then how terrible it must have been, waiting back at the inn, guessing and second-guessing the fate of Cody Rivers.

I placed my hand over one of hers. "He did, and he's going to be fine. He's in a coma right now but the doctors assured us he's going to make a full recovery. He'll be plenty sore for a while, though."

"My God, Whit!" she exclaimed, taking her eyes off the road to look at me. Tears stained her cheeks. "And you? How are you? I was so scared when you were trapped in that burning building. I thought I'd never see you alive again."

"Me too." It was a sobering thought, and it was the first time I'd had the chance to think about it. I didn't want to think about it.

"I'm so sorry," Hannah sobbed.

"The road. Keep your eyes on the road," I encouraged her, gently redirecting her head with two fingers.

"Yeah. Right. But I was so mad at you before, and for what?" Her red-rimmed blue eyes darted to mine and back. "Over some ... some stupid super-hot rich guy? You almost died, Whitney! You. Almost. Died," she reiterated dramatically. "And all I could think about was what a shallow, petty, terrible friend I'd been. I mean, he's just a stupid guy, right? And like, you're my best friend. I swear it, I'm not going to let some arrogant, stuck-up yacht-man get between us again. Do you forgive me for acting like that?"

How could I not? Hannah, for all her yoga and centered living, still gave voice to her every thought and emotion. She was honest and faithful, and those were the two best qualities in a friend. "Of course," I told her. "And I'm sorry too, Hannah. I didn't mean to flirt with him. I wasn't trying, honestly, but I was kind of flattered by the attention. I mean, you have to admit, Carleton Brisbane is like a perfect ten. But he's just a guy. They're virtually all the same. It won't happen again."

And with that it was settled. We were besties again.

It was eleven thirty when Hannah dropped me off at Grandma Jenn's to prep the elements for my deconstructed pie. Competition at the bake-off was fierce, and, after all I'd been through since arriving that morning, I was of a mind to win the darn thing.

My car was still in the driveway from my earlier visit, parked next to hers. I couldn't believe that my first suspect had been my kind-hearted, free-spirited gran. Seeing my car there reminded me of what a long day it had been. The cafeteria coffee had helped but my energy was fading fast.

The moment the door opened, a gentle calm settled over me. My gran was there, framed in the light of her doorway with a welcoming smile on her face. It was a look of unconditional adoration, and I felt like a child again, happy and carefree as she beckoned me to her kitchen.

Everything I needed had already been arranged on her spotless granite countertops. It was as if she'd read my mind, but she hadn't. Gran was the master baker. Everything I knew about baking and cherries, I had learned in her kitchen. As I baked the layers of flaky, sugar-dusted crust and mixed the brandy-infused cherry filling, we chatted and drank more coffee. I told her about the note, Cody, and the fire. I told her about the unsettling pagan twig-face that seemed to be taunting me as I hunted for Jeb Carlson's killer. I even drew it for her in a shallow pan of flour. The image didn't frighten her as much as the fact that Tay and I were the only two who'd seen it. I also told her of the skulking shadow I'd shot at in the processing shed and my suspicion of Brock Sorensen. We talked of the odd behavior of the young people working at the inn.

After this, Gran deftly guided the conversation, prompting me to talk about the three men that occupied my thoughts more than they should have: Jack, Tate, and Carleton Brisbane. I even told her about Hannah and the flare of jealousy that had consumed her when Carleton began flirting with me. Grandma Jenn listened as I talked away, adding her thoughts, concerns, and some suspicions of her own. By the time I'd prepared and stored all the elements of my pie for tomorrow's assembly, my heart felt lighter, my mind relieved of its weighty burden. There was no better medicine than cooking with Grandma Jenn. I was ready to drive back to the inn and fall into bed.

There is no rest for the wicked, and even less for those who pursue them, I mused a bit sarcastically the moment I walked through the doorway of the family quarters. Giff was there, his face glowing with elation, his form-fitting V-neck and jeans streaked with soot. He was beside Tay, the two talking animatedly with my parents.

The moment I entered, Mom, stifling a yawn, turned. "Whitney!" she exclaimed, happy to see me. "Gifford's here, thank heavens. And what a night it's been! How are you holding up, dear? How's Cody?"

I brought them up to speed on what was happening, after which Tay said, "Giff got here just as you all left for the hospital. Came right to the processing shed, rolled up his sleeves, and pitched in, selflessly helping the volunteer firemen put out the fire." Her dark eyes oozed adoration as she looked at him.

I took one look at my former assistant and rolled mine. Selfless? There was nothing selfless about it. Giff knew Tate was head of the volunteer fire department. He would go to any lengths to meet Tate in person, and from the wide grin on his face, I knew he had. Great. There'd be no living with him now that he'd met Tate.

"And look what he found," Tay continued, holding up what was left of the airsoft gun I'd used to shoot the suspected killer. The entire thing had melted in the fire, and the barrel now had a nasty right hook to it. "Todd's not gonna be happy with this."

"I'll buy him a new one," Dad offered flatly, turning his all-knowing eyes on me. "Tay told us what happened in the processing shed. For cripes sake, Whitney! What were you thinking going in there alone?"

"I was thinking," I said, casting an apologetic look at my parents, "that I could get some information on the killer, and I nearly did. We believe Cody knows who's responsible, but, as I told you, he's in a coma. You can imagine how eager Jack is to talk with him, but he's just going to have to wait. Jack's also keenly aware that the boy's life is still in danger. Cody's parents are at the hospital, but Jack's taking no more chances. He's placing a guard outside his room."

I could see that Mom was horrified. Dad appeared overburdened with sadness. "There you have it," I told them. "Two more tragedies at the orchard. Mom, Dad, why didn't you tell me what's been going on here?"

Mom looked surprised by this. Dad looked pensive. "What do you mean?" he asked, his silver-blue eyes shooting to mine in guarded question.

I had been up a long time. I was dead tired and over-caffeinated. It was not the best combination for level thinking or polite conversation. It was unfortunate that Tay and Giff were there as well, but I couldn't help that. I felt myself snap. "What do I mean?" I cried. "How about the inn's software getting hacked, or the rats in the kitchen, or all the petty thefts, not to mention Jeb's murder. Dad! Mom!" I held them both in an accusatory stare. "Bad things are happening here and you never bothered to call me and tell me. Why didn't you tell me?"

Mom, standing beside Giff, gave a little gasp and grabbed his arm for support. Dad just looked at me and shook his head in the way people do when they have nothing good to say. "Don't take this the wrong way, my dear, but you've had enough problems of your own in Chicago. We didn't want to burden you with our petty little problems here. This place is our responsibility," he said, gesturing to Mom. "We've always managed the orchard and inn before, and we'll continue to do so. We've just run into a string of bad luck of late, that's all."

"Dad, this is more than bad luck. And what do you mean by 'I have enough of my own problems in Chicago'? I can handle my problems in Chicago just fine. But this place is my home. I grew up here. For heaven's sake, I'm your daughter! I think I have the right to know what's been going on."

"It looks like you already do, dear," Mom offered softly. "Who told you? Was it Grandma Jenn?"

"Brock Sorensen, if you must know. By the way, don't you find it a little odd that all this started when you hired him? What do you know of the guy, Dad?"

Dad's silvery head tilted as he looked at me. "You think Brock has something to do with this? Whitney, he's a good man. I know he is. This string of bad luck might have started around the time he took over, but believe me, without Brock and his diligent work we'd be

Thirty

'll tell you about Brock Sorensen," Tay said. She and Giff were in my room, the three of us sitting on my bed, ensconced in a floral wreath of sheer bed hangings. It was midnight. We each had a glass of tart, fresh-pressed cherry juice. Grandma Jenn swore by it. She always drank a glass before bedtime. Tart juice aside, it might have had the feeling of a slumber party if we'd been hitting each other with pillows instead of discussing a suspected murderer.

Tay looked pointedly at Giff. "Get this. That lean strip of jerky who calls himself your business manager is wonky as a stiffy in church—a thing that should never occur, but Lord knows that it does. Point in fact, the one I saw belonged to the man himself."

Giff was easily enchanted by scandal. I, however, found Tay's remark disturbing. "Wha … wha … what?" I chirped.

"It's true," Tay said. She proceeded to tell us a sordid tale that had taken place a few weeks before Sorensen was hired at the inn. Apparently he hadn't been wearing his wedding band when he first arrived in Cherry Cove, showing up in December at Shenanigans, the local pub. There he hit on Tay, and she, being between boyfriends at the time, took pity on the "uptight, nerdy newcomer." She took him home, some awkward snogging commenced, and just when things began to get hot and heavy, the man burst out in tears.

"I didn't know why," she said. "He wouldn't say. Instead he asked if I would make him some bacon." Tay grinned. "I thought it was code for some kinky nerd thing, but no. He really wanted bacon."

Giff, amused, asked, "And did you make him some, angel?"

"Yep. A whole pound, in fact."

After that, Brock had left, promising Tay he'd call, but *surprise, surprise,* he never did. A month later Tay spotted him in church with his skinny, lank-haired wife and two waif-thin kids.

"He kinda freaked when he saw me," she admitted with a look that made us all smile. "I mean, what had he been expecting? It's a small town. He was bound to run into me sooner or later, although I got the feeling he thought he'd be safe in the pews of St. Paul's Lutheran. He wasn't. I could tell he was kinda turned on when he first spied me, but then he got really nervous. He did his best to avoid me, so I waited until he went to the little boys' room and cornered him in there. I was pissed. I mean, look at this hair!" she demanded, pointing to her chic, bright red do. "I don't judge, but the dude was married—with kids! What a dirtbag!"

"Totally," Giff halfheartedly agreed, running a hand through his thick black curls. "I take it you're not a fan of the new manager?"

Tay gave a noncommittal shrug. I couldn't say I blamed her. I had mixed emotions about Sorensen myself. Although he didn't come off as a creep, and he'd been very forthcoming about the disturbing incidents at the inn, his sudden appearance by the pine trees still spooked me. The timing was just poor, and I really couldn't help but be suspicious of him. However, it was all circumstantial. I had nothing solid on him, and being a cheating pig doesn't make a man a killer. But I would keep my eye on Brock Sorensen.

"I mean, he's supposedly a great accountant," Tay continued. "I don't run into him often, but when I do he's cordial enough. But any dude who takes off his wedding band to flirt with chicks is despicable. He was here in Cherry Cove interviewing for a job and thought he'd sow some wild oats while he was at it. The fact that he couldn't seal the deal's not my problem. He's still a dirtbag in my book."

I nodded, then asked, "What's his relationship with Cody Rivers?"

"I don't know that they have one," Tay replied. "The kid works here. They're on friendly terms, I suppose."

"Unless he's the killer and found out that Cody was going to talk to Whitney," Giff offered. He set his empty juice glass on the bedside table and continued. "Think about it. Baggsie mentioned that the man would be foolish to jeopardize his career here by instigating a string of damaging events. But what if that was his intent in the first place? What if he was purposely trying to ruin this place, forcing it into bankruptcy so that he could snap it up for a bargain price? A major software hack, a sudden infestation of rats before a health inspection, a murder—these are all hits against the Cherry Orchard Inn brand—damaging hits. Whit knows a little something about damaging a brand. Isn't that right, princess? She's living proof that the results can be catastrophic."

"Gee, thanks."

"No problem, angel. But say Sorensen purposely damages the image of the Cherry Orchard Inn. Maybe the kids knew about it, and even applauded it in their stick-it-to-the man youthful way. But then he takes it one step further—"

"—and kills Jeb Carlson," I finished, picking up on the thread of his idea just like in our advertising days. "He kills Jeb because Jeb was onto him too. Jeb had begun to figure out what was going on and tries to tell Dad, but Dad's too upset about the stolen wine to listen. Sorensen could easily be behind that too. Maybe that was intended to be just another hit on the image of the inn. But it's too close to home. Jeb knows about Sorensen, and therefore Sorensen has to murder him. To cover his tracks, he frames Dad. It would be easy for him to do and it serves his purpose. Framing the owner of the inn is a catastrophic hit to the brand as well. It's all over the news and people are talking. But the murder of Jeb Carlson is too much for the kids. Murder is real. They can't talk to Jack because they've been warned against it. So they get nervous. Their lives are threatened. Then Cody's conscience kicks in. He sees me snooping around and dares to take the risk because I'm not the police. He arranges a private meeting. Sorensen somehow finds out about it and tries to stop the kid before he can tell me what he knows. He then tries to kill me too, because I'm getting close to the truth."

"Oh my God!" Tay exclaimed, fear rippling across her pretty face and blossoming in her night-dark eyes. "Oh my God! I ... I might have nearly boinked a psychopathic murderer!"

"A married, cheating, closet-cigar-smoking psychopathic murderer with a penchant for bacon, darling," Giff corrected her. "But that's the least of our worries. If our suspicions are correct, Sorensen's now onto our Whitney as well, and we can't let that happen."

"Oh! Oh, show Giff that creepy twig-face we found," Tay urged.

I pulled out my phone, found the picture, and handed it to Giff. He studied it for a moment, then sat back.

"You recognize it, don't you?" This I didn't find nearly as surprising as Tay did. Giff was a savant at recognizing logos, icons, taglines, and jingles.

"Nothing that primitive, but yes, I have. That, my darlings, is either a fair self-portrait of a Sasquatch or a poor rendition of Green Man, a leafy icon of obscure Celtic origin thought to represent rebirth and leafy fertility, as in the cycles of the seasons. Very common throughout Europe. It wouldn't be so unusual springing up in an orchard here, I shouldn't think. Was Jeb superstitious?"

I thought a moment, then remembered something Doc Fisker had started telling us. He'd been speaking of Jeb, and mentioned something about how in the spring he'd seen Jeb, Mom, Grandma Jenn, and Tay holding hands and dancing around the budding trees. He'd called it 'suspiciously pagan.' I said as much to Tay, and she nodded.

"Yeah. I forgot about that until you mentioned it, but it's kind of become our spring tradition. Three years ago, Jenn thought it would be fun to have our own May Day celebration. She and Jeb kinda had a thing for Scandinavian folklore and talked your mother and some of us younger ladies into getting up at the crack of dawn on the first of May. We come to the orchard, throw on a white robe, put a wreath of wild flowers in our hair, and dance around the budding trees while holding hands. It's a gas. I had no idea you didn't know about it."

"No. I didn't," I told them, feeling a little low that no one had bothered to tell me about May Day. "Do you remember if Jeb ever made a Green Man face on the ground?"

"No," Tay said. "That I would have remembered."

Tay left shortly thereafter. Giff went to my brother's room, where he was staying, but came back a few minutes later wearing only pajama bottoms and with a toothbrush hanging out of his mouth. He was in the middle of a thought. The only thought I had was to get into bed.

"Sorensen," he said, and pulled the toothbrush from his mouth. "He has no motive that we know of to destroy the inn, right? But he came here from somewhere. Everyone's got secrets, Whit. Tomorrow, before the pie judging, I'll do a little snooping around on the internet and see if I can find one."

"Thanks," I said, just as there was a knock on my door. Without thinking, Giff crossed the room and opened it. The toothbrush dropped from his mouth. Only one man in Cherry Cove could have that effect on a city boy like Gifford.

"Hello, Tate," I said, getting off my bed.

Tate looked good, standing at the threshold while holding a small bouquet of wildflowers and a bottle of wine. His eyes, however, were glued to Giff, and not in a good way. It was then that I realized Tate's face was as red as a glass of cherry wine.

"I … I didn't know you had company," he stammered. "I was at the processing shed putting out the fire. I … I met your friend there. Heard what happened. I just … I just, dammit, Whit, I just wanted to make sure you were okay."

Giff, the little sadist, stood blocking the doorway, enjoying himself. "Oh, she is, my friend. Had a little scare, but she's fine now. You know our Whitney, she takes a licking and keeps on ticking." Giff loved quoting ads. "Where are my manners? You brought us wine. Would you like to come in? We were just going to bed, but you can join us if you'd like."

"No. No. I've got to get going. It's been a long day. I didn't know he was … I mean … I don't know what I mean. I'm going to go."

"Now that was a shame," Giff stated, leaning against the door and turning to me with a wide grin. "You haven't dated a man in over eighteen months and here struts in Adonis himself, groveling at your bedroom door with flowers and wine. Some people have all the luck, but I see the problem. Were he my problem, I'd likely forgive him anything. But clearly he still has feelings for you. My advice? Don't cave just yet, angel. You need to make that man walk through fire if he's to have another chance at you." Giff handed me the flowers.

"I think he already has," I said.

"Well, yes, literally. But I'm speaking metaphorically. Don't tell him just yet that we're only friends."

And with that, Giff placed a brotherly kiss on my forehead, said good night, and walked out the door, taking the bottle of wine with him.

It was a habit, but as soon as Giff left I crawled into bed and opened my laptop. It had been a traumatic day, and exchanging a few lines with the enigmatic C-Bomb always helped me get to sleep. He could be anyone, anyone who loved cherries, and he might even be here at the inn. I conjured up an image of Carleton Brisbane, then pushed it from my thoughts. Dear heavens, that would spell trouble, especially if I wanted to remain friends with Hannah. But what was I thinking? Carleton was hardly a man who'd hide behind a name like C-Bomb, no matter how badly my pesky hormones wanted him to be. I pushed all thoughts aside and typed, *Hi. You there?*

No answer. Of course not. It was nearly one in the morning, far too late for C-Bomb. I sat a few minutes longer, staring at the blank computer screen. I was just about to close my laptop when he answered.

Good evening, Ms. Bloom. You left our little chat rather abruptly last night. I was worried. That's not like you. Are things all right?

Not really, I typed. *In fact, they're pretty terrible. I'm in Cherry Cove at the inn. I had to drive here early this morning because last night, while I was typing with you, I learned that one of our employees was murdered in the orchard. He was the manager of it, in fact. A dear old gentleman named Jeb Carlson. And just a few hours ago another employee was nearly murdered as well.*

Dear God! I'm aghast. Your parents must be devastated. Are you there offering moral support?

That and I'm determined to find the murderer.

He was stunned by this, clearly stunned, but also intrigued. *Dear God!* he typed. *Isn't that what the police are for? Do they have police in Cherry Cove?*

They do. Only one, and he's a friend of mine. That's part of the problem. I then told him a little bit about the situation as things stood.

Well, I do love a good mystery. Tell me all about it. Draw me a timeline, describe the suspects, and I'll see if something doesn't jump out to me that you might have missed.

I told him everything I could remember, including a little personal history about both Jack and Tate, which he annoyingly focused on.

Tell me about Officer MacLaren, C-Bomb asked. *What's he like? What are his methods? Is he capable of finding a murderer?*

Jack's an old friend. I grew up with him. He can be a real pain sometimes, but he's also incredibly smart. He's doing the best he can on this case.

And is he, Ms. Bloom, good-looking?

What kind of question is that? I typed.

An important one. You're easily distracted. If you want to find the murderer you can't be distracted.

I frowned at the screen, thinking he was teasing me. *Yeah, he's absolutely flipping adorable! But don't be jealous. Officer MacLaren is also oblivious. He called me Whit-less today, his high school nickname for me.*

He's got a sense of humor. And what about Tate?

I've told you about Tate before, remember? He's the reason I stay clear of Cherry Cove. In my absence, however, he's been hanging out at the inn a lot, helping wherever needed. Truthfully, I'm a little envious. My parents adore him, as does everyone in Cherry Cove. But don't worry. I'm not distracted by him any longer. This was somewhat of a lie, but I was holding to it. *And what about you?* I typed. *Perhaps if you told me who you are, I could call you instead of typing to you over a computer? Oh! (says she, answering her own stupid question), I can't call you because your wife will get suspicious.*

There was a long pause, and then, *No wife, just a dog.*

It was my turn to stop typing. After all this time, the man was finally revealing something personal. He had a dog. I could really love a man with a dog. It was an opening. I pressed him a little more. *So, you're not married, but you do have a dog? What kind?*

A faithful one. Ms. Bloom, it's getting late, so listen up. There are two things that stand out in my mind about this murder. While there are many persons of interest, I'm a little puzzled about Tate. He's your ex-boyfriend. He lives in Cherry Cove. He's gotten particularly close with your parents. He was a basketball coach at the high school and has a relationship with Cody Rivers, who was nearly murdered, and Erik Larson, the kid who disappeared when you tried to question him. What I find most interesting, however, is that terrible things are happening and yet this man seems oblivious to everything but seducing you.

I looked at the screen to see if I was reading it right. Yep. I was. Incredible. *You don't seriously think Tate has something to do with these murders, do you?*

I'm not saying that. All I'm saying is that I think you should keep your eyes open to the possibility.

Noted, I typed with a frown. *And the second thing?*

The missing wine. How does wine just disappear from a lighthouse without a trace? If I were you, I'd get up at the crack of dawn and pay a visit to the old lighthouse. You might find a clue others have missed. Find the wine, Ms. Bloom, and you just might find the murderer.

Thirty-One

 awoke to my phone chirping away. It was my wake-up alarm. Why had I set it? It was still dark outside. My head was foggy with disjointed dreams. Dear God, it was early.

I had to bake pies! I sat up abruptly at the thought, then saw my Victorian love-nest surroundings. It was all coming back to me. I was in Cherry Cove, in my old bedroom. This was the day of the cherry pie bake-off. I had only two pies to bake today, and I had done most of the work already. That was a relief. But why the alarm? Snatches and pieces of memory were pushing through my sleep-muddled head, but they didn't make much sense. Something about Tate looking magnificent, standing in my bedroom doorway with flowers and a bottle of wine. Did I drink the wine? Did I invite him in? Did we ... ? I quickly looked at the mound of rumpled bedding beside me and made sure it was only pillows. It was, thank goodness. No sign of Tate anywhere. It had only been a dream.

I forced my mind to back up. I was missing something. Try it again. A comfy bed void of Tatum Vander Licious. Giff, shirtless, opening the door. Giff giving Tate the wrong impression, bless him. My laptop on the bedside table. My laptop. I'd been talking with C-Bomb. We were talking about the murderer. He mentioned wine. The missing wine! Now I remembered. I was on a mission to find the missing wine.

I eased out of bed, got dressed, and slipped downstairs to brew a pot of coffee. I might have been on a mission, but I wasn't a sadist. I waited until there was just enough to fill a travel mug; then, with a key and a flashlight, I quietly slipped out the back door.

It was not only dark but foggy as well. I thought about leaving a note for Mom and Dad, then thought better of it. Why advertise my whereabouts? Besides, I'd likely be back before anyone was out of bed. If not, there was no harm in letting them think I was still in my room, fast asleep.

I hiked across the dark lawn, now striated with patches of fog, heading toward the long, meandering stretch of Lighthouse Road. I'd been wanting to investigate the lighthouse for a while now but it was C-Bomb who had reminded me of it. He'd also suggested I get there early, before anyone was awake at the inn. This was because Jack had taped off the lighthouse as part of the crime scene, and snooping around a crime scene, as he'd been so quick to remind me, was against the law. Jack couldn't know I was at the lighthouse. No one should know, for that matter, except the mysterious C-Bomb. And I believed he was right. Find the missing wine and I'd find the killer.

That was all well and good, but what I hadn't expected was the eerie feeling that hounded me as I traveled down the rutted gravel road in the pre-dawn darkness. I'd walked this way hundreds of times before and never experienced such a feeling. It was all in my head, I told myself, trying hard not to think about the fact that there was a murderer on the loose. I then chided myself for not taking Giff with me. I should have wakened him, I mused, until I recalled that the whole idea of mornings, in general, sickened him. Waking Giff before dawn would be akin to poking a sleeping bear; a thing only fools attempted. Besides, he was judging the cherry pie bake-off. I wanted to stay on his good side. I wanted that darn Gilded Cherry taking up precious shelf-space in my kitchen.

However hard I tried, thoughts of the prestigious Gilded Cherry trophy soon crumbled under the more pressing, unsettling sounds that floated through the foggy darkness. I consoled myself with the thought that dawn wasn't far off, but that did little to stop my overactive imagination from turning every creak of a branch, every soft moan of the wind, every rustling of leaves into something sinister. It was also, admittedly, the wrong time to recall the old Indian curse and the legend that these woods were haunted. Everyone assumed that a human being was responsible for the death of Jeb Carlson … but what about that invisible, chilling presence Tay and I had felt in the cherry orchard?

The rational part of me knew I was being ridiculous. But the other part of me—the open-minded, easily impressionable reality TV junky—was more than willing to entertain the possibility of a ghost or woodland monster. And why not? The world was full of unexplained phenomenon. Then again, there usually was a logical explanation for even the most baffling cases.

I continued making my way toward the old lighthouse, gripping my steel flashlight with one hand and sipping coffee with the other. My flashlight wasn't turned on. It was a bright one, and my eyes had already adjusted to the darkness. Besides, the light might draw attention. I was walking quickly; the screech of an owl induced me to run, and I didn't stop until the lighthouse loomed before me.

I'd like to say that the sight of the old brick tower, attached to the lightkeeper's house of the same design, was reassuring, but it wasn't. The lighthouse had been abandoned for over ninety years, and I'd always found it a little creepy. My brother, Bret, swore that it was haunted—swore that he'd seen the light on one night, and on another occasion witnessed the ghost of an old sailor pacing down by the rocky shore. I didn't really need to think about that … but I was. The sight of the yellow crime scene tape across the front door of the keeper's house was also unsettling, yet it was nothing compared to the fact that when I went to put the key into the lock, the heavy old door creaked back on its hinges. Jack would have locked it after he came here yesterday, wouldn't he? Maybe he hadn't, I told myself, because there was nothing left to steal. The door was already open, so I gave it a little push, turned on my flashlight, and walked inside.

"Hello," I called out, not really expecting to be answered. I swung the powerful beam in an arc, illuminating the dilapidated parlor of the old keeper's quarters: a small room of crumbling plaster walls, boarded-up windows, and neglected hardwood floors. As children we used to think it fun to play in the lighthouse, but now I couldn't imagine why. "Any one in here?" Apparently not. It had the feeling of a long-abandoned dwelling, complete with stale air and centuries of dust motes.

Where had Dad stored the wine, I wondered, illuminating the untouched plaster where pictures had once hung, along with strips of musty old lace frayed by broken glass. When my light hit the floor, the answer became apparent. Footprints, a whole slew of them, overlaid by the tires of a handcart, disturbed the layers of dust. They all seemed to flow in a general direction. I set my now-empty travel mug on the floor and followed them.

As the footprints moved through the old keeper's house, I made note of the different sole patterns and sizes. Dad had moved through here, and so had Jeb. Dad was partial to boat shoes, and his were easy to spot. There was also a larger pair, a men's twelve or thirteen from the look of it. Those most likely belonged to Jack. So what about the other sets? One of them, obviously, had belonged to Jeb, but which one? I studied the shoeprints all the way to a painted metal door. It was the door to the light tower. Dad had said that he wanted the wine to be unique—made in a lighthouse. Since the old lighthouse shed lay in ruins, this obviously meant that the wine had been aged on the cold cement floor of the light tower.

I opened the door and saw that I'd been correct. It wasn't a spacious room, but I could tell by the marks on the floor that this is where the barrels had been, tightly packed on either side of the circular, ascending staircase.

I walked farther into the light tower, studying the jumble of footprints in the dust, and then suddenly froze. No, I thought. It can't be. Not here! On the floor, partially hidden by the rise of the first step, was a twig-face—the same menacing twig-face that had been hounding me. Frightened, and with every nerve in my body aching with terror, I backed out of the light tower and ran for the door. He's been here, my head screamed. The murderer has been here! And somehow he knew that I would be too.

I came bursting out of the keeper's house and paused outside the door, bending over to catch my breath. That was when I noticed something I hadn't before. In the fresh, fog-dampened dirt there was another set of footprints. I recognized the pattern of the sole as one of the patterns I'd seen in the lighthouse. The tread was similar to what one might find on a good pair of hiking boots. My best guess put the size at around a men's ten. What made this set stand out from the others, however, was not only that it looked fresh, but after leaving the lighthouse, the boot prints turned and headed straight for the woods.

The words *find the missing wine, find the killer* sprang to mind. Darn right, I thought as anger consumed my better judgement. I was laying odds that hiking-boot guy was the killer, and there was no way I was going to let him terrorize the inn or me any longer. Although the sky overhead was brightening with the first fingers of dawn, it was still foggy. I kept my flashlight glued to the footprints and followed them into the woods.

Granted, it had been quite a while, but I'd hiked these woods all my life and my recollection was that they were dense, interwoven every now and then with narrow deer trails. Therefore I was surprised when I followed the boot prints down an embankment and came upon a well-worn path. The moment my foot hit the exposed dirt, I felt that odd, skin-prickling sensation that suggested I wasn't alone. I brushed it off as paranoia and followed the tracks. I had only gone a short distance when a twig snapped not far behind me, confirming my deepest fears. I turned, knowing even before I did that I wouldn't see a thing. And I didn't. I was met with the same tangle of colorless, fog-shrouded branches and leaves. The sun was getting higher. The fog should be burning off shortly. I'd be fine.

I took a deep breath and continued.

The rustling of a bush—as if someone or something had walked past it—made me stop dead in my tracks. Maybe I should climb back up the embankment to the lighthouse? I hadn't found a trace of the wine yet, and wasn't likely to find it down here. I could always come back later. Yeah. Good idea. I'd come back later. I was about to turn and head straight for the embankment when I made the mistake of looking down.

"Holy cobbler!" I whispered, staring at a pair of tire tracks. I was standing between them, and they looked suspiciously like the tracks of a Gator to me. But that couldn't be right? I looked at them again, and my heart started beating a little wildly. I would have laid odds it was one of the orchard's Gators, but what on earth was it doing down here? It came to me then: wine. This was how the barrels of wine had been taken from the lighthouse—on this private path hacked through the dense woodland near the rocky shore. And whoever took the wine had access to the Gators. Brock Sorensen had access to them, that's who. Then, however, another face popped to mind, one I desperately wished hadn't. Tate. Tate had access to whatever he wanted. C-Bomb had mentioned him—had pointed out his odd behavior. Everyone at the inn was focused on the murderer, but Tate was focused on me. Dear God, I thought. Please don't let it be Tate! I probably should have turned around then, but I couldn't. Violent curiosity propelled me forward.

The fog was still thick as pea soup. It was hard to tell where exactly I was, or how far I'd followed the tracks, when the sound of another twig snapping hit my ears. In the still air, it had the same effect as a gun firing. My head flew up like a startled deer as the hair on my neck prickled. I turned in the direction of the sound. I was met by the same milky-white nothingness. But the sound was definitely getting closer. I picked up the pace, heading away from whatever it was that was following me.

And something, or someone, was most definitely following me.

Knowing that I was heading away from the inn and civilization wasn't a comforting thought either. However, the fog was beginning to thin a bit. Oh, who was I kidding? That changed nothing! With the snap of that first twig the forest had turned menacing.

My heart was racing.

I should bail. I should just head for the bluff and bail!

The trouble was, I was still a bit disoriented. I knew that if I ever wanted to see my mom and dad again I should probably abandon the path I was heading down, take a sharp left, and work my way back to the lighthouse. But would I make it that far? Maybe not.

I spied the shadow of a large, prickly yew and decided to take cover there, just until the menacing presence passed. I was about to dart for it but made the mistake of looking down … again. Like a wolf's eyes pulled to the full moon, my eyes were drawn to it—the shiny white porcelain of a diner plate and the deep red of cherries. Unbelievably, it was a slice of cherry pie.

"Oh, for the love of Pete!" I exclaimed, dropping to my knees to inspect the pie. I had the feeling that someone was just yanking my chain now, and it pissed me off. I grabbed the plate, inspecting the pie. From the dull, crumbly crust and the electric red of the cherries, I knew it was store-bought. That figured. The psychopathic killer who was plaguing me couldn't even do me the curtesy of baking a pie. And to add insult to injury, those most definitely weren't Bloom Orchard cherries!

Fuming at the absurd pastry in my hands, I now made the mistake of looking up. Just visible through the blanket of fog was a shadow— a shaggy, utterly horrific man-size shadow. It had no face, no definition, and it made no sound, yet I most definitely knew what it was.

The shadow took a step closer.

The piece of store-bought pie slipped off the plate and fell to the ground.

And then I screamed.

Thirty-Two

*C*orrection. I tried to scream, but all that came out was a terror-constricted squawk. I was too paralyzed with fear to even move a muscle. Great. All I could do was stare at the shadowy face, thinking how I was about to become the first-ever victim of abduction by Sasquatch in Wisconsin. Then again, maybe I wasn't. After all, every year a staggering amount of missing person cases went unsolved. It wasn't a pleasant thought.

Encouraged by my paralytic fear, the Squatch took a step toward me and raised a shaggy arm. It was holding a rock. Dear God, it was going to knock me over the head! But before the fur-fringed arm could descend, the creature froze, drawn to a spot in the fog just behind me.

I heard it too. Something was moving through the forest with lightning speed. It was nearly upon us when it let out a frightful bark. A dog! Somewhere in the back of my mind I recalled hearing that Sasquatches didn't like dogs. I'd thought this a suspicious fact at the time, since I'd heard it on one of those reality TV shows about Bigfoot. Apparently it was true, though, because this Bigfoot turned and disappeared into the fog.

I faced the oncoming dog and ducked as it leapt. It cleared my head and raced after the shaggy, two-legged creature. It was a hunting dog, a long-eared spaniel from the little I saw of it. The dog kept barking as it traveled farther away in pursuit of the creature. And then it grew quiet. I cowered on the ground beside the dirty slice of pie, fearful that something might have happen to the dog—that timely, brave dog.

A moment later my fears were allayed when the dog appeared beside me. I was still shaking as I stared into the soulful brown eyes of a large black-and-white Springer Spaniel. "Swingin' dingles," I breathed, "wherever did you come from?"

The dog, encouraged by my voice, attacked my face with gooey kisses, its little stub tail wiggling happily. Its enthusiasm was a balm to my nerves. Unable to resist, I threw my arms around it and buried my face in its silky fur. I'd been so scared.

"Who are you?" I asked, releasing him. "Who do you belong to?"

Of course, the dog didn't answer. Instead it followed its nose to the slice of cherry pie and gobbled it down before I could stop it. A terrible thought occurred to me then. The pie had been placed between the tire tracks by the murderer. What if it had been poisoned? Oh God, I didn't need this too! I quickly grabbed hold of the dog's collar. Should I make it throw up? How would I make it throw up? I didn't know, but I assumed making a dog vomit was probably like making a human vomit. I grabbed hold of the spaniel's neck and attempted to pry open its jaws. The dog stubbornly resisted and clamped them shut, squirming away from my probing fingers like a trapped piglet.

"I'm sorry!" I cried, "but it's for your own good!"

"What's for my own good?"

The voice startled me. I looked at the dog, confused. Did it talk? I had nearly been abducted by a Sasquatch, so why did that surprise me?

"Jesus, Whitney!"

I looked at the dog again. It knew my name? But its lips weren't moving. Then, "What the hell are you doing to my dog?" I spun around and saw the form of Jack MacLaren emerging from the fog, dressed in jeans and a sweatshirt. In all my life, I'd never been so happy to see him. I could feel myself blush, then, not only from embarrassment but from the fact that I found him incredibly handsome.

"This … is your dog?" I asked, attempting to look unfazed at the sight of him. I released the spaniel and watched as it ran straight to Jack, its stubby tail wagging double time. "What … what are you doing here?"

Jack, after showering affection on his dog, straightened. "I could ask you the same question, but I think I already know." He held up my abandoned coffee tumbler. "You were snooping around in the lighthouse, weren't you? I went there myself to have a look around this morning and found the door already open. Then I found your mug on the floor. I went back into the light tower and saw that twig-face, Whit. The same as the ones you told me about. You're right, it's super creepy. The moment I saw it, alarm bells when off and I called your mom directly. She confirmed that you weren't in bed. Then I saw your footprints by the lighthouse heading into the woods, and that other set of prints. MacDuff and I decided to follow. He tracks much faster than I do."

"Thank God," I said. "Your dog saved me. I was seconds away from being abducted by a Sasquatch."

Jack's head tilted as he stared at me. "Whitney, seriously, this is no time for joking around."

"I'm not joking, Jack! I decided to check out the lighthouse this morning to see if I could find any clue pointing to the whereabouts of the missing wine. The door was already open when I got there. I thought you'd left it open, but realized when I saw that twig-face that you probably hadn't. The killer was in there, Jack. Not with me, but I think he knew I would be snooping around in there. Then I saw the footprints leading into the woods and decided enough was enough."

Jack's face was anything but teasing. "You should have called me. Jesus, Whit," he breathed, looking truly upset. "Whoever is making those creepy twig-faces is trying to frighten you. Don't you get that? Why would you follow his footprints into the woods?"

"I told you, I want to find the killer."

"Great. And let's say that you found him. What were you going to do then?"

I hadn't really thought that far ahead, but I didn't want him to know it. Instead I held up my flashlight and gave the air a good whack.

Jack crossed his arms and shook his head.

"Okay, I didn't find him. What I found, however, was a Sasquatch." Even to my own ears it sounded a little crazy, but I was beyond trying to sugarcoat the truth. "It had been following me. I could hear something, only I could never see it until it stood in my path. See this plate? There was a slice of cherry pie on it. Someone had placed it in the middle of those tire tracks." I pointed. "Yep, those are tire tracks— from a Gator, I believe. I was following the tire tracks until I came to the pie. I was so stunned by it that I bent down to take a closer look. When I looked up again, the Squatch was standing right there, about ten feet away. I recognized it because I've seen it before, last night in the processing shed. It was only a shadow, but I saw it right before the fire broke out—a big, shaggy, butt-ugly creature on two legs. Only I didn't know then what it was."

"Why didn't you tell me about that?"

I raised a brow. "Well, because it sounds crazy, and also, I forgot about it. Last night was very traumatic." It was then that I looked at the dog sitting at Jack's feet. "Jack, your dog ate the pie. I thought it might be poisoned and was trying to make him throw it back up when you found me."

"That's what you were doing?" Jack smiled for the first time. "Risky if you value your fingers, but thanks. However, I think the MacDuffster will be just fine, won't ya, boy. Because that piece of pie in the middle of the woods is the killer's way of toying with you. He's mocking you, Whitney—using cherry pits for cyanide, using cherries as the eyes in the twig-face, and now pie. Why? I don't know, but I doubt he thought you'd actually eat it. There's no use wasting poison on something the target is not going to eat, so I don't think it was poisoned. But we'll keep an eye on Duffy all the same. I didn't notice the tire tracks before," he said, and walked over to them to take a closer look. "Damn," he uttered, running his fingers over the tracks printed in the soft dirt and leaf mold.

"And right there, that's where the Sasquatch was."

Jack's eyes narrowed in disbelief.

"You know, Bigfoot? Yeti? Don't look at me like that. I'm just telling you what I saw."

"And you think it was following you?"

"I know it was following me," I told him, recalling the unsettling feeling I'd had.

"And you got a good look at this thing?"

"Not a good look, but enough to know what I saw."

"How tall was it?" Jack probed.

"I don't know? Taller than me but shorter than you, I suppose."

A troubled look crossed his face. "Whit, even if I believed in Bigfoot, we can both agree that they don't wear hiking boots, right?"

"What are you saying?"

"I'm saying that whatever it was you saw standing here, it was wearing hiking boots, and it was a heck of a lot closer to you than ten feet. Christ, Whit, it was standing right here." Jack pointed to the boot prints in the dirt between the tire tracks, uncomfortably close to the abandoned diner plate. Somehow, I'd missed them. But he was right. They were the same prints I'd seen in the lighthouse—the ones heading into the woods—and they'd gotten too close for comfort. The thought made me nauseous.

Jack reached into his pocket and pulled out his keys. "I'm parked at the lighthouse. The red hard-top Jeep. It's the only vehicle there. I want you to go back to the lighthouse and get into my Jeep. Lock the doors and wait for me there. There's a bag of Danish on the front seat. Help yourself. I was going to stop by the inn after Duffy and I were done here, but ... Look, Whit, if I'm not back in half an hour call the station in Sturgeon Bay. Okay?"

"What? You're going to track down ... this Bigfoot alone?" Although it was clearly wearing boots I was nonetheless having a hard time reconciling what I had seen. "Not a chance, Jack. You need backup. I'm coming with you."

"Whitney. Jesus! This guy's dangerous."

"He is," I agreed, reminded of the truth of this statement by the little shiver that ran up my spine. "But you're not in uniform. Do you even have your gun?"

"Always," he replied, and patted a mysterious bulge on the side of his sweatshirt.

"Wow. Okay." Why did I find that a total turn-on? What the heck was wrong with me? I didn't know but fought hard to regain my train of thought. "Here's the thing, Jack. I don't want to hike back up to the lighthouse. I'd rather take my chances with you, MacDuff, and your gun." He was about to argue. I held up my hand. "Don't bother. You know how stubborn I can be, just as you know there's nothing you could say that would make me change my mind. These are Gator tracks. They shouldn't be here, and you and I both know what we're going to find at the end of them."

"I have a hunch," he acknowledged. "And the man you saw, Whitney—if he is our killer, he's not going to want us getting too close to the truth. That changes things."

"I'm still not convinced that what I saw even was a man."

Jack, exasperated, closed his eyes as he shook his head.

"Look, I understand your concern," I told him. "But I think we'll be okay." Without awaiting his reply, I turned and started walking along the tire tracks into the fog, my new buddy MacDuff bounding beside me.

"You think? YOU THINK?" he cried. "I prefer to be sure," he added, and ran to join us.

Thirty-Three

Although I really should have been thinking about the killer as we followed the tire tracks through the woods, all I could really think about was Jack and the fact that he had a dog. I found it relevant insofar as it seemed a pretty important clue in another little mystery I was working on, namely the identity of C-Bomb. After all, it had been just last night that C-Bomb revealed he had a dog. He'd also been the one to suggest I search the old lighthouse at dawn. Was it mere coincidence that Jack and his dog had showed up as well? I already knew Jack liked cherries. He might like me as well, possibly even more than I realized. How did I feel about that? Truthfully, I didn't hate it. In fact, if anything I was intrigued by the prospect. My old buddy Jack MacLaren, I mused, staring at his lean, muscular back. He had a nice back. My eyes scanned a bit lower. Very nice, I thought, and dared to entertain the thought that Jack was my secret admirer C-Bomb.

"You never told me you had a dog," I said to his swiftly moving backside.

"You never asked," he replied without breaking stride. He was like a hunter, treading silently, his senses on high alert, all the while keeping one eye on the ground and the other on MacDuff in the vanguard, sniffing and just visible through the fog. "You might also be surprised to know that I have two kids."

I stopped walking. What? Two kids? Holy cobbler! I didn't think he was married. Matter of fact, I was pretty certain that he wasn't. Jack MacLaren, you dog.

"Whit," he said, pausing to look at me, "don't worry. I'm not talking about little humans. I'm talking about little goats—little stub-horned hellions. I don't love 'em. I don't even want 'em, but I kind of inherited them. They live at my station." He grinned and continued walking. "The tourists get a kick out of 'em. I keep them on the roof during the day, mostly to keep them out of MacDuff's and my hair. They eat everything—grass, dog food, paper. Mostly paper."

"Oh yes," I said, utterly charmed by the notion of Jack keeping goats. "I saw them yesterday on the grass roof. They're really noisy."

"They are. They don't bleat like normal goats. They yell, hence the reason they're on the roof. Better than guard dogs, present spaniel excluded."

"Your dog is my hero."

"Because he saved you from a booted Yeti?" Jack turned just long enough to flash an ironic grin. He didn't believe I'd seen a Sasquatch, and the presence of boot prints on the ground was pretty damning evidence. Still, I knew what I'd seen, and in both encounters it hadn't appeared entirely human. To be fair, it probably didn't resemble a true Sasquatch either. And if I was being totally honest with myself, I should be more than a little disturbed that my mind had made the leap so willingly. I needed to think more like a real detective and not a sleep-deprived, over-caffeinated baker with an addiction to weird reality TV. Yet I had to wonder. If it wasn't a Sasquatch or a man, what the devil had I seen? That was the question that troubled me most, the question that made my heart thump as I stared at the man-sized boot prints.

I was so busy staring at the ground and the tire tracks that I didn't notice that Jack had stopped walking.

I ran into his unmoving back. *"What?"* I hiss-whispered.

"MacDuff," he answered softly, still facing forward. "He's heading for the shore."

I looked in the direction of Cherry Cove Bay. "Well, that makes no sense. The Gator obviously continues this way."

"But your booted Yeti went that way."

That was when MacDuff started barking. The moment he did, an outboard motor fired up, the sound penetrating the fog like a jack-hammer. Jack drew his gun and bolted into the fog. I ran after him.

The chase ended at the water's edge. I found Jack standing on the smooth, damp rocks peering at something beyond the wall of gray mist. A gust of wind fell from the bluffs behind us and rippled the water, parting a cottony swath of fog. And then I too caught sight of the sleek spaniel head forty yards out, sticking just above the water. MacDuff had given chase and was still paddling like a champ into the fog. The boat was far out of view, but the motor could still be heard.

"Damn it," Jack breathed, and then he turned to me. "I think I just saw what you saw—just a brief glimpse—far out in the fog, in the boat—but … damn, it did look kind of Squatchy. Duffy! Here boy!" His attention grabbed, MacDuff circled around and began paddling back to shore. "I apologize," Jack said. "I can see where you might have been confused. But, Whit, that thing is no Squatch."

"How can you tell?"

"Seriously?" He cast me a grown-up echo of his best condescending high school look. "It's driving a fishing boat. A fishing boat! Why would Bigfoot need a fishing boat when he's got two giant hands"—

Jack thrust up his hands to illustrate— "and the animal cunning to catch fish? Besides, I doubt he's got a fishing license, or passed his boater safety course. I could be wrong, but I doubt it." A smile was attempting to break through but he fought it.

"Jack," I began, totally playing along, "don't you watch those Bigfoot documentaries on cable? Bigfoot's your classic kleptomaniac. He doesn't hunt or fish. Whatever he needs he steals, like that boat."

"Exactly," Jack said, and the smile broke through at last. "I told you I caught a glimpse of your Squatch—not a good one, but I did see the boat. It's one of Tate's, the kind he rents out to vacationing fishermen. Let's hope your old boyfriend can help us sort this one out." Jack pulled out his cell phone, scrolled through his call list, and pressed a number. He looked at me. "He *is* your old boyfriend, right? Or are you two ...?"

"Old. Definitely old," I was quick to assure him. "All that's in the past."

Keeping his ear to the phone, Jack gave a meditative nod, not even flinching when MacDuff bounded beside us and shook the water from his fur.

"Hey, this is Jack," he said into the phone. "You missing a boat? You don't know if you're missing a boat? It would be one of the little fishing boats you rent. I think I just saw one speeding into the fog. You didn't rent any out this morning? Can you go check and see if one's missing? I'll hold." Jack looked at me and rolled his eyes. Then they narrowed. "What? Why can't you jump down to the docks and check? Where are you? Where am I? I'm standing at the water's edge, right below the bluffs half a mile down from Cherry Cove Lighthouse. I'm virtually across the bay from you. I believe one of your fishing boats was beached here early this morning, and I just caught a glimpse of it speeding away. I don't know where it was headed. It's foggy. But I can tell where it wasn't headed. Back to the marina. This is very important, Tate. I need to know who's in that boat."

Jack then paused a moment, looking confused. "You're not at the marina? Where the hell are you?" As he listened, his eyes shot to me with a dark look. He covered the phone with his hand and whispered, "Apparently after I called your mom, she called Tate. He's poking around the woods looking for you." He put the phone back to his ear. "No need to worry. She's here with me. Here, talk to her yourself." Jack thrust the phone into my hand, gave a deprecatory shake of his head, and headed back into the woods, aiming for the tire tracks.

I looked at the phone and cleared my throat. Tate, Tate, I thought, what the heck are you playing at?

"Holy Mother! That's one of the inn's Gators, MacLaren. And five casks of wine. Nice work, dude. You found the missing wine!" Tate, standing beside me at the mouth of a little cave, leaned across and gave Jack a fist bump. Shortly after sighting the motor-boating Sasquatch, we'd run into Tate in the woods.

Jack grinned and met him knuckle to knuckle. "Thanks, bro. But I can't take all the credit. It was Whitney who discovered the tire tracks, and they led us here." Jack shifted his attention back to the wine. "Five casks? That means there are still a few missing."

The cave in question was one of the more accessible natural fissures in the face of the limestone bluff. And it was feeling a little cramped, sandwiched as I was between the two men and their budding bromance. Truthfully, I was happy to see them getting along so well, yet a part of me was a little disturbed by it too—the part that had grown a little suspicious of Tate. Especially since he'd been trouncing around the woods looking for me. Apparently Mom had made it clear when she called him that Giff wasn't my boyfriend.

Then again, what if Tate had already been in the woods when Mom called? What if he'd been the one following me? What if he was the creature Jack had spied in the boat, dressed as a Sasquatch? It was Tate's boat, after all, and he more than anyone knew how my mind worked. The thought was as distasteful as it was unsettling.

"Whit, babe," he said to me now, "did you know all this was here too?" He smiled as if the awkwardness of last night had never happened.

"Not until a second ago," I said, taking a step away from him. "I told you, I came out here looking for the missing wine. When I stumbled on the tire tracks under the bluff I was confused, but I'm not anymore. Did anyone know this Gator was missing?"

Tate shook his head. "I never thought to look. But it's the one Jeb used to drive."

Jack looked up from his cell phone. "No one realized it was missing? Tate," he said sharply, "don't touch anything! I'm calling this in to the station in Sturgeon Bay. They'll want to take a good look at this. Hopefully they can lift some prints."

The moment Jack ended the call, he pulled a pair of latex gloves from the back pocket of his jeans and began examining the Gator.

"So," I said, standing beside him, "I'll bet whoever stole this thing murdered Jeb. He's probably been using it to travel back and forth to the orchard."

Jack looked up and gave a confirming nod, then winced as Katy Perry's voice blurted out in the small, echoing cave, singing the refrain from her song "Firework." I winced too. MacDuff started howling. Jack spun around and stared at Tate's crotch.

"What?" Tate reached into his pocket. "It's an awesome song."

"Yeah, if you're a thirteen-year-old girl," Jack told him.

"Dude. Don't judge." Tate smirked and put his phone on speaker. "Mrs. Cushman! What's the verdict? Is there a boat missing?"

I looked at Jack. *"Mrs. Cushman?"* I mouthed. *"His housekeeper?"* Jack nodded. A moment later an elderly voice could be heard shouting on the other end.

"Tatum? Are you there, dear? You sound like you're in a tunnel again. Ooh, it's the oddest thing. I popped down to the docks and counted those little fishing dinghies of yours like you asked and I think one's missing again. Oh, and that Lori Larson stopped by this morning to see you. She dropped off another plate of those lumpy, dried-out little hockey pucks she calls scones. Honest ta Pete, they're foul little buggers … unless you're all bound up. In that case they're better than a pound of prunes stewed in Metamucil. Its colon blow, I tell ya. I can't figure out what she puts in 'em. Lard for sure. Rhubarb? Goat chow? A hand full of Grape-Nuts cereal? I'm stymied, but I'll tell you what's not in them, mister. A scone! And do you know what else? I think she's what they call a cougar. You don't want to get mixed up with a cougar, Tatum. I hear they have baggage, and your closets are too full already. I shooed her away. Told her you weren't home, but she left her dried-out old buns anyway, so I brought them down to the docks and was about to toss 'em in the lake when that nice man on the yacht, that real classy gent, came over and took 'em. He was starving. I tried to warn him. Told him they looked better than they tasted, but he just laughed and ate one. You'd best check in on him when you get back home."

"Will do. Thanks, Mrs. Cushman." The woman was still talking when Tate ended the call. "Well, looks like you're right again, Mac-Laren. One of my small rental boats is missing."

"I thought I heard Mrs. Cushman say 'again,' as if it's happened before." Jack cast Tate a friendly, questioning look.

"Yeah," Tate replied nonchalantly. "Thought I told you about that? Back in April I rented one to a fisherman. The poor guy got halfway

242

across the bay and ran out of gas. It shouldn't have happened. I always have Hank top off the tanks at the end of the day. Then, a week later, I found a slew of empty beer cans in one of the boats. One morning I even found a condom. Someone, and it wasn't me"—affecting the look of a virginal choir boy, Tate focused on me as he spoke—"was getting busy in one of my fishing boats. However, whoever is borrowing them always brings them back by morning, so no harm no foul. Right?"

"Well, I'm calling foul," Jack said. "Because the boat we saw wasn't heading back to the marina this morning, Tate. It was heading around the point, aiming for state land or beyond. Whitney found the guy's boot prints this morning coming out of the lighthouse. She followed them into the woods and down the bluff, where she found the tire tracks."

"I saw him through the fog," I added. "He was going to knock me over the head with a stone."

"Christ, Whitney!" Tate exclaimed, and to his credit he did look highly alarmed. He was filled with indignation, looking every part the Viking as he cried, "You saw this creep? What did he look like? Describe him and we'll hunt him down."

Describe the Yeti. That was the problem. "I ... ah ... didn't get a *good* look at him. The fog was too thick."

"Surely you saw something. How tall was he? What was he wearing? Can you describe the shape of his head?"

Jack looked at me, humor touching his eyes as he waited for me to reply. Damn him, I thought. If he really was C-Bomb he'd come to my defense. But Jack just stood there, looking oddly curious.

"Ah ... the shape of his head. All I can say is that it was really shaggy."

"Shaggy or squatchy?" Jack prodded with a muted grin.

"Squatchy?" Tate was lost. "As in Sasquatch?" Jack nodded. Tate then turned his dreamy blue gaze on me. "Whit, babe, I don't judge, but were you, by chance, drinking this morning? Jani says you're under a lot of stress—says you're baking a lot and that you don't even know that your own boyfriend Giff is gay."

"He is not my boyfriend!"

"Obviously. But a Sasquatch, babe? There's no such thing as a Sasquatch. I know you'd love to think differently, but it's mere folklore and legend."

"Ask Jack. He saw it in the boat."

"Only a glimpse," Jack was quick to reply. "I have no idea what she's talking about, but I do have a question for you, Tate. Who's stealing your boats?"

"I told you. I don't know."

All humor left Jack's face as he gave Tate a penetrating look. "Don't you?"

Tate's expression turned pensive and he paled under the scrutiny. I'd never seen his sun-bronzed face look so white or so worried.

How did Jack know that Tate wasn't telling the truth regarding his boats? What was Tate hiding? Who was he covering for? I looked at my former boyfriend again and thought that maybe C-Bomb was right to be suspicious of him.

If Tate's face was pale, Jack's was flushed with high color. Obviously the thought that his new bro-buddy was withholding information from him wasn't sitting too well. An unspoken guy-rule had been broken, and the mood in the little cave suddenly turned chilly.

A sharp pain seized my stomach as my mind spun out of control, reeling over the possibility that Tate might know the identity of the man-creature stalking me. Worst case scenario, it was Tate himself. It took a moment before I realized Jack was speaking to me.

"Whit, I'm asking if you'd mind taking MacDuff back to the inn with you. Tate and I are going to have a little chat down at the station in Sturgeon Bay once Sergeant Stamper and the forensic kit arrives. I'll call you when we're done. Okay?"

"Yeah. Okay," I said, suddenly feeling the need to get out of there. I took one last look at the former love of my life and felt a dull ache in my heart.

Jack attached a leash to MacDuff's collar and handed it to me.

"Well, MacDuff," I said, looking into the soulful eyes of the spaniel, "looks like you're coming with me to the Cherry Orchard Inn."

MacDuff, still damp and still bursting with energy, wagged his happy little tail.

Thirty-Four

We'd barely made it through the door of the inn when MacDuff caught whiff of something warm, fruity, and delicious. I unhooked his leash and followed him to the kitchen.

Mom was at the counter in one of her Barefoot-Contessa-on-steroids modes. The sink was full of mixing bowls, measuring cups, and empty pans. She was busily arranging slices of warm cherry coffee cake on a doily-topped silver platter. It was unbelievable. I didn't know how long she'd been up, but obviously long enough to bake three of her famous cherry coffee cakes. Dad was also in the kitchen, dressed in a dark gray suit with a light blue tie that matched the color of his eyes. He was lathering butter onto a slice of warm coffee cake. One look at the delectable treat in Dad's hand and MacDuff's little stub tail kicked into high gear.

"Whitney!" Mom cried, spinning around to look at me. Her white apron, smudged with cherry juice and white flour, covered a form-fitting black dress. She still had a great figure, I thought, but her face looked older, pinched with anger as it was. "Dear Heavens!" she scolded. Then, catching sight of MacDuff, her eyes softened. "Is that

Jack's dog? Of course it is. Thank goodness he found you. He called us this morning, as you must already know, to ask if you were here. Why wouldn't you be, I thought. However, when I went to check your room and found you gone, your father and I grew worried. There's a murderer on the loose, Whitney! What were you thinking?"

"Obviously she wasn't," Dad replied for me, feeding half his slice of coffee cake to the dog. They both seemed familiar with MacDuff. Was I the only one who hadn't known Jack had a dog?

"We called Tate then," Mom continued, "Tate being such a dear. He always did have a way of finding you."

"Well, if you must know, Jack and I found *him*," I retorted, experiencing another sharp pang of remorse at the thought of Tate as a suspect. By now he would be on his way to Sturgeon Bay with Jack for questioning. It was still hard to believe Tate knew who was stealing his boats. What else was he covering up, I wondered, staring at my parents—two of his most ardent supporters.

I couldn't tell them about Tate, not now, and so I didn't. Instead I added, "We found something else, Dad. We found your missing wine along with one of the Gators, likely the one Jeb used to get around the orchard. We didn't know it was missing. The Gator, we think, was used to transport the casks of wine. Both are in a little cave under the bluff about half a mile down from the lighthouse. I left Jack and Tate waiting there for backup from Sturgeon Bay."

"It's all there?" Dad asked, his silver-blue eyes brightening. "You recovered my wine?"

"Not all of it," I said, and then told my parents a highly watered-down version of my morning, omitting all mention of the eerie twig-face in the lighthouse, my near-abduction by Sasquatch, and Tate's stolen fishing boat and possible involvement. It was just as well. Mom reminded me that Reverend Dahl was holding a special memorial service for Jeb in a few hours and that the whole community was coming together to pray for Cody. Mom's coffee cakes would be part of the after-service fellowship, held in the community room in the basement of St. Paul's. The entire town of Cherry Cove would be there, with the probable exception, of course, of Jack and Tate.

"We need to come out in force as a community," Mom added, wiping a tear from her eye. "And we need to come out strong as a family, because ... because this doesn't look good for the Blooms. Not at all. A murder, a poisoning, and a fire in less than twenty-four hours! And I don't even want to think about what might happen at the cherry pie bake-off this afternoon. We just have to get through the day, Whitney. But I feel so ... so G-damned helpless!"

Mom never swore. It was sobering. Unfortunately, I knew exactly how she felt.

"So, Jack thinks Tate knows who's been stealing his boats? Interesting."

"It is," I replied, casting a thoughtful look at Giff, who was riding in the passenger seat of my car. We were running late for the memorial service. I'd showered and changed into a navy skirt, white tights, white blouse, and my favorite cherry-red sweater. But that's not why we were running late. It was Giff's lengthy Hollywood shower and slavish devotion to fashion that had really put us behind. I had to admit, though, that it worked for him. He looked like a movie star on Oscar night in his black tailored suit and a gold-and-black silk tie.

I glanced in the rearview mirror and saw MacDuff—another vision of silky black-and-white elegance, only he was sprawled across the back seat in peaceful slumber. Jack had sent a quick text asking me to drop him off at the Cherry Cove police station on my way to the church, but I was of half a mind to keep him. Then again, I lived in an apartment in Chicago. I couldn't even afford a free cat, let alone a stately Springer Spaniel like MacDuff. I would have to return him, but I would visit. After all, the dog had saved my life.

I'd told Giff all about that too, sparing no detail. Giff was a creative soul. Whether or not he believed in Bigfoot didn't really matter. He was still open-minded enough to be intrigued by the notion.

"Erik Larson," he said.

"What?"

"The boy, Erik Larson. Think about it," Giff suggested. "Who disappears the moment you try to speak with him? Erik Larson. Who is Cody Rivers best friend? Erik Larson. What if these boys were protecting a dark secret and one of them cracked—one of them decided to tell the boss's daughter what was really going on? Would the other go so far as to kill him to protect this secret?"

"Holy cobbler," I breathed. "Do you think Erik Larson was the person in the processing shed last night—the one who tried to kill Cody and me?"

"It's super twisted, but kids these days are super twisted. I wouldn't rule it out. Look, the kid worked closely with Jeb. He also had access to the processing sheds. I've never met him, but I'm told he's a big, strapping young lad. And if he caught wind that Cody had sent you a message, he might have been desperate enough to try and stop him."

"His best friend. Dear God, what are these kids involved in?" I uttered. Giff shrugged. "Well, what about Brock Sorensen and his sudden appearance near the processing sheds last night?" I asked.

"He might have been telling the truth," Giff offered. "Look, I know Tay's not a fan and rightly so. While you were out hunting Bigfoot this morning, I did a little checking up on him. The guy graduated at the top of his class from the University of Wisconsin, worked as an accountant for the Miller Brewing Company in Milwaukee, met his vegan wife while protesting the treatment of circus animals, got married, and shortly thereafter started working for a large organic grocery store chain. Got tired of that and moved here. He likes golf, he's on a fantasy football team, and he subscribes to *Aficionado*, which he has sent to the inn. Sorensen make's good money but he's not ambitious. He's plenty smarmy, but what motive does he have to kill Jeb?"

Giff paused for breath, then galloped on. "Sorensen was working late at the inn when Jeb's body was discovered, but Tate was hanging around in the lounge. Both men accompanied Baxter when he went to the orchard to find the body, but only one of the two has any real tie to those two boys—Tate. You told me Tate was their basketball coach at the high school. You also said that both Cody and Erik had had a run-in with the law. They were caught stealing bicycles last summer, and then got their whole basketball team disqualified from the championship for using steroids. What if Tate knew about the steroids? What if he was the one supplying them?"

"No way," I said, quick to jump to Tate's defense. "Tate may have his fair share of shortcomings, but drugs aren't one of them. He'd never use the stuff, or suggest others use them."

"Maybe not, way back when you were still in love with him, but what about now? Remember, I've met him, angel. Maybe you drove the poor man to it."

I shot him a dark look. "Thanks, but I doubt it. Besides, Tate's in perfect health. No dark circles under his eyes, no sallow, saggy skin."

"True. He's beautiful as a Norse God, and I'd like to trust him too. It would be such a waste, locking away a man like that for life. But darling, consider this. What if Tate does know that those boys were stealing his boats? He also knew about your Dad's secret wine. You told me once, when you were very, very drunk, that you and Tate used to break into the old lighthouse and make out in there. Tate's very familiar with the layout, and I would bet he'd still know how to break in if he needed to."

"Oh my," I blurted out, interrupting him. "I just remembered something. Tate was on the phone this morning, taking with his housekeeper, Mrs. Cushman. She's an older lady, and he put her on speaker phone. She mentioned that Lori Larson stopped by the marina this morning to drop off a plate of scones for Tate. Tay's mom, Char, also talked about Lori Larson and a possible reason she might have had for hating Jeb. Lori's a notoriously bad baker, and yet she was stopping by Tate's house with baked goods. Why?"

"This Lori Larson wouldn't happen to be Erik Larson's mom?"

I looked at Giff and nodded.

"Looks like we need to pay Lori Larson a visit."

"Indeed," I said, stepping on the gas. "Lori Larson will be at the service, I expect. Erik too. The whole village of Cherry Cove will be there to say goodbye to their old friend Jeb Carlson, while praying for that poor boy, Cody Rivers."

Thirty-Five

The town of Cherry Cove was jam-packed with parked cars, a scene reminiscent of the height of the summer tourist season, not a lazy weekend in late May. Having little choice, I pulled into the handicapped parking spot at the police station, the only spot available, certain Jack would understand. We then walked MacDuff around to the gated backyard, where Jack's adolescent goats were busy grazing. The moment they saw us they ran for the gate. Giff was enchanted, until the two little billys lowered their heads, revealing their pointy horns. MacDuff ran in, barking. Giff shut the gate and leaned against it.

"Who is this guy?" he breathed, his dark eyes glittering with humor. "He's got an awesome dog, two crazy goats, and lives in a turf-roofed police station. What a badass. Can't wait to meet him in person."

St. Paul's Lutheran Church stood on a hill overlooking the town. It was a short walk, and although we were already late, Giff and I lingered. I'd like to think it was because of the beautiful scenery. The early morning fog had lifted, revealing the languid, dark blue water of Cherry Cove Bay. The midmorning sun hit the waves at such an angle that the water sparkled like a sea of diamonds, while hungry gulls cried overhead. The black roof of the Cherry Orchard Inn could be seen across the bay, sitting on the point and poking above the forested bluff. It was a sight I never grew tired of, and I'd missed it. Giff was swept up by it too. But there was something else—the town was deserted. Every living soul was already in the church, paying tribute to the man who'd been so brutally murdered in our orchard. *Our orchard*. That oasis of an inn on the bluff. It was going to be a difficult day.

Giff and I continued along the water, walking in companionable silence until somebody shouted my name. We both turned. Carleton Brisbane was running toward us. Giff, having never seen the man before, removed his sunglasses in reverence at the sight of his suavely elegant demeanor.

"Damn," he breathed. "This town's just full of delightful surprises. Who is he? He looks familiar, like I've seen him on the cover of a magazine or something."

"Maybe you have. He's Carleton Brisbane, a frequent visitor and Hannah's latest heartthrob. He's the other judge in the great cherry pie bake-off you'll be working later. Don't get any ideas, though. She's guarding her claim on him like a hawk."

"Noted. Then should I be concerned by the way he's looking at you?"

"Don't be silly."

"Angel, if I know anything, I know men."

Perhaps he was right. When Carleton caught up to us he was smiling at me. Only me.

"I'm heartened to find I'm not the only one running late this morning," he quipped. Then, shifting his focus to Giff, he thrust out his hand. "Carleton Brisbane."

"Gifford McGrady. I'm a friend of Whitney's. I hear we're to be the judges today in the cherry pie bake-off."

"Well, that's great news. Miss Winthrop volunteered me for the honor. I do have a passion for cherries, especially a great cherry pie, but I've never done this sort of thing before. I'm happy to have another discerning palate to help make what is certain to be a difficult decision."

"Not sure what kind of help I'm going to be," Giff admitted. "Whit's making me do it. Of course, she knew I'd agree. I'm intrigued by the notion of a giant gold-plated cherry trophy." Carleton laughed, thinking Giff was joking. Giff played along.

"I'm going to be honest," Carleton said. "I'm a little worried I won't be able to uphold my end of the bargain. You may have to do most of the tasting, Mr. McGrady. I think I ate something this morning that I shouldn't have—a truly horrible scone made by one of today's contestants. I've been dealing with it for that last hour. It's why I'm running late." He grimaced and patted his stomach.

Mrs. Cushman's story sprang to my mind again, particularly the part about the man who'd ended up with Lori Larson's rock-hard scones. "Tell me, you didn't, by chance, happen to eat one of the scones Mrs. Cushman was trying to feed to the fish this morning?"

The question shocked him. Carleton's light green eyes narrowed. "Yes. That's exactly what happened. How … how did you know about that?"

"It's a small village," Giff replied for me, tossing in a private wink. "I'm told one hears everything in this town. It's a miracle the identity of the murderer hasn't been bandied about yet by the Cherry Cove gossip mill."

"Deeper secrets take a little longer to uncover," I said, "and this one is pretty deep. Carleton, you really should've let Mrs. Cushman toss those scones in the lake. Never go against the wisdom of an old baker, especially where baked goods are involved."

Carleton laughed. It was a charming sound. "Yes. Wise advice. I'll just have to cling to the thought that I might have saved a fish or two. Seriously, though, how did you know about the scones?"

I thought about keeping the information to myself but caved under his probing look. It hit me, then, how similar these two men were. It was like staring at father and son, the older man embodying classic elegance while the younger man sported a modern, fresh, and slightly disheveled take on the original. The thought made me smile.

"Okay, but you need to keep this to yourselves. No adding it to the gossip mill." The two glossy black heads nodded in unison. "Giff knows most of this already, but the short answer is, I heard Tate talking with his housekeeper, Mrs. Cushman. Jack and I had seen a boat speeding across the lake this morning, and we asked Tate if one of his boats was missing. He called Mrs. Cushman to check, and one was."

"Someone stole one of Tate's boats?" Carleton looked troubled. "I was at the marina last night. As you know, I have a room at the inn for the festival, but after that damnable fire in the processing shed I decided it might be safer on my yacht. I was sleeping like the dead. Didn't hear a thing."

"I'm glad you didn't. With all that's happened at the inn, you're likely to think Cherry Cove is a pretty dicey place. It really isn't, you know."

"I know," he assured me. "But it's highly unsettling all the same. Did Tate ever find his boat?"

"No. Whoever stole it wasn't heading back to the marina."

"Did anyone see this person in the stolen boat?" Carleton looked both concerned and intrigued.

The trouble was, I had seen him … or it. I chanced a look at Giff. His expression screamed, *For the love of God, do not mention the Sasquatch!*

"Ahh, no," I replied. "We were in the woods, just down from the lighthouse, when we saw the boat. It was too foggy."

"What were you doing in the woods at that time of the morning, may I ask?"

"Looking for the missing wine."

"Interesting. And what made you think you could find it when Officer MacLaren couldn't?"

"Hubris," Giff added. "Pure hubris."

I cast him a reprimanding look and replied, "Truthfully, I don't know, but I did find it, or what was left of it. Jack was in the woods too. We were both following the same set of footprints when we met up. Someone had been there with us—the same person who stole Tate's boat, we think. Then we found out that Tate was in the woods too, looking for me. We all met up shortly after the person in Tate's stolen boat raced away. We're not sure who's been stealing the boats, but we believe it's the same person, or people, responsible for stealing Dad and Jeb's cherry wine. It could be some of the high school kids. But I doubt they killed Jeb. Whatever the case, Jack and Tate won't be at the service this morning. They're both at the Sturgeon Bay police station. And we best get going too, before we miss everything."

The church was packed. It was standing room only, except for one tiny space in a pew Tay and Hannah had been protecting. I urged Giff to take it because I had another plan. Erik Larson was somewhere in the church, and I meant to find him.

Since Carleton was a visitor to Cherry Cove, I brought him with me to a little door, tucked away at the side of the church, marked *Do*

Not Enter. We entered and quietly made our way up the rickety stairs to the roped-off balcony.

We took a seat in one of the antique pews, the sturdiest-looking one. Carleton sat quietly beside me, lost in thought as I began my observation of the mourners below. In the first pew on the left sat the couple I'd seen last night in the hospital, Cody's worry-worn parents. A young girl sat with them, presumably his sister, and beside them, more family. Across the aisle I recognized the family of Jeb Carlson: his two vaguely familiar middle-aged children and their respective families. They didn't live in Cherry Cove any more, and it gave me a jolt to see them sitting once again in the village church.

My own parents were three rows behind Jeb's family, with Grandma Jenn beside them, crying silently into a handkerchief. My heart went out to her, especially now that I knew Jeb had been so much more than a friend. Sitting on the other side of my parents was Brock Sorensen. I assumed the thin, blonde-headed woman next to him was his wife, Gwyneth. Poor woman, I thought, and couldn't help glancing at Tay. Tay and Brock. I shivered at the thought and continued searching.

Reverend Dahl, the rock of the little community, stood behind the pulpit. As he spoke to his parishioners his face was lined with agony— agony mirrored by everyone in the church. The sermon, I thought, had to be one of the hardest he'd ever given; how does one make sense of the senseless murder of an old man, or the beating and forced poisoning of a boy? He was speaking in solemn tones as he recalled the life of Jeb Carlson and all that he'd done for the community. There wasn't a dry eye in the entire church, including a whole group of teen-aged girls who were openly crying, albeit not for Jeb but for the handsome youth lying comatose in Door County General. I didn't blame them one bit. What had happened to Cody Rivers was a glimpse into the brutal, desperate mind of the killer.

And yet, somewhere in the back of my mind was the fact that both Jeb and Cody knew who he was. It was a chilling thought. The killer could be anywhere. He could even be in this very church. The thought chilled me to the bone. That's when the warm, solid hand of Carleton Brisbane was placed over mine.

"This must be incredibly difficult for you," he whispered.

My response to this was to squeeze his hand just as tightly. It felt so good to be held by a man—a real man. For the second time that morning, I dared to believe I'd discovered the true identity of C-Bomb. And what a perfect discovery it would be, I thought. Carleton was polished, wealthy, incredibly handsome, and had the most mesmerizing green eyes.

"Do ... you have a dog?" I whispered.

He quirked a brow, looked at me oddly, and then nodded. "I do. Molly. She lives on my yacht."

"And ... are you married?"

"I was actually hoping you'd get around to asking me that question, my dear." Carleton leaned in and whispered in my ear, "No, I've never been. Not yet. And please know that I have no romantic feelings for your friend, Hannah. Only for you. Have dinner with me. I might even introduce you to Molly."

It was hardly the time. We were in church—at a funeral. But I said yes, sure, we should do that sometime. Tate was my past, Jack was my friend, but Carleton ... Carleton Brisbane could very well be my future.

I never gave a thought to what Hannah might think, because just about then I realized that Erik Larson wasn't in the church. I scanned the pews three more times to be certain. I could be wrong, I knew. I needed to check the lobby. Dear God, how I hoped he was in the lobby. I could feel my pulse elevate at the thought, and what it might mean.

The sermon was drawing to an end. I quietly stood up, pulling Carleton with me, and left the balcony.

Thirty-Six

We snuck out the forbidden balcony door at the same moment the congregation began streaming out of the chapel. The lobby had been crowded when we came in. Now, however, the solemn mob was on the move, sweeping everyone along like a cleansing wave as it headed for the community room and coffee cake.

I stood on tippy-toes and craned my neck, attempting to find Erik's face in the crowd. I had no luck, but I did spot Giff, Tay, and Hannah. "Over that way," I told Carleton, still pulling him along, and realized too late that I was still holding his hand.

"Hey," Hannah said by way of greeting. Her smile faded the moment her eyes dropped to our entwined hands. Immediately I let go.

"Can't have Carleton getting swept away in the crowd now, can we?" Giff was quick to add, shooting both Carleton and me a reprimanding look.

"No," I replied. "St. Paul's has never seen such a turnout. I was afraid Carleton would be trampled by a coffee cake stampede. I've heard it can happen. By the way, have any of you seen Erik Larson?"

"Holy Mother of Mischief!" Tay cried, nearly coming to a stop. "No. No I haven't," she said, regaining her place in the surging crowd. "I knew something seemed odd, but I couldn't place my finger on it."

Hannah, momentarily forgetting her jealousy, added, "Erik worked with Jeb! He's Cody's best friend! He should be here!"

"Do we know if anyone's seen him since he disappeared yesterday, during the wine and cheese tasting?" I asked.

The blank looks, the utter silence, did not bode well.

The moment we entered the community room, I caught sight of my parents. They were standing with Jeb Carlson's family, talking. At times like these there were no words that could bring comfort, and whatever Dad was saying, I could tell, fell short of the mark. Jeb Carlson's son refused to shake his proffered hand. Then the words "irresponsible," "money-grubbing capitalist," and "lawsuit" rang out, filling the room.

"Holy cobbler!" I uttered under my breath. I was about to jump to my parents' aid when Tay and Hannah blocked me. Carleton took the hint and steered me toward the refreshment table at the other end of the room.

"I'm sorry," he whispered, "but you must have expected that people would be angry. That man's father was murdered on your father's cherry orchard. Their son," he began, gesturing toward the Rivers family, "was nearly murdered as well. Tensions are running high, and understandably so. Nothing anyone could say now would be of help. Best let the storm blow over."

"Blow over? I was in advertising, Carleton. A storm this size doesn't just blow over without a healthy dose of damage control."

"Damage control?" he said, and for the first time the sparkle left his compelling aqua eyes. "Death, scandal, lawsuits, costly repairs—this, Whitney, will be the end of your family's cherry orchard and inn, I'm afraid."

"My God. My God," I uttered, feeling my stomach drop to my knees. "Isn't there anything we can do? You're a successful businessman, Carleton. You must deal with things like this all the time. There has to be something we can do to help my parents and save their business."

Carleton studied my face. "I've had my share of challenges, and what I've learned is that a wise businessman knows when to cut loose a sinking asset before he's dragged to the bottom with it. I know you don't want to hear it, but this is a sinking asset, my dear. There's no kinder way I can put it. Unfortunately, it also happens to be the life-blood of your family. Be prepared, Whitney—when the Cherry Orchard Inn goes down, the Blooms will go down with it."

His words hurt more than a knife to the heart, but there was some truth in it. I looked at my parents, my heart pounding double time. The Rivers family had joined the group, and the anger was compounding. "You may be right," I told him. "But the Blooms won't go down without a fight."

It took a while to defuse the anger of the grieving parties, but with the help of friends, we did it. Fortunately the Blooms had more friends in the room than enemies, including Reverend Dahl and Dr. Engle, both influential men in the village. Between them they managed to bring back order. Dr. Engle even reminded everyone that this was a memorial service. "No one can bring your loved ones back," he told the crowd, "But what we can do is to help the authorities find the person responsible for these tragedies and bring him to justice. That's what we should be focusing on, not pointing fingers."

Yes, I thought. Good. Bring the focus back to the problem at hand. Find the murderer!

"Here," Giff said, coming up to us and handing me a tiny paper plate weighted down by a lumpy scone. "That's all that's left. Just those. Clearly they weren't up to par with the quality of the other baked goods, but hey, how bad can they be?" He winked, then picked up the scone on his own plate. He was just about to take a bite when Carleton knocked it out of his hand.

"Don't eat that! That's one of the nasty things I ate this morning, and I'm still suffering for it."

"Lori Larson!" I cried, remembering the connection between the scone and the baker. I scanned the room. I hadn't seen her son, but if Lori's scones were here, there was a pretty good chance she was too. I was just about to search the crowded room when my phone rang. It was Jack.

"Whit. Are you at the church? Good. Listen. I need you to find Erik Larson. Is he there?" At the sound of the name, I inhaled sharply. It was a little spooky that Jack was asking after the same person I happened to be looking for.

"No," I said, "but Lori's here. Why?" I had a sinking feeling that I already knew the answer.

"Christ!" Jack swore under his breath. "I'm sorry to have to break this to you over the phone, but I think you should know. I'm still at the police station in Sturgeon Bay with Tate. During the questioning, he revealed that Erik Larson and Cody Rivers were the ones taking his boats. I'm not sure what else he knows, but the boys definitely knew something. Look, I know these kids too, and they're not murderers. If someone tried to kill Cody, it stands to reason that Erik is in danger as well. We need to find him, Whit. Quickly! He's not answering his cell phone."

In one lurching beat all the blood drained from my heart. "Right," I said, fighting to remain calm. "Got it. What does Lori Larson look like?" I roamed the room as Jack described the woman I was after. I

263

found a person who fit the description standing in a far corner with a small group of middle-aged ladies. "Excuse me," I said, breaking in on their conversation. "Mrs. Larson?"

The woman stopped talking and stared at me.

"My name is Whitney Bloom and I'm looking for your son, Erik. Do you know where he is?"

"I know who you are," Lori said curtly, glaring. "Why ya looking for my son?"

I could have told her, yet under the circumstances I felt it best she hear the news from Jack. I handed her my phone. "Officer MacLaren is on the other end. He'll explain it to you."

With visible trepidation Lori took the phone and held it to her ear. The moment she did, the fair skin beneath the heavy sheen of makeup turned the color of ash. "No," she breathed, "Oh no. Please, God, no…"

"Lori. What is it? What's going on?" The women in her circle were stricken with concern.

"It's Officer MacLaren," she told them, handing back my phone. "He's been trying to get ahold of Erik. He believes my son is in grave danger."

Thirty-Seven

"He should be at home," Lori said, heading for her car. "I don't understand. Last night, after hearing about the murder attempt on Cody, we were so distraught. It hit us hard. Cody and Erik are like brothers."

"What time did he get home last night?" I asked.

She cast me a nervous glance. "Ashley, my daughter, came home from the inn around ten. She was pretty upset when she told me about the fire and Cody. She said Erik went to visit Cody in the hospital and would be home late."

"Do you know around what time he came home?"

"He didn't," Lori admitted, biting her lower lip as she strode across the parking lot. "But that's not unusual. He's a high school senior, ya know. They usually crash at whoever's house they're hanging out at for the night. But he's always home for breakfast."

"Hopefully he's home now," I said, and prayed it was true. "He probably just turned the ringer off on his phone. Happens all the time. Watch, we'll find him in bed, sleeping like a baby."

"Right," she agreed, looking utterly unnerved. It was eleven o'clock now, so by all accounts Erik should be home. And that's what was so alarming. Immediately after getting off the phone with Jack, Lori had tried calling her son's cell phone. She'd tried three times. Each unanswered call was like a private death. She gasped; her chin and lower lip quivered, and her red-rimmed eyes filled with tears. Like a pebble tossed in a glassy millpond, her plight had rippled through the community room on concentric waves of anguish and fear. It had stopped the finger-pointing and threats, working as a cohesive force on the congregation. Everyone present understood. Erik Larson, friend of Cody Rivers and loyal employee of the Cherry Orchard Inn, was missing.

I jumped into the backseat of Lori's car, along with Ashley. Carleton, undeterred and unwilling to return to his moored yacht when crisis was so thick in the air, rode shotgun. Hannah and Giff ran with Tay to her car. In fact, half the congregation of St. Paul's Lutheran got in their cars and followed Lori as she shot out of town, pedal to the floor.

The Larsons lived down a dirt road on the fertile interior of the peninsula in a freshly painted old farmhouse. This was prime Wisconsin farm country. The house was surrounded by sprouting green fields with a handful of dairy cows grazing near a copse of trees. As Lori drove up the long winding drive, she moaned. Her son's car wasn't there.

Pulling out her keys, she ran up the front steps. Carleton and I followed, but on the wide front porch I turned and instructed him to bar the door. "Let me go with her," I told him. "We'll know soon enough if he's here. She doesn't need the entire village milling about."

"Right," he agreed. Tay, Hannah, and Giff joined him.

Lori, Ashley, and I did a quick search of the first floor, then headed upstairs to Erik's bedroom. Tension was running high; Erik wasn't responding to his name, and my heart was pounding in my ears like a hammer on an anvil because of it. Lori reached the bedroom door first and threw it open. I gasped, falling into the room open-jawed, staring at the carnage around me.

"Oh my God!" I cried. "It's been ransacked! Erik's been abducted!"

"What?" Lori looked at me and started screaming.

"Jeez! Mom! Get ahold!" It was Ashley. The girl had a death-grip on her mother's arm. "Erik's room always looks like this. The kid's a flippin' pig," she told me, rolling her eyes. She then walked over to a cluttered dresser, picked up a can of Old Spice Wolfthorn, and proceeded to crop-dust the pigsty.

"Right," Lori said. "Right. Enough, Ashley!" She took a deep breath and shrugged. "Teenage boys."

Teenage boys? The place looked like the subterranean den of a feral child, and smelled like one too under the spicy spray-on deodorant scent. Correction. It looked like the den of a feral child with cash.

As I wandered through the piles of discarded clothing, dirty plates, and open soda cans and energy drinks, I noted the knots of wire connecting game controllers to an Xbox One, a PlayStation 4, and an old Nintendo 64—all sitting beneath a flat-screen TV the size of a small car. There was a pair of expensive looking headphones, and another pair that had a mouthpiece for live gaming. A sizeable pile of video games sprawled along the floor like a lumpy volcano. All of them were rated Mature, I noted, and most were first-person shooters. It was an expensive setup for the kid of a struggling single mother, I thought. When I asked if Erik's father had bought the gaming equipment, Lori shook her head. Erik, she said, had bought it all himself. The kid did have cash.

A pair of sizable stereo speakers sat beside the TV stand, one holding up a pair of dirty gym shorts and the other a white button-down, complete with sweaty pit stains. There were basketballs, footballs, a lacrosse stick, and a tennis racket. I did a quick search for the bed and found a likely suspect perched along the far wall. Erik could have easily still been asleep in the thing for all I knew, it was so lumpy and messy. Aside from the piles of clothing and wrinkled blankets there was an unseemly number of pillows. Lori, picking up on my thought, walked over to it and began peeling the layers away like it was a giant banana. The bed held a lot of things, but an eighteen-year-old boy, unfortunately, wasn't one of them. As I fought to make sense of what I was looking at, a buzzing noise grabbed my attention.

"It's coming from the bed," I said, "or under it."

After searching the rumpled bed, I dropped to my knees and lifted the blankets. Among a pile of dirty, mismatched socks and dust-bunnies on the floor was a phone. If it was Erik's, I knew Jack would want to dust it for fingerprints. With a slight shiver of disgust, I slipped one of the dirty socks over my hand and grabbed it. It was still buzzing.

"It's Erik's," Lori confirmed.

"I don't suppose he leaves this behind often?"

"Are you kidding me? That thing's practically attached to him." As Lori spoke, her red-painted lips twitched nervously.

I peered at the screen. *BabyGirl*, whoever that was, was calling. There was only one thing for it. I took off the dirty sock and pressed answer.

A frantic female voice cried, "Erik!? Oh my God! Where've you been? I'm so worried. I've been trying to call you all morning—"

"Who's this?" I asked, cutting her off.

"What? What d'ya mean, who is this!? Are you smokin' weed again or somthin'? It's Kenna, asshole."

"Kenna who?"

"Jesus, Erik. Have you been huffing helium? You sound like a girl. Stop messing around. I'm worried sick."

"This isn't Erik, Kenna. This is Whitney Bloom. I have Erik's phone."

"Holy ****," the girl swore and ended the call.

"Kenna McKinnon," Ashley supplied. "She's a waitress at the inn, same as me, and she's Erik's girlfriend."

"Right. Dammit!" I muttered. "I don't suppose you know the password to Erik's phone?" Thankfully Ashley did, and she told me the numbers. The moment I unlocked it, I called Kenna's number back.

"Kenna, don't hang up. Where are you? Sitting in a car outside Erik's house?" I went to the window and pulled back a curtain. There were a lot of cars outside the Larson house. "Do me a favor," I said. "This is very important. Get out of your car and wave." A moment later, Kenna got out of a white Ford Fiesta and waved her hand. "Gotcha. Okay. Stay right there. I'll be down in a few minutes."

I ended the call and saw that there were fifteen missed calls since last night, and six unanswered voicemails. Most of the missed calls were from BabyGirl … aka Kenna. I checked the time on the first unanswered message again: four thirty yesterday afternoon, about the time Erik had gone missing from the wine and cheese tasting event. I scrolled further and saw the last text Erik sent: it was to Cody.

Dude, don't do it, it read. Cody had never replied. The message was sent at 8:28 p.m.

If Erik's phone was under his bed, it obviously meant he'd been home at some point yesterday. He'd been home and gone, and nobody had seen him, including his girlfriend. Did Erik know that Cody was planning to meet with me? Was his text a warning … or some kind of threat? If he ran home after leaving the inn, he would have had plenty of time to go back to the processing shed and set a fire, but would he really be able to murder his best friend? Or perhaps Erik knew that by talking with me, Cody was taking a terrible risk. This would mean that whatever Cody was involved in, Erik was involved in too. Was he afraid? Or was he a monster? Either way, the fact that he was missing without his phone sent a wave of cold panic running through me.

"Lori, what time did you come home last night?"

She thought a moment. "Nine," she said. "I was having dinner with a friend."

"Erik had his phone on him yesterday, and we found it under his bed, so he must have left the house before anyone came home. I believe he knows what's going on, and we need to find him. Meanwhile, I'm going to need to keep this." I held up the phone. "Officer Mac-Laren will want to look at it."

Lori nodded. I slipped Erik's phone into my pocket and ran my eye over the room once again. Then I stopped.

"Lori, can you tell me if you see anything missing from this room—anything at all?" She swept the room with her eyes, then shook her head.

"Really Mom?" Ashley, standing aside with arms crossed, uncrossed her arms and stormed over to the desk. "I'll tell ya what's missing, Miss Bloom. His backpack, that's what." She cast her mother another disparaging look. "He always throws it there," she told us, indicating a clean little space on the floor beside the desk. "Those are his books, his papers, and his calculator. He dumped them all out."

"Very good," I said. "What else?"

"His Doc Martens," she added, pointing to the closet. "And his Carhartt jacket. It's usually over there."

"Whitney." Lori not only looked frightened but highly annoyed. "What does this mean?"

"I'm not sure, but I'm going make a guess. Since all the doors to the house were locked, and there's no sign of forced entry or a struggle, and your son went to some effort to shove his cell phone under the bed, I think that for whatever reason, Erik doesn't want to be contacted—by you or by anybody. Without a cell phone he can't be traced, either." As I spoke, some pieces of the puzzle were beginning to fall into place. I looked at Lori and said, "Tell me the truth. You knew that your son was stealing Tate's boats, didn't you? That's why you were bringing a plate of scones to his house at the marina this morning, wasn't it?"

"How ... how did you know about that?"

The way she looked at me made me think that Mrs. Cushman had been right. Lori Larson was a cougar. "Because Tate was with me this morning," I said, feeling oddly proprietary about the ex-love of my life. "Mrs. Cushman told him that you came by with a plate of scones. They were a form of apology, weren't they? When Erik didn't come home last night, you assumed he'd taken one of Tate's boats."

"You're right. Please, please don't be hard on Tate." It was kind of sad, but the woman sounded like a child begging to keep a lost kitten. And the look of adoration on her face as she spoke Tate's name was, quite frankly, disgusting. "Ever since his dad left us," Lori continued, with a beseeching look in her eyes, "Erik's been acting up. A couple of months ago I found out he was paying someone to buy him beer, and then he and Cody would steal one of Tate's boats and drink out on the lake. Tate followed the boys one night and caught them in the act." She looked squarely at me and added, "He called me instead of Officer MacLaren, thank God, and I was so grateful he did. Erik already has a criminal record for a minor indiscretion last year. Tate knows he's a good boy and didn't have the heart to add theft to the list. Tate's taken Erik and Cody under his wing. He was the one who got the boys their job at the orchard. When I realized that Erik didn't come home this morning, I assumed he was depressed about Cody and had taken one of Tate's boats by himself. I was going to … talk with Tate. He's such a good listener."

Tate? A good listener? Ha! I'll bet she wanted to do more than just talk with him. I shook the thought from my head and focused back on the matter at hand. Something had been following me in the woods this morning. Erik stole boats. Was Erik my Sasquatch? I looked at Lori and asked, "Does, um, Erik have a Sasquatch costume by chance?"

I could tell by the cross look she gave me that the answer to this was no. "What the hell kind of question is that? My son is missing and you ask me if he has a Sasquatch costume? Of course he doesn't have a Sasquatch costume! He spends all of his money on video games! And anyhow, why am I talking to you? You're not the police. Shouldn't we be talking to Officer MacLaren about all this?"

"Jack's on his way. And yes, there was a boat missing at the marina this morning. And it was never returned."

"Oh God!" Lori cried. "Did he have a boating accident? Do you think my son might have drowned?"

"I doubt it," I said, recalling the boat speeding away in the fog. I looked at Ashley then, suddenly remembering that she'd said she worked at the inn too.

"Ashley, you know what's going on here, don't you?"

For the first time since we'd entered the house Ashley looked scared. She cast a nervous glance at her mother. That was it! Ashley wouldn't talk in front of her mother.

"Lori," I said, "would you mind stepping out of the room for a moment?"

"Yes, I would mind! What is it, Ash? If you have something to say, just say it. Say it!" Lori howled in a fear-crazed voice. "Say it!"

"You already know what it is, Ma, but you won't allow yourself to see it!"

I was confused. Ashley glared at her mother.

"You don't want to see it because you don't want it to be true. But it is true, Mom. It is. Erik's back on drugs again—just like Cody, and Kenna, and her sister, and Finn. Mostly Finn! He's the one they all go to."

"Finn? Who's Finn?" I asked.

"He's the new guy. The hot bartender all the girls are trying to sleep with."

"Oh God!" This, Lori and I uttered at the same time. She was aghast at the fact her daughter was trying to sleep with a man. I was aghast at the fact that I knew exactly who Ashley was talking about. And, dammit, not that I hadn't thought about jumping in the sack with him too.

"You know this guy?" Lori rounded on me.

"I ... I don't really know him. It's more like I know *of* him." Lori's eyes widened. "I mean ... I know him if by 'Finn,' Ashley's referring to a dark-haired Irishman with flirty aqua-green eyes?" At her nod, I continued. "Yep, I saw him yesterday. He was chatting up two high school girls." I looked at Ashley. She blushed. "Oh dear, you were one of the girls he was hitting on, weren't you?"

Lori, who was already whimpering, let out a loud gasp.

"Oh for cripes sake, Mom. Get ahold!" Ashley's pink, glossy lips twisted in disgust. She looked back at me. "Yeah, I was talking to him. Who wouldn't? He's smokin' hot, and I hear he's a really great kisser.

Anyhow, maybe Erik went to see him, you know, to get some more drugs or something?" Lori gasped again.

"Where does Finn live?" I asked.

Ashley shrugged. "Don't ask me. I'm not sleeping with the guy, and I certainly don't do drugs. But I'd bet my iPhone that slut Kenna knows."

Thirty-Eight

Kenna. I needed to talk with Kenna and hoped she was still waiting for me. If anybody knew where this Finn guy lived it would likely be her, I thought, running down the stairs. I leapt down the last two steps and made for the door, nearly colliding with Jack.

"Whitney!" he said, holding me by the arms. "They said you were in here with Lori. What's the rush?" He looked up at the stairs, expecting Lori. She wasn't coming just yet. Lori and her daughter were having a little heart-to-heart in Erik's room.

"Let's go in here," I said, pulling him into the old farmhouse kitchen. The smell of cherries took me by surprise until I spotted a pie on the messy counter. The crust was lumpish and under-baked. I suddenly felt sorry for Lori. Her son was missing and her pie was a flop. She'd never win the Gilded Cherry with a pie like that. Jack saw it too and shook his head. Then I handed him Erik's cell phone and filled him in on what I had learned.

There was a part of Jack that was obviously miffed I'd gotten there first, and a part of him that was truly grateful. The guy had a lot on his plate.

"Gotta be honest," he said after listening to all I had told him. "I'm gravely concerned about the kid. The way I see it, it can go one of two ways. The boy's terrified and he's running from someone, or he's been involved in all this nasty business from the start. I'm not sure which."

"Those were my thoughts exactly. Do you really think Erik murdered Jeb?"

"God, I hope not. But whenever drugs are involved anything's possible, even the unthinkable."

"But why? Why would a boy like Erik do such a thing?"

"Same reason he was stealing bicycles and selling steroids to his teammates last year. Money. You told me about his room. Lori told you that her son bought all that stuff? I know my gaming systems, Whit. And with a fifty-inch TV and all those games? That doesn't add up."

"Erik does have a job, Jack. He works at the orchard and inn."

"True. But a pusher makes *just a wee bit more* money than a busboy or day laborer." Jack was being sarcastic, but I got his point. Still, the notion of anyone murdering their best friend over something as senseless as drugs just didn't make any sense to me.

"This Finn guy," Jack said. "I'd like to speak with him. Maybe your dad can help with that."

"What's the verdict? Is the boy in there?" Dad looked anxious. He and Dr. Engle had joined my friends on the porch, all six of them holding what looked to be the rest of the village at bay.

Jack shook his head. There was no easy way to say it. For a town where crime was virtually unheard of, a murder and a poisoning within two days had everyone on edge. Now they were about to learn that another employee of the Cherry Orchard Inn was missing. One look at Dad's face and I could see he was keenly aware that his dream of keeping his beloved inn was swiftly slipping from his grasp.

Dammit! I could not let that happen!

"Was he abducted?" Carleton asked.

"No," Jack answered, then announced to the crowd, "Erik went missing yesterday and never came home. That's all we know. We need to find him." He stopped talking, and I realized he was staring at someone. I followed his gaze.

"That's Kenna," I whispered. "Erik's girlfriend."

Kenna looked up, locked eyes with Jack, and turned. She was trying to get away.

"I got this," I said. "Give me your keys."

"What?" Jack hesitated.

"Look, you're the law. You have to manage this crowd. You have to let them know what's going on and how they can help. That's not my bailiwick, and we both know I'm far better at talking to girls than you are." Jack raised a brow at the insult and dropped his keys in my awaiting hand.

Kenna was fumbling with the keys to her own car when I grabbed her by the arm. "Wait!" I said. "We need to talk."

"I can't! I can't talk to you," she cried, looking scared. Apparently Kenna had had a change of mind. Then, lowering her voice, she added, "I promised I wouldn't."

"Did you promise someone you wouldn't talk to the cops?" Kenna's response was a deer-in-the-headlights look. "Well then, we're good, because I'm not a cop. Come on. We're going to sit in that Jeep and have a little chat. Erik's life might very well depend on it."

We were securely seated in Jack's Jeep, which, aside from a bag of uneaten Danish and the prevailing smell of cherry-stuffed pastry—

with a hint of wet dog—was remarkably tidy. I opened the bag and offered it up. "Who made you promise not to talk to the cops, Kenna? Erik or Finn?"

She pulled out a Danish. She was just about to take a bite when she replied, "How do you know Finn?"

Ah, so it was Finn. A man that hot who was working over a couple of teenage girls had to be up to no good. I applied my friendliest smile. "I don't, really. I saw him at the bar during yesterday's event. He's kind of hard to miss."

She swallowed a bite of Danish. "Totally. He's so raw, so wild. He's not like the others, ya know?"

"I get it. I really do," I said, nodding my head. Unfortunately, I actually did get it. "I grew up here too," I told her. "A man like Finn's not quite the same as a boy like Erik or Cody."

"Right?" she agreed, pronouncing the word as a question. There was a dreamy look in her eye as she continued nibbling the pastry.

"Probably has a tattoo." This I said out of mere selfish curiosity.

"Yeah. He does. Right here." She brought her right hand over her left breast. "It's so badass."

My heart, blast it, was beating a little too rapidly as I said, "Don't tell me. It's a gold-dusted Quidditch ball, isn't it?"

"What? No! God, that's so flippin' lame. It's a wolf!" she declared, with a look that let me know she had at least seen the guy shirtless. "With mesmerizing aqua eyes, just like Finn's. It's so hot, looking at that wolf. It's like you're staring right into his soul, or something."

"Hmm," I mused aloud, conjuring the image. It sprang to mind a bit too easily, and I had to admit it was kinda hot. I shook my head, attempting to expunge the thought. "So, you and Finn are pretty tight. You guys hang out together and smoke pot?"

Kenna narrowed her eyes and took another bite. She stared at me in silence, measuring me up as she chewed.

"Look, I'm not a cop," I said. "I don't judge. But I do need you to answer the question. Does Finn give you pot?"

The girl, coming to some conclusion, swallowed the Danish, then sneered with attitude as she said, "Finn gives me whatever I want."

I didn't know quite what to make of that, although I assumed that whatever Kenna wanted from the bartender was probably illegal. "Does Erik know that you hang out with Finn?"

"*Yyyeahhh*. He, like, introduced me to the guy. He's the one who brings us there. It's not like I'm sleeping with him or anything."

"Who else goes with you?"

"Me, Brynn, Bill, sometimes Kayla … " She looked at me and frowned. "Cody used to."

I gave a respectful nod and pressed on. "And where does Finn live?"

Kenna grew quiet, suddenly losing interest in the half-eaten pastry. She set it down and stared at me. "Like, I don't even know how to explain it."

This threw me for a moment. How could she not explain where the guy lived? "Kenna. This is very important." I placed my hand over hers, forcing her to look at me. "We're all worried sick about Erik, and I know he was selling drugs, drugs he got from Finn. I need to talk to Finn. You're going to have to try to explain where he lives."

Her eyes glistened with unshed tears. "You … you think Erik was selling drugs? No. No way. Why would he? He's got a good job. He works at the orchard and does odd jobs for Mr. Vander Hagen."

Erik worked for Tate? Tate never mentioned this. Interesting, I thought, and asked, "But if Erik wasn't selling drugs, why was he hanging out with Finn?"

She looked at me as if I had just asked the stupidest question in the world. "Duh, because Finn's a total badass. He gets us, and he gives us whatever we want. Who wouldn't hang out with him?"

Who wouldn't indeed! It was a dangerous combination—a badass-hottie-dirtbag with an unlimited supply of drugs and alcohol, and a pack of bored teenagers. Yet if I had learned anything from my stint in advertising it was that nothing, nothing, is ever really free. My God, hadn't any of these kids watched *Pinocchio*? What happened to foolish little boys (and girls) when they went to Pleasure Island? Sure it was all fun and games…until they all turned into donkeys. And what do donkeys do? Donkeys do whatever their handler tells them to do, that's what.

I had a sinking feeling that Cody, Erik, Kenna, and whoever else had fallen under Finn's spell were now essentially nothing more than his donkeys. And donkeys were expendable.

"Kenna, I'm not joking." I stared into her large brown eyes. "Where does Finn live?"

"I…I don't know where he lives!" she snapped. "I only know where he stays, where we find him."

"And where's that?"

"In the woods."

Her declaration made the hair on the back of my neck stand on end. The man stayed in the woods, and I would bet my iPhone he would know how to walk through them silently and not be seen. I had looked right at him yesterday, and he had looked right at me. He knew who I was. I opened the glove box and searched for a pad of paper, knowing Jack would have one. He did, and a pen. "Here," I said, and put the paper and pen in her hand. "Draw me a map. Show me how to get there."

I watched as Kenna sketched a rough outline of Cherry Cove, and I watched as she carefully placed an X in the vicinity of the place they meet Finn.

The pieces of the mystery were beginning to fall into place.

Thirty-Nine

The crowd in front of the Larson house was breaking up as Kenna and I finished our conversation. I made her promise that she'd go home directly, lock her doors, and not leave until Erik was found. Despite the glaring moments of pubescent-stupidity, Kenna was a sweet kid, and I could tell she cared deeply about her friends. She also promised to call me if she heard anything regarding Erik.

Shortly after Kenna left the Jeep, Jack opened the passenger-side door and got in.

"The search parties have dispersed. Everyone's been instructed to keep an eye out for Erik and to call me if they find anything. So, how did it go with Kenna?"

"Surprisingly well." I handed him the pad of paper. Jack buckled up. "Where should we go?" I asked.

"Police station. I met your friend Giff. He told me you left your car there, and also said to remind you to stop playing detective and get your pie ready for the bake-off. It begins in two hours, I'm told. As for Mr. McGrady himself, he's getting a ride back to the inn with Tay and Hannah. Your dad took Carleton. So, what am I looking at?"

I put the key into the ignition and started the Jeep. "A map. Kenna drew it. That's where they meet Finn."

Jack stared at the picture a moment. "Oh, it is a map—a really crappy one, though. Nothing's to scale."

"So Kenna's not an artist. However, lucky for us she happens to be a minor with a penchant for weed, alcohol, and bad-boy hotties."

Jack turned his fiery head to me. "A girl after your own heart."

"Funny. But I don't do drugs." This I added while strategically omitting the fact that I didn't really do the whole bad-boy hottie thing either, but I'd hardly admit that to him.

As I drove us back to town, I told Jack everything that Kenna had told me about the high school kids and their relationship with the inn's new bartender, Finn. When I was done, Jack looked impressed. I don't know why, but that look, coming from him, filled me with pride.

When we reached the police station, I parked the Jeep next to my car. I marveled anew at the sixteenth-century Scandinavian log cottage replica, complete with its decorative carvings and blooming window boxes. And I marveled a little at the man sitting next to me.

"So," I said, "now all we have to do is find this Finn character. I think he's the key to everything that's been going on at the inn. I can't believe you live here," I added, not sure why I'd said it.

"Yeah. I live here. It's got electricity." Jack shrugged, feigning nonchalance.

"And plumbing?"

"Supposedly. It's rumored to have all the modern conveniences, including an eco-friendly roof maintenance system."

I peered out at the thick sod roof and grinned. "Ah, for your 'kids.' I met them when I dropped off MacDuff."

"The goats prefer to be called by their names, Thing One and Thing Two." Jack grinned back. "Although I'm not entirely sure which is Thing One or Thing Two, but they know. Duffy knows too. He's the alpha. But enough about my awesome police station and cool pets. Back to this Finn character, if that even is his real name. The first thing we have to do is find the guy. Did you actually look at this map? It makes no sense. Look where she put that X. It's clearly on state land, but Whit, there's a lot of state land here. Another thing—I doubt the guy lives in this spot. It's more probable that the place he brings the kids to is a makeshift campsite, or party den, and not his actual home. Believe me, he's not the first one to think of partying on state land. And then there's the problem of motive," Jack continued. "So, we know that Finn is a squatter, a drug pusher, and likes to party with underage teens. There are many violations here, clearly, but it doesn't necessarily make him a murderer."

"But what if he has bigger plans, Jack? What if he's masterminding a lucrative drug ring and he's using our cherry orchard as his base? Maybe that's what Jeb overheard? Maybe Finn was the guy Cody was going to squeal on? And maybe he's the person Erik is running from?"

Jack nodded, then added with a troubled look, "Or running to. The point is, we're never going to know until we find him. And, little thanks to this map, we still have to figure out how to do that."

"Brock Sorensen!" I said. "He does the payroll. He's got to have contact information for every employee of the inn."

"You're right. Excellent thinking, Bloom." Jack took out his phone.

"I got this," I said, and called Dad. A moment later I had Brock Sorensen's phone number. I watched as Jack made the call. He scribbled an address and phone number next to Kenna's map and thanked Sorensen.

"Well?" I asked.

"Sorensen doesn't have much on the guy. Name's Finn Connelly. Says he picks up his checks at the inn. No phone number for him, and the only address he has on file is the same one he has for the other bartender, Bill Bachman. He assumes they live together, because he's seen them drive to the inn together on occasion. Sometimes, he says, Finn just shows up, no car, no bike. He just shows up."

"Interesting. I assume you got the address for Bill Bachman?"

"Of course."

"Good. Buckle up," I told him and started his Jeep back up.

"What are you doing? Don't you have a pie to bake?"

"Don't worry about my pie. I'm a professional. I have two hours, and you have an address. Between you and me, I believe I can help you find this creep Finn *and* win a pie bake-off."

"Such confidence. Such drive. Now that's the Whitney Bloom I know."

As we raced across the peninsula in search of Bill Bachman, Jack searched Erik's cell phone, calling some of his contacts. None, unfortunately, were very helpful.

"No one's seen Erik since he left the inn yesterday afternoon. Another thing of interest? It doesn't appear Erik or any of his friends have any contact information for Finn. It's actually pretty smart on Finn's part, especially if he's engaged in illicit behavior. The guy knows how to cover his tracks, which means he's no amateur. And get this. No one's actually seen him in the town of Cherry Cove. The only place this Finn person seems to exist is at the inn and on state land. It's as if the guy's a ghost or something."

"Or a Sasquatch," I added pointedly. "Ever since I arrived, I've had the feeling something is watching me from the woods. And then I keep seeing those twig-faces. They look like a Sasquatch! What if it's him, Jack? What if it's Finn? But why me? I never saw the guy before yesterday. And believe me, I'd know if I had."

I could feel Jack staring at me from the passenger seat. "I don't know, Whit. If I had to guess, I'd say it's because you're the owner's daughter. Your inheritance is at stake here. You've come all this way to snoop around, and maybe he feels that you pose the greatest threat to whatever game he thinks he's playing."

"Oh," I said, feeling a little deflated. "I thought maybe it was because he's attracted to me."

"Seriously?" Jack was grinning.

"Of course not. It was a joke."

"I mean, he could be," Jack added, and this time, I was happy to note, he wasn't grinning. "Guys can do some pretty strange things to get the attention of the woman they fancy. Take Bill Bachman, for instance."

"What about him?"

"He's obsessed with Greta Stone, the reporter."

"What? Are you serious? How do you know about that?"

"I noticed it last night, when I went over the tapes of the interviews Greta dropped off—"

"Greta Stone was at your police station last night?" Why did that bother me so? And why did Jack look amused?

"Yeah. I asked her to bring over the tapes. Remember when I told you that Greta was really great at getting people to talk on camera? Well, she got nearly everyone staying at the inn to talk, and also Bill Bachman. In fact, he was one of the only employees to speak with her. Mostly so he could flirt with her on camera, and partly to cast blame on your dad as the murderer. The guy could barely focus on the interview due to his eyes being glued to Greta's—well, you know. He tried to speak with her a couple more times after that, but it was only a ploy to chat with her."

"Creepy."

"Nah. It's just normal guy behavior."

"No, I'm talking about Greta Stone being at your police station. Creepy. You were just talking with her, right?"

Jack grinned. "Do I detect a hint of jealousy?"

"Don't be ridiculous." I lifted a hand from the wheel and waved it nonchalantly, ignoring a very real surge of anger at the thought of Jack and Greta. It was unsettling, that feeling. More unsettling? I didn't even know why I felt it. "You're a grown man," I added in an attempt to prove my point. "You can … you know, with whoever you like."

"Thanks," he said, then quickly changed the subject to continue talking about the case. Unfortunately, I wasn't paying much attention to what Jack was saying. I was too busy imagining him and the gorgeous, long-legged Greta entwined together up on the lush green grass of the police station roof. I didn't know why I was picturing them on the roof, but I was. I pulled into a parking lot, thinking about Jack and naughty, naughty Greta! Grrrretah!

"Whit. Were you just growling?" Jack was staring at me through narrowed eyes.

"What? No. Just clearing my throat." There was a very real possibility I'd just lied.

"Really?" he said, opening the door. "Because I distinctly heard growling. You coming?"

Bill Bachman lived in a unit of a building that once, quite obviously, had been a motel. It was the type of low, one-story motel that had sprung up all over the peninsula during the 1950s, and from the looks of this one it should have been bulldozed out of its misery years ago but wasn't. The owner, who had put just enough money into the place to keep it from being condemned, rented out the tiny, ramshackle units on a monthly basis to those who couldn't afford better. And from the *No Vacancy* sign out front, there were apparently quite a few folks working on the Door County Peninsula who couldn't afford better. That was the dirty underbelly of the tourist industry: grossly inflated prices that drove the locals to live in places like old, run-down motels.

I followed Jack to door number five and stood aside as he knocked. No one answered. "Bill," he called out, "this is Officer MacLaren of the Cherry Cove police department. I need to speak with you." No answer. Jack knocked again, and again.

"How convenient for Finn," I remarked. "Everyone connected to the guy mysteriously goes missing." Jack shot me a troubled look and gave the door one more fervent knock.

"You lookin' for Bill?" The voice came from the graying head of a woman who was peeking out of door number six. "Not gonna find him here, hon. Bill cleared out twenty minutes ago. You just missed him."

"Do you know where he went?"

"Nope. Not a clue." The woman, a round, pleasant lady in her sixties, shrugged. "I saw him loading up his car. Officer MacLaren, isn't it?" She looked Jack up and down and grinned. "Bill drives an old Chevy Impala," she offered. "Dark green. You gonna write this down or what?"

"Yes. Thank you." Jack pulled out his little notebook and scribbled.

The woman continued. "I thought it odd, him packing up like that on a Sunday. I've never seen Billy out of bed before noon on a Sunday. When I asked where he was going, he said that he had quit his job at the Cherry Orchard Inn and didn't feel like stickin' around no more."

"He moved?"

"Moved, or went away for a while." The woman stepped out of her doorway and came over to us. "What's he done?" she asked in a tone that invoked motherly concern. "Is he in trouble or something?"

"No. We just need to ask him a few questions." Jack was speaking gently to the woman, steering well clear of the fact that Bill was now a prime suspect.

She stared at Jack a moment longer, then reached under the door mat and pulled out a key. "Here," she said, handing it to Jack. "His friends know where he hides it. Billy may be a little squirrelly, and too fond of the weed for his own good, if ya know what I mean"—here the old woman winked—"but he's a good boy at heart. Go on in and have a look around. Just replace the key when you're done."

Bill's apartment was tiny, and just a wee bit nicer than the outside of the building. Of course, he wasn't there, and it didn't take long to determine that he'd left in a hurry.

"We really need to talk to this guy," I told Jack, feeling panic taking hold. "He's the only one who seems to know anything about Finn. How are we going to find him now? Got any bright ideas?"

"Of course," Jack said, pulling out his phone. "You know me. I'm full of bright ideas." He hit a number. I assumed he was about to report an All-Points Bulletin on the dark green Chevy Impala, but to my extreme annoyance he didn't. "Greta," he cooed into the phone in a voice that was pleasant and cheerful, "hope you're not busy. Hey, I need a huge favor."

Forty

"Why, you ask? Because men are silly, shallow, vain creatures, that's why." The look Jack cast me after this explanation was ironic and resigned, which annoyed me to an even greater extent. He was driving twenty miles an hour over the speed limit in his unmarked Jeep Wrangler, weaving through cars like a race car in a video game. It should have unnerved me, but it didn't. I was too focused on the fact that he'd called sexy Greta Stone instead of real backup, and that her number was readily available on his phone.

I leaned back in the passenger seat and crossed my arms. "Yeah, I get that. But why Greta?" As soon as the words left my mouth I instantly regretted them. I sounded whiny and jealous.

Keeping his focus on the road, Jack replied. "You obviously didn't watch the tapes or you wouldn't be asking that question."

"Okay, so she's beautiful—if you're attracted to that long-legged, bimbo-esque, Barbie sort of look—but do you really think Bill, who's obviously scared and running for his life, is going to fall for it?"

The coppery head turned to me. "Whit, you're overthinking this. You're also overestimating Bill's intelligence and underestimating the power of Greta's long-legged charm." At his mention of Greta's legs, a wry grin touched his lips. I gave him the eye, which was enough to wipe the grin off his face. He whizzed past two more cars, then said, "Don't be jealous. The first rule of catching criminals is to think outside the box, and that's exactly what I'm doing."

"Obviously. Way, way outside the box. And I'm not jealous."

"I'd believe you if it wasn't written all over your face. Trust me. Greta's okay once you get to know her. Sure, she's the media, and a bit of a bimbo, but she's our bimbo. She's on our side, Whit."

"That I believe. However, you're utter poop at reading expressions. This isn't jealousy," I lied. "This," I said, gesturing to my face, "is skepticism. The reason this expression is glued to my face, if you must know, is because I don't think your silly plan is going to work."

"You sure about that? Want to back it with a bet … like dinner at the place of one's choosing?"

"I could use a good dinner," I said, and flashed a well-practiced, confident grin. "Oh, you're on, MacLaren, on like Donkey-Kong!"

As much as I hated to admit it, Jack had a better grasp of male vanity than I did, or so it appeared the moment we stepped through the doors of Ed's Diner in Sturgeon Bay. Marge, our waitress from yesterday, had gone deep undercover, hovering near the cash register while holding a tray laden with two cups of coffee and two slices of cherry pie à la mode. She'd been waiting for Jack. The moment he appeared, her eyes nearly popped out of her head with excitement.

"Favorite booth's already taken, love," she offered with a wink. I wondered how long she'd been standing there practicing that line. "A friend of yours has arrived. *A lady friend*," she added covertly, then noticed me standing behind him. She cast me a look that could only be described as confused. "Oh, Miss Bloom. Nice to see ya again." She cast a questioning look at Jack before hoisting her tray. She then indicated for us to follow.

Jack leaned near my ear. "Looks like you're out a steak dinner."

Great. Another blow to my pride delivered by Jack. First Greta, then his crazy plan involving Greta, and now a dinner I could hardly afford. Was he planning on inviting Greta to that too? Probably, I mused, staring at the glossy blonde head and blinding sheen of air-brushed make-up poking above the top of the booth. You can do this, Bloom, I told myself. She's on our side, remember? Correction, Jack's side. Grrrrrr.

Before Jack had the chance, I plopped down on the bench next to Greta, enjoying the shock on her face.

"Greta Stone. What a surprise seeing you here. You were at my orchard the other day interviewing murder suspects. Whitney Bloom," I said, hoping my smile didn't look as forced as it felt as I held out my hand. "A pleasure to meet you."

Greta's smile was forced too, and she looked baffled as she shook my hand.

I then turned to the startled man sitting across from her. "Oh my gosh! Bartender Bill! I didn't know you two knew each other? What a surprise!"

"Bill, honey?" Greta, regaining her composure like a pro, placed her hand over the bartender's. "You've met Whitney Bloom? Of course you have. You work for her daddy." For a hearty, corn-fed, cheese-curd loving Wisconsin girl, she was certainly oozing Southern charm.

"He does," I said. "But we've never been formerly introduced." Before Bill could protest, I took hold of his other hand. Bill smiled cautiously. He was right to be cautious, because at that moment Jack slid into the bench beside him, trapping him between the wall and the table.

"Bill," Jack said softly. "We need to talk, buddy."

Apparently Bill wasn't in the mood. A primordial fear seized him. His thin face paled, his body went limp, and his hand slipped from my grasp. Then, like some disjointed rag doll, he slid under the table. Marge was about to plop down the pies when he struck the floor, taking out her legs. Marge and her pies toppled onto the booth, landing on top of Jack. At that same moment, Bill shot out from under the table and headed for the door.

"I got this!" I cried, peering under the table at Jack. He was kind of adorable, squished as he was between sticky pleather and grease-splattered polyester. He grunted in reply. Marge was flailing her arms and legs like an upturned turtle. I gave a thought to pulling her off him, but then thought better of it. Bill was getting away.

I sprang from the booth and gave chase, my red church-going sweater billowing out behind me like a baby cape. I caught my reflection in the glass of the door as Bill ran out. I looked pretty flippin' cool, I thought, and kicked it up a gear. People were watching! I didn't see the giant shadow rise up in the glass until it was too late. I hit the door at full tilt and bounced back, landing flat on my bum and skidding across the floor. Gasps, oohs, and a late warning of "Oh for cripes sake! She's gonna hit the glass!" filled the diner. I rolled to my knees and tried to stand, but I was trapped in my sweater. I was just about free when something grabbed my arm and yanked me to my feet. It was, to my astonishment, Tate.

"Whitney?" He was just as confused as I was.

293

"What the heck are you doing…?" My jaw dangled a bit as I stared at him. There was really no time for talking. "Quick," I cried. "Bill Bachman. We need to get him before he gets away!"

If Tate was anything, he was fast—high school wide receiver fast. Bill was just opening the door of his car when Tate grabbed him by the arm and spun him around.

Intelligent people didn't try to fight Tate, especially those with the build of a string bean. Bill, apparently, wasn't intelligent. Desperate is what he was. And desperate people do stupid things, like kicking other dudes in the giblets. His aim was solid, and Tate, doubling over as a stream of colorful expletives poured from his mouth, went down like a stone.

"Bill. Stop!" I cried. Like that was going to work! The guy was in flight mode, entirely forgetting about his car and heading for the busy road. I had no choice. I climbed on the hood of his car and jumped, launching into the air like a short-caped Wonder Woman in sensible white tights. I wasn't nearly as graceful, but I did fly—six whole feet across the pavement into Bill. We both went down with a thud. Bill fought to get away. I held on like a clingy girlfriend, digging my nails into his skin. Jack and Greta caught up to us as we were flopping across the parking lot like a couple of dirty fish trapped in the same fishing line.

"Help," Bill croaked from beneath me. "For God's sake, help me!" He was trying to look up at Jack.

Jack pulled a pair of handcuffs from his pocket and knelt beside us. There were still remnants of pie on his face and clothing. "I'd like to, buddy, but honestly, I don't know where to begin."

Forty-One

Bill Bachman was in a heap of trouble. He had thirty thousand dollars cash in his car and refused to answer Jack's questions about where he got it, or his relationship to Finn Connelly.

This infuriated Tate, given that he'd spent the morning at the Sturgeon Bay police station answering questions. Now it was Bill's turn, and Tate wasn't having any of Bill's tight-lipped stubbornness. Removing the bag of ice from his crotch, my ex-boyfriend stood up from the curb, ready to make the guy talk the old-fashioned way, when Jack intervened.

"Easy there, big fella. Haven't you heard? We're PC now. Can't touch 'em no matter how badly we want to. Besides, the squad car's here. Best leave this to the professionals. Don't want to spend any more time in the station than you have to."

"But Erik's life is on the line!" Tate protested. "He knows where Erik is, by God, and I'm going to make him talk."

"We'll make him talk," Jack assured him. "Don't you worry. And while we're doing that, you need to get Whitney back to Cherry Cove.

She told me she can take down creeps and win a pie bake-off. She took down a creep, all right. Let's see if she can go two for two."

Tate was unusually quiet as he drove Jack's Jeep back to town. The moment he spoke, it became instantly clear why.

"Babe, I can't believe you thought I was somehow involved in all this." He looked sullen and hurt. "Has your opinion of me sunk so low? I was only trying to help those boys."

"I'm sorry, Tate. I wanted to believe you had nothing to do with it, but... well, I've believed in you before..."

"And I've let you down," he finished for me, looking remorseful. "I know. But we're not exactly talking apples-to-apples here. This is murder. It takes a huge leap of depravity to commit murder."

This was true. Murder wasn't exactly the same thing as cheating, and I felt pretty awful that I'd believed the worst of him. For both our sakes, I thought it best to change the subject. "Did you know the kids were into drugs as well?"

"No," he said, and gave a remorseful shake of his head. "I thought the alcohol was bad enough. I mean, I even talked to them about it— the dangers of getting drunk and operating watercraft. Or how alcohol can alter your judgement, making you think you can do things you know you shouldn't do."

"And they didn't listen. Don't beat yourself up over it. Men, I find, can be exceptionally difficult."

"Obviously not your friend Giff," Tate challenged. "I had no idea you two were so chummy-chummy."

I crossed my arms. "We're friends. Giff used to work for me. And, for your information, he is super difficult, but in a whole other way. That reminds me. I never did thank you for helping put out the fire last night. I heard you were quite the hero."

"Just doing my job as a volunteer firefighter. I'm glad you and Cody got out before something even … even worse happened. Jesus, babe, you could have been killed. Do you think it was Bill who started it?" Tate's face darkened at the thought. "I should turn this Jeep around and beat him to within an inch of his life, Jack MacLaren be damned."

"No, you shouldn't. Bill's in trouble enough. The irony is that he could have gotten clean away with all that money, at least for a while, but was stopped because of Greta. Jack knew Bill had a thing for her, but I never would have believed he'd risk so much for a cup of coffee and a slice of pie."

Tate was unnaturally quiet. I stared at him, opened-mouthed, until he shrugged. "Well, you know, he's a guy. And she's *Greta Stone*. You met her. She was interviewing you back there, wasn't she?"

"She was trying to. Her mistake was that she live-streamed the entire takedown on her cell phone. Great legs or no, when one calls someone's dad a murderer on the news and doesn't apologize, one doesn't get the answers one is looking for. She asked me what was going through my mind when I took Bill down, and I told her I was thinking about the cherry pie bake-off at the inn. I took the opportunity to keep plugging the event, and my online bakery, until she got the hint and left."

Tate chuckled. "So that's why she left. I didn't know. Was in too much pain to pay attention to Greta. Believe me, Whit, great legs aren't so great when they're attached to a grasping, self-centered bimbo. But hey, she helped MacLaren, so that was pretty cool. It's the craziest thing, but now that he's a cop he does pretty well with the ladies. You should be proud of him. He was your geeky little shadow back in high school. And I'm proud of you for entering one of your pies in the bake-off. About time. But you, ahh … might want to rethink your outfit. No offense, but you look like you've been rolling around in the gutter."

∞

I was used to working fast, but rushing the presentation of a pie to be judged isn't a great strategy. Thankfully, Grandma Jenn was still at her house waiting for me. She and Mom had gone straight there after Jeb's memorial service. It had been a rough day for my gran, yet she was happy to hear that we were closing in on Jeb's killer. The moment Tate and I walked through her door, she rushed us to the kitchen and made Tate tell her everything while I attempted to make a deconstructed pie look good enough for the cherry pie bake-off.

It helped that I'd made all the components last night. All I had left to do was assemble the layers. My first task was to cut the flaky sugared phyllo crust into triangular slices and place them on individual fluted papers. I then piped on the almond cream, topped it with the brandied cherry filling, and repeated the layers. Once my pie slices looked perfect, I place them on a round cake plate in the shape of a pie. When two plates of eight slices were completed, I garnished each with a dollop of whipped cream and put a cherry on top for good measure. Since Tate was starving and had been deprived of his lunch at Ed's Diner, I made him a huge slice of his own.

"Ammashing!" he exclaimed through a mouthful of pie.

"And they look even lovelier, dear. These have got to be the prettiest pies the bake-off has ever seen. Now run along upstairs to the guest room. I hung a dress on the door that'll look just darling on you." Grandma Jenn placed the pies in a carrier and turned to Tate. "Be a dear, Tatum, and open the door. Whitney will be down in a minute."

It was more like ten minutes, really, after squeezing into one of Grandma Jenn's 1950s classics. I felt like an elegant June Cleaver as I swept down the front steps to the car in Gran's vintage red cocktail dress, the one with the white polka-dots.

"Babe. You look stunning." Tate was no judge of fashion, but his open adoration was a real confidence booster after I'd literally rolled in the gutter with a slimeball.

"She does indeed," Gran chimed in. "That's my lucky dress. I won a lot of cherry pie bake-offs in that dress."

"I'll bet." Tate remarked, turning his dimpled grin on Gran. "After all, what self-respecting pie judge could resist a woman in a dress like that?"

The gathering under the tent was even larger than it had been for yesterday's wine and cheese tasting, which made me a little nervous. So many participants, and so many cherry pie enthusiasts, Giff and Carleton being chief among them. They were already seated at the head table with their judges' hats on. Giff waved when I walked through the door. Carleton was busy chatting with one of the contestants. Oddly enough, I felt a welling of pity when I realized that Lori Larson wasn't under the tent. She'd baked a pie, had probably given it her best effort too. But all that seemed trivial, I supposed, when your son was missing.

"Whitney!" Hannah cried, shifting my attention. Her bright smile and infectious enthusiasm were enough to wipe all thoughts of murder and missing boys from my mind. She waved me over to the sign-in table, where she and Tay were working.

"You nearly gave us a heart attack, waiting like that until the last minute. Holy Mother of Sugar! Are those your pies?"

"Indeed they are." Tay grinned. "Bursting with tart cherries, almond cream, and a hint of brandy. You need to try one, Hannah, only we'll have Whit add more than just a hint of brandy."

Hannah liked that idea and handed me my number. "Quick, fill us in on what's happened." As she scribbled my name on the sheet, Tate and I briefly told them about Bartender Bill.

"Bill Bachman, that little weasel!" Tay exclaimed. "Well, can't worry about him now. Whitney has a pie contest to win. Probably shouldn't be telling you this, but that old busybody Edna Baker has a real nice-looking entry this year, and she's been kissing up to Giff something fierce. She's invited him to her place tonight for dinner. I heard her tell him that she's already baked him her famous Sunday night chicken potpie."

"*Edna*," Grandma Jenn seethed. "Ooh that's low, even for her. What single young man can refuse a home-cooked meal from a woman who purposely dresses like Marie Callender's grandmother?"

"Her *ugly* grandmother," Tay added with a wink.

Grandma Jenn ignored our giggles. She continued her tirade. "And Gifford's so skinny. That old frock she's wearing practically oozes home-cooked goodness. And I have to admit, she does make a mean chicken potpie. I should have known she'd stoop to bribery. She used to promise Jeb all kinds of things before the judging began, most of which can't be mentioned in polite society."

Tate glanced at Edna and shivered.

"Shameless old busybody," Tay added. "Char told me how Edna thinks you have a secret cherry tree, Jenn. Edna said that's how you win every year—that and the fact you were literally in bed with..." Tay wisely stopped there.

"Don't worry, dear. It's all true but for the part about bribery. Practically from the day she moved here, Edna's been trying to find my prized cherry tree. Jeb even caught her poaching cherries from the orchard. But she hasn't found my tree. It's my best-kept secret. I tried to keep my love for Jeb a secret too, but I didn't do a very good job of

it. The truth is, I loved him. I should have said it sooner—more often."
Gran's chin began to quiver, and her pretty blue eyes filled with tears.
I wanted to hug her but my hands were holding pies. Tate, bless him,
beat me to it.

"There now, Jenn," he said, wrapping her up in his muscular arms.
"Jeb knew it. Believe me, he knew it, and likely still does. Let's get to
our seats."

I set my pies on the appropriate tables and joined them.

"Ladies and gentleman," Dad said, talking into the microphone.
The crowd fell silent. "Jani and I are overjoyed at this wonderful turnout for what has become a very special event here at the Cherry Orchard Inn. The cherry pie bake-off is the final event of our weekend-long
Cherry Blossom Festival. As I'm sure you are all aware, this year's
festival saw its share of tragedy, and our dear friend and expert pie
judge, Jeb Carlson, is no longer with us. We thought about canceling
this event, but then we thought what better way is there to honor Jeb's
memory than by making this year's cherry pie bake-off the best one
yet."

After the applause died down, Dad gestured to the table at the
front of the tent. "This year I'd like to welcome our two guest judges,
Mr. Gifford McGrady, all the way up from Chicago, Illinois, and Carleton Brisbane, currently living on that lovely yacht moored in the
Cherry Cove Marina. I'm sure you've all seen it—that giant white
dream of a boat that Tate Vander Hagen's trying to pass off as his
own?" This elicited a wave of laughter. "This year, it was also suggested that the judges be blindfolded, focusing on mouth feel and
taste instead of presentation. I liked that idea. Our very own Tay Robinson will assist Mr. McGrady. Hannah Winthrop will assist Mr. Brisbane. Now, without further ado, let the tasting begin."

Each pie was brought to the head table, one at a time, to be sampled by the blindfolded judges. I had to admit, it was far more entertaining to watch than in previous years. The hand-feeding created its own hilarious challenges. Then, as the judges tasted each pie, they made witty remarks, each man trying to outdo the other with choice words and descriptive imagery. Giff was a master at this, yet Carleton caught on quickly. At times it was like watching stand-up comedy instead of a pie contest. But it felt good to laugh after so much tragedy. The entire community had come together for this celebration of the tiny stone fruit that had put us on the map. And it all came flooding back to me, why this place was so special. Cherry Cove was about friendships, and families, and helping each other through hard times. Sure, there were rivalries, but that was just a part of human nature. This was my home, and I'd missed it.

I cheered Tay and Hannah on as they struggled to feed their chosen judge. Giff had Tay in a fit of giggles. Sometimes he'd turn his head right before the fork hit its mark; sometimes he'd start responding to a heckler in the crowd.

Carleton, on the other hand, was being more flirtatious with Hannah, fanning the flames of her crush on him, which was hardly a secret. What was he playing at, I thought, leading her on like that when he'd asked me out to dinner? As I watched Hannah blush with joyful embarrassment, I felt a sharp pang of guilt. Because I knew how she felt. I'd fallen under Carleton's spell too. But Hannah was my friend. I'd promised her I wouldn't let a man get in the way of our friendship again, and I intended to keep that promise. It was a pity, but there was nothing else for it. I would have to cancel my dinner date with him.

The pies kept coming, and the judges kept plugging away, relaying their comments about each pie as the girls hastily wrote them down. They'd narrowed it down to just a handful of their favorites, mine and

Edna's among them, when Brock Sorensen caught my attention. He was standing at the side of the tent, indicating that he wanted a word with me.

"When I couldn't find a real address for Finn Connelly, I decided to check all the information he gave me when he was hired back in February," Brock whispered. "Nothing about the guy checks out. It's all fake." The cheating vegan looked utterly depressed by this revelation.

"What? But shouldn't you have checked it when you hired him?"

"I should have," he admitted with a self-admonishing grimace. "But he was a really good bartender—has an engaging mannerism about him. I didn't want to risk losing him."

"So you suspected the material he gave you wouldn't check out?" I found this a little troubling.

"Not exactly. He said his green card had expired and he was in the country illegally. I thought, hey, there are millions of illegals in the US. What harm would it do to turn a blind eye to one more? Besides, he's Irish. Women love his accent."

Troubling as this was, Brock did have a point. "Okay, but from now on, never again. This Finn guy is a serious scumbag. I can't say for sure he's the one who murdered Jeb, but it's not looking good. We need to find him."

"I'm sorry, Whitney. I have no idea how to help you with that."

I was pretty upset when I got back to my seat. Tate wanted to know why, so I told him.

"Damn it," he whispered, his face darkening again. I understood now that for Tate, this had become personal. "I'm going to find that Irish bastard if it's the last thing I do."

It hit me, suddenly. "Tate, you knew that Erik and Cody were stealing your boats. Do you know where they went in them?"

Tate shrugged. "Not exactly. But I did follow them one night. They took the boats across the bay and about a mile or so down from the old lighthouse, well past the bluffs and the cave where we found all the missing wine. I watched them pull up on a weedy stretch of shoreline located on state land, in the middle of nowhere."

I thought of the shoddy map Kenna drew—where she'd put her X—and suddenly grew excited. "Do you know how to get there? Could you find it again?"

"I don't know. I suppose I could. Why?"

"I'll tell you why," I said, "after they announce the winner. Look, it's between my pie and Edna's. Their blindfolds are still on. Holy cobbler!"

"Dear God, did Giff really choose Edna's?" Tate couldn't believe it.

"Yes, he did," Grandma Jenn added with a frown. "Never underestimate the power of a potpie bribe. Looks like she's pulled out all the stops this year, her pie included. Cherry chocolate surprise. She must have caught wind that Whitney was entering a nontraditional pie as well. *Ooh, Edna.*"

I shook my head. "Cherries and chocolate. That's just about the best combination on earth. Hardly the thing a person like Giff could resist. Still, why do I feel as if I've just been bitten by the dog I've been handfeeding for five years?"

"Because you have. Hey, wait. Look. Briz has chosen yours! Whitney," Tate said, staring intently at me, "it's a taste-off!"

Forty-Two

It was a taste-off, one of epic proportions. There had never been a taste-off in the history of the cherry pie bake-off before—likely because there had never been two judges—and the entire tent was abuzz with excitement. Dad consulted the judges on the rules, and it was decided that everyone without an entry in the contest would get to decide the winner. The two pies were cut. A bite of each was placed on a tiny paper plate. Then, once every crumb of the pies had been plated, they were handed out to the awaiting spectators. After sampling each bite, the tasters were then required to head to the judges' table and place a tally mark under the pie they liked best—either my deconstructed cherry pie or Edna Baker's cherry chocolate surprise.

"Don't worry, dear," Grandma Jenn said, patting my hand. I was staring at her plate—at the dark smudge where the sample of Edna's pie had been. "It's good, but a little heavy on the chocolate. It overwhelms the delicate balance of cherry."

I took the fork from Tate's hand and scooped up his bite of Edna's pie before he knew what hit him. He was about to protest but was too late. "What?" I mumbled through a mouthful of cherry-chocolate bliss. It was, I had to admit, surprisingly phenomenal. "Like you were really going to vote for her." I swallowed and turned to Grandma Jenn. "It's good, Gran. Really good."

"But so is yours, dear."

A crowd had formed at the judges' table. Everyone was casting their vote, and I'm sorry to admit that the sight of the Gilded Cherry trophy, sitting up there for all to ogle, had really super-charged my competitive side. I wanted to win. I wanted to get my hands around that dang Gilded Cherry trophy! And Giff knew it.

I looked at Giff then. His blindfold was off and he was staring right at me, feigning surprise—surprise that he'd picked Edna's pie over mine. As if he couldn't taste the chocolate in there! And I wasn't buying his manufactured air of "innocent mistake" either. There was nothing innocent in his impish grin. Edna's pie was really good, but Giff was my friend, or at least he'd been my friend when he'd entered the tent. Either his judge's hat had been too tight or Grandma Jenn was correct—Gifford McGrady had sold his vote for a homemade chicken potpie dinner.

"Ladies and gentlemen, the votes have been cast. Will Edna Baker and Whitney Bloom please come to the judges' table."

Grandma Jenn squealed and crossed her fingers.

As Edna and I stood together on the raised platform with the great golden cherry of a trophy before us, Carleton spoke. "We've had the pleasure of tasting fifty-seven delicious pies, and while you all are wonderful bakers, we've had to make a tough decision on which pie will be the winner of this year's Gilded Cherry award. Gifford and I were doing pretty well until we came across the two extraordinary pies you've all just had the pleasure of tasting. We couldn't decide, and it looks as if you couldn't either. It was a dead split down the middle, with half of you voting for Whitney's deconstructed cherry pie and the other half for Edna's cherry chocolate surprise. And the pity is, there's not even a scrap left for one more person to cast the deciding vote. What this means, ladies and gentlemen, is that we have a tie!"

The crowd cheered. Edna and I were both awarded the Gilded Cherry Trophy, and pictures were taken. Since there was only one actual trophy, it was decided that I would get it for the first six months and Edna would keep it for the remainder of the year. Both our names would be added to the prestigious list of winners. I'm not going to lie—it felt good to have the Gilded Cherry Trophy in my hands, even if it was for only half a year.

But it also meant that the Cherry Blossom Festival had come to an end. The nineteen guests staying at the inn had fulfilled their obligation; Jack had cleared them all as murder suspects and they were free to go home. They might have been traumatized by the murder of the orchard manager at the beginning of their stay, but thankfully the real terror of the weekend had been restricted to the staff. My parents had bent over backward to make sure everyone's stay had been as pleasant as possible. And each guest had been given a voucher for a free weekend. It was the best my parents could do. Only the McSweenys had denied their voucher, stating that one visit to the Cherry Orchard Inn was enough.

Once all the guests had checked out, the remaining employees were told they had the next two days off. It really wasn't safe at the inn with the killer still on the loose. Hopefully he would be apprehended soon.

And for that I had a plan.

Giff, having earned his Sunday night chicken potpie dinner at Edna's with his vote, begged Tay to accompany him. "She was so grandmotherly, but I may have given her the wrong impression. Once she got hold of that giant gilded cherry she became very handsy. Couldn't keep her old dough hooks off me. Come with me! Whitney, for obvious reasons, wont. It'll be fun," Giff promised. "After dinner, we can go back to your place and shop online for rare antiques."

"Stop," Tay told him, holding up a hand. "You had me at potpie."

Hannah, meanwhile, had to run off to teach her Sunday evening yoga class at the retirement center. The moment my friends left and the inn was relatively quiet, I pulled Tate into my bedroom and shut the door.

"Whoa. Hands in your pockets, lusty dutchman," I reprimanded him, realizing he'd gotten the wrong impression.

"But babe, aren't we celebrating your sweet victory?"

"No. You're still on probation. Listen, we have to call Jack and see if he's learned anything from Bill Bachman."

Tate lounged on my bed while I made the call. Jack, I could tell, was frustrated. Bill had been in the interrogation room since I'd tackled him to the pavement and was still refusing to talk.

"It's okay," I told him. "Just get back to the inn as soon as you can. I've learned a little something about Finn. Sorensen's just checked his references and they're all fake. Also, his green card's expired and he's an illegal. And you're not going to believe this, but Tate once followed the boys to their party spot. Remember Kenna's map? Well, Tate thinks he's been there and believes he can find it again."

The plan was simple. At midnight, Jack and Tate would slip into a canoe with MacDuff and paddle to the place Tate had seen Erik and Cody land their stolen boat weeks before. Standing off-shore, providing backup, would be Sergeant Stamper and Officer Jensen in the police boat. Hopefully MacDuff would pick up Finn's scent and lead Jack and Tate through the woods to the party spot. They hoped to catch Finn sleeping there, or at the very least unaware. Jack had a hunch that Erik might be there as well. Because even more than catching

Finn, he wanted to find the boy. If Finn ran, or posed a threat, Stamper and Jensen would rush in, flooding the area with light and extra manpower. Jack was aiming for simple, silent, and quick.

Simple, maybe. But this plan had a few hitches, namely the fact that I had taken a refreshing nap and was determined to tag along. My argument was sound. I deserved to go because I was knee-deep in this case as well. I'd also had my share of encounters with whoever it was that was terrorizing the cherry orchard. Although Finn was the suspected culprit, I harbored some doubts; the creature I'd seen in the woods still haunted me. This, wisely, I kept to myself.

Jack eventually relented, mostly because the rallying point for the midnight mission was in my family kitchen and a little because it was my canoe they were borrowing. I even promised to stay with the canoe once we'd landed, although it was a promise I wasn't entirely committed to keeping.

It was nearing midnight when Dad sauntered into our command center with his buddies Dr. Engle, Brock Sorensen, and Briz. Jack was just getting ready to slip on his bulletproof vest. He stopped and threw them a questioning look.

"We've been thinking," Dad said. "Wouldn't hurt to have some backup for your backup. We've unmoored the cabin cruiser and will stand off unless you need us."

"You just want to watch, don't you?" Jack asked them.

"We've all endured a lot at the hands of this man. The boys and I want to see justice done."

Jack nodded, told them to keep their distance, and disappeared under his bullet-proof vest. Both he and Tate were dressed head-to-toe in black—black cargo pants, black turtlenecks, black knit caps, black makeup under their eyes. I wasn't sure why just under their eyes, but Tate had insisted. Jack was armed with his police-issue Glock and had on his utility belt. Tate wore an athletic cup and carried his old baseball bat. Not gonna lie, they both looked darn good—hunky-special-ops-dudes-getting-ready-for-a-night-raid good—only Jack was a cop and Tate a recreational sailor. Nonetheless, I found I was actually excited to be alone in a canoe with them. It might be a little awkward, given my past history with Tate and my newfound interest in Jack, but hey, we were all friends. Right?

Then Hannah arrived, wearing her skin-tight yoga clothes and breathing like she'd just run all the way from the retirement center, which she actually might have done.

"Hannah," I said, giving her a hug. "Have you come to wish us luck?" One look in her eyes and I knew luck wasn't involved. But Carleton Brisbane was.

"Yeah. Exactly. Hey, Carleton. Fancy meeting you here."

It wasn't fancy at all, and no one in the room was fooled. Hannah looked at me, invention blazing behind her eyes, and then exclaimed, "Whit called me. She wanted me to be here for moral support."

"I'm going in the canoe with Jack and Tate," I admitted. "But Dad and his friends are going in the cabin cruiser. There's plenty of room in there."

"Cool," she said, staring boldly at Carleton. "That's a great idea."

"Actually," Carleton said, throwing that same bold look at me, "I think you should go in the canoe with Whitney and the boys. They've made her promise to stay with the canoe once they reach their destination. It might be a good idea to have another body there to make sure that she does."

Forty-Three

We're all fitting in that canoe?" Hannah was a little miffed, especially after watching Carleton climb aboard Dad's big motorboat with a freshly brewed latte in his hands. Mom had packed the men a stakeout cooler containing roast beef sandwiches, kettle chips, and cherry chocolate-chip cookies. She offered some to us, but Jack declined. We were, after all, on a mission.

"Great," Hannah continued, "so where do you want me to sit?" She lowered her voice and whispered, "In other words, I'm asking who you have the hots for. Come on, Whit. I've seen you staring at them both. Pick one and I'll sit by the other. It's going to be a long paddle. Might as well enjoy it."

I looked at the canoe with Jack in the bow and Tate in the stern. Where to sit? Truthfully, I wasn't entirely certain myself. Tate ... or Jack? There was a real possibility it might be Carleton instead. I wanted to kick myself. Had it really been so long that I couldn't even decide which man I liked anymore? Cheek-dimpled Tate, tall ginger Jack, or savory suave Carleton? Did I really just think that in my head? Holy cobbler! This wasn't an ad. This was a seating choice, and I was failing miserably. I looked at Hannah and clearly saw that Carleton was off the menu. For me it was a Tate or Jack dilemma, and in their current special ops state, I couldn't decide.

"You have three more seconds," Jack offered softly. "Then we're shoving off, with or without you two."

"Coming," Hannah said. She got in the canoe, making the choice for me. She chose the spot at Tate's feet, leaving me to sit directly behind Jack. I took up my seat and a moment later found MacDuff in my lap as well.

It was a beautiful night, clear, cool, star-strewn. The moon, a perfect crescent, was just bright enough to help Tate guide the canoe along the meandering shoreline to the spot he'd visited weeks ago. Paddling under the stars always had a touch of romance about it, but that mood was thoroughly broken by the thought of Finn Connelly and the fact that there were four people crammed into the canoe. Also, MacDuff was the only one getting his belly rubbed, the needy pooch.

"Is it just me," Hannah began softly, breaking the silence, "or does anyone else feel like we're in a *Scooby Doo* adventure? We even have our own Scooby Doo." She leaned forward and ruffled the fur on MacDuff's head.

"I totally get what you mean," I said, smiling. "Two guys, two girls, and a dog all squished in a little canoe at midnight heading for the spooky woods. It's a real *Scooby Doo* adventure, all right."

"I'm Daphne, of course," Hannah declared.

"Really?" I hiss-whispered. "You're Daphne? On what grounds?"

"On obvious grounds. I'm tall, blond, and flexible. Tate's Fred, and Jack's Shaggy."

"So I'm Velma?" This seemed unfair. "Velma's chunky and wears glasses," I protested. "How am I Velma?"

"Velma was also smart," Jack was quick to add. "She had grit. Hey, didn't Daphne and Fred have a thing?"

"I thought that was Fred and Velma," Tate added, his white teeth glittering in the dark night.

"No," Hannah shot back. "It was totally Shaggy and Velma."

Hearing this, Jack hesitated. He missed a paddle, throwing off his steady cadence.

"What? No. That's totally ridiculous," Tate replied, frowning at Jack's back. "They were just friends."

"Were they?" Hannah quipped, her simple question dripping with innuendo.

"Hey," Jack hiss-whispered. "Be quiet. We're almost there."

"You two stay here," Jack said as he and Tate got out of the canoe. We'd run aground on a muddy bank at the end of a reedy little stretch of water. Tate had guided the craft through a narrow inlet that sheltered this particular landing. It was well hidden and would have been nearly impossible to detect by those who didn't know what to look for. Thankfully, Tate had known what to look for.

MacDuff, the first one out of the canoe, was bounding along the bank with nose to the ground and stub-tail wagging. He caught a scent, bounded to the reeds, and stilled. "Over here," Jack whispered to Tate. He pulled out a small flashlight and turned it on. MacDuff spun from the reeds and ran to Jack's side, tail wagging excitedly. "There's a footpath leading up this way." Jack turned off his light again. "Wait here, okay?" he whispered through the darkness. "And, Whit, if anyone but us should come this way, don't be a hero. Cry out and wait for backup. Got it?"

I didn't reply, feeling it was more of a rhetorical question. Jack wanted to believe that Hannah and I were going to sit quietly in the canoe, and I was going to let him.

The moment Tate, Jack, and MacDuff disappeared up the path, I turned to Hannah. "Okay, ready? I want to find the bastard responsible for terrorizing the cherry orchard and bring him to justice." I was already out of the canoe, my Skechers sinking slightly in the mud. I pulled a small flashlight from the pocket of my sweatshirt, flicked it on, and swung it in a wide arc.

"What are you doing?" Hannah hissed.

I pointed my flashlight at her face. "I'm trying to find that path." She had her arm up, blocking her eyes. "Are you coming, or are you really going to stay here and wait?"

"I'm coming," she said. I dropped the light and continued scanning our surroundings. "So, what's your plan? You do have a plan, don't you?"

"I do, and my plan is to not be seen until our help is needed." My flashlight scanned a row of scrub pines, tall grass, bushes. "Say the guys find Finn," I continued, "and Finn puts up a fight. We come in, create a diversion, and BOOM! Finn gets distracted and Jack and Tate take him down. We get profuse thanks for our help. You get to tell Carleton all about it, and I get to kick Finn Connelly square in the giblets when no one's looking." I pointed my flashlight at the reeds. "Only don't tell anyone about that last part, okay? I don't want that blowing up on Twitter or anything. Giblet-kicker's not a great tagline for a baker. Wait. What the devil is that?" I caught a glint of metal through the reeds.

Hannah stumbled out of the canoe and got her shoe caught in the mud. She panicked, left it, and ran behind me as I continued to investigate. "What is it?" she whispered. I felt her peering over my shoulder as we ventured further into the reedy water.

I stopped walking. "It's a boat," I replied, slightly unnerved. I nearly panicked when the reeds started moving, wiggling and swaying as if someone or something was in there. I felt the wind then and took a deep breath. It's nothing, I told myself. Stay calm. I lowered the light and scanned the boat. Just as the beam of light dipped, my heart caught in my throat. I thought I saw something big move in the darkness. I hit it with the light, but nothing was there, only reeds. My imagination was working overtime. And no wonder, because the boat I was looking at was the exact same one Jack had seen fleeing the shore that morning. According to Tate, it was one of his.

"So, what's it mean?"

"It means Finn's probably here, and possibly Erik Larson as well."

"You got all that from that little boat?"

"Shhh!" I hissed. It was still so fresh in my mind—the feeling of being watched—the memory of that creature. I knew that beyond the reeds, sitting near the entrance to the cove, was Stamper and Jensen in the police boat. Dad was out there too somewhere. Now, however, all was dark and quiet, with the exception of Hannah's heavy breathing and the quiet rustling of the reeds.

"I should have gone with Carleton," she moaned.

"About that. Hannah, I think you're far more into him than he's into you."

"What? How can you say that?"

"Because you're here with me and not sitting beside Carleton on my dad's boat." She thought about this and frowned. "Don't worry. Truth is, you're too good for him. Just stay close, okay?" I whispered. Then I turned from the boat and headed up the embankment, traveling the path taken by Jack and Tate. I still had my flashlight on. I didn't think it mattered. It wasn't very bright; certainly not enough to keep Hannah from stumbling over logs and stubbing her one bare foot on rocks.

"Ouch!"

"Shhh! Do you hear that? MacDuff's barking. They're somewhere over there." A few more yards and I saw the clearing. I could still see the red glow of a hastily banked campfire, the wan light softly illuminating what looked to be a couple of casks of wine sitting beside it. And beyond that were the dark, humplike shapes of a grouping of dome tents.

"Is that pot?" Hannah whispered, giving the air another good sniff. "Damn. Someone's been having a good time."

"Where are Jack and Tate?" I pointed my flashlight at the campsite but the beam was too dull to reach that far. Besides, both men were wearing black, and if they were still in the area they'd most likely be hidden from sight. "Did they miss this?" I wondered out loud. "How could they miss this? Oh my God, maybe they were captured and need our help." Curiosity kicked in and I walked forward, suddenly filling with visions of taking down Finn, rescuing Jack, Tate, and Erik, and solving the mystery of who killed Jeb Carlson all without the aid of a man. I'd be the hero. I'd tell the world that Hannah helped me, even though clearly asking her to help was out of the question. She was still miffed at me for voicing my concerns about Carleton.

"Whit. Where're ya going?" she hissed. "I thought your brilliant plan was to stay out of sight?"

"I have a new plan. It's called find Jack and Tate. I don't see them over there, or MacDuff." No sooner had I stopped talking than I heard a twig snap directly behind Hannah. I spun around, pointed my flashlight, and froze.

"Hey, Veronica Mars. Get that fudgin' thing out of my eyes!" Then Hannah stilled. "What? What is it? Stop staring behind me like that. You're totally freakin' me out."

"No. No, don't look."

Too late. Hannah spun around and came face to face with the hideous creature, the same looming, faceless Sasquatch that had shadowed me through the woods that morning. It was creepy—*Creature From the Black Lagoon* creepy—all covered in dead leaves and dripping with spindly moss. It was here, and even without seeing its face, I could tell it was pissed.

"What the ... " She never finished the sentiment. The Squatch jerked quickly, bringing the butt-end of a rifle hard against her head. Hannah collapsed on the ground like a rag doll.

"No!" I breathed, starring directly at the creature. It had a gun. Did Squatches use guns? I might be wrong, but I didn't think they did.

The barrel of the gun lowered, pointing directly at me. "Whitney Bloom," the Squatch said with a distinctly Irish lilt. The accent took me off guard. I was staring down the barrel of a gun held by a hideous beast, yet the voice was all man. I was a sucker for a good accent, and damn me if he didn't have a deep, lilting, seductive voice. The sound of my name rolling off the Irish-speaking tongue captivated me a moment too long, and then fear kicked in. I saw the situation clearly. Every nerve in my body exploded.

"Holy mother of moss," I croaked. "You're not a Squatch at all. You're Finn Connelly in a flippin' ghillie suit! And you've just attacked my friend!" It all made sense—how he could hide in the woods in plain sight—how he could sneak around, undetected. All he had to do was stand still, or lie flat on the ground and no one would see him. I tried to see the face behind the moss but couldn't.

"I've been watching you," he said. "Because, you see, you and I, we were destined to have our moment. And now, m'dearie, that moment has come." He jerked the barrel of his gun, indicating that I should walk back to the lake with him.

There were really only two options as I saw it. The first was to do a quick about-face and dash into the woods, screaming for Tate and Jack as I ran. But he could shoot me before I took two steps. The second choice was to go with the deranged Irishman, wait for my moment, seize his gun, and be a hero.

Jack had told me not to be a hero.

I wasn't in the habit of listening to Jack, so why start now?

The Irishman had a hot accent, but his gun looked dangerous. Would he really shoot me?

I was pretty sure he would. That was the whole point in pointing a gun at someone's face.

Screw it! You only lived once. I made up my mind. I looked at the sinfully ugly beast with the gun and changed my mind again. Dammit!

"Jack!" I cried, and gave Finn a swift kick to the gibs.

The ghillie suit was thick. The kick didn't have quite the effect I was counting on. Finn was still standing. He redoubled his hold on the gun.

I dropped my flashlight and ran.

Forty-Four

Somewhere in the distance, MacDuff barked. The dog had heard me, and I clung to that thought as I made a mad dash for the tents, half expecting to be shot in the back as I ran. But Finn didn't shoot. Instead, he let me go a dozen paces before hitting my legs from under me with the barrel of his gun. The impact was unexpected and painful. I stumbled forward, scrambling to find my footing. Jack's name was on my lips and I wanted to cry out, but the gun came again, this time hard on my back, knocking the air from my lungs. I flew forward and landed face down in the dirt, just like poor Hannah.

He was on me like a hunter on a fresh kill, pinning me with his knees while his hands grappled to secure my arms behind my back. I fought to catch my breath. Finn was quick, skilled, and painfully efficient. He was doing his best to prevent me from warning Jack and Tate. I rolled violently, trying to throw him off, but all I managed to get was a mouthful of dirt and a better view of the dark, lifeless form of Hannah on the ground. It scared me. I felt ill thinking of the hard blow she'd taken to the head and prayed she'd be okay.

My wrists were zip-tied behind me. A dirty rag had been shoved in my mouth. I was yanked to my feet and slung like a sack of potatoes over Finn's shoulder. Then he ran, back down the trail to the reed-infested shore. Every breath I managed to take was hard-won because my face kept slamming against the moss on his back while my stomach was pummeled by his broad shoulder. Finn was in a hurry because MacDuff was barking, and that barking was growing louder. I thought I'd even heard Jack's voice as well, or maybe it was Tate. Maybe they would get to me before the psycho did me in, just like he'd done to Hannah.

My hopes were dashed the moment Finn splashed through the reeds and dumped me into the boat. His rifle landed beside me, but with my hands zip-tied behind my back, it was useless. As Finn unmoored the little craft and pushed it free of the weeds, I struggled to a sitting position. I focused on the shore and thought I saw the reeds shimmy, as if displaced by a bounding dog. Jack would be close behind. Hope surged through me. I stood, took a step to the side, and was about to tumble overboard into the muck when Finn grabbed me and threw me back into the bottom of the boat. I hit hard. He removed the hood of his ghillie suit, allowing me to see the malicious grin on his handsome, night-dark face. Finn Connelly was a man keenly aware of his good looks and the impact it had on women and men alike. He was still smiling when he took his seat in the stern and cranked up the motor.

"Whitney!" Jack's frantic cry rang out from the shore, along with the faint sound of splashing water.

I raked my mouth along the edge of the bench and managed to pull the rag free. "Jack!" I croaked. But it was too late. We were deep in the reeds, Finn navigating the narrow waterway by the light of the moon and stars. All Jack had was a canoe, and a canoe was no match for an outboard motor.

"I have a question," I said, glaring at the man before me. Finn's eyes flashed at me as he guided the boat. He made no move to shove the rag back into my mouth, probably because it didn't matter now. He also knew I wasn't about to try again to jump into the unholy tangle of aquatic plants that surrounded us—because it was gross, and because I'd drown before anyone found me. I stared at him a moment longer, able for the first time to really get a good look at the guy. Although he was dark and edgy, I thought him more beautiful than handsome. There was a fragile sort of air about him—as if his looks had been more of a burden than a blessing. I actually sighed then, thinking it a pity that the guy had to be such an insufferable dirtbag. After all, Finn Connelly was rumored to be pure white-hot dynamite in the sack. I sighed once more. "So, if you can sell your filthy drugs anywhere, why set up business here in Cherry Cove, on my dad's cherry orchard? It's a pretty odd place. Probably not the best location for what you do."

He leaned toward me, looking slightly amused. "Ye'll be thinking this is about drugs?"

"Isn't it?"

White teeth flashed in the darkness. "Drugs, alcohol, sex ... certainly I give these freely to my young friends."

"You mean to tell me you're just giving your product away?" I was intrigued, and yes, slightly aroused—and not about the drugs or alcohol. "Far be it from me to criticize a murderous Irish drug dealer-slash-gigolo in a ghillie suit, but that's not very good business sense."

"O dearie, dearie," he admonished with a teasing shake of the head. "But drugs are not my business."

I raised an eyebrow at him. "Really? Then what is your business?"

321

His eyes narrowed. I wasn't sure he was going to tell me. Why would he? He owed me nothing, and clearly he had the upper hand in our current situation. Then, however, he relented. "I'm after cultivating friends," he said in his soft Irish accent. "I'm after building a special bond between us, a bond my friends are mindful not to break. And in return for my gifts, they'll be doing me favors."

My jaw dropped. It was utterly diabolical. The man had created a cadre of killer, drug-crazed teens. I glared at him. "You used your friends to murder a harmless old man and poison a boy?"

The dark brows furrowed as the lips pulled into a contradictory grin. "O dearie, I never ask my friends to kill, only to keep secrets."

"And when one of your friends is about to talk, like Cody Rivers was, you ... you try to kill them?"

"I'm afraid that's the deal, dear lass. An' what a pity 'tis. I hear he survived. He won't for long. To be fair, he didn't seek out Officer Ginger Nuts back there, but he did attempt to meet you, thinking no one would be the wiser. Foolish, foolish boy."

A cold shiver traveled down my spine at the callous way he talked about attacking Cody, and suddenly the beauty of the lethally handsome Irishman faded and I saw him for the soulless devil he really was. "And what about Erik Larson?" I asked. "He didn't talk. Did you attack him too?"

He raised a brow. "I did not. Unlike your wee man Cody, Erik understands the rules. He's just, shall we say, laying low for a while."

I didn't like the sound of that, but at least he'd indicated the boy was still alive. I wanted to strangle Finn, but the zip tie binding my wrists wouldn't budge. My plan was to keep him talking until I could cut through it with the sharp metal edge of my seat. Unaware of what I was attempting to do, the Irishman kept navigating the boat. "And

Jeb Carlson?" I asked him. "Don't tell me Jeb was one of your *friends* as well, because I won't believe you."

"Nay, he was no friend, and more's the pity. Because old Jeb, he was like me." Finn's dark gaze held mine. "Always snooping around in the woods, he was. Always watching. Well, dearie, I was watching too. Only he couldn't see me. Not with me dressed in my ghillie suit. But old Jeb, he knew I was there. He could feel me—sense me as I moved though the orchard. The old man had a habit of standing motionless. He was nearly as good at camouflage as myself. Sometimes I had to lie in wait, barely breathing, not moving a muscle, until he got tired of listening. Old Jeb Carlson suspected many things, including the drugs, and the alcohol I was after in the lighthouse, but he never hit upon the real reason I'm here."

"So you killed him?"

"I bludgeoned him with your father's own mallet and dumped him in the orchard. 'Twas easy, really."

"You're mad!" I seethed. "And what about the creepy twig-faces. That was you, wasn't it?"

"Aye, that was me. That was my wee game with you. I'm glad ye came, Whitney Bloom. And here I was thinkin' you'd never come. All the little tricks I played at the inn, none of that was enough. But Jeb's death, that got your notice."

"My God. You did all this so that I would come home?" I was, to say the least, aghast. "Do I even know you?"

Finn's only answer to this was an infuriating, sardonic, heart-stopping grin.

I needed to think fast. The guy was a cold-hearted murderer, and he was insinuating that I had been the target all along. Why? What had I done to him? I had no idea, but I was pretty darn certain I'd never laid eyes on him before this weekend. He wasn't about to tell me any more, so I tried another tactic.

"Well, we know who you are now, and what you've done. There's no escaping, Finn. Your only recourse is to tell me what it is you want from me, and I'll see what I can do."

He waited until I finished talking and then laughed. The sound was magical, and for a moment I fell back under his spell... until he opened his mouth to speak. "O dearie me but that's a grand one. Somebody told me they thought ye were smart. I heard ye baked pies, and now you're pokin' your wee nose into murder. But ye have failed to detect the simplest thread of this one. You may be fine at baking pies, but you're utter shite at solving mysteries. You disappoint me."

"Umm, *hello?*" I said, grabbing his attention and staring boldly back at his mocking gaze. "I'm sitting in a boat with the killer. How is this not solving the mystery?" I wanted to slap the insolent grin off his face. Finn quirked a brow, then shifted his focus to the bow of the boat. I turned and saw that the reeds were thinning. We would be in open water soon, where the police boat was waiting off shore in the darkness, along with Dad. I needed to keep Finn occupied until we came close enough for them to blind him with their lights. *Shite at solving mysteries?* I was about to open a can of whoop-ass on this dirtbag!

Finn was still grinning when he said, "Does it bother ye at all that you're missing two key pieces to this puzzle?" As he spoke he began ramping up the boat's speed. I frowned, wondering what he could possibly mean by that.

"Ah, you're thinking now. But you'll be strainin' your wee pretty head over this one for longer than we have, so I'll give ye a clue. The first is this. You'll be after finding my motive, I suspect, but ye never will have it. So, let's skip along to our second and final key to this puzzle. I told ye that I'm after causing trouble here, and I have. But now I'm after throwin' this place and your poor parents over the edge. Can ye guess how I might be doing that?"

"Seriously? You're a flippin' psycho. I have no idea what's going on in your demented little hea … " I stopped talking. All the blood left my heart in one gigantic thud. "Oh God," I uttered, knowing that the surest way to devastate any parent was to take away their child, no matter how old or unworthy that child might be. The Irish psycho was going to kill me.

"Ah," he breathed, staring into my soul with his night-black eyes, "so ye have figured it out at last. Maybe you're not utter shite at solving mysteries after all." I didn't even notice the rope in his hand until he tried to tie it around my legs. With the same practiced skill he'd used to bring me down, he bound my legs together. He then picked up the other end, revealing the anchor.

We were in the bay. The police boat was primed and ready. I looked Finn Connelly in the eye, stood up, and then I screamed.

Searchlights from the police boat exploded in the darkness and began scanning the area. They were farther away than I'd imagined, and it took a moment or two before they focused on us. I kept screaming. Another motor kicked on and I saw the flashing police lights. The boat was coming for us. I looked at Finn. The expression on his face sickened me. He was grinning again, and I realized that he'd known all along that the police boat would be there. He'd wanted them to see me. He'd wanted them to see the anchor held aloft in his hand. They would know the other end was tied around my legs. They would see me go in, and then they would have to make a terrible decision: save me or go after my murderer. If they tried to save me, they likely wouldn't get to me before I drowned. If they went after Finn, they had a chance.

It happened quickly. Finn pulled me to him with his other arm and placed a searing kiss on my lips, stifling my screams. It was heady and stomach-turning at once—a sickly sweet welcome to the watery death that awaited me. His lips had barely pulled away from mine when I heard the splash of the anchor. "Goodbye, Whitney Bloom," he whispered in my ear, the subtle Irish accent making my last farewell sound oddly nostalgic. Then he picked me up and tossed me over the side.

The moment I hit the water, I was engulfed in paralyzing cold. Then the rope around my ankles tightened and I was dragged helplessly down into the cold murky depths of Cherry Cove Bay, the memory of Finn's parting kiss clinging to me like a parasite. It sickened me that his would be the last lips to ever touch mine.

And worse than his kiss? As I sunk to my cold, quiet death I could hear the sound of my killer racing away.

Forty-Five

I was used to water. I'd spent all my life around it. I'd been a lifeguard in high school, and a sailor for longer than that. It was my second favorite element next to air, and yet I had never contemplated drowning until now.

Drowning was a cold, dark, lonely business. The mere thought infuriated me, causing me to fight against the weight of the anchor as it pulled me toward the bottom. But it was a useless fight. My arms and legs were bound, and although I'd tried to cut the zip tie around my wrists, I hadn't made it all the way through before Finn threw me overboard. As I sunk helplessly, I thought about my friends—about Jack and Tate, and Tay and Giff, and poor dear Hannah—but mostly my parents. How would they feel knowing I'd never be able to hug them again?

It would rip them in two. It would destroy them. And that was exactly what that freakin' crazy Irishman had wanted. Well, not on my watch, mister. Not if I could help it!

I waited until the anchor hit bottom. It was a deep bay, and my lungs burned. But I needed to act. There was no time to wait until someone found me. I doubted I'd even last that long. The thought was terrifying. I tried to relax and focus. I needed to focus. If I was ever to get that Irish dirtbag, I needed to get free. I exhaled slowly, relieving some of the pressure building up in my lungs. Then, using the best dolphin kick I could muster, I worked my way to the bottom, running my bound hands along the rope until I reached the anchor. I hooked my wrists around one of the sharp flukes and began to finish what I'd started: cutting the zip tie.

As I frantically fought against my bindings, I cursed the fact that my lung capacity wasn't what it used to be. I should have hit the lap pool daily. I should have run more and drunk less. Oh, who was I kidding? None of that mattered now.

I worked on the zip tie until the pain in my lungs was unbearable. My diaphragm was stricken with spasms. I was going to pass out, but I fought it. If I passed out it would be game over, and the Irish creepo would win. And I was not about to let that happen. I had an orchard and an inn to think about, not to mention my burning desire to avenging my friend Hannah. With that thought pumping through me like pure adrenaline, I pulled against the anchor fluke with all the strength I had left. My wrists burned with pain, but suddenly my hands came free. I quickly untied my legs, releasing another small string of bubbles as I did so. I could see them rise to the surface because this time there was light—just a small shaft reaching down through the murky blackness. Light! Someone was there. Someone had come to find me. It was a comforting thought. I didn't feel so alone anymore. With my last ounce of remaining strength, I kicked toward the light and the surface.

A strong hand grabbed mine, pulling me upward. The moment the cold air hit my face, I gasped and hungrily began filling my burning lungs.

The light on the surface was blinding. It came from the police boat, and right next to me was the canoe with Jack and MacDuff peering over the side.

"Whitney! Whitney, are you all right?"

I looked beside me and saw Tate. I realized he still had a strong grip on me and was treading water for the both of us. I'd never been more grateful to see him. Tate was the strongest swimmer I knew. Still gulping air, I nodded. "Finn," I uttered. "My God, don't let that dirtbag get away!

I was sitting beside Hannah in the police boat, wrapped in a blanket, with a cup of hot coffee in my hands and a warm dog at my feet, wondering why they'd let Finn get away.

"Why?" Jack cried, anger and frustration blazing across his face. "Because we saw that bastard throw an anchor into the water with you following after it! My God, it was the most gut-wrenching thing I've ever witnessed. I'm sorry, Whitney, but it was either you or Finn, and I'm not going to have another murder on my hands."

"Besides," Tate added, wrapped in a blanket of his own, "we like you a whole lot better."

"True," Jack concurred, then frowned. "But I explicitly told you to stay in the canoe!"

"I tried. But I thought you needed backup."

"Backup?" he seethed. "Stamper and Jensen are backup. You and Hannah were supposed to stay in the boat, and don't blame this one on Hannah."

"What?" Hannah, holding an ice pack to her head, sat up and looked at Jack. She squinted, grimaced, and slumped back against my shoulder.

"We need to get this one to a doctor," I whispered. "Finn gave her a good whack on the head."

"The truth is, Whitney, we'd never have found you if it wasn't for MacDuff." Although Jack still looked frustrated, the anger had left his voice as he spoke. "We were in the camp. We'd just found Erik. The kid was in one of the tents, lying on a cot and stoned out of his mind. Then MacDuff started barking. I came out of the tent in time to see him take off through the woods, heading for the canoe. He wouldn't have done that if something wasn't up, so we ran after him. Halfway down the trail we find Hannah, stumbling around like a drunken sailor and mumbling something about a Sasquatch abduction. Then an outboard motor fired up and we heard you scream. Tate picked up Hannah and we ran to the canoe, paddling after you like we've never paddled before. We broke through the reeds in time to see you being tossed into the lake by a shaggy manlike creature. Thank God Stamper and Jensen had the spotlight trained on you, marking the exact spot you went in."

Sergeant Stamper came over then. "The moment we heard you scream," he began, "we turned on the spotlights and cranked up the motor. It was an odd sight until we realized the guy was wearing a ghillie suite."

"Looking like that helped him sneak around without anyone noticing him," I said.

Jack nodded. He'd already guessed as much.

"Then you went in," Sergeant Stamper continued, "and Finn sped away."

"And you let him go because of me." I sighed.

Sergeant Stamper smiled. "You're far more important to us, Miss Bloom. But I don't think our ghillie-suited perp will get away so easily. A chopper's on its way, and the League of Extraordinary Gentlemen back there fired up the cabin cruiser the moment Finn went barreling past them. They'll run him to ground for what he did."

Sergeant Stamper had been correct. As the police boat swung in an arc, ready to head back to Finn's camp to retrieve an unconscious Erik Larson, Tate suddenly got to his feet.

"Oh my God!" he cried, pointing across the water. "They're going to …"

A loud bang rang out, followed by a column of fire shooting up from the darkness.

"Oh fer cripes sake!" Jensen exclaimed, and changed course once again.

The moment we came abreast of the accident, we were met with a gruesome sight. Apparently Dad and his League of Extraordinary Gentlemen, as Stamper had called them, had caught up with Finn. It was a dark night. Carleton had been driving the cruiser because Dad, after seeing me plunge into the lake tied to the business end of an anchor, had been beside himself with anguish and grief. It had been a smart move on Carleton's part to take the wheel. Anger had taken hold of him as well, and he was on a mission. He took off after Finn like a demon possessed, determined to drive the Irish psycho into the shore.

Finn had refused to comply.

Dad's boat was bigger and faster. Finn's stolen boat was easier to maneuver, and he was desperate—we now knew who he was and what he'd done, and we'd found the place where he'd been hiding. As Carleton explained it later, Finn made a sharp cut across the bow of the cruiser after realizing he was heading straight for a rocky outcrop. He almost made it, too. But the cabin cruiser was going full-out, and it slammed into the back quarter of the little fishing boat. The boat exploded on impact, and Finn, still in his ghillie suit, went flying headlong into the lake. By the time we arrived, all that was left of Tate's stolen boat was a scattering of burning carnage.

"Where is he?" Jack cried, desperate to get his hands on the man. He'd crossed into Dad's cruiser the moment we'd pulled alongside. I stood up as well and cried out to my dad. The look of tortured joy on his face when he saw me nearly broke my heart. He clearly thought I'd drowned.

The moment Dad was in the police boat, he gave me a hug that surely would have cleared all the water in my lungs, had there been any.

Not long after our little reunion, the police chopper arrived. It hovered over the site of the crash, scanning the black waves with its powerful searchlight. There was still no sign of Finn. It was assumed he had drowned. After all, he was wearing a cumbersome ghillie suit. All the faux leaves and moss dangling from every inch of the fabric would have swelled like a thirsty sponge, making the suit heavy and impossible to swim in. It would act like an anchor. Having literally been tied to an anchor myself, I felt there was some real poetic justice in such an end for Finn Connelly. Still, after Stamper ordered the divers to commence a search, I found myself hoping the guy was still alive. Yes, he was a ruthless killer, and he'd totally wreaked havoc on our cherry orchard. Nonetheless, standing on the deck of the police boat as I stared at the flaming carnage, I couldn't help from being haunted by his parting remark: *You'll be after finding my motive, I suspect, but ye never will have it.*

His words were oddly prophetic, and the longer the police searched for his body, the more likely it became that Finn Connelly had indeed taken his secret to the grave. It was his final senseless slap in the face, and it stung me nearly as deeply as being tied to an anchor and left to drown.

Forty-Six

There never was a Sasquatch lurking in the woods, just a vengeful drug-pushing Irishman in a ghillie suit, and to be honest, I'm a little disappointed."

"Me too," Grandma Jenn said sympathetically, plopping down in the chair next to mine. "A Sasquatch would have been easier to forgive, and it would have done wonders for tourism." There was a twinkle of mischief in her eyes as she spoke, but deep down a part of me knew she would have preferred it. After all, Grandma Jenn was a lot like me. We both found it easier to believe that the evils of the world were the result of otherworldly forces rather than the guiles of humankind. I gave an affirming nod and took another sip of coffee.

After the trauma of being in the hands of a killer, and after my near-death experience anchored to the bottom of Cherry Cove Bay last night, I'd emerged from my ordeal with an entirely new perspective. Nearly dying had changed me. For the first time in my adult life, I saw with crystalline focus what was truly important to me, namely my family and friends. The thought of never seeing any of them again was overwhelming. So was the thought of never again being able to sit in the magnificent sunroom of my childhood home and stare across the diamond-capped water to the picturesque town sprawled along the hillside—a town that was so intricately linked to my very existence. Although yesterday's bright sun had been replaced by a cool, overcast sky, it was still lovely. So lovely that I failed to notice the mug between my hands shaking until Mom gently took it from me and set it on the table.

"It's all right," she said, drying my cheeks with her warm hands. Her eyes were watering too, and I hugged her tightly.

"I'm sorry. It's just that I'm so thankful to be here—so thankful to be alive—and yet I'm so ... so damned pissed off! Why did he do it? The monster corrupted the young employees, killed Jeb, tried to kill Cody, and nearly succeeded in killing me—all for no better reason than to damage this place. And he targeted me. Why? What kind of crazy, demented flippin' psycho does that?"

There was no good answer to this. And because there wasn't, I was seized with the same sick, helpless feeling that had been haunting me for the past twenty-four hours.

After the devastating boat crash that killed Finn, Hannah and Erik Larson were taken to the hospital. Poor Hannah. She'd suffered a serious concussion and was held overnight for observation. Tay and Giff met us at the hospital and we stayed with her for an hour, making sure she was going to be okay.

Since Erik Larson was in the room next to hers, we couldn't resist sneaking a peek at his toxicology report. The kid was in a blissful state of inebriation and had barely been conscious when he was found. When we read the list of drugs in his system, Giff inhaled scandalously, Tay covered her mouth in shocked disbelief, and my eyes nearly popped out of my head. Aside from high levels of alcohol and marijuana, it appeared that Erik had also ingested the date rape drug Rohypnol. Finn

Connelly, nasty bastard that he was, had taken no chances with the young man. He'd wanted Erik hidden and incapacitated. Thank God he hadn't killed him. Erik knew that Jack would eventually want to question him, and knew that Finn knew this as well, so in order to avoid being murdered for a possible breach in their disturbing relationship, Erik chose the only course he saw available to him. He was smart. Oh, sure, he was going to have a hell of a hangover and he would have to face the wrath of his mother, as well as an uncomfortable interview with Jack, but at least he was alive. And there was more good news. Cody Rivers had come out of his coma. Our prayers had been answered—he was going to be okay. The fact that Finn didn't pose a threat to the kids any longer was a blessing.

After the excitement of the previous night, I was anxious to talk to Jack. We had a lot to discuss. Jeb's murderer had finally been identified and effectively stopped, and yet it seemed a hollow victory without a body, or knowing why Finn Connelly had done what he'd done. Giff, feeling the same pestering unrest, had gone to Tay's house while I was taking a nap. He'd decided to stay a few extra days in Cherry Cove and thought he and Tay could put their computer skills to the test and see if they could come up with anything on Finn Connelly that might indicate why he had terrorized the Cherry Orchard Inn. It was a long shot, and they knew it, but they wanted to try.

I leaned back in my chair and picked up my coffee again. "Mom," I said as another thought occurred to me, "where's Dad?"

A troubled grimace crossed her lips. "He went with Brock to meet with the bank and the insurance people." Her lip began to tremble as she continued. "They're trying to determine if the inn and the orchard can be saved."

"My God," I moaned, feeling all the blood drain from my face. It was the last nail in the proverbial coffin. "I'm so sorry." I said, holding her as she cried. I couldn't imagine what she was going through. Last night she'd learned how close she'd come to losing her only daughter, and this morning she was facing the imminent demise of her livelihood. I'd never thought it possible. I never would have believed that Mom and Dad could lose the Cherry Orchard Inn. Financial troubles were hard for any business to overcome, yet it still might have been possible. Now, however, the reputation of the inn had been damaged. That was harder to fix. In the ad business, it would mean serious rebranding and a pricey ad campaign, and there were still no guarantees. In a small, close-knit community where everyone knew everyone's business, rebranding often backfired. But it was worth a shot. I'd do anything I could think of if it might save my family's inn.

I pondered Mom's statement that Dad was with Brock. Why did it ruffle me so? Probably because Dad was awfully trusting of the guy. Jack had seemed to think Brock was okay, and Giff had even done a quick background check and found nothing that was cause for worry. But I nevertheless had a healthy amount of suspicion where Brock was concerned. He'd hired Finn without doing a background check. Really, who does that? And he'd seemed a little too surprised when he'd told me at the bake-off that none of Finn's information checked out. What if Brock had some connection to Finn Connelly? He'd only worked at the inn since the beginning of the year, and Finn had come aboard shortly thereafter. Although they were both willing to break the rules for their own self-serving needs, there was nothing further that linked them together. Still, it was definitely something worth looking into. I picked up my phone and sent a quick text to Giff with my request.

While I was busy consoling Mom, Grandma Jenn reappeared with a tray of sandwiches—rare roast beef and Havarti cheese on freshly baked Kaiser rolls. "Just a little something I whipped up," she told us, setting down the tray. It was just the thing. And I'd been starving.

"Did I mention that Jack called while you were napping?" Mom said a short while later.

"What?" I swallowed a bite of my sandwich. "No. You should have woken me. What did he want?"

"They found Finn's body in the lake this morning."

I set the sandwich back on the tray, suddenly losing my appetite. So Finn Connelly had indeed died. I was slightly dismayed by this. "Where'd they find the body?" I finally asked. "Did it wash up on shore?"

"I don't think so," Mom said. "It's at the morgue, but I don't think you should go see it. Anyhow, I doubt they'd let you in there again." Her eyes shot to my forehead, searching for the telltale lump. It was nearly gone, but I still sported a lovely bruise. Mom frowned sympathetically. "Besides," she continued, "from what Jack said, the body's not in the best condition."

"I can imagine. He drowned. It's bound to be mottled and bloated, and maybe even a little nibbled if we're lucky." This last bit I added out of pure spite. I reached into the pocket of my jeans for my cell phone, suddenly burning with the desire to call Jack. I looked at the phone and realized I'd turned the ringer off before my nap. I was just about to press Jack's number when Tate appeared in the doorway. I shoved my phone back in my pocket and smiled into his sparkling sky-blue eyes.

"It's true. Finn's body was found in the lake, Whit," he said, walking over to me. "But he didn't drown. Doc Fisker said he was dead before he ever hit the water. It was the direct hit from the bow of Baggsie's boat that did him in. And if on the off chance he wasn't killed on impact, the exploding ball of flame finished him off. Either way, there wasn't any water in his lungs, and not enough skin left on his hands to pull a good set of prints. MacLaren was fit to be tied when he found that out. Seems Finn's going to take his secrets to the grave after all. MacLaren's going to try dental records, but that could take weeks." Tate reached down next to me, picked up a sandwich, and took a huge bite. "Make's no sense at all," he said chewing. "The guy went to all that trouble to ruin this place, and now he's dead. Makes you wonder, doesn't it?"

"It makes you realize that you never really know what another person's thinking," Mom added, staring out the window. "He always seemed so polite."

"It was that accent." Grandma Jenn cast me a knowing look. "Accents can be very disarming."

Tate shoved the rest of the sandwich in his mouth and took my hands. "Enough talk about that bastard." He pulled me to my feet. "How ya feeling, babe? I nearly had a heart attack watching you tumble into the water tied to the end of an anchor. Can't believe you managed to break free. Thank God you did. I had a nightmare last night where I couldn't get to you in time. Christ, Whit, I thought I was going to lose you, babe. And I'm not going to let that happen. Not now, not ever."

"We can't thank you enough, Tate dear, for diving in after Whitney." There was adoration in Mom's eyes as she spoke, and a gin and tonic in her hand that she offered to him. It was Tate's favorite drink. Dammit! How did she do that? When had she had time to pour it? None of this concerned Tate, however. He took a hearty sip of the strong drink, made an appreciative sound, and set it down next to my coffee. My hand was back in his, and I had to admit, it felt good. It wasn't quite enough to erase the painful mistakes of our past, but perhaps having a near-death experience was enough for me to realize that Tate and I deserved a second chance.

We were in the middle of the sunroom, Mom and Grandma Jenn staring at us open-mouthed, when Tate employed his dimples to their fullest effect. I felt my knees weaken at the sight as butterflies took flight in my belly. And then he brought his lips very close to mine. He was going to kiss me. Holy cobbler! Was I ready for this? So soon? I had just come back to Cherry Cove. I had gone after a murderer. I'd almost drowned! And yet … and yet I found that I wanted him to kiss me.

Tate's lips were nearly on mine when a loud buzzing sound erupted in the room, breaking the spell and causing my recently frayed nerves to fire like buckshot from the gun of a spastic hunter. I squirmed out of Tate's grasp. "Sorry. Poor timing. I should probably get that," I told him and ran for the door.

Standing on the doorstep, holding a stunning bouquet of flowers, was Carleton Brisbane. My hand flew over my mouth. "Carleton!" I breathed, suddenly recalling that I'd agreed to have dinner with him. We'd never set a date; obviously that hadn't stopped him from taking the matter in hand, and I found that I liked that. "Those are … gorgeous," I said, taking the flowers. I inhaled their fragrance and smiled. Carleton. He was like a breath of fresh air—suave, handsome, and so very civilized. And he had money. Maybe even enough to save the Cherry Orchard Inn. Without another thought, I took his proffered hand and slipped out the door.

Tate and his kiss would just have to wait.

Forty-Seven

hope you don't mind that I took the liberty of setting up a little picnic for us? I thought it would be a charming first date." Carleton took my hand and led me down the inn's back walkway to an awaiting Gator.

"Where are we going?" I asked, utterly intrigued as I climbed into the passenger seat.

"You may find this a little cliché, but the orchard is still in bloom. The white of the blossoms look magnificent under this dull gray sky, and I thought it would be such a shame if every memory we have of your beautiful cherry orchard is blighted by death. The murderer has been found, and we are going to celebrate."

"Yes, yes we are," I agreed, smiling.

It was a scene from a fairy tale, I thought, spying the intimate table deep in the heart of the orchard. It was covered with a white lace tablecloth and set with fine china and crystal. A silver candelabra stood in the center, and beside the table was a bottle of wine chilling in a silver ice bucket. I was enchanted. The man had thought of everything.

Carleton lit the candles and pulled out my chair. Then he poured me a glass of the chilled wine as delicate petals fell like snow around us. It was everything I had dreamed of as a child. I felt like a princess, with Carleton my charming prince. Maybe he was my destiny, I mused, and smiled at him across the table. Beside him on the ground was a picnic hamper. Carleton excused himself and leaned over, pulling from the basket a plate of smoked Coho Salmon, a wedge of Brie, and a bowl of red grapes. Next he pulled out a tray of perfectly arranged crackers. He then picked up a cracker, loaded it with the tender salmon, and handed it across the table to me.

"Was that Vander Hagen's car I saw parked near the family wing?"

"Yep," I said with a nod, shoving the salmon-loaded cracker into my mouth. It was kind of a mistake. An explosion of smoke-tinged salty goodness awakened my taste buds, rendering me speechless. I grinned appreciatively and kept nodding, chewing until I could swallow again. "Fabulous stuff," I remarked, then explained. "Tate, I've learned, is like my parent's house elf—always there, always showing up where you least expect him. I took a nap this afternoon and when I awoke—*POOF!*—he was there, standing like a hero in the sunroom."

"Yes, he's quite the hero, but I hear you were the one who actually freed yourself from what was sure to be a tragic death."

I swallowed the lump that had suddenly risen in my throat and nodded. "True, but I was on the verge of passing out. If Tate hadn't been there ... "

"It's all right. No need to talk about such a terrible night so soon. Let's change the subject and focus on something more pleasant, shall we? How about that wine? Do you like it?"

Truthfully, I hadn't tried it. With Carleton watching expectantly, I picked up my glass and took a tiny sip. I was immediately struck by the flavor of cherries. It was cherry wine, and not a very good one. It was a little too sour and a hint too vinegary for my taste. However, I was not about to let a little glass of wine get in the way of my romantic dinner under the blossoms with Carleton. I set the glass back down and smiled. "Very nice. This whole dinner is so wonderful. I can't believe we're finally alone. Now that we are, I realize I hardly know anything about you."

"What would you like to know, Whitney Bloom?" Carleton rested his elbows on the table, folded his hands, and leaned in, grinning.

"Oh, like, everything," I said. He raised a brow at this, then reached for something in the picnic basket. While he wasn't looking I covertly dumped out my wine, pretending I'd finished it.

"Here," he said, "let's just skip to dessert, shall we?" He placed a plate before me, on which sat a piece of my deconstructed cherry pie.

"What's ... this?"

"Don't you remember? I told you that one day I would sweep you off your feet and you would know who I was. Do you recognize the pie? You ought to. It's your own recipe."

My eyes flew wide. "C-Bomb? You're C-Bomb? You're the man who's been writing to me over the internet?" I was intrigued, delighted, and yet a little disturbed as well. "Holy mother of mischief! Why didn't you say anything? I thought it might be you, but I never dared to dream ... "

An odd sort of look crossed his features as he stared at me. "It's truly amazing. I thought you would figure it out sooner." He reached over to refill my wine.

As Carleton spoke, the phone in my pocket vibrated. He kept talking while I looked at it. It was a message from Giff. My heart stilled. *Struck out with Sorensen and Finn, so Tay and I did a little poking around on Carleton Brisbane. Not his real name. Thought I recognized him. He's Francis Flannigan, CEO of Flannigan Industries, which is the holding company for*

Stay Fresh Feminine Products—the brand you single-handedly ruined with that ad!"

All the blood drained from my face as realization dawned on me. The final, heart-rending pieces of the puzzle fell in to place. Dear God. That Ad.

Help. With him now, I texted. *Call Jack.*

I had just hit send when the phone was yanked from my hands. I looked up and froze. Carleton had a gun pointed straight at me. He looked at the phone, snarled, and then threw it into the orchard.

"You lied to me," I said accusingly. "You lied to us all, Francis Flannigan." At the sound of his true name, his lips twisted into an ironic grin. "We've never actually met," I pointed out.

"Funny, that. And yet you took it upon yourself to make an ad that destroyed my brand. I lost millions, millions I couldn't afford to lose, because of you, Whitney Bloom."

"Now hold on a minute!" I cried, ignoring the gun to properly glare at him. "Your marketing department encouraged it. They loved that ad!"

"All a parcel of overeducated morons. They were charmed by you, their judgment impaired by your enthusiasm: 'A modern-day Dutch girl saves her boyfriend and all of Holland by stopping up a leak in the dyke with a super-absorbent Forever Free tampon!' How clever of you to make such an ad, and how foolish of my marketing department to unveil that rubbish during the Super Bowl. They've been dealt with, Whitney. But you needed to be taught a lesson as well. My nephew, Finley, convinced me of it."

My jaw dropped. "Finn Connelly? He's your nephew?" I'd never connected the two, likely because of Finn's Irish brogue, but it did make sense. As I stared at Carleton, I saw the slight family resemblance. Both men were handsome, but it was their mesmerizing aquamarine eyes and dark hair that were so remarkable ... that and the fact that they were both psycho killers.

"Finley Flannigan is his real name," Carleton added. "You met him last night, I believe? A crazy, baseless bastard with a winning smile and the soul of a thug? He was my late brother's son, you see, and my legal heir. When my brother passed away five years ago, Finn came to live with me in America, bringing his rough Irish ways with him. He was like an incorrigible pet. I spoiled him rotten and encouraged him to continue his education in substance abuse and fornication because he was so good at it. Finley liked money and all the things it could buy him. When he realized your ad spelled doom for the lavish lifestyle he'd grown accustom to, he convinced me that you needed to be taught a lesson. I wholeheartedly agreed. But, sadly, you'd already destroyed your career and were reduced to selling cherry pies on the internet by the time I caught up with you. That's when Finn encouraged me to strike up a relationship with you. He told me to toy with you—to draw out any thread of information that might be helpful. You see, he thought you were a desperate and lonely woman, and he was correct."

"What?" I cried. "I'm none of those things!"

"Then why were you so willing to chat with me online—a perfect stranger—and share with me your most intimate thoughts and the pathetic details of your life? That's the definition of desperate, my dear. I actually enjoyed our chats, and was even a little smitten as well, once I realized there was nothing left to take from you. But then you told me all about the Cherry Orchard Inn in Cherry Cove. Finn looked into it and became obsessed. It's quite a little gem."

"That's ... that's diabolical! You let your pathetic nephew talk you into ruining my parents?"

"Not just ruin, my dear. We were planning a hostile takeover. You're sitting on prime real estate, or haven't you noticed? This property alone is worth a fortune. Imagine what it would be worth with hundreds of upscale condos littering this bluff?"

"No," I exhaled, scandalized.

"Anyhow, while I worked you over on the internet for the past year, I also made several visits to Cherry Cove. Your former boyfriend, Tate, was quick to make me feel at home. He was enamored of my yacht, you see, and took me under his wing. He introduced me to your parents. And while I was elbowing my way into this charming little village, Finn got a job at the inn. He can be utterly charming when it serves his purpose. He was hired on the spot and began working his magic on the younger employees. While cultivating his young workforce, he also began to plague the inn. He had the kids do little things, like steal money or break things. They gathered rats and put them in the kitchen. These were just pranks, and the kids loved pleasing Finn. They loved the drugs and alcohol he gave them. His aim, you see, was to ruin the inn's pristine reputation. We'd always planned that our final blow would occur during the Cherry Blossom Festival, as we were certain that you'd come home and help your parents with the event. You were to witness firsthand your family business implode, which would remind you that your actions do have consequences. But you didn't seem inclined to come to the inn on your own. That surprised me. I thought you were a better daughter than that." Carleton's admonishing look shamed me.

"Hey, I am a great daughter!" I rallied, trying to ignore the crushing guilt. It didn't work; and Carleton's soft, condescending smile only made it worse.

"*Tsk, tsk,*" he said, waving the gun. "Continue to live in your own fantasy, my dear, but we knew how it was. And because we did, we had to take matters into our own hands. Jeb was the obvious choice. Finley knew he was getting close to the truth. Jeb was smart, and wily. He had to die, and I felt that if we framed your father, you were sure to come home. So I ordered Finn to steal the wine before the festival began. Then, on Friday night, I stole the croquet mallet out of Baxter's office. I was the one who pulverized the cherry pits in your grandmother's blender and poisoned Jeb's rum. Knowing his habits, I then ordered Finn to bludgeon Jeb's body with the mallet once the poison had killed him. He was to bring the body into the orchard and sprinkle some cherry pits by the old man's hand. That was for you, my dear—to pique your interest and induce you into a little snooping around."

"You planted those cherry pits?" I was aghast, mostly because it had worked.

Carleton, popping several grapes into his mouth, nodded. "Finn wanted to kill you for what you'd done to his inheritance, and I was happy to oblige him. I let him toy with you, hunt you, scare you with that little twig-face he was so fond of. When you survived the fire, that only made him want you more. He's a real woodsman, you see— an expert hunter who always catches his prey. When he wasn't staying on my yacht reveling in luxury, he was living in the woods where he could give voice to all his animal desires. I made sure he never had a shortage of drugs. And because of his looks and charm, he never had a shortage of friends either. But Finley was most excited to get his hands on you, my dear. Because with your death, your parents would surely part with this place, and for mere pennies on the dollar. I already had their confidence. Tate—loyal, trusting, big-hearted Tate— would see that they sold it to me. Your parents listen to him; he's so much like a son to them. But Finn screwed up last night. He hadn't counted on you surviving a drowning too. When I realized he was in danger of being caught, I was forced to make a hard choice. Part of me really loved that kid. But I was driving Baxter's boat, you see, and I couldn't risk Finn being apprehended. I had to run the crazy bastard down and kill him. And now, Whitney dear, it is time for me to finish what I began all those months ago."

Carleton stood. With the gun still trained on me, he turned to the picnic hamper and pulled out a metal can. It contained kerosene, I saw. I could only look on in horror as he began dousing the bases of the cherry trees with it. He tossed the empty can aside and pulled out a long rope.

"Come," he ordered with a flick of his gun. I stood up but didn't move. In the distance I could hear the sound of a motor approaching. Jack, I thought. Help was on the way. Carleton, too focused on burning down the orchard and killing me, just continued talking. "I'm tying you to this tree. You won't feel anything, my dear, once the tranquilizer takes hold. Damn," he said, looking levelly at me. "It should have taken effect by now."

I inhaled sharply and looked at my refilled wine glass. "The wine! You drugged the wine?"

"Very good. I thought you'd recognize that too, but you didn't. That's the wine your father and Jeb were making. Not very good, but the young people seemed to enjoy it."

"You are a despicable man! And to think I actually liked you!"

"Truthfully, my dear, it would have never worked between us, because I have my sights on Tate too."

That's when I screamed.

And that's when a Gator came crashing through the orchard, narrowly missing the table. But it wasn't "help" at all. It was Tate and Hannah.

Forty-Eight

Hannah, fresh from the hospital and consumed with jealousy, jumped out of the Gator and stormed up to Carleton, totally ignoring the fact that he had a gun in his hand.

"How could you?" she cried, hitting him square in the chest with her balled fists. "I fed you pie while you were blindfolded! You flirted with me for, like, an hour. And now this? With my best friend?" Her voice grew whiney. Carleton laughed. Hannah's punches had little impact, likely because she'd been released from the hospital too early and was still woozy.

While Hannah was accosting Carleton, Tate marched over to me. I'd never seen him so angry or so hurt. He looked like a jilted lover. He looked like I'm sure I looked on the night I found him in bed with another woman.

"Jesus, Whitney! How could you just sneak out of the house like that? After all we've been through? Babe, I saved you last night. I thought we had a thing going on."

I didn't really know what he meant by "a thing," but I was stunned by the situation. Carleton, the mastermind behind Finn and all the terror, was pointing his gun at me, and Tate and Hannah were so consumed by their personal jealousies that they hadn't noticed. Then, before I could stop him, Tate grabbed my full glass of wine and tossed it back angrily.

"No! Don't! Holy cobbler, Tate. It's been drugged."

"What?" He looked at me, then at Carleton. His eyes dropped to the gun in the other man's hand and he uttered a thoroughly disgusted "Dude."

"Horse tranquilizer, to be more specific, Tatum. Are you surprised? It was me all along. And now that you two know, I'm going to have to kill you as well. Such a pity. Don't worry. I'll make it look like an accident." Carleton picked up the candelabra from the table and threw it on the ground. The kerosene-soaked petals exploded. The trees were on fire.

"Oh, crap," Tate muttered, and fell onto the table, unconscious.

Hannah, in a full-blown girl rage, swore and kicked at the same time. It was a hard kick, right to Carleton's crotch. "You dirty rotten scumbag!" she spat as he dropped to the ground. She kept kicking him.

"Quick!" I shouted, pulling her away. "Help me get Tate into the Gator!"

Hannah was still a little disoriented, but she got the hint. She ran with me, albeit clumsily, back to Tate and together we managed to get him into the bed of the Gator they'd just arrived in. Hannah jumped into the passenger seat and I took the wheel. The moment I stepped on the gas, a shot rang out. Carleton was back on his feet and he was blazing mad.

"Whit, I forgive you!" Hannah shouted. "He's sooo not worth it. Just get us out of here!"

I drove through the burning orchard, heading for the inn, but the fire and thick black smoke were making it difficult. The fire was moving through the orchard at an alarming speed, the hungry flames dancing from tree to tree consuming whatever they touched. It was a gut-wrenching sight. So too was the sight of Carleton in the other Gator, swiftly closing the distance between us. Every chance he got, he took a shot. Bullets ricocheted off tree trunks. Branches thick with white petals exploded. I kept swerving, slaloming through the trees, desperately trying to keep Carleton's bullets from hitting Tate or Hannah. Carleton's Gator was carrying a lighter load, but I knew the orchard like the back of my hand. My only hope was to evade him. And to do this I took the Gator deeper into the orchard, heading for the woods.

Carleton was fast on our trail.

I kept my foot on the gas as I crashed through bushes, mowed down weedy plants, and rambled over rocky terrain. No matter what I tried, Carleton kept gaining on us, firing his gun as we wove our way through the forest. And his aim was getting better.

Then I remembered a narrow opening in a thick scree of pines. Below the trees was a steep ditch, and on the other side was Lighthouse Road. "Hold on to Tate!" I yelled to Hannah as I spun the Gator around. Hannah yelped as Tate's body slammed against the other side of the cargo bed. Ignoring both, I headed for the pines. The opening was narrow and just barely visible through the thick branches. But we went for it. We didn't really have a choice.

The Gator hit the thick branches, launching an explosion of needles into the air. The impact rocked us, but I held firmly to the wheel. We flew out of the trees and bounced down the steep side of the ditch. Hannah screamed as she clung to Tate. I screamed and clung to the violently shaking wheel. By the time we were at the bottom of the ditch, I'd gained control once again and wasted no time forcing the Gator up the other side. We'd just landed on the road when Carleton came flying through after us. I hit the gas, then stopped when Hannah cried, "Carleton's flipped his Gator!"

It was true. Carleton's Gator was upside down in the ditch, all four of his wheels spinning in the smoky air. The scumbag himself was trapped beneath it. His gun, I was happy to note, had been thrown ten feet from the vehicle and was wedged between two rocks.

"Call Jack," I told Hannah, turning off the ignition. "Tell him we need backup. Then call the fire department."

"The fire department's lying unconscious in the back of a Gator!" she cried, pointing to Tate. Tate wasn't the whole fire department, but he was a big part of it. And he was still out cold.

"Well, just make the call. You can tell them they'll need backup, too." Then I ran down the embankment, scooping up the gun as I went. The moment I peered beneath the Gator, Carleton snarled at me.

"Get this blasted thing off me!"

"Can't," I said, feeling a perverse form of satisfaction that the despicable murderer was trapped. He wasn't going anywhere anytime soon. "The Gator's too heavy, and Tate's been knocked out with horse tranquilizer. Oh, wait," I said, the moment I heard the sirens. "Officer MacLaren's on his way. Hang on a sec. Don't move a muscle." Carleton didn't appreciate the humor in that.

The moment Jack alighted from his car, I waved. "Down here, and you're not going to believe this."

"Whitney Bloom," he marveled, staring at the wreckage and the smoke-filled orchard beyond. "What have you done now?"

"Caught the real killer, just like I told you I would. It's Carleton Brisbane, aka Francis Flannigan. But you already know that, don't you?"

Jack nodded. "Tay called. Told me all about it, including the fact that you were with him. Whit, what were you thinking?"

"Well, obviously I didn't know about this until a few minutes ago."

Jack gave a curt "got it" shrug and added, "Nice work, Bloom." He looked truly impressed and, quite frankly, a little disturbed by what he saw. He joined me by the Gator and peered beneath it.

"Carleton Brisbane, aka Francis Flannigan, I'm placing you under arrest. You have the right to remain silent—"

"Oh, for Christ's sake, MacLaren!" Carleton barked. "Just slap me in handcuffs and get me out of here. This whole town's crazy!"

"Mister, you don't know the half of it." Jack winked. "Just hope backup gets here before that fire does or we're going to have to bail. You've managed to drug the main firefighter in Cherry Cove, and everyone knows better than to mess with the fearless Whitney Bloom. And, for the record," Jack continued, staring at the trapped killer, "I thought *that ad* was hilarious."

Forty-Nine

It had been a long, emotion-filled, heart-pounding few days, and yet for the first time since graduating college, I wasn't in any rush to leave the beautiful little village of Cherry Cove. In fact, as I drove down Main Street, I realized it was quite the opposite. A real sense of joy swept through me at the sight of the charming array of buildings nestled along the lakeshore. I felt at home, at peace, because I was staying.

This wasn't entirely due to the fact that Mom and Dad needed me, which they did. Carleton Brisbane, aka Francis Flannigan, had burned down a quarter of the orchard in his final attempt to destroy my family and me because of *that ad*—that fifteen-second, misplaced feminine hygiene product ad. It had been a stunning blow to learn that something as insignificant as that ad had instigated all the corruption, murder, and mayhem at the cherry orchard and inn. It shook me to the core and rattled my confidence. Of course, Mom and Dad didn't blame me. And Jack and Giff had soundly convinced me that Brisbane and his tragically hot Irish nephew were total psychopaths. Still, the situation got me thinking. Brisbane had almost gotten away with it. Both Hannah and I had been infatuated with him, and I'd been flirting with him online for over a year, although I hadn't known it. Holy cobbler, what a couple of suckers we were, and all because of a handsome face and a super sweet yacht! The yacht, we learned, was the only asset Carleton had left, and it was still moored in Tate's marina. Mrs. Cushman had just moved onboard, partly out of spite, but mostly to care for Carleton's little West Highland terrier, Molly.

Due to the current state of the orchard and the fact that we no longer had the wisdom and guidance of Jeb Carlson, Dad had decided to step away from his duties at the inn and focus all his attentions there. This left an opening at the inn for me, and how could I refuse an offer like that? I'd be working with Mom and Grandma Jenn. I'd be able to help restore the image of the Cherry Orchard Inn, in addition to continuing with *Bloom 'n' Cherries!* I'd have a professional kitchen to work in, and the best tart cherries in the country at my doorstep. No longer having to pay my high Chicago rent would be pretty cool too.

It was all wonderful, but it wasn't the whole reason I'd decided to stay. There was another factor too, a more personal thing that I couldn't quite put into words. Tay and Hannah were definitely a part of it. It would be great living in the same town as my best friends once again. Then there was Tate, dear Tate, who'd finally persuaded me he deserved a second chance. That had been his first request while coming out of his tranquilized stupor. He'd looked so earnest and contrite that I couldn't refuse. He was also covered head to toe in bruises from the Gator chase. I agreed to give our relationship one more try, but this time, I knew that my heart wasn't entirely in it. And that's what I couldn't understand. That's what intrigued me the most. Had I finally conquered my infatuation with Tatum Vander Hagen? I was heading to the Cherry Cove Marina to figure that out, but I had a stop to make first.

The moment I pulled into the little parking lot, the screaming began. I got out of my car and peered up at the police station roof.

Thing One and Thing Two had stopped their brotherly antics and were now standing on the edge of the thick sod, welcoming me in their own disconcerting way. Somewhere inside, MacDuff started barking. It was a sure sign that Jack was in the building. I lifted the tailgate and retrieved the basket of goodies Mom and Gran had prepared for him and his dog.

I'd taken only a few steps when the police station door burst open and Jack flew out with MacDuff at his heels. "For Christ's sake!" he cried. "Would you two demon spawns stop your rack…" He saw me and fell silent. "Whitney. What a pleasant surprise! I've been meaning to call you. I still need you to sign your statement."

"That's why I'm here. That and to give you this." I held up the basket.

"For me?" He looked genuinely surprised, and then he smiled.

My heart started beating a little faster because of that smile, and there might have been some fluttering in my stomach as well. I ignored both, adding, "For you and MacDuff." I handed Jack the basket, then reached down to stroke MacDuff's long, silky ears. "It's a little thank you for all you've done for us at the orchard, and, of course, for arresting Brisbane."

"As much as it pains me to admit it, you had a pretty big hand in that too." Jack cast me a teasing grin and peeked under the lid. "Whoa. There's a lot of vacuum-packed New York Strips in here … and a container of bacon-topped mashed potatoes, Caesar salad, French bread, home-made dog cookies—"

"And a cherry pie," I added. "Wouldn't be dinner without that."

"No it wouldn't," he agreed. "Did you make it?" I nodded. "Now I feel honored—to have a pie made by the Gilded Cherry winner herself. So many surprising talents, Ms. Bloom." Jack's grin was wide and slightly teasing.

Thing One and Thing Two, having fallen silent after being repri-manded, realized Jack wasn't paying attention to them any longer and started back up with their weird bleating goat-scream. MacDuff re-taliated by barking at them. Jack ignored them all. He was too busy staring at me. Then he took me by the hand. "Come inside, Whit. The kids'll stop screaming, eventually."

He grilled two steaks while I prepared the salad. I'd had no inten-tion of staying for dinner, but I did. I couldn't help it. Jack insisted. Besides, he'd opened a bottle of wine just for me.

"I wanted to thank your friend Giff," he began, putting a steak on each plate. He then placed the lid back on the Webber. "But I was told he left this morning."

We sat at a little table in the garden and began eating. "He had to get back to work," I explained. "He didn't really want to, being a hero of sorts and all, but the pull of bragging about his cyber-sleuthing skills to his boss, Mr. Black, was pretty strong. Also, Mr. Black told him that if he didn't get back soon he'd lose his job. The man's an unbending tyrant."

"Well, thank God that he and Tay are good at snooping around on the internet. The scary part is that Briz wasn't even on my radar. I never made the connection between him and Finn. It was Giff who thought he'd recognized Brisbane from somewhere. Turned out to be an old article he read in *Fortune* magazine featuring Francis Flannigan."

"Giff has a passion for magazines and one heck of a memory."

"Thank God for that," Jack said reflectively. "Without Giff's hunch and Tay's dogged expertise on the web, I might not have gotten to you in time." He looked at me, all trace of humor gone from his face. "That's the thought that keeps me up at night, Whitney." And by his pensive, intimate expression, I knew that it did.

I swallowed, producing a watery smile. "Thank you. But I'm pretty resourceful, you know."

"I do know," he said, raising his bottle of beer in a toast. I returned the gesture with my wineglass. "So," he continued, deftly changing the subject. "When are you heading back to Chicago?"

"Friday," I told him, and watched his reaction to my news. My old pal Jack MacLaren was visibly disappointed by the thought of me leaving—so disappointed that he stood up from the table and actually began clearing the dishes.

"So soon?" he remarked, unable to look me in the eyes as he busied his hands. "I thought you'd stay a bit longer."

"Well, I'm coming right back." I waited until these words had sunk in. Holding our two plates and an empty beer bottle in his hands, Jack stilled. And then he looked at me. "Didn't I tell you? I thought I told you," I said.

"No. No you didn't. Why are you coming right back?"

"Because I've decided to move back home for a while. You know how it is. I mean, things are going great in Chicago and all," I glibly lied, "but I feel totally responsible for what's happened, and my folks could really use my help with the inn. I'm also taking you up on your suggestion. I'm going to run *Bloom 'n' Cherries!* out of the inn bakery. You won't have to order online anymore, using your mom's name and address. You can just swing by any time you like."

"I will," Jack promised, grinning. "I'm amazed. You're really doing this? You're really moving back?"

"Why is that so hard to believe? I'm not as self-centered and heartless as you seem to think I am, Jack MacLaren."

"I've never thought that." He was trying his hardest to look sincere. "Your folks must be thrilled." He turned and, to my horror, set the plates and serving dishes on the ground where they were immediately set upon by the eager tongues of his awaiting menagerie. "Come," he demanded. "The boys'll take care of these. I'm taking you out for ice cream. This calls for a celebration!"

Before I knew it, I was in his arms, being whisked off my feet for a celebratory whirl in the garden. When my feet were back on firm ground once again I realized that Jack's arms were still holding me tightly. Then, with his soft, honey-brown eyes holding my own, he slowly, very slowly, brought his lips down to mine.

Time stopped. My knees became jelly. Every nerve in my body burst to life with a heady, all-consuming tingle. Then my entire backside started vibrating. Somewhere close by, above the sound of animal tongues lapping up steak scraps and leftover salad, piano music tickled the air with a familiar, melodic riff. With his lips still attached to mine, Jack slipped his hand into the back pocket of my jeans.

The vibrating stopped.

"Hello," he said huskily, momentarily removing his lips from mine.

I looked up. Jack was holding my iPhone. Dear God! Jack had answered my phone!

The look in his eyes was intimate and playful as he replied to the voice on the other end. "This is Jack. Who's this? Yeah. She's right here. Hold on a sec, bro." The playful look turned to one of suspicion as he looked down at me and whispered, "Were you, by chance, supposed to have dinner with Tate tonight?"

Holy cobbler! I'd forgotten about Tate and the marina. Completely! As Jack's eyes bore into mine, a wave of white-hot embarrassment coursed through my veins. My ears burned, my face grew uncomfortably hot, and I found that for once I was utterly speechless.

"Whitney, were you heading over to Tate's place tonight?" Jack asked again, this time sounding suspiciously like an interrogating cop.

"Because I thought you two were broken up? I had the distinct impression, just now, that you were over him."

Still breathless from his kiss, and feeling like a guilty criminal under his pointed stare, I stammered, "I ... um ... I'm sorry, Jack," and took the phone from his hand. I held it to my ear, watching as Jack's expression oscillated between pleasure and humiliation.

"Babe. You were supposed to be here, like ... hours ago. I was getting worried. Hey, quick question. Why's MacLaren answering your phone?"

"Long story. I'll be over in five," I told him, ending the call. I shoved my phone back into my pocket and looked at the man standing before me.

"Jack. I'm sorry." I could tell he was angry and he wasn't buying it. "Look," I said a little defensively, *"you* kissed *me.*"

"I did. And *you* didn't seem to mind it."

"I didn't—not one bit. And I'd like to stay, really I would, but I ... can't."

"Because you're still not over Tate?"

Wasn't I? I thought I was, but maybe he was right. I was so confused. "Look," I pleaded, "I don't have any good answers for my behavior. I have a lot on my plate right now, but you of all people should know that eventually I will figure it out. All I ask is that you please, please bear with me." I took his face between my hands, stood on my tiptoes, and pulled his lips down to mine. This time Jack was the one who was left breathless. "Bear with me," I told him again, and let him go.

I slung my purse over my shoulder and headed for the garden gate, MacDuff and the goats following me. My hand was on the latch when I suddenly froze. What the heck was I doing? I turned back around, ready to abandon all my plans.

But I was too late. Jack was gone.

I closed my eyes and released the breath I'd been holding. With one last look behind me, I left the garden, grateful that I had made the decision to stay in Cherry Cove.

Whitney's Cherry-Tastic Recipes and Other Delights

Decadent Deconstructed Cherry Pie
Makes 6 generous servings

Who doesn't love cherry pie? No one that I know of, surely. However, there are times when a slice of pie just isn't enough to wow that epicurious foodie who really likes to push their taste buds to the limit. That's why I came up with this little gem. It's got all the basic elements of a great cherry pie, but with a hint of brandy in the cherries and two layers of almond cream. Yum, yum! Go on, give it a try. You know you want to.

Ingredients

For the Filling:

5 cups fresh Montmorency cherries pitted (or any variety of baking cherries will do). If using canned cherries, drain cherries, keeping one cup in reserve.

1 cup sugar

¼ cup Kirschwasser (cherry brandy)

½ teaspoon cinnamon

1 teaspoon lemon zest (lemon rind)

3 tablespoons butter

3 tablespoons corn starch

For the Phyllo Dough Crust:

10 sheets phyllo dough, thawed

½ cup butter melted

½ cup sugar

2 tablespoons cinnamon

For the Sweet Almond Cream:

4 oz cream cheese, softened to room temperature

½ cup powdered sugar

2 teaspoons almond extract

1 cup heavy whipping cream

For the Whipped Cream Topping:

1 cup whipping cream

¼ cup powdered sugar

½ teaspoon vanilla

Make the Filling

Preheat oven to 375°F.

Put fresh cherries in large bowl. Add 1 cup sugar, ¼ cup cherry brandy, 1 teaspoon lemon zest, and ½ teaspoon cinnamon. Stir and let stand for 20 minutes.

Put the cornstarch in large saucepan over medium heat. Drain the juice in the fresh cherries and add to cornstarch, stirring until blended. Cook over medium heat, stirring occasionally until liquid becomes thick and bubbly.

Turn off heat and add cherries. Stir to blend.

Put cherries in an oven-safe dish. Dot with the three tablespoons of butter and cover loosely with tinfoil. Bake for 30 minutes. Remove tinfoil, stir, and bake for 10 more minutes. Remove from oven and let stand.

Meanwhile, while cherries are baking...

Make the Phyllo Dough Crust

Brush cookie sheet with melted butter.

Lay one sheet of phyllo dough on the baking sheet, keeping the rest covered with damp paper towels to keep them from drying out while you're working with the dough.

Liberally brush phyllo layer with melted butter, then sprinkle with cinnamon sugar mixture. Repeat the layers.

Bake in 375°F oven for 10–15 minutes, or until golden and crisp.

Cool completely.

Meanwhile, while the sugared phyllo crust is baking…

Make the Almond Cream

In mixer, mix the cream cheese, powdered sugar, and almond extract. Beat until soft and creamy. Transfer to bowl and set aside.

In mixing bowl, beat heavy whipping cream until soft peaks form. Gently add the cream cheese mixture a quarter at a time, mixing until stiff peaks form. Store in fridge.

Time to Assemble!

Carefully cut phyllo dough into 12 squares. Place one square of sugared phyllo directly on dessert plate. Place a dollop of almond cream (I like to pipe it on using a pastry bag) and carefully spread on crust. Next, add a spoonful of cherries. Repeat this layer.

Top with a dollop of freshly whipped whipping cream and serve immediately!

Some fun variations I make for my friends:

Whenever I make this for Tay I add an extra splash of brandy to the cherries. What can I say? She loves her brandy!

Another fun way to make this deconstructed pie is to make a very simple version of it, one that's perfect for a quiet dinner or intimate gathering of friends. I made this version when Giff came over once and I was out of my fancy phyllo crust. Since I still had plenty of the cherry filling I whipped up a quick batch of Grandma Jenn's trusty pie crust (see recipe below), rolled it out, cut it into wedges, sprinkled a little sugar on top, and baked it at 375°F for 10–15 minutes—just until the wedges were a nice golden brown. I then placed a scoop of vanilla ice cream in a dessert dish, topped it with a generous helping of the warm, brandied cherry filling, and finished it off with a decorative pie dough wedge. Although not as elegant as the original version, it's still delicious, and Gifford McGrady couldn't get enough of it!

Grandma Jenn's Classic Door County Cherry Pie
Makes one 10-inch pie (can be used in a 9-inch pie as well)
No kidding—this basic, old-fashioned cherry pie is good enough to win a cherry pie bake-off without your having to sleep with the judge…unless, of course, you want to (wink, wink). It seems ridiculous, but the secret to baking a fabulous cherry pie is all about the cherries. A good, tart baking cherry is essential. You don't need a secret pie-contest-winning cherry tree at your disposal like Grandma Jenn. All you need to do is take a trip to an orchard that grows tart cherries. They'll have what you need. At the Bloom Family Orchard, we also pit and flash-freeze our cherries to preserve that fresh-picked flavor. Grandma Jenn does this as well, and actually prefers to use frozen cherries for this recipe. However, if fresh or frozen cherries aren't available, bottled or canned from any grocery store will do.

Ingredients

For Grandma Jenn's Flaky Crust:

1½ sticks chilled butter

⅓ cup chilled vegetable shortening

3 cups all-purpose flour

1 teaspoon salt

1 tablespoon sugar

1 teaspoon cider vinegar

½ cup ice water

For Grandma Jenn's Fabulous Filling:

6 cups of fresh or frozen tart cherries

1 cup sugar

4 tablespoons corn starch

1 teaspoon fresh lemon juice, or ½ teaspoon concentrate

3 tablespoons butter

1 tablespoon milk, to brush over top crust

1 tablespoon sugar, to sprinkle

Make the Crust

Dice the butter and the vegetable shortening and put in the refrigerator to chill.

While the butter and shortening are chilling, place the flour, salt, and sugar in the bowl of an electric mixer. Fit the mixer with the stir attachment and add the chilled butter and shortening.

Mix until the butter and shortening are the size of peas.

Next add the vinegar to the ice water and stir. While the machine is still mixing, pour in the liquid and keep mixing until the dough begins to form a ball.

Turn the dough out on a floured cutting board and shape into a ball, being careful not to work the dough too much.

Wrap the dough ball in plastic wrap and chill for about thirty minutes.

When the dough is ready to handle, sprinkle cutting board with flour so dough won't stick and cut the dough in half.

Using a rolling pin, roll half the dough into a large circle about a quarter of an inch thick, making sure the surface of the cutting board has enough flour so the dough won't stick.

Once the dough is rolled out, fold it in half and place in the bottom of the pie plate. Roll out top crust and set it aside.

Time to Make the Filling!

Preheat oven to 375°F.

Place cherries in large saucepan over medium heat. Add the teaspoon of lemon juice, cover, and stir occasionally. After a few minutes, the cherries should start releasing juice. Keep covered and remove from heat.

In a small bowl, mix sugar and cornstarch together until combined. Pour this mixture into the warm, juicy cherries and mix well. Return the mixture to the stove and cook over medium heat, stirring continuously until the liquid loses its cloudy appearance and becomes thick and bubbly. Remove from heat and stir in the butter.

Pour cooled cherry filling into the prepared pie crust.

Using a pastry brush, moisten the edges of the bottom crust with a little water. Place top crust on and flute the edges of the pie.

Make a slit in the middle of the top crust to vent steam.

Brush on a thin layer of milk over top crust, then sprinkle with sugar.

Place pie on baking sheet, cover the edges of the crust with tin foil, and place in the middle rack of the preheated oven.

Bake for 30 minutes. Remove foil from edges and bake another 20 minutes until crust is golden brown. Remove from oven and cool.

When pie has set and is ready to be served, plate a generous helping and serve with a scoop of your favorite vanilla ice cream!

Edna Baker's Bribe-Worthy Chicken Pot Pie
Serves 8 to 10

While I don't generally condone outright bribery, it's not a bad idea to have at least one resolve-weakening recipe in your arsenal—just in case you need it. Edna's chicken pot pie is that recipe—a rich, savory chicken stew topped with a golden flaky crust. It's comfort food at its best, and I'm sure if Edna found out how Grandma Jenn "accidently" snapped a picture of this recipe during a Cherry Cove Women's Club meeting at her house, she'd be furious. So don't tell Edna. But seriously, a recipe this good shouldn't be squirreled away and kept under lock and key. It should be shared. So go ahead and try it yourself. Just don't invite Edna over for dinner when you do.

Ingredients

For the Crust:

Ask yourself, do you want to make individual pot pies in oven-safe personal dishes, or do you want to make a family-style pot pie? If you want to make individual pot pies, I recommend doubling the crust recipe below.

2 cups all-purpose flour

1 teaspoon salt

⅓ cup butter cut in small cubes and chilled

⅓ cup shortening, chilled

6 to 7 tablespoons ice water

For the Filling:

3 pounds boneless, skinless chicken breasts

4 cups chicken broth

1 heaping tablespoon of minced garlic

3 tablespoons vegetable oil

1 onion, finely chopped

4 carrots, peeled and sliced

2 celery ribs, cleaned and finely chopped

Table salt and pepper

10 oz. cremini mushrooms, washed,
   stems trimmed and thinly sliced

2 teaspoons soy sauce

2 teaspoons tomato paste

4 tablespoons butter

½ cup all-purpose flour

1 cup whole milk

2 teaspoons fresh lemon juice

3 tablespoons fresh parsley leaves

1 cup frozen baby peas

Make the Crust

In mixing bowl, mix the dry ingredients. Add chilled butter and shortening. Cut into flour until shortening is the size of small peas. Add ice water and continue mixing until soft dough forms. Turn dough onto floured cutting board and form into a ball. Cover with plastic wrap and put in the refrigerator.

Make the Filling

Preheat oven to 450°F if making individual pot pies.
Preheat oven to 375°F if making in 11x14 baking dish.

Bring chicken, broth, and minced garlic to simmer in covered Dutch oven or large stock pot over medium heat. Cook until chicken is just done, 8–12 minutes. Transfer chicken to large bowl. Pour broth through a fine mesh strainer into liquid measuring cup and set aside. Do not wash pot.

Heat 2 tablespoons vegetable oil in empty Dutch oven over medium heat. When oil is hot, add onions, celery, and carrots. Add ½ teaspoon salt and ½ teaspoon pepper. Cover and cook until tender, about 7 minutes. While vegetables are cooking, shred chicken into small bite-sized pieces. Transfer cooked vegetables to bowl with chicken and set aside.

Heat remaining tablespoon of oil in empty Dutch oven over medium heat. Add mushrooms and cover. Cook, stirring occasionally, until mushrooms have released their juices, about 5 minutes. Remove cover and stir in soy sauce and tomato paste. Increase heat and cook, stirring frequently, until liquid has evaporated and mushrooms are browned, about 5 minutes. Transfer mushrooms to bowl with chicken and vegetables. Set aside.

Heat butter in empty Dutch oven over medium heat. When melted, stir in flour and cook 1 minute. Slowly whisk in reserved chicken broth and milk. Bring to a simmer, stirring to loosen browned bits on bottom of pan. Raise heat to medium and continue to simmer, stirring continuously until sauce fully thickens. Remove from heat and stir in lemon juice and parsley.

Add chicken-vegetable mixture to sauce. Add peas.

Place mixture in baking dish/dishes.

Remove dough from refrigerator and roll out crust, making a 12x16 rectangle for the baking dish, or five-inch circles for individual pots. Place dough over rim of dish and flute edges, sealing the dough to the dish. Poke a hole in crust to vent steam. Place pots/baking dish on cookie sheet.

For individual pot pies, bake in 450°F oven for 12–15 minutes. For 11x14 baking dish, bake in 375°F oven for 30 minutes, or until crust is a light golden color. Let cool ten minutes before serving.

Acknowledgments

To these stars in my personal universe, without whose light this author would still be wandering in the wilderness:

The gracious Sandy Harding, agent extraordinaire, for taking that first leap of faith and following it up with a whole lot of patience. Terri Bischoff, Sandy Sullivan, and the entire talented staff at Midnight Ink for their love of books, humor, and vision.

Robin Taylor, cherished friend, antique collector, whisky aficionado, and creative soul whose encouragement and enthusiasm for my work is partially responsible for the preceding pages. Jane Boundy, cherished friend and joyous spirit whose passion for yoga is inspiring, but not quite enough, and who never fails to make me laugh.

Debbie and Todd Coy, for the adventures, the Friday night dinners, and all the entertaining character name suggestions. My coworkers at the reference desk—Hey Girls!—and the entire amazing staff at the historic Howell Carnegie Library. You are the heart of our community and great people to know.

Dave and Jan Hilgers, the best parents in the world, seriously! I wouldn't be who I am today without your love, laughter, guiding wisdom, and love of cherry pie. Jim, Dan, and Matt, my three amazing sons, and the most loving, intelligent, adventurous, and hysterically funny millennials I know. Feed your passions, cherish the ones you love, and never give up on your dreams.

And to my dear husband, John, the wind beneath my wings. Always and forever.

About the Author

Darci Hannah is the author of two previous works of historical fiction, *The Exile of Sara Stevenson* and *The Angel of Blythe Hall* (Ballantine). When she isn't whipping up tasty treats in her kitchen, she's hard at work writing. *Cherry Pies & Deadly Lies* is her first mystery.